VIRULENCE

TONI DUARTE

Book two of the Bioluminescence Trilogy

Hardcover edition ISBN: 9781068716683

Paperback edition ISBN: 9781068716690

Cover illustration by Nastya Litepla @litepla

Interior design by Toni Duarte

www.toniduartewriter.com

Content Warning

This book contains material relating to:
alcohol consumption,
suicidal thoughts,
attempted suicide,
violence,
grief,
drug abuse,
addiction,
death,
murder,
PTSD,
mass shooting,
psychosis,
gaslighting,
& panic attacks.

It also references off-page:
sexual assault &
human trafficking

Please remember to take care of yourself
and respect your limits.

To the ones searching for home

Also by Toni Duarte

The Bioluminescence Trilogy
Bioluminescence
Incandescence (coming soon)

The Anchored Duology
The Hollow Dark

Virulence is book two of the Bioluminescence Trilogy.

SCAN ME

For a full summary of characters & events from book one

Or go to https://www.toniduartewriter.com/bioluminescence-summary/

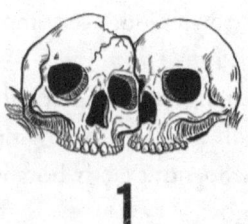

1

Invisibility was crucial for survival. Blend in. Don't draw attention.

But for Oliver, that wasn't exclusive to the post-collapse world. He'd spent his entire life trying to disappear.

When the emotions would bubble up, he'd fight the gnawing urge to fidget with his shirt hem or shake out his hands. Push the feelings down until they hit critical levels and the energy pulsing inside him would erupt, leaving him a blob of human pudding on the floor.

Blend in. Don't draw attention. Don't rock. Don't bounce. Don't mumble.

Oliver pulled the door to the shed closed behind him, his fingers wrapped around the fan in his pocket as he crossed the empty yard.

The farm was eerily still, the sky just beginning to brighten overhead, and the air was a sharp sort of cold that made his lungs ache.

Autumn had barely made an appearance, freezing into a bitter winter before the last of the dead leaves even hit the ground. He slipped inside the farmhouse, tensing as hushed voices spilled out from the living room, the firelight from the giant hearth stretching lazily into the hallway.

Don't draw attention.

Gaze locked on the floor, Oliver hurried past the wide archway.

Was he acting suspicious? Did he always walk like this? Were his sneakers always so heavy? God, every movement felt like it was screaming *hey, look at me, I stole from you.*

But it wasn't really stealing. It was borrowing. Stealing was wrong, but borrowing was...well usually borrowing was consensual. He hadn't asked permission. So, not exactly borrowing either.

Oliver scrunched his nose.

He was overthinking this. As he always did.

Three flights of stairs and one drop-down ladder later, he was back in his own space, and his fingers finally loosened their grip on the fan.

The small attic was hardly warmer than it had been outside. The old wood was drafty, and the cold seeped through the round window over his bed, but he appreciated it for what it was; a place where he could be alone. He could focus here.

Oliver sank onto the wooden chair, placed the fan gently on the desk, then flipped on the portable generator and small work lamp, wincing at the high-pitched buzz as it came to life and doused the room in harsh white light.

He wasn't sure how Vivian would feel about him taking things from the workshop, but if he could get this air filter working, she'd understand.

No, not if. *When.*

Oliver pulled on his goggles—a worn-out pair with a magnifying lens in the bottom that his brother had given him—and turned on the soldering iron, the tension in his muscles already fading.

People made him nervous. They always had. People were unpredictable. Indecipherable. They said one thing while meaning another and left him questioning everything. But this...this he understood.

Everything else faded into the background as his attention zeroed in on the project before him.

When Oliver looked up again, he found himself surrounded by daylight.

How long had he been working?

The hours had an inconsiderate habit of slipping by without warning.

He lifted the safety goggles, letting them rest on his head as he held his breath and flipped the switch on the purifier.

And...nothing.

What was he missing? The circuit board was in decent shape. Not perfect, but better than the rest of his collection. It was one he'd found over the summer during a run with Adam.

Oliver winced as the name rippled through his thoughts, disrupting his focus and draining his motivation.

He set the soldering iron down and tore the goggles from their spot on his head, his dark hair falling into his eyes.

The filter still didn't work.

Why didn't it work?

What if he was trying to fix the wrong part?

The thought tugged at him as he studied the metal box. The machine was simple compared to BUG, but the potential was what made it special. This little purifier could ensure an entire room was clear of spores, and, theoretically, if he could figure out how to scale it up, it could protect an entire building.

It had been a fun side project at first, just to keep his mind busy, but they'd recently realized that the fungus was spreading again, stretching out beyond the city, which meant Spring Valley was at risk. Their daily checks made them *feel* safe, but if they actually saw that glow on the walls, it'd be too late.

Oliver could help. He could do something important. Make amends for the terrible things he'd done.

Okay, if he was being honest, yes, those were the thoughts that had sparked the idea, but it was a different thought that had turned the project into an all-consuming obsession. One that, admittedly, was a whole lot more selfish.

Successfully pulling this off, getting it to function at a level that would make a significant impact, would give Oliver leverage. Something to offer Haven. He could be with Adam again without asking him to leave his safe place.

This was the solution. Now, he just needed to finish it.

Oliver blew the strands of hair away, then dropped his face into his hands.

Why couldn't he figure this out?

The buzzing of the light grew from a dull hum to an earsplitting whine that burrowed through his skull, and then everything came down on top of him at once. The wooden chair was suddenly unbearable, his jacket too heavy, the cuffs too tight, even his skin felt wrong, like it was two sizes too small. He forced his eyes closed and tried to shake the feeling out through his hands.

Even alone in his room, Oliver's brain chided him for the stim and he tucked his hands under his legs to keep them still.

That makes you stand out. Stop it.

It wasn't fair that he had to work so hard at things that seemed to come so easily to everyone else.

Oliver had always known he was different. Even as a kid, he could see it. It didn't bother him; it was just a fact. And he was okay with it. He liked who he was. Until he started middle school, and *different* became *weird*.

Weird made him stand out, and *that* definitely bothered him. Standing out drew unwanted attention. So, he started watching and learning and mirroring, all in a desperate attempt to blend into the scenery. To disappear.

Blend in. Don't draw attention.

In high school, he tirelessly crafted his mask, made a few friends, and had a couple short-lived relationships. But the connections were shallow, and they never felt right. *He* never felt right. So, he tried harder. Fought against all the things that made him stand out. But the harder he tried, the more frequently the meltdowns hit.

It was like everybody had received a blueprint except for him, and he was left struggling to reverse engineer what they had so effortlessly achieved.

When he got his autism diagnosis at fifteen, his parents seemed *relieved*, of all things, like this medical term would make everything easier. But it didn't make Oliver feel any better. It didn't change anything. It didn't make life easier for *him*.

The point of identifying an issue with anything mechanical is usually to repair it. Replace the parts with different, better ones to get it running smoother. This wasn't something he could change or repair. What good was knowing the error code if he couldn't fix it?

Oliver squeezed his eyes tighter, but the feeling kept building, the threat of a meltdown looming.

It wasn't a single thing sending him over the edge. It was a whirlwind of unfortunate events, all happening simultaneously, stacking on top of each other.

The hyper-fixation of the air purifier had whisked away entire weeks, keeping him from obsessing over the grief and self-pity, but this snag had brought the entire thing to an abrupt dead end, and without the project to keep his mind busy, it inevitably drifted, and it always drifted to the same face.

It had been sixty-two days since he made the call to Haven, a decision that would shatter his life and save Adam's.

Sixty-two days of trying to establish enough of a routine to keep his sanity. And he was finally getting there. He was managing.

But all it took was one failing project and a handful of people from his past to ruin it all.

Spring Valley had recently agreed to take in the last remaining people from the Campus. People he and Adam had shared a home with for months.

Kye had been here for four days, and so far, he'd been successful in avoiding her, opting to stay in his room whenever possible. Not that he wasn't happy to have her there. She was one of his favorite people. She was kind and patient and protective. And honest. She always said what she was thinking. Which was probably the reason Oliver had been avoiding her.

He didn't want to answer the questions he was sure she'd ask. Didn't want to explain why he left. Why Adam wasn't here. He didn't want to hear her response. Not when he knew it wouldn't be in his favor.

Of course, Kye knew Oliver was here. It was part of the conditions for Vivian allowing him to stay. She wasn't going to keep secrets from Kye. They had known each other since before the collapse, and despite their disagreement—Spring Valley, like all the other communities, had refused to help when Kye wanted to stand up to the cult—there was a mutual respect between them.

When Oliver's skin finally stopped crawling, he pried open his eyes and tried to direct his focus back to the project, but it was no use.

A knock on the hatch made him jump, and he turned to stare at the square in the floor.

Maybe if he ignored it, they'd go away.

Another knock.

Or not.

With a sigh, Oliver switched everything off, then shoved up from the desk. He opened the hatch, watching as the ladder slowly unfolded on its own—one of the first adjustments he made after arriving—and looked down at a girl with brown skin and a crown of tightly coiled black curls on her head.

His face tightened into a frown. So much for avoidance.

"Hi to you too," Kye said, folding her arms. "Can I come up or are we just going to glare at each other from a distance?"

Oliver hesitated, then nodded, and as she climbed up, he swiftly tucked away the various stolen items on the desk, hiding them under the clutter.

Kye looked around the room as she leaned against the wall in that nonchalant sort of way that he'd never been able to pull off. His eyes bounced from her to the hatch and back, the silence painfully uncomfortable.

Why wasn't she talking? Was he supposed to say something? *She* was the one who came to find him.

Finally, he met her gaze—only for a second before his eyes slid to her temple because it took a lot less effort—and raised his eyebrows. "Did you need something?"

"It's cozy up here," she said.

Oliver cast a glance over his shoulder at the room. The attic was small, a wooden desk pressed against one wall, overflowing with circuit boards and tools, his messenger bag hanging off the edge. A mattress on a metal frame was crammed against the other.

Cozy was an interesting way to put it.

His attention caught on the controller peeking out from beneath his pillow.

BUG wouldn't power up, but the GPS tracker still worked, so he kept the controller close, checking the location every time his mind drifted to Adam. Thankfully, the location was always the same. BUG was still at Haven. Adam hadn't gone searching for him.

Which was a good thing. It was what Oliver told him to do. What he wanted. But some traitorous, selfish part of himself wished he'd check the GPS one day to find Adam on his way here.

Oliver's brow knitted. He really was an awful person.

"You okay?"

He tore his eyes from the controller, turned back to Kye, and nodded, the movement sharp and clunky. "Peachy."

It was selfish to grieve over a choice he made. Selfish to think about showing up at Haven, begging Adam to forgive him, to leave with him. How could he even consider tearing him away from all that? Adam had spent months doing everything he could to protect him, while the best Oliver managed was almost destroying the Campus to save him from Cassira. And even that failed.

This was his way of making up for being a burden, and if that meant suffering through this never-ending, self-loathing spiral, so be it.

"There's breakfast downstairs," Kye said.

"Not hungry."

She slid the chair out. "Can I sit?"

He nodded, and she dropped into it.

"Viv tells me you've missed every meal for the past two days." Her fingers idly traced the items closest to her. She lifted a caliper, inspected it, and then returned it to its spot. "You've eaten *something* since you got here, right?"

He rolled his eyes. "Sixty-two days without eating, and I'd be dead." Oliver followed her lead and sat on the bed, which felt too awkward with someone else in his room, so he hopped right back up.

"I was worried," Kye pressed. "You left without a word, and then Eduardo told me..." As the sentence trailed off, her expression shifted. Oliver tried to decipher the meaning, but it changed again before he could figure it out. "I'm not sure what happened between you and

Adam," she continued as Oliver fought the urge to cover his ears. "But I just wanted to check in and let you know I'm here for you if you need to talk."

"I don't."

"Fair enough." Kye stood slowly. "Oh, Viv wanted me to tell you to stop sneaking into the workshop."

Oliver's gaze snapped up, and she responded with a knowing look.

"And that if you need supplies for whatever it is you're working on, just let her know. She can help you find it."

His cheeks went hot.

"Go eat. Apparently, there's a blizzard coming. Viv sent a few people to the cabin to chop firewood and wants you to help bring it back here."

He nodded, and Kye gave him a warm smile before heading down the ladder.

With his focus completely obliterated and his energy sapped from the interaction, Oliver gave up on any hope of productivity and dropped flat onto the bed, hand automatically going to BUG's controller to check his location, which, of course, hadn't changed.

Everything was okay, because Adam was still there. Still safe.

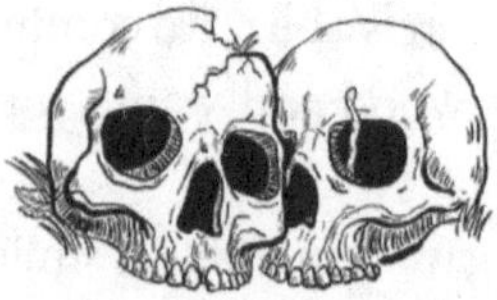

2

The frozen puddles cracked beneath Adam's boots as he trudged forward, his teeth chattering uncontrollably and his fingertips numb.

That probably wasn't a good sign.

The gnawing hunger had faded to an ache in his stomach, dulled by the medley of other pains, and his movements were sluggish, though he wasn't sure if it was from lack of sleep or lack of food.

It didn't matter, really. The cold would kill him long before either of those.

As Adam approached the front of a boxy warehouse with metal siding, the wind howled around him, throwing him slightly off balance. The street was lined with mismatched industrial buildings pieced together like an ugly collage, but he'd been watching long enough to know *this* was the one he needed.

The muffled voices inside confirmed it.

"Help me," he said, the plea barely a whisper, scraping his throat as he limped unsteadily up to the warehouse. "Please." Louder this time. "Help." His voice bounced off the buildings and echoed down the empty street.

Within seconds, the warehouse doors burst open, and two men emerged, their guns aimed cautiously at him.

Adam's steps slowed, then faltered, and his knees buckled beneath him. He winced as he hit the icy ground, hands splayed against the concrete.

The men stared, dumbfounded, and as Adam peered up at them from beneath heavy eyelids, the tension in their frames immediately faded. He'd never looked like much of a threat—always too thin, with a face that made him look younger than he was—and the scraggly waves of hair falling over his forehead only emphasized that. He sat back on his boots and huddled into his coat, shivering against the cold as he studied the men.

They didn't have the telltale tattoos of collectors, so they weren't the ones dragging people back to the Hub to be rented out or sold. Instead of the small black spade beneath the corner of their eyes, these each had a diamond. Dealers. They managed trade goods. Guns, ammo, meds, drugs, food. Anything that might interest their clientele. Not exactly who Adam was looking for, but what was the saying...a gift horse's mouth is...something. Adam searched his memory for a moment before giving up. His mind was fuzzy at the edges, and he kept getting lost in the fog.

Focus.

"Please, help me. I don't want to die out here."

The men exchanged glances. One was short, with jet black hair tied into a tight ponytail at the nape of his neck, and the other was bald, with muscles on top of his muscles.

"Hold up," Muscles said before disappearing back through the doors. Within seconds, he returned with a small length of rope. "Hands out in front of you." When Adam recoiled, the man added, "It's a precaution. If we were gonna kill you, why would we waste our time with this bullshit?"

Adam gave a nervous nod, and the man wrapped the rope around his wrists, pulling it tight enough to cut off circulation before tying it into a triple knot. He grabbed Adam's arm and hoisted him to his feet like he weighed nothing.

Muscles opened Adam's coat and quickly patted him down, taking the pistol from its holster and tucking it in the back of his pants before shoving him forward.

He'd had a plan when he left Jardine yesterday morning, and he was pretty sure it was flawless, but exhaustion and Oxycodone clouded his thoughts, and now he couldn't remember the second half, so he was improvising from this point on.

He worked better under pressure, anyway.

Adam's muscles vibrated, and he almost smiled.

Do you want to watch them burn? Desmond had asked after Haven fell, and Adam had thrilled at the possibilities.

Des was going to help take out the Hub. Adam could finally put that place behind him and maybe he'd be able to sleep. The thought was the one thing that kept him going.

Lots of big promises, but still no follow-through.

Des was more worried about finding his stupid plant, and the waiting was driving Adam crazy.

Yes, him going off on his own was a risk. No, Desmond wouldn't be happy about it. But Adam could handle it, and maybe Des would realize that he was done waiting and actually lift a finger to help.

Killing a couple dealers wouldn't make a dent in the Hub's business, but it was a start. It was better than wasting away at Jardine doing nothing.

They entered the warehouse, and the heavy metal doors creaked shut behind them. Faint beams of gray morning light streamed through the high, dirty windows.

"Sit," Muscles ordered. "Don't move."

As Adam sank to the floor, his eyes roamed the room, taking in every detail. One exit, if you didn't count the large loading doors, which he didn't. The shelves, towering to the ceiling, were mostly empty, while three rows of solid wooden crates were neatly arranged near the entrance. Two men. Each had at least one gun. Probably a knife, too.

The men met up a few feet away, arguing in low voices, Ponytail leaning casually on a half-opened crate. If they were trying to be secretive about the conversation, they were failing miserably.

"I ain't dropping everything to run all the way back. Not our job. Just shoot him."

"One of our ammo reloaders up and died last week," Muscles countered, flicking a glance in Adam's direction. "We can't pass up laborers."

When the man's attention shifted back to Ponytail, Adam slid his hand into his boot, discreetly pulling his knife free from its sheath. With his bulky boots acting as a vise, he secured the blade and began sawing through the rope, his gaze never leaving the men.

The rope gave, and as the men finished their argument and headed back toward him, Adam pulled up his knees, hands in his lap, fingers wrapped tightly around the hilt of the knife.

Now for the fun part.

Ponytail leaned down to grab Adam's arm. "We're go—" Adam's knife opened a clean slice across his throat, the words cut off by a low gurgle. His hand flew up to cover the gushing cut, but it wouldn't help him.

The corner of Adam's mouth lifted. One down.

He jumped to his feet, then spun and swung at the second man, but Muscles caught his wrist before the blade could land.

"You little shit." His fist crashed into Adam's cheekbone, snapping his head back and lighting up his vision like the fireworks over Navy Pier. Muscles twisted his arm, stopping short when he noticed the tattooed letters peeking out from beneath Adam's coat sleeve. His lips curled into a feral grin. "You're one of Stanton's."

Adam tried to tug his arm free, but the man's grip tightened, beefy fingers digging into his forearm.

"You know, I'd be doing you a kindness by killing you," Muscles said. "It'd be better than what Stanton'll do."

He was right. Adam would rather take a bullet to the head than see what kind of fresh hell Stanton would think up to punish him for running.

Adam's eyes narrowed. "Then do it." The words should have probably given him pause, made him afraid, but he was too tired to feel anything.

"Hell no." Muscles twisted the knife free from Adam's grip and tossed it aside, then brought his other hand up, clamping it around his throat. "I gotta get a new partner 'cause of you, so I'm not feeling very generous."

Adam tried to pry the man's hand away, but it wouldn't give.

As his lungs screamed for air, adrenaline surged, and the numbness faded, allowing room for a sickening panic to take hold.

Muscles slammed him against the wall, hard enough to knock the air from his lungs—if he'd had any left.

Just when it felt like his chest was going to implode, the man threw him to the ground.

Adam gasped for air as he clambered toward his discarded knife.

"You must be a special kind of stupid," Muscles growled.

Run, Adam, a familiar voice pleaded.

Ignoring it, Adam grabbed the knife and pushed to his feet. The man snatched a crowbar from the top of a crate and swung, landing a hard blow to Adam's thigh. With an anguished cry, he collapsed to his hands and knees.

"Do I have to break both your legs and *drag* you back?"

"Yeah, probably." Adam swung the knife, slicing across the man's calf and dropping him to his knees. He plunged his knife through the man's throat, then yanked it back out.

Despite the throbbing in his cheek and the pain lancing through his leg, despite the exhaustion and the cold and the hunger, a grin spread across Adam's face as the man collapsed.

That was what he'd been waiting for, and it felt *good*.

What were you thinking? the soft voice chided, and his smile fell away.

"Leave me alone."

Adam sheathed his knife and took his handgun back from Muscles. He struggled to his feet and when he pushed through the front doors into the cold, he paused a moment, his breath forming billowing clouds of white as he exhaled deeply.

The sound of distant voices pricked his ears. He gripped the gun tighter, ready to do it all again.

You're hurt.

Adam grimaced. "I told you to leave me alone."

Please. Stay alive.

He bristled at the words he'd heard a dozen times before in that same voice. "You have no right asking anything from me, Oliver," he spat. "You're—" He was going to say that *he* was the one who left. The one who'd abandoned him. But Adam knew he wasn't *actually* there.

His eyes flicked toward the voices—the real ones—as he holstered his gun.

"It's fine. I have a plan."

You mean, like the plan that just almost got you killed?

Fair point. Things hadn't gone as smoothly as he'd hoped, and now, with the fresh pain coursing through his body, the odds were definitely against him. He should scout it first, see how many show up. He'd take out a couple more, and then head back to Jardine in time for lunch.

"Fine." Adam turned and dragged himself away from the warehouse, the limp in his step no longer a ruse. "But, for the record," he added airily, "the plan itself was solid." At least, he was pretty sure it was. He couldn't remember.

From the upstairs window of a hardware store, Adam kept an eye on the warehouse entrance, his fingers tapping against his leg. Stillness blanketed the neighborhood, the silence broken only by the gentle chirping of birds as the sky steadily brightened.

Maybe the voices weren't dealers.

Maybe nobody was coming.

Maybe he should go back to Jardine.

No, he wasn't ready to go back yet. Someone would show up. He just needed to wait a little longer.

You need to sleep.

Adam chuckled, the sound bitter and humorless. "Pass." He hadn't been able to sleep for more than an hour at a time in weeks, and the little he managed was plagued by things awful enough to haunt him long after waking.

He pulled an orange container from his vest, studying the quickly diminishing supply of pills inside. Just one shape now. One color. The only one that worked to settle the nagging ache in his muscles, the ravenous clawing at the back of his brain. The one that would stop the throbbing pain in his leg and cheek and throat.

He popped two and tucked the bottle safely back in his pocket.

You can't keep this up.

Adam let his eyes close, just for a second, putting Oliver's face with his voice.

This, he quickly realized, was a huge mistake. The pain that came with those ice-blue eyes and messy dark hair was debilitating, almost knocking him off his feet. He clenched his fists and waited it out, and when it finally faded, Adam tugged up his gloves and settled into the chair by the window, eyes back on the warehouse.

He fought sleep, mostly out of spite, but eventually it pulled him under.

Wake up.

Oliver's soft voice pried Adam free from the relentless grip of nightmares, but he lingered in the hazy void between sleep and consciousness.

"Leave me alone."

You need to open your eyes.

Adam groaned. "Make up your mind." He dragged his blurred vision into focus, slowly making sense of the new shapes. With a jolt, he sat up straight.

He wasn't alone.

His hand went reflexively for his pistol, but found nothing.

A man with a bandana tied over his head had his gun trained on Adam. Another with a short, patchy beard was examining a pistol. Adam's pistol. He popped out the magazine to check the bullets, then snapped it back into place. Both had a single diamond tattoo beneath the corner of their eyes. Dealers. And they were blocking the only exit.

"Morning," Patches said, leveling the gun. "We need to have a talk."

Adam wrinkled his nose. "Were you watching me sleep? That's really weird."

"You killed two of our guys."

"I did," he answered with a shrug.

Adam's gaze jumped to the exit, listening for any sign of movement.

The last time he left Jardine without telling anyone, he'd climbed the stairs to the roof of a tall building close by, desperate for the space to breathe. He didn't realize that Eris had followed him until he stepped up onto the ledge and she yanked him back down.

He wasn't going to jump, only enjoying the view. But they watched him closer after that.

They probably still were.

"Why are you here?" Patches asked.

Adam gave him a tilted smile. "I'm here for *you*."

The man frowned. "Who sent you?"

"Nobody sent me. I just want you dead."

"Sorry that didn't work out for you."

"Oh, it will."

Patches spat a laugh.

"How about this," Bandana chimed in. He held up an almost empty bottle of pills and gave it a quick shake. "You got some more of these stocked away, we could be convinced to let you walk."

Adam's hand instinctively jumped to his empty vest pocket as an animalistic growl resonated in the back of his mind, the claws digging in.

The man twisted open the bottle and dumped two into his hand.

Take them back, the voice roared as darkness coiled around Adam, causing his vision to tunnel and his jaw to clench shut.

As Bandana popped the oxys in his mouth and swallowed them dry, Adam fought with every ounce of willpower he had to stay in that chair while the voice urged him to carve the man open.

You can figure this out.

Oliver's voice pushed back the other. Adam's jaw loosened, the darkness fading, and he glanced over his shoulder at the space behind him, at the mess looters had left behind during the collapse.

The second floor of the shop was stocked with household products. Storage bins and garbage cans and useless junk that would be no help right now. And the pegboards along the walls were mostly bare.

But he could feel the knife still tucked into his boot. All he needed was a second to grab it.

"Okay, yeah, there's more," Adam said, shoulders slumping in defeat. "If I show you, you swear you'll let me leave?"

Patches nodded. "Yeah. Simple as that."

Adam inwardly rolled his eyes at the lie. "There's a whole box over here. I'll show you."

He stood, and Patches followed as he backstepped through the store, Bandana a few paces behind.

"In there," Adam said, nodding to a tall garbage can.

Patches stepped closer, but stopped and gave Adam a skeptical look. "*You* get it."

"Fine." Adam bent like he was reaching inside, and in one quick movement, he plucked the knife from his boot and spun around, driving it into the man's outstretched arm. The gun fell from Patches' grasp as he jerked his arm back, Adam's knife still lodged in his muscle.

As Adam went for the gun on the floor, Patches grabbed the back of his head and slammed it down against the metal shelf, the impact echoing through the room like a gunshot.

Sparks of pain exploded in his skull, the world fracturing around him as he crumpled.

Not good.

He dragged his gaze up just as the man's head kicked to the side, the hilt of a throwing knife protruding from his temple.

There she was.

Adam grabbed the gun and turned it on Bandana.

"Hey, easy, wait," the man sputtered, dropping his weapon and raising his hands in surrender. "It's just a job. I'm trying to survive, just like you. I never even killed no one. Don't got the stomach for it."

Adam gave him a sharp grin. "It's not so bad."

"Please do—"

He pulled the trigger, the shot landing between the man's eyes.

"Took you long enough," Adam muttered, wiping the blood from his forehead with his sleeve as the man fell.

"Bite me," Eris replied in her usual feathery voice.

"You couldn't have done that *before* he tried to crack my head like an egg?"

"You're lucky I showed up at all. If it were my call, I'd leave you to dig yourself out of your own mess."

"Liar," he said with a smile. "You like me."

"But you know how Des worries," she added, ignoring the comment.

His smile fell away at the name. "Then maybe he should keep his word."

Eris rolled her eyes and pulled up her hood, then took her knife back from the man's head. "Bitch to *him* about it. It's freezing, and I literally couldn't care less."

Adam dug his pills out of Bandana's pocket and tucked them away before tugging his knife free from Patches's arm. He grabbed his gun from the floor, then followed Eris down the stairs and out onto the street.

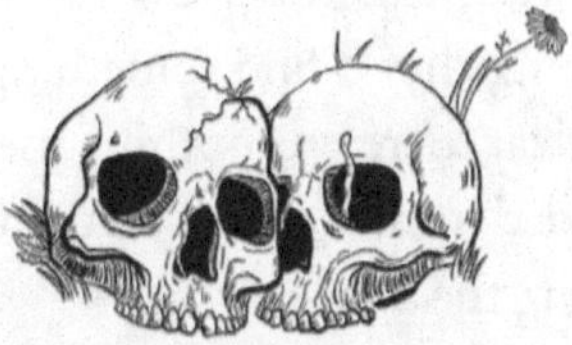

3

Haven felt haunted. More like a collection of tombs than a town.

The bodies were gone now, laid to rest beside the others in a graveyard just outside the walls. The task had been massive and had taken weeks. Not that Georgie had been able to help. The last two months had passed with her confined to a house a half hour away, healing from her stab wound, her days spent pacing and stewing and checking injuries whenever Grayson would accept her help.

The daily trips had kept the soldiers busy for a while, and the funerals brought some closure, but every moment they spent inside Haven was a risk, so after the dead were buried, they kept their distance.

There were enough supplies at the house where they'd been hiding to get by while they recovered. Food and water. Clothes. Blankets. Firewood. Even a working pickup truck. Plus, the small amount they'd scavenged from Haven. But with twenty-six people, it went quickly.

Georgie winced at the number as she headed down the street, away from the center of town. There were twenty-six left. Hundreds lost in the span of a night.

With the low supplies and the long journey ahead, the soldiers had agreed to make one more run to Haven. One last sweep before leaving for Indiana. And this time, Georgie went with them. They were optimistic, hoping they'd find something, but now, after hours of searching, it was clear there was nothing useful left.

Haven had depended mostly on the verti-farms for food, and those were decimated during the attack.

Three explosions.

Boom. Boom. Boom.

One to wipe out the soldiers and the radios after someone called them back to the base. A tactical move to neutralize Haven's defenses.

One to destroy the verti-farms. A ruthless move to eliminate any chance of Haven being revived.

And one, apparently, for revenge.

Georgie stood in the road, staring at the place she'd called home only months before. The back corner of the top floor was partially caved in, the windows all shattered.

Her fingernails dug into her palms.

Life's too short to hold grudges, right, love?

Petty bastard.

It was her first time back since that night, and the memory of it left her breathless, the sharp rattle of gunfire reverberating in her mind. For a brief, fragile moment, she let herself sink into it. Let the pain surface.

Then footsteps approached behind her, and she quickly settled her expression into a mirror of her father's—brave and unwavering—because *that* was what she needed to be.

"They're loading the truck." Grayson's voice, edged with impatience, as usual. He'd insisted on joining them for the last scavenging trip, worried that if he didn't go himself, they'd miss something at the med center.

"I'll be there in a few," Georgie mumbled, adjusting the bag on her shoulder, keeping her eyes locked on the house. It had rained nearly nonstop for the past month, so everything in the back of the house was most likely ruined—her parents' bedroom and her mom's office—but the front half of the house was still intact. Her room. Where she'd left her mom's notebooks. Her green jacket.

This was their last trip. She wouldn't get another chance.

"You're going in there?" Grayson asked.

"I need to grab something. I'll meet you guys at the gate."

He gave an indifferent grunt, and she waited for him to turn and walk away before she started up the porch steps. Her healing stomach wound still throbbed with a dull, distant sort of pain, and her hand went automatically to the spot as the muscles beneath her skin protested the movement.

The door stood slightly ajar. Georgie reached out and pushed it open, recoiling from the repugnant smell of mildew and rot. She didn't need a gas mask anymore—the only positive thing to come out of the days she'd spent with the cult—but sometimes, she wished she still carried one.

Her shadow spilled across the threshold onto the beige carpet, and for a second, she almost lost her nerve. She could feel Desmond's presence in the destruction.

Fear plucked at her nerves like guitar strings as she stepped inside, and when she closed the door behind her, the gray daylight gave way to a familiar, hazy green.

Georgie froze, her gaze following the wall up, goosebumps raising on her arms as she studied the intricate colony of glowing stalks.

How was that possible?

The fungus could follow walls and spread short distances through spores, but without a host, it couldn't go far. Or at least, it shouldn't have been able to.

What was it doing *here*? Haven was far from the city. Isolated.

She was thankful Jax had insisted on everyone else wearing masks.

The sound of voices outside brought her back to herself, and she headed further inside. The stairs were still intact, but they groaned beneath her weight, and when she made it to the second-floor landing, she breathed a sigh of relief.

Her chest filled with a hollow ache as soon as she set foot in her bedroom. Even surrounded by destruction and decay, it felt safe. Comfortable. A pocket universe away from all the terrible things that had happened.

But it wasn't real.

It wasn't safe.

She crossed the room and pulled the curtains aside, then pressed her forehead to the window glass. In the neighboring yard, Grayson searched through a plastic container while Banks scanned the street, gripping his rifle, the only movement in a stationary ghost town.

Georgie closed her eyes, picturing the town the way it had been that first day. Before the governor ruined it. Before she lost her mom. The frigid, damp air around her faded into a warm, dry summer heat, the empty streets suddenly bustling, chatter filling in the space where the silence had been a moment ago.

The pandemic was just beginning to reach its crescendo when they'd arrived at Haven. She had just been ripped from her normal life and thrown into a new house with someone else's stuff, sulking in self-pity as the world outside fractured and fell.

Selfish and entitled and weak.

Georgie had understood the severity of the pandemic. She'd watched the news reports. The death toll was already in the millions, and full lockdown had been in effect for almost a week before they left the city. But it wasn't unprecedented. It had happened once before when her mom was younger. A worldwide pandemic, just like this one.

She figured it would be awful for a while, but then things would go back to normal. She wanted to go home. Back to Chicago. To their apartment.

"How long?" she remembered asking.

Her mom's voice came from behind her. "If the doctors are right, it'll taper off in a few months."

"And if they're wrong?"

"Then we'll wait it out. Together." She gave a worn-down kind of smile and tucked Georgie's hair behind her ear. "I'm just glad you're here, Gigi. That you're safe."

The cold slid back in as she opened her eyes, the streets empty again. She pulled in an unsteady breath.

I'm just glad you're here.

But Georgie wasn't *supposed* to be. Her spot didn't belong to her.

If her parents had realized their mistake earlier, updated the paperwork, would Desmond have been there with them? Would Haven still be standing? Would they have been able to finish their vaccine?

Boom. Boom. Boom.

This mess, it all came back to *her*.

The room closed in around her like the house was taking a breath of its own, and Desmond's voice crept into her mind, knotting her stomach.

You didn't deserve any of this. I could've made a difference.

Georgie sank onto the hardwood floor. This was her fault. She let him inside and he destroyed everything.

Dark water rose around her, and she turned her focus to the cold against her skin, to the sturdiness of the floor beneath her.

All that time spent trying to be like her mom, fighting to save a dying world, and all she'd managed to do was make things worse.

What mattered now was keeping her people safe. Getting them to another Haven, handing over the plant and the notes and hoping like hell that Indiana had the resources to finish the vaccine.

Once her people were behind another Haven's walls, Georgie would find a way to get to Desmond, end this before he had the chance to track them down.

Her breathing gradually slowed, the wave of panic subdued before it could crest. Georgie dragged herself to her feet, eyes landing on the green jacket hung across the back of her desk chair, discolored and tattered. She shrugged off her bag and her winter coat, letting them drop onto the bed, and then grabbed the jacket and slipped it on, the feel of it comforting.

As she pulled her heavy coat back on overtop, her gaze swept across the room and landed on the cluttered desk where she'd left the notebooks before the party.

Georgie combed through the mess and when she came up empty, went to her bookshelf, her movements growing more frantic with each book she tossed onto the bed. When every surface in the room was bare, she stood in the center, surveying the mess.

The notebooks weren't here.

Of course Desmond had taken them.

Wood groaned in the hallway, and Georgie whipped around, her hand already on her holstered pistol.

"Wicks?" Grayson's voice.

She let her hand fall away. "Coming."

Grayson peeked in the open bedroom door, a gas mask covering his face. "How is this place contaminated?"

Georgie shrugged.

"Find anything useful?"

"No, nothing."

"A spare gas mask? Ammo? Painkillers?" The skepticism was visible in his expression, even through the scratched lenses. "Your parents really kept nothing like that here?"

"I haven't looked," she admitted. "I was trying to find—"

"Fine, I'll do it," Grayson cut her off. "This is precisely why I insisted on coming." He stormed out, muttering something under his breath.

Georgie stuffed her hands in her coat pockets, fidgeting with a small metal cube the size of an apple. She'd found BUG on their way in, and though it seemed broken, she'd held onto it, just in case.

With a sigh, she cast one last look around her room before following Grayson out.

The door across the hall stood open, Grayson already inside, which made Georgie's muscles tense. It had been an unspoken thing between her and her dad that the room was off limits. They both avoided it, pretending it wasn't there, because going in would be painful, and disturbing her mom's stuff felt wrong.

Until the day Georgie built up the nerve to go inside. She'd spent the afternoon in the office, enveloped by her mom's belongings, sobbing and reading through journal entries until she'd found the one that set her off on her vaccine tangent.

She hadn't been inside since.

The back corner of the room was a mess of rubble, one of the wooden shelves torn to pieces, the contents strewn across the floor. Daylight streamed through the broken ceiling, illuminating the dusty floor where a large puddle had accumulated. The explosion had collapsed the wall between the rooms, exposing her parents' large closet and the fittings for the master bathroom, with broken pipes jutting through the debris.

Georgie inched forward. The air no longer smelled of flowers or fresh soil; the plants were long dead, reduced to shriveled leaves in their planters. Now, it reeked of mold and stagnant water.

Grayson hastily rifled through the items on the desk.

"Not in here," she said through gritted teeth. It felt wrong, someone else being in here.

"There we go," he said, ignoring her.

She followed his line of sight to a bookshelf against the back wall, loaded with thick textbooks. It was far enough from the blast that only a few items had been knocked out of place.

A Ham radio sat in the center of the top shelf.

Why was that in here? Radios were supposed to be kept at the base.

Jax's voice carried up the stairs.

"We're up here," Georgie called back, watching as Grayson slid along the wall, carefully avoiding the puddle. "Let's go, Grayson."

"We need it," he countered. "Check the desk. See if there's anything else."

Georgie sighed, then crossed to the desk, pulling open the drawers and sifting through the clutter. A small box labeled *emergency kit* was tucked into the bottom drawer, which sounded promising until she opened it. It was the kind of thing people used to keep in their trunks for roadside emergencies. She dug through the contents, pocketing a small wind-up flashlight, but the neon vest, bulb replacements, and seatbelt cutter didn't seem particularly useful.

A small orange cylinder caught her attention, and she picked it up to read the side. *30 Minute Red Emergency Flare*. She frowned and put it back. The last thing they needed was to broadcast their location.

"Got it," Grayson said as he grabbed the radio and coiled the cords.

Georgie closed the box, then hesitated. Being able to light up somewhere dark could come in handy. She grabbed the flare and stuffed it in her coat pocket before pushing back to her feet.

The floorboards groaned louder with every step as Grayson passed the debris along the destroyed wall. He stopped suddenly, expression tightening.

"What's wrong?"

"It's fine. I'm just caught on something." He twisted, trying to free his coat from whatever had snagged it.

Georgie moved toward him, her footsteps cautious and deliberate. They shouldn't have come in here. It wasn't safe.

When she made it to Grayson, she crouched and worked the coat free of the metal bracket.

"Everything okay?" Jax asked from the doorway, his arm in a sling secured tightly across his chest. Like Grayson, his face was concealed by a gas mask, though his was just for show. The fact that he was vaccinated like her was a secret they kept between them.

As Georgie stood, her eyes landed on a silver box amid the rubble—something between a mini-fridge and a safe. The door was askew, the sides dented, and the word *cryo*-something was barely legible in the top corner. It was too bright to see the glow up here, but the wall behind it was overtaken by fungus stalks.

Samples from the lab, she realized.

Seriously?

Most people packed clothes and sentimental items. Her mom had packed her work. Because of course she did.

Always so busy trying to be a hero.

Two years they lived with this thing in their house, and Georgie had no idea.

She looked back at Jax. "Yeah, we're fine."

The floor bowed slightly beneath them, enough to throw Georgie off balance. She caught herself, but Grayson lost his footing and crashed to the ground, the radio tumbling from his hands as he let out a guttural groan.

"Get up," Georgie urged, her heart pounding against her ribcage. The floor wasn't going to hold.

"I can't!"

It took her a second to register the broken pipe through his thigh.

Jax rushed forward, his working arm reaching out to help Grayson up. "We need to get out of here."

Georgie grabbed Grayson's other hand.

"Three, two, one."

He bellowed as his leg came free, blood spurting from the wound like a garden hose.

It hit an artery. They had to work fast.

"The box," Georgie said, thoughts buzzing. "You had a box outside. Did you find any medical supplies?"

Grayson started to answer, but the words twisted into another groan. He steadied himself and tried again. "Yeah, bandages."

The floor creaked beneath their weight.

Jax's gaze flicked up to meet hers, then everything seemed to happen at once.

The sudden sound of rushing water filled the room. Jax shoved her, and she hit the floor hard, pain surging through her body. A sharp crack—and Jax and Grayson were gone.

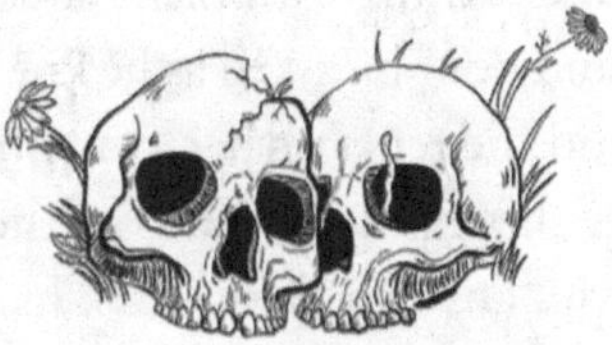

4

Georgie scrambled forward on her hands and knees until she reached the edge of the hole in the floor.

"Jax!"

No response.

Please, no.

She pushed off the ground, wincing at the sudden jolt through her stomach, and bolted down the stairs, taking them two at a time.

Two soldiers, Banks and Thompson, pushed inside as she clambered through the living room and into the kitchen. Like the room above, a portion of the far wall had collapsed, leaving the floor covered in drywall and dust and splinters of wood.

Jax was already climbing shakily to his feet.

"Are you okay?" she asked through gasping breaths.

"I...yeah, I'm okay," he muttered, dazed, and the sudden burst of relief made Georgie dizzy.

Until she realized Grayson was flat on the tile floor, his leg still gushing.

Georgie hurried to him, her knees colliding hard with the tile as she dropped and pressed down on the wound with both hands. "I need the box from outside."

Banks disappeared, returning a moment later with the small stock of supplies. "What can I do?" he asked as he knelt beside her.

She grabbed his hand and replaced her own, pushing it down. "Keep pressure on it." After shrugging off her bag, she glanced back at the other soldier, a tall woman with short black hair. "Find me a butter knife. The drawer closest to the fridge." Georgie's hands shook as she dug a roll of bandages from the crate. There wasn't much left, but she could make it work. She unwrapped it, then slanted a look at the soldier still frozen in place. "Now!"

Thompson bolted to the cabinet, returning a moment later with a metal butter knife.

Georgie took it and pulled in a steadying breath. She could do this. It was one of the first things Grayson had taught her.

After wrapping the bandage once around his leg, Georgie set the knife overtop and tied the bandage around it, creating a makeshift tourniquet. She twisted the knife, turning it like the handle of a wind-up toy, again and again and again, the bandage tightening until Grayson was shouting in pain.

"What are you doing?" Thompson asked, voice shrill with panic. "You're making it worse."

"Almost done."

The screaming abruptly cut off as Georgie tied up the ends of the bandage.

"He's not breathing," Thompson said.

Georgie's heart sank. Thompson was right. The heavy rise and fall of Grayson's chest had stopped.

What now?

She'd done everything exactly the way he'd taught her. It was supposed to work. Why didn't it work?

Do something!

There was no time to think. No time to second guess. If she hesitated, she'd miss her chance.

Georgie cursed as she crawled up and tore the gas mask from Grayson's face. She cupped her hands together over his chest and started compressions, counting out loud while her heartbeat pounded in her ears. She winced as his ribs cracked beneath the pressure.

Jax said her name, his voice quiet, but she couldn't stop. Not yet.

Keep going.

When she made it to thirty, she tilted his head, pinched his nose, and blew air into his lungs, once, twice.

She paused long enough to check for a pulse, but there was nothing, so she started again, repeating the cycle three times before Grayson finally sucked in a breath.

Georgie checked his pulse again, and this time she found it.

Calm down.

Grayson was unconscious, but he was breathing.

She tugged off her winter coat and lay flat on the floor, letting the cold tile soothe her as she caught her breath.

Finally, Georgie sat up. "We should get him out of here." She looked up at the others, who were still stuck in place, eyes somber behind their masks. Why were they just standing around? They needed to move. "Guys!"

Jax's eyes slid pointedly to the glowing corner of the room where the daylight didn't reach.

No.

Georgie scrambled to get the mask back over Grayson's face. "It was only a couple of minutes."

Still, nobody moved.

Exposure meant infection. Infection meant death. Not a damn thing they could do about it without the vaccine.

She had stopped the bleeding and gotten him breathing again, but it didn't matter. None of it mattered. She'd killed him the second she removed his mask.

She fucked up. Again.

And to add icing to the shit cake that was this scavenging trip, the radio sat in pieces a few feet away.

Why was it that no matter how hard she tried, it never seemed to matter? She was so sick of failing.

Georgie grabbed Grayson's mask and hurled it against the wall, shouting a slew of curses.

"Oh, shit, Hale," Banks said, dragging her attention back.

Jax's hand lifted slowly, touching the crack in the lens of his mask, and for a split second, ice spread through Georgie's veins.

But the mask was only for show.

He's okay.

He's fine.

Thompson drew her gun, and without a second thought, Georgie did the same, pointing it at the woman's chest.

"Put it away," Georgie growled, her finger on the trigger, face burning. There was a time when she would have cowered at the thought of firing that gun—a version of herself that had never hurt anyone. But that version was gone, and now she had no doubt that she would pull the trigger.

"Thompson," Banks urged.

The soldier held her ground, even as her hand began to shake. "There a protocol change I'm not aware of?" she asked. "'Cause I'm pretty sure y'all had the same training I had. I don't like it either, but it has to be done."

Georgie shook her head. "This is different."

"How?"

"He's vaccinated," she blurted. "He can't be infected."

Jax's mouth set in a straight line, and for a moment, the resentment she'd seen in his face at the train station returned, and as much as it stung, she was relieved to finally see it surface. He'd been pretending to be fine, but she could sense it in their strained interactions and the way he skillfully avoided being alone with her.

Banks's gaze jumped to her. "Since when?"

"Since the night the cult fell," Jax answered flatly.

"Cassira tested him," Georgie lied, wishing she would've said he was immune instead of vaccinated. If the others knew what she did, she wasn't sure how they'd react. "When the cult took him. She used her vaccine."

"Why would she waste a dose if she planned to kill him?" Banks asked.

"Don't know," Jax replied with an awkward shrug. God, he was a terrible liar.

Thompson shook her head. "You're clearly full of shit."

"I don't know what you want me to say," Jax replied.

"I want to know what you two are keeping from us. Why you're lying."

"It was me," Georgie said. "I vaccinated him."

"But Emery took the vaccine," Banks interjected.

"Well, he missed one."

Thompson's voice was a snarl. "You had a vial of the vaccine, and you, what, called dibs?"

"I wasn't going to let him die!" Georgie snapped. "He's not infected, so back off."

"Okay," Banks said. "Thompson, put the gun down."

The woman let her gun hang at her side. "That's all you have to say? *Okay*? If we had that dose, we could've made the vaccine ourselves. We wouldn't have needed to take in some asshole scientist to help us. Haven would still be standing."

"That's bullshit," Banks argued. "A single dose of the vaccine wouldn't have changed a damn thing."

"I bet Dr. Williams would disagree." Thompson turned the brunt of her anger back to Jax. "You think your life's worth more than *his*? You both just royally fucked us all. I hope it was worth it." She turned and stormed out.

Banks crouched beside Grayson and placed the barrel of his gun to his temple.

The gunshot cut through the room, a sharp bang that pulled forward a chorus of screams and staccato gunfire in Georgie's mind—the memory of a crowd mowed down in one fell swoop.

She bolted through the door and around the corner of the house, disappearing from sight just before the dark water reached up and pulled her under.

5

The gate to Jardine slid open, and three heavily armed guards watched as Adam and Eris stepped through.

Adam's boots felt like lead, each step sending a throb of pain through his leg. He struggled to keep pace as Eris strode ahead.

She pushed back her hood, the long scar on the side of her face visible for only a second before her black hair tumbled over it, then spared him a quick glance. "You look like hell, by the way."

Yeah, he figured. He could feel the patchwork of rising bruises. His cheek was swollen, forehead throbbing. Every time he spoke, his voice scraped against his bruised throat.

Adam tilted his head and flashed her a playful sideways smile. "Are you flirting with me?"

Eris rolled her eyes. "You're an idiot."

Behind them, the gate slid closed, and footsteps sounded on the concrete as the guard moved back into place.

Adam's eyes scanned the massive building, landing on one of the many surveillance cameras scattered across its exterior. He gave it a quick wave, sure Colette was watching.

"So, if you're here," he started, "I'm guessing Des is back."

"We got back yesterday," Eris answered.

"Where is he now?"

"Go sleep, Adam," both her and Oliver's voices urged in unison.

"Later. Where is he?"

"I don't know. I was out tracking some dumbass with a death wish all night."

As they stepped inside, Eris veered left, disappearing a second later. Adam checked his watch. 9:00. Comms or the command room would be his best guess. He dragged himself down the hall and pushed open the door to the latter, not bothering to knock.

Desmond Emery sat at the end of a long table, leaning casually back in his chair with his legs propped up and crossed at the ankles. Even this early, he looked as polished as the switchblade in his hand. His face was set in its usual steady calm, mouth perpetually on the verge of a smile.

His gaze lifted to meet Adam's. "Welcome back."

A man with leathery skin—Marshall, or maybe Hershel—shot Adam a glare, and the handful of people sitting at the table turned.

Adam moved further into the room and leaned against the wall, his sore muscles straining to keep him upright, and with a sweeping flourish, he urged them to continue.

The attention shifted back as Marshall went on. "The guy, he flat out refused to give us shit. Said we're not holding up our end of the deal."

"And why exactly would he think that?" Des asked, his slight English accent giving the words a smoothness that contrasted with the other man's rough, clipped way of speaking. He kept his dark eyes fixed on the knife as he casually closed and reopened it.

Marshall shifted in his chair, gaze also lingering on the knife. "There was a thing. Not a big deal." He shrugged. "It's a long story."

Des flicked the switchblade closed, studied the curled engraved lines on the handle, then set it flat on the table before he turned his full attention to the man. "Then *summarize.*"

"Okay, so, my guys and I, we run into some of their people right outside Spring Valley. It was after you left. I don't know. Friday afternoon, I think." When Desmond's lips tightened with impatience, Marshall cleared his throat nervously. "They just pull their weapons on us and start firing. So, my guys and I, we shoot them."

Des blinked. "That's a lot to throw at me before breakfast."

Marshall shifted again in his seat, the muscles in his jaw moving beneath his weathered skin.

"I left for three days," Desmond continued, his words measured. "You realize, this reflects poorly on us. We're supposed to be protecting these communities. It's difficult to do that while you're shooting at them."

"They don't know it was us. Vivian thinks it was the assholes harassing the Campus."

"It doesn't matter who they think did it," Desmond said. "Just that we let it happen."

"They didn't give us much choice. It was self-defense." Marshall kept his expression steady as he spoke, but his hand gestures were delayed, and he'd itched a spot on his arm after every sentence. His tells were subtle, but they were still there. He was lying.

Of course, Des already knew that. He wrinkled his nose and gave a smile that was somehow both delighted and cynical. "Was it now?"

"Yeah."

"Great," Desmond chimed as he ran a thumb absently over the scar on his hand. "I'd like to talk to the rest of your team when we're done here."

"Sure. Yeah, of course."

Desmond's expression darkened, his entire demeanor shifting in a breath, and when he spoke again, his voice was cloying and smooth. "Let them know that whoever caves first and tells me what really happened gets to take your place."

Des had many sides, all of them unshakably calm. Most were charming, a few were scary, but this one, it was lethal.

"I—" Marshall's face hardened as the words sank in. "Fuck you, Emery." He shot up from his seat and reached for his gun, but before he could get it free from the holster, Adam fired a round into the side of his head. He went down hard, head catching the side of the table, leaving a dark red smear behind.

Des rewarded Adam with an approving quirk of his mouth and a subtle raised eyebrow.

A wiry man in a worn leather jacket pushed to his feet. His mouth opened to speak, but he must have lost his nerve, because it snapped shut again.

"Is there a problem?" Des asked, his voice tinged with something. Not anger—there was never anger—but a cold, prickling displeasure.

The man, Jay, shrank back, and after a moment, he dropped into his chair.

The room fell into a hushed silence, and nobody seemed to breathe until, finally, Desmond's face softened into a warm grin. "Well, that's a way to start the day."

They continued, ignoring the corpse on the ground and the puddle of blood that was slowly spreading toward the center of the room as they discussed the handful of other settlements and the contributions from the last week.

Once they were done, the others filed out through the door, and Desmond, who hadn't moved from his spot at the table, leveled his gaze at Adam.

"Good to have you back."

Adam forced a smile. "I just couldn't stay away. Especially when you send Eris to shadow me."

Desmond gave him an evaluative look. "Take off that mask when you speak to me. I don't need you sugar-coated."

The smile fell away. "Okay, fine, how about this?" Adam crossed the room and sank into the chair beside him. "It's been over two months and you still haven't made a move to take out the Hub. I'm not staying here if—"

"If you want to leave," Des interrupted, his tone indifferent, "then, by all means, go. I'll call Eris off right now. I'm not forcing anyone to be here."

The chair squeaked as Adam leaned back, a feeble attempt to mimic Desmond's nonchalance. Adam was bluffing, and not only did Des know it, but his poker face was way better. He had nowhere to go. Nobody else that wanted him. This was the closest Adam had come to having a family since Alice. Even Oliver and Georgie turned out to be just like everyone else.

Leave, Adam, Oliver's voice begged. *You've survived on your own, and you can do it again.*

Adam shook his head. He didn't want to be alone.

"Brilliant. Right now, my concern is finding the strays and my plant. After that, I'll have whatever resources you need." His head tilted slightly. "You *do* understand?"

Exhaustion snuffed out Adam's frustration. "I guess," he said, stifling a yawn as he placed his elbow on the table and propped his chin in his hand. "So, what was this big run I wasn't allowed to go on?"

Desmond and a handful of his best fighters had taken off days earlier, armed to the teeth. When Adam had asked to join them, Desmond brushed him off. *Next time*, he'd said, like he was placating a child to avoid a tantrum.

With them gone, Adam had opted to go after the Hub's people on his own. Reckless, yes. But it was an experiment, not a tantrum.

He needed to find a way to sleep, and pacing Jardine wasn't helping.

"Just a quick errand," Desmond answered, and when Adam rolled his eyes, Des's mouth quirked. "The Missouri Haven."

Adam frowned. "So, you can make time to clear out a Haven, but not the Hub?"

"The two are vastly different endeavors," Desmond replied. "I had inside sources at that Haven. Those people were untrained, lazy, and complacent. It was only a matter of time before someone stumbled upon their location. I was merely putting a dying Haven out of its misery." He tapped the table with his finger. "Now, The Hub, that will be a real challenge. And as much as I love a challenge, now is not the time."

Adam nodded, fighting against heavy eyelids.

Des watched him for a long moment, assessing, and Adam wondered how visible the damage on his face was.

"Come with me tomorrow," Desmond said suddenly.

Adam sat up straight. "Where?"

"Hershel's mistake appears to have caused some discontentment." *Hershel. Not Marshall.* Not that it mattered anymore. "I think I'll pop by Spring Valley to smooth it over."

"I'm in."

"Thought you might be. I'll have someone bring by some ammo for your rifle."

A smile tugged at Adam's lips. His sniper rifle had been empty since he messed up a run his first week here, and though Desmond had promised to restock it, he'd yet to follow through. Another promise he kept putting off.

The absence of the gun left Adam feeling unbalanced, and he still reached for it like a phantom limb, so the thought of having it back was exhilarating.

"Try to get some rest."

"Sure," Adam replied dismissively.

Desmond's expression sobered. "You know you're safe here. You don't have to be on guard all the time. Sleep."

He knew Des was right. This was the safest place in the city. It was guarded, monitored, protected.

Adam liked being at Jardine, and it wasn't just the security of the place. All these people who had been screwed over and left for dead, Desmond understood them. Fought for them. And better yet, he delivered consistent results. He could strategize, pick out pressure points, and bring an entire settlement to its knees with a few well-placed jabs, and the others were more than happy to deliver the final blows when necessary.

Cassira and her cult.

The Illinois Haven.

Both done with careful precision and lots of planning.

Meticulous, formulated chaos, he'd heard Desmond say once.

With a reputation like that and the charm to top it off, the other communities were eager to make him an ally. He offered them protection, and in return, they willingly offered supplies. A business transaction built on a thin layer of trust.

But where the subtle jabs were enough with the settlements, the less civilized factions that had popped up in the cult's absence responded better to violence, and Desmond could play both roles perfectly. Fear and respect kept those ones at bay, kept them from attacking anyone under Des's protection, and if they dared to overstep, a single brutal display would reignite that fear.

And the people at Jardine, Des had this way of doing things—clever and ruthless—that made them hang on his every word. They *wanted* to be here. Wanted him on their side.

Why, then, wouldn't the Havens? Why would they turn him away?

"How'd you lose your spot?" Adam asked.

Desmond arched a brow.

"I mean, I know you blame Georgie, but what actually happened?"

"Nepotism," Des answered plainly. "Bigotry. And a bit of nationalism. All the fundamental principles upon which Project Noah was built. Those with power have never had a problem exploiting those without, especially when they can dress it up as patriotism. Why do you want to know?"

Adam shrugged. He knew the Havens were filled with terrible people. They'd proven that when they tried to hold him against his will, eager to poke and prod him like a lab rat. But Georgie had seemed different. She was his friend. And he thought, maybe if he had proof that she was terrible just like them, he'd be able to forget the look on her face when she thought he'd betrayed her.

And maybe he'd feel less guilty now that he actually *had*.

"Our team was part of Project Noah," Des said. "Planning for the future of humanity. Self-sufficient communities. Top-level technology." He picked up the knife again, absentmindedly flicking it open and sliding it closed, the rhythmic *click, click, click* pulling Adam's attention. "Georgie's mother, Elaina, was my boss. Our role was plant genetics. Cultivating resilient plants to provide sustenance for entire communities in space-constrained environments."

Click. Click. Adam's vision blurred at the edges as the light glinted off the polished blade.

"Elaina, Arthur, Isaiah, and myself, we developed the verti-farms together. Towering vertical planters with highly intricate self-filtering irrigation systems. It earned us an official spot when these little communities came to fruition. After all, they couldn't exist without our contribution."

Adam thought of the building he'd seen at Haven as he wandered the streets. The massive glass structure filled to the ceiling with planters.

"Near the tipping point of the pandemic," Des continued, "our team was moved to a different part of the lab. Top secret. High security. They had tried everything to find a solution for the infection, and we were a last, desperate stretch. We worked for weeks on end, staying at the lab long after everyone else left, neglecting sleep, skipping meals. Four brilliant minds set on solving one catastrophic problem." His face brightened. "And we did it. The human trials were successful, and we produced the first round of vaccines for distribution. Thirty vials. Enough for a couple hundred doses."

"From the plant?" Adam asked.

Des answered with a nod. "But something went wrong. Out of the blue, the trial participants died. All of them within hours of each other. And because I happened to be the one present during the incident, they tried to place the blame on me. But before anything could come of it, Project Noah was initiated. They locked down the lab, put it in preservation mode, and we were told to evacuate the city."

Click. Click. "When I made it to Haven, they turned me away. Elaina even had the nerve to show her face, giving me the full sob story, like she expected me to understand. But it was *their* incompetence that I was being punished for. They'd forgotten to re-register their daughter as an adult. When the collapse happened, she didn't have a spot, so they took mine."

"Why you? Why not pick someone else?"

"I was under investigation. My job was already on the line." He gestured with the knife as he spoke. "That, coupled with the little detail that Elaina made sure to point out to them. I was born in India, raised in England, and I'd only moved here from London a couple of years before they hired me. I'm a foreign national. Apparently, I should never have received the spot in the first place." With a shake of his head, he added, "She had no trouble getting their consent to make the switch."

"That's messed up."

Des closed the knife with a harsh finality and tucked it away. "I agree. But I think we're even now." A sharp flicker of a smile.

That proved that Georgie's parents were terrible people, not her. And it certainly didn't make Adam feel any better.

"Did you ever find out what happened with the vaccine?"

"Turns out, betrayal was a recurring issue within our team." Des's tone was clipped in a way that said to let it go, and he pushed up from the chair, signaling that the conversation was over.

Adam dragged himself to his feet.

"Where'd Eris disappear to?" Desmond asked as he pulled open the door, leaning against it to hold it ajar.

"Couldn't tell you."

"I think she may be angry with me." He motioned for Adam to go first, then followed him out, the door falling closed behind them. "Wish me luck," Des added before whirling and striding down the large hallway.

Adam smiled. He missed this place.

6

When Oliver finally peeled himself off the bed, the weight of everything came with him. He plucked a sweater from a pile of neatly folded shirts and slipped it on over his green flannel button-up, then added his coat overtop. It was freezing, and even inside his room, he could see his breath.

As he passed his desk, the partially assembled purifier seemed to taunt him, adding to the pandemonium in his head. Oliver hated leaving things unfinished. Especially something this important.

But, as much as it irritated him, Viv had a strict *everyone chips in* way of doing things. Fair was fair. She'd let him stay when she could've easily turned him away.

Oliver pulled open the hatch door, and as the ladder unfolded, he tugged on a gray and black striped beanie, tucking the overgrown strands of hair out of his face. He slipped a pair of cotton gloves into his coat pocket and wrapped a heavy scarf around his neck before descending to the floor below.

The sound of overlapping voices echoed up the stairs, and he paused by the window, taking a moment to brace himself for the submersion while his gaze slid over the yard outside.

The sky was the usual dreary gray of Illinois in winter, and through the bare trees of the forest, he could just make out the lake and the weathered wooden dock.

Spring Valley sat on a hundred acres of forests and prairies, smack dab in the middle of the suburbs, set up as some kind of historical recreation used in field trips. A living museum. The farmhouse was beautiful, with enormous living spaces and a spacious kitchen.

When Oliver was twelve, he moved to a cookie-cutter suburban house from a tiny two bedroom. He remembered thinking it was too big. He would lose things all the time, and their beagle, who had slept at the foot of his bed since they brought her home nine years prior, had a hard time making it up to his room.

But as big as it was, it had nothing on this place.

Even with the six extra added to Spring Valley's population of fourteen, there was enough room for everybody.

They had goats for milk, chickens for eggs, and even a few pigs. There weren't a ton of crops, but the ones they had were thriving and protected from not only the elements, but the infection by the thick cover of the greenhouse. And the basement was stocked with jars of miscellaneous preserves.

It was incredible, really, what they'd accomplished here, which kept Oliver constantly on edge, knowing there were people who would kill for this setup. Literally. And nobody here carried weapons. Vivian's rule.

She had a whole lot of faith in their protection deal.

Oliver sighed and glanced at the stairs. The faster he finished his chores, the sooner he could get back to work.

He reached the bottom level of the farmhouse, making a beeline for the front door, but the savory smell of something buttery slowed his steps like an electrical current hitting a resistor. His stomach growled, reminding him how long it had been since he'd taken time to eat.

Maybe he could grab something small before heading out.

The crackling fire in the living room radiated warmth, and the handful of people spread across the floor picked at the plates propped in their laps, talking loudly between bites.

Oliver tensed.

Blend in. Don't draw attention.

It wasn't that he hated being around people. At the Campus, he didn't mind it at all. Kye had always been straightforward about what was expected of him. She didn't leave things up to interpretation. He knew the rules, knew the people by name, knew who he was there. But these people were strangers. He still didn't know what they expected of him, and the fear of doing something wrong made it impossible to relax when any of them were around.

As he moved through the living room, Oliver zipped his coat up to his chin and shoved his hands in his pockets. The space was too enclosed, too loud.

Someone sneezed. A fork scraped on a plate.

Slurp. Chew. Scrape.

The sounds sent a shudder through him, and he clenched his fists in his pockets to prevent them from slapping over his ears.

Why was everybody so loud?

He stared at the scuffed wooden floors as he entered the kitchen, where the bulky cast-iron stove emitted a dry, suffocating heat.

As he reached for a slice of fresh bread, an old woman with deep wrinkles greeted him with a warm smile.

"Good morning."

When Oliver tried to respond, his body fought back, his voice buried somewhere deep inside him. He breathed a frustrated sigh through his nose, his face tightening into a frown, which, guessing by the woman's scowl, she assumed was directed at *her*.

He knew that wasn't polite, but he couldn't shape the expression into anything different.

Oliver's body always seemed to be working against him. When his brain felt overloaded, it would shut down certain functions, like it was trying to conserve power for the essential ones. Usually, this would manifest in subtle ways, like quiet shutdowns in his room or missing a meal or two. Nobody would even notice. But other times, it was less subtle. Meltdowns in public. Shouting, crying. His parents used to have to drop everything to take him home.

During the really bad times, when the world felt particularly impossible, his words would stop coming altogether. A switch would flip, making even the *thought* of speaking unbearable.

The first time, at least the first Oliver could remember, was when he was ten. When Patrick left for vacation with one of his friends.

Patrick wasn't just his brother, he was his best friend.

Every day after school, Patrick would remove his implants to shut out the sounds of the world, and they'd have entire conversations in sign language, both of them relishing the silence.

He never judged Oliver for the ways he was different.

When Patrick left, Oliver had a meltdown. He locked himself in his room for the rest of the day, and when he finally resurfaced, the words didn't come with him. They stayed gone for two days. Well, not *gone*. Just hard to reach. Painful, almost.

It happened again the day he lost everything. He was sure he'd never say another word after that, not that there'd been anyone left to talk to.

That was when Cassira found him and took him in.

Oliver placed a piece of thick bread on a plate and covered it in blackberry preserves, then flattened himself against the wall. He took a bite, the faces of everyone he'd lost whirling in his mind as the sounds of the kitchen scraped across the inside of his skull.

Kye and Vivian were planted at the table in the kitchen, deep in a heated conversation with a man in Carhart coveralls.

"It's extortion," the man growled, breaking through the other noises. "Plain and simple."

"No, it's insurance." Viv's voice was quieter, and Oliver had to strain to hear her. "And it wasn't your place to turn them away."

"They're gonna bleed us dry. We just took in more people and can't afford to keep handing over our supplies."

"We have a lot here to protect. It's worth the payment."

The man stood and slammed his hands down on the wooden surface, and Oliver jumped at the sound. "They aren't even keeping up their end of the deal. We lost four people."

"If we didn't have this agreement," Viv said, leaning in, "we'd lose a lot more. We can either give these people a fraction of what we have and stand together against whatever may come, or we can stand alone and face losing all of it. This was the first incident since we made the deal. They're helping."

The man spat a bitter laugh. "They're thugs taking advantage of the fact that they're better armed than us. We're not giving them nothing else."

"With all due respect, Hal, it's not your call."

"Should I take a vote?" Hal asked.

"By all means. While you're at it, you can explain how you told the people dangerous enough to keep all the other threats away to fuck off."

There was a noticeable shift in the man's expression as that sank in. "It's not a big deal," he said. "They weren't mad or nothing."

"You kicked the hornet nest. You think they're just going to let it go?"

Hal said something Oliver couldn't hear, then turned and left.

Kye must have said something then because Vivian's head tilted to look at her.

"You agree with him."

Kye shrugged. "Protection's a good thing. There's a lot of bad out there, and this group seems like they're doing more good than harm at the moment. But it's a thin line. How long before they cross it?"

"If we go back on our deal," Vivian responded, "well, you know as well as I do how that would end." She pushed her gray braid off her shoulder, and it hung down her back as she stacked their empty plates. "Anyway, that's a problem for another day. We have more important matters to worry about right now with this blizzard coming."

Kye nodded once. "What can I do?"

"The livestock need fresh water. Heat it first so it won't freeze. The snow's already starting."

"On it."

Vivian noticed Oliver then, and he quickly dropped his gaze to the plate in his hands, pretending he wasn't just eavesdropping. Her chair scraped against the floor as she stood.

"Good morning, Mr. Brennan. Did Kye relay your assignment for the day?"

He managed a slight nod.

"Great. We'll see you for lunch, then. Stay warm." She placed the stack of plates on the counter before heading out the door.

Oliver shoved the last bite in his mouth and added his plate to the top of the stack, the sensation of Kye's eyes on him making him itchy.

He should leave. He had his assignment. But if he went now, Kye might tag along, and he was looking forward to walking alone.

He'd just wait her out.

Oliver shifted the stack of plates, pretending to straighten up, and when she still didn't go, he gave in and looked at her, his mouth pinched. *What?* he wanted to ask, but the words were still stuck, and he didn't currently have the energy to force them out.

She stood and joined him at the counter. "You've been here a little while," she started. "Do you know anything about these people?"

Oliver considered the question, fingers twisting the strings on the bottom of his scarf until they formed a tight coil.

He shrugged, answering silently. *Not really.*

Over the past two months, he'd gathered enough details to suspect they were the same group Art had mentioned. His people had struck the same deal: supplies in exchange for protection. It added up. How many groups had the influence to offer something like that?

He also guessed they were the ones responsible for gunning down the cult. The same ones who'd tried to recruit Adam. Again, it made sense. There were too many overlapping factors to be a coincidence.

But he didn't actually know anything about them.

"Do you trust them?"

Not even a little. He shook his head.

"Yeah," she muttered. "Me either."

This group was clearly dangerous. Adam's deal was the reason Oliver had to push him away. Had to find somewhere they couldn't get to him. The reason he had to leave the Campus so Adam wouldn't come looking for him.

Then again, Adam wouldn't have had to make that deal if it weren't for Oliver. If Cassira hadn't sent two members of the family—Oliver cringed at the word, quickly correcting himself—two members of the *cult* to the Campus.

She wanted revenge for her brother's death, and she gave Oliver a choice. Come back to her and bring Georgie, or she'd have Adam killed.

Oliver may have owed Georgie for getting him out of the train station, but he'd always choose Adam over anybody else. So, he ran back to the cult to save him, and Adam made a deal to get him back. Oliver couldn't have foreseen that happening, but it didn't make it any less his fault.

He knew those people would come for Adam. For a while, they kept him hidden inside the Campus, but it wasn't a permanent solution. They couldn't keep people like that out.

Plus, being confined made Adam miserable.

When Oliver realized that their current path wasn't viable, he found a new one. And it worked. Adam was safe. He was at a Haven, surrounded by walls and soldiers and people who were better for him than Oliver. Better for him than some group out to use him as a weapon.

"I know you don't want to talk about it," Kye started, bringing him back to the present, "but can you at least tell me that Adam's okay?"

He sunk into his shoulders and nodded once.

"And you?"

Not even a little, thought Oliver, but he just shrugged.

Kye sighed and pushed away from the counter. "Guess I should get to it." She hesitated, like she wanted to say something else, but a moment later, she turned and headed out of the kitchen.

The interaction left Oliver feeling drained, and he stayed there in the kitchen, staring at the worn wallpaper until he finally found the strength to move.

Oliver spent the rest of the morning shuttling between the farmhouse and the cabin, the worn-out wheelbarrow rattling along the uneven path. He tried to focus his attention on the task, on the bare branches of the trees, the squeaking of the wheel, but his mind inevitably drifted, sifting through memories.

Mornings in a sun-drenched tent.

Nights in the bay window of an apartment lit by flickering candlelight.

A boy with a smile so bright that, when genuine, it could warm the entire room.

On his fifth trip back to the cabin, Kye's questions intruded on the peaceful memories, and after obsessing over those for a while, his thoughts settled on the day they first stumbled upon the Campus—the day he first met her.

It had been a while since they'd come across any other people, so the sound of voices had stopped them both in their tracks. When they found a handful of survivors fumbling with a broken security light outside the University of Chicago, Adam wanted to keep going. Avoid them. But Oliver wanted to help.

It ended up being a simple fix. The transformer wasn't doing its job. Within the hour, the light was up and running, and he and Adam had a new place to call home.

Oliver stopped short, the wind rattling the tree branches as it cut through the forest.

His brow cinched.

The transformer.

It couldn't be that simple, could it?

He closed his eyes, replaying the dozen different solutions he'd tried while working on the purifier, but not one of them involved replacing the transformer. He hadn't even considered it. Not once.

As his eyes fluttered open, he couldn't help but let out a small laugh.

A simple fix.

"How did I miss that?" he asked the empty forest, the words coming without issue now.

Oliver's fingers curled on the handles of the wheelbarrow, fighting the sudden urge to abandon it. To run across the street and search the houses, to fix it now.

But he couldn't afford to be reckless. Besides, he'd told Vivian he would help, and he couldn't go back on his word.

He'd finish the chores, and first thing tomorrow, he'd go find a new transformer and get back to work.

7

They buried Grayson in the graveyard alongside Haven's other fallen. No one had spoken for over an hour, and by the time the soldiers finally laid down their shovels and shouldered their bags, the sun was touching the horizon. Jax's face glistened with sweat, flushed from the exertion of trying to keep up with one arm tucked in a sling.

Two months had passed since the bullet tore through his shoulder, damaging the brachial plexus, and he still hadn't regained mobility in his right arm. The damage was likely permanent. He refused to acknowledge it or talk about it, but it weighed heavily on him. Georgie could see it in the way he pushed himself, like he was always trying to prove something.

She clasped the dog tags hanging around her neck as she followed the soldiers to the truck, tracing the engraved letters with her thumb.

This was supposed to be a simple scavenging trip. They should've all made it back. They'd only managed to gather two crates worth of supplies, and none of it was worth the price they'd paid. Even the radio was a lost cause after the fall, the pieces littered across the kitchen tile.

There was nothing left.

Georgie was eager to leave, ready to put this place behind her.

She joined Banks in the cab of the truck, the others climbing into the back, and they pulled away from Haven in silence, the loss hanging heavy in the air around them.

Grayson was gone.

Twenty-six. She flinched as she corrected herself. Twenty-*five*. Twenty-five survivors and no doctor.

What were they going to do? They'd eaten their way through the stock of food in the house. The plan was Indiana. They'd all agreed it was the best solution. Jax had been there once, so he knew where it was. But the truck wouldn't fit everybody, and the gauge was hovering just above *E*. It was too far to go by foot, especially in this cold.

Banks straightened suddenly, his fists clenching onto the steering wheel. "That's not a common sight these days," he muttered under his breath.

Georgie followed his line of sight, tensing as she picked out the shape on the horizon, a small silhouette with pinprick headlights. "Is it coming this way?"

Banks didn't answer, but he slowed the truck to a crawl and flipped off the lights. The other vehicle was definitely getting closer.

"We need to get off the road," she said.

Banks shook his head. "There's nowhere to go."

Georgie eyed the cornfields on either side. The stalks were dead and wilted and thin, spread too wide to provide any cover, but it was better than the alternative. "Go through."

"We'd leave an obvious trail. And damage the truck." He pounded on the back windshield three times. "Company."

The warning sent Jax and Thompson into action. They fumbled noisily in the truck bed, readying their weapons.

"We'll pass quickly," Banks said. "They'll probably be more freaked out than we are."

With a forceful push on the gas pedal, the truck lurched forward, its engine roaring as they picked up speed.

What were the odds that these were just other survivors? They were an hour's drive from the city, surrounded by farmland. The only thing out this way was Haven.

An icy cold crept into her bones as the other vehicle took shape.

No.

"Get off the road, Banks."

When he started to argue, Georgie grabbed the wheel and forced the truck off into the shallow ditch, plowing through the layers of dead cornstalks. She pressed her hand to her stomach, trying to stop the sparks of pain that tore through her with every jarring bump.

When the truck finally came to a stop, they were deep in the field, not hidden, but far enough from the road to give them a chance of not being noticed, if the other vehicle hadn't spotted them already.

"What the hell are you doing, Wicks?" Banks snapped, slamming the shifter into park, but his scowl dissolved when he saw the look on her face.

Georgie twisted around to look out the dirty back window as a bulky Humvee flew past.

Their Humvee. The one Desmond had stolen.

Her breathing stuttered, her lungs tightening as her shirt clung to her damp skin.

The back window slid open. "We can't go back to the others," Jax said. "We need to find a place to wait it out until we're sure they're not following."

Banks shifted into drive, and the truck tore through the field. By the time they reached the next town, Georgie's soaring pulse had slowed slightly. They parked the truck in a garage and settled in to wait.

When they finally deemed it safe to head back to the others, twilight had given way to night.

Banks pulled the truck around to the back of the house, out of sight from the street, and as Georgie slid out of the passenger door, she shaped her expression to hide the fear rattling through her nerves.

She gripped the edge of the truck bed, steadying herself as she looked up at the house. Smoke billowed from the chimney, leaving a smudge of gray across the dark sky.

When they reached the patio, Banks stopped and scrubbed a hand over his messy beard.

"We keep the vaccine thing between us," he said, giving Thompson a pointed look. "It happened. It's in the past. Bringing it up now will only cause more problems, and we already have a stockpile of those."

Thompson's eyes narrowed, but she didn't respond.

"I mean it," Banks added. "Not a word. That's an order."

The soldier scoffed and shoved past him.

As they followed her through the back door, a boy hopped up from the couch. Levi Banks had the same dark eyes and umber skin as his older brother, though his face was soft and boyish where Chris's was made up of hard lines.

"How'd it go?" he asked. "Did you find any more food?"

"No, but I found this." Banks set a crate on the ground at his feet and pulled something from inside.

Levi's face brightened. "My chess board!" He took the board from Banks, running his fingers along the smooth surface.

Georgie's gaze swept over the group in the living room. A handful of people were huddled on the couch beneath a blanket, a few more beside the brick fireplace, the flames casting a warm glow over their faces. Large mattresses were arranged on the floor, the rest of the group sprawled out across them, some already asleep.

"Put that out," Jax ordered as he crossed to the window and pulled the curtains closed. "You can see the smoke from the main road."

Wren shot him a scowl. "We'll freeze."

"Double up on clothes. Stay huddled."

As Jax rushed to the next window, Wren's expression softened with understanding. "What happened?"

"We saw another car on the road, out by Haven," he responded.

"That's twenty miles from here. Why does—"

"It was our Humvee," Georgie interrupted.

Wren's expression fell. "Oh."

"Yeah."

The others worked to extinguish the fire as Reese slid past to pluck the large pot from above it.

"I guess we're having lukewarm corn chowder tonight." He set the pot on the floor in the center of the room, then disappeared into the kitchen, returning with a stack of bowls and a fistful of spoons.

This had been his evening routine ever since they found this place. It was his way of thanking them for letting him stay with their group after Haven. He was an excellent cook, and could make canned goop taste surprisingly decent with a few thoughtful add-ins.

Reese lifted the lid and scooped a small portion into a bowl before handing it to Wren. "If it's terrible," he said with a playful smile, "feel free to lie."

"I'm sure it's delicious. Thanks, Reese."

Georgie wanted to trust Reese. They had the plant because of him. He seemed like a good guy who got caught up in a bad situation, but every time she looked at him, she saw his twin sister. He and Flora had the same face shape, the same dark skin speckled with vitiligo patches, the same golden-brown eyes. Although her resentment wasn't aimed at him, at least not directly, she couldn't let go of it.

When he finished distributing the bowls and spoons, Reese sat beside Piper on the couch. Neither of them had taken a bowl for themselves.

Piper searched the room, eyes landing on Jax. "Where's Grayson?"

A pit formed in Georgie's stomach as she looked down at her hands. She had washed them three times before leaving Haven, but her skin was still stained red from Grayson's blood. Or was it in her head?

Jax answered Piper's question with a quick shake of his head, sending a palpable wave of dread through the room.

"What happened?"

"Exposure. Contaminated house."

"At Haven? How?"

The conversation continued, but Georgie was no longer listening. She perched on the windowsill, staring out into the darkness through the thin opening in the curtains, arms crossed to hide her trembling hands.

Since Haven fell, her anxiety had been at an all-time high, locked in a constant power struggle with her anger. She kept hoping the anger would overpower and smother the fear, because anger was manageable. Anger she could use. But this fear—the perpetual state of fight-or-flight—it made her reckless. Made her weak. It left destruction in its wake.

She had hoped that when it came time to face Desmond again, the anger would be enough to drive her forward. But it wasn't. Fear won out. She saw the Humvee and panicked. Even now, it was all she could feel, and she was terrified that it would snuff out the embers that kept her going.

As long as they had the plant, he'd never stop looking for them, and this close to Haven, he *would* find them. Maybe they should leave the damn thing at Haven. Let him have it. Maybe then he'd leave them alone. Her throat constricted, blocking out the air as the room pressed in against her.

It was too much. She couldn't breathe.

Stop it.

This wasn't who she was supposed to be.

Georgie shot up, determined to get out of sight before she fell apart. She stumbled clumsily through the back door, pouring out onto the patio and lowering herself onto the cold concrete, legs folded beneath her, before her body stopped responding. Her stomach churned as she fought back the bile rising in her throat.

He was going to find them.

Gunfire echoed through her thoughts.

Her heart slammed against her ribcage, one word echoing in time with her pulse. *Run. Run. Run.*

They needed to go. Needed to get further from Haven. Needed to make it to Indiana.

Georgie's breaths came in ragged gasps as the dark water turned to tar, seeping in through her nose and mouth. Desperately, her lungs strained for air, the world spinning viciously around her. She folded forward, hands splayed on the ground, fighting to remain upright.

After what felt like an eternity, she resurfaced, feeling tattered and brittle, like she would crumble under the slightest breeze.

Usually, as her pulse settled, the dread would ease, at least a little. But this time, it held on tight.

Startled by the sound of approaching footsteps, Georgie turned to find Banks standing beside her, a bowl in his hands

"Did you get anything to eat?" he asked, holding it out to her.

Georgie grimaced at the potent smell of corn chowder, swallowing hard as she shook her head. She burrowed deeper in her coat, trying to hide the turmoil she knew was etched on her face.

Why was she like this? She was supposed to be strong. She was supposed to be fighting for these people, like her parents had. How was it that she inherited so much from them, but she seemed to have missed out on all the qualities that truly mattered? She would have gladly traded the copper hair for her mother's rational intelligence or her hazel eyes for her father's unwavering courage. Instead, she was a terrified bundle of anxiety with only a superficial likeness to them.

If they were here, they'd know what to do. They wouldn't be afraid.

After a long stretch of silence, Banks set the bowl on the patio. His face softened, and for a moment, he looked like the boy she'd grown up with. Her stand-in family when her own was too preoccupied to give a shit.

She missed that version of him. Missed that apartment. The way his parents would set her a plate without even asking. Missed feeling like she was part of something.

She missed Mabel.

"We should get back inside," Banks said finally. "It's starting to snow."

Georgie tipped her head back, the cold biting at her face as a large snowflake landed on her lashes. Another on the tip of her nose. She stared up at the dark sky, dragging in a deep breath as the snow fell around them.

Without warning, everything she'd been holding in came pouring out. She doubled over as a sob ripped through her, tears spilling uncontrollably.

Apologies had never been her strong suit. It wasn't pride or stubbornness. It was the vulnerability they demanded. But, in that moment, she didn't have the strength to fight back the words she'd been dying to say.

"I'm so sorry." Georgie dropped her face into her hands. "For Grayson. For Haven. I fucked everything up."

"Neither of those were your fault."

She looked up at him and the words tumbled out before she could stop them. "And I'm sorry about Mabel."

"Don't," he warned through clenched teeth.

She had been fighting so hard to keep that night from her thoughts, but it was there now. "I'm sorry I left her at that party. I'm sorry I came back too late."

"Georgie," he growled.

"I'm sorry I kissed her. I'm sorry I ruined everything. She told me to go, and I listened. I should've stayed. It's my fault, and you're right to hate me."

"I didn't..." Banks started, but the sentence tapered off. "That wasn't the story we got."

"She was wasted, and I left her there. I should've tried harder to convince her to go home."

"Like anyone could convince Mabel to do anything she didn't want to do." A hint of a smile crossed his face, and then it was gone. He held out his hand. "Come on. It's freezing."

She wiped away her tears, then pulled in a deep breath before taking his hand and climbing to her feet. She'd said her piece, allowed herself a moment to grieve.

Now, there were bigger things to worry about. They all needed rest because tomorrow, they had to leave.

8

Georgie was exhausted, but when Jax offered to take first watch, she volunteered to stay up with him.

"I'm fine on my own," he argued.

"I know you are, but we need to figure out our plan before morning."

He had no argument for that, so they both stayed up, planted at the front windows.

A lantern sat on the coffee table, turned down low. Just enough light to push the shadows back to the edges of the room. The gentle, steady rhythm of breathing filled the space as the others drifted off to sleep, tucked under blankets.

"We could search the towns around here. Find another working car."

"We need gas," Jax replied from his spot in the window. "It's a long drive, and the tank is almost dry."

Thompson should've been sleeping, but instead she had propped herself against the couch and was busy organizing the items from her bag. If she was listening to their conversation, she didn't show it.

"We'll check the gas stations," Georgie said. "Garages. There's got to be something. We can avoid the city. The country roads are empty. It'll be a straight shot to Indiana."

Jax kept his gaze locked on the window.

"We have to leave, Jax." Georgie studied his profile in the dim light, wishing she could read his thoughts. "You're sure you remember how to get there?"

Jax had only been to the Indiana Haven once, when he thought she was dead—while she was being tortured by a pair of psychopaths with God complexes.

Her fingers instinctively landed on her arm, tracing the place where, beneath the layers of thermals, the raised scar formed the shape of a diamond-tipped cross.

"Yeah, I think so. It's just..." His words trailed off.

"We *are* leaving, right?"

"I agree we should search the towns in the morning," he said. "To look for a radio. We need to see if there's any chance Indiana will come pick us up. We should stay put until we have an actual plan to get there safely. There are twenty-six of us and—"

"Twenty-five," Thompson corrected without looking up. "Ya'll killed one, remember."

Georgie shot her a scowl.

"If you're not gonna sleep," Jax told Thompson, "go check the attic for any warm clothes we might have missed. Snowsuits. Boots. Anything. We'll need them for tomorrow."

Thompson zipped her bag and climbed off the floor. "Fine, but I'm taking second watch when I get back." She turned and stormed up the stairs.

When they were alone, the tension sat between them like a dense fog. It was strange how far someone could feel while sitting five feet away.

Georgie wanted things to go back to how they were before.

She missed the easiness between them, the sort of silence that didn't need filling. She missed the hours they'd spend together in his cozy box of a house or sprawled in the grass at the edge of town, sometimes talking about their lives before the collapse, other times not saying a word. Jax would clean his gun or practice his guitar—he was just starting to get the hang of it—while Georgie studied her medical books or doodled in her sketchbook.

From the first time they spoke, amidst the aftermath of the uprising, there had been an undeniable magnetic pull between them.

The Locals were finally allowed to join Haven's military, and one day, he came into the med center with a cut beneath his eye, thanks to a couple assholes who didn't agree with the new rules. He and Georgie spent an hour talking—she couldn't even remember what about. But that pull was there, and it had been ever since.

But it felt different now.

Despite her efforts to prevent it, she still lost him, and she wasn't sure she'd ever get him back.

Georgie glanced at the staircase. "Think she'll be a problem?" she asked, desperate to fill the silence and stop the downward spiral of her mind.

"Thompson?" Jax shrugged. "She's just pissed. She'll get over it."

"What if she tells everyone?" Georgie might not see her choice as a mistake, but she wondered how the others would react. How they would treat Jax. He was battling so much, and protecting these people seemed to give him purpose. What if they turned on him, blamed him for something that wasn't even his decision? Something she'd forced him to do.

"Worst-case scenario," Jax said, "they're pissed for a while, too. But Banks had a point. Even if you'd taken that vaccine back to Haven, a single dose wouldn't have fixed things. It wouldn't have stopped what happened. The game was rigged against us before we even knew we were part of it."

Georgie met his gaze, her brows drawing together. "Then why are you still mad at me for using it?"

He matched her frown. "I'm not mad that you used the vaccine, Georgie. I'd pick saving you over fixing the world, too."

She flushed. "You would?"

"Of course I would. But I didn't *want* you to save me. I told you not to, and that should've mattered." His tone was steady, and he spoke carefully, like he'd thought this through extensively. "It was my life and my decision, but you didn't care about what I wanted—only how my choice would affect you."

Silence returned, and Georgie's eyes instinctively shifted downward, fixating on her lap as the uncomfortable conversation lingered in the air.

Thompson's footsteps sounded overhead and someone beneath the blanket shifted and sighed.

"I won't apologize for saving you," Georgie said finally.

"I don't expect you to."

"And, honestly," she added, "I can't tell you I'd choose differently if given another chance."

"I know."

"But I *am* sorry for not considering what the decision meant to you."

Jax blew out a long breath. "And *I'm* sorry for pushing you away. I'm trying to get past this. I really am. I'm just—" He paused. "I'm still mad."

More footsteps overhead, crossing the second-floor landing.

"We should probably get some rest," Georgie said, pushing up from the windowsill and crossing to where the others were sleeping. "Thompson wants second watch, let her take it. I'm tired."

"I'll get her," Jax said. He stood and started for the stairs, but before he made it, Thompson's voice called down.

"Guys, I think someone's outside."

Jax's eyes went wide. "Everyone up," he ordered, drawing his pistol. "Now!"

The others barely had time to stir before the room erupted in a deafening burst of gunfire and shattering glass.

Georgie dropped to the floor, arms flung over her head.

As quickly as it had begun, the shooting stopped, leaving only panicked voices and Georgie's pulse pounding in her ears.

They had just been sitting in those windows. If they hadn't moved...

"Get everyone to the basement," Jax said, already back on his feet.

The others scrambled toward the basement, but the front door crashed open before they made it.

Another cacophony of gunshots and screaming.

Everyone scattered, and Georgie rounded the couch, ducking behind it with Jax and Thompson.

The soldiers returned fire at the man in the doorway as he retreated outside. A bullet must have clipped the lantern because the room plunged into darkness.

"Go," Jax ordered. He flipped on a flashlight, lighting the way to the basement as he hurried to close and lock the front door. "Stay down."

Where the flashlight pushed back the dark, Georgie noticed two of their people on the floor, shirts bloodied. She crawled to their side and checked their pulse.

Shit.

And there were more.

How many were down?

The last of the survivors vanished down the stairs, and Piper slammed the basement door shut, crouching with her back against it as she cradled her assault rifle, looking to Jax for orders.

Jax clicked off the flashlight, sending them back into an oppressive dark. "Keep your lights off and guard the doors. Try to get eyes on them. We need to know how many."

"How?" Piper's voice was high and thin. "We're blind."

"Do we have another lantern?" he asked. "Something to light the yard."

"No, nothing but a couple crappy flashlights."

Oh!

Georgie's hand went to her coat pocket, swallowing hard as she grabbed the long cylinder.

She felt her way to the window, leaning against the wall beside it as she stood.

Please let this work.

She pulled the cap off and flicked it across the top of the flare, and as a burst of light flooded the room, the soldiers raised their hands to shield their eyes.

Georgie held her breath and flung the flare through the broken window, bathing the front yard in a fiery orange glow and illuminating the trees as if they'd been engulfed in flames.

"Now," Jax barked, and the soldiers rose to their feet, guns pointed toward the light, faces bathed in the glow from outside. "Ten o'clock."

Shots rang out in the room, quickly met with return fire from outside that dropped two of their soldiers. Georgie couldn't tell who. The rest took cover, and the quiet returned.

Her ears rang painfully, her hands shaking as she drew her pistol.

"One down," Banks called.

"We should run," someone shouted.

"We're not leaving the others trapped in the basement." Jax's voice. Thank god, he was okay.

"You know what we're after," a deep voice called from outside. "We could end this now. Don't know about you, but I'd rather move on with my fucking night."

Jax stood, the light bathing his face as he fired three rapid shots from his pistol, then ducked back into cover, cursing under his breath. He couldn't use his assault rifle anymore, and he wasn't used to shooting with his left hand.

Thompson pushed to her feet and unleashed a barrage of gunfire through the window before swiftly vanishing back into cover. "One more down."

"All right," the man outside shouted. "Fine. We'll do this the hard way." A brief pause, then, "Colette, you copy?"

A quick crackle of static, followed by a cheery voice through a speaker.

"Copy, Warren. Whatcha got for me?"

"Tell Emery I found the strays. They're holed up in a house. Not sure how many. I got my tracker on me, so you can ping my location."

"Already did," the girl answered, and Georgie's heart leaped into her throat.

Piper's blonde hair caught in the light as she hopped up from behind the couch. She slid out the back door, pulling it silently closed behind her. Georgie couldn't blame her for running. They were all screwed.

"You sure I can't just burn the house down?" the man outside grumbled. "It'd spare me the waiting."

"You burn that plant and Des will burn you. Why don't you finish them yourselves?"

The man didn't answer.

"Oh, shit," the girl said, her tone laced with amusement. "You guys got your asses handed to you by a few privileged *hijueputas*?" She spat a quick laugh. "Is it just you left?"

"It's fucking dark," the man snapped. "And we weren't expecting a fight. Thought we took care of their military. How the hell were we supposed to know they were armed?"

The girl laughed again. "I'm sending someone now. Stay put and try not to die."

"Fuck you Col—"

Bang.

"Warren?" A crackle of static, then silence. "*Carajo.* You jackass. I said *don't* die."

"Guys," Piper's voice called from out front.

They all rose cautiously to look out the window.

Piper crossed the yard to the body of a wide-set man. "We should probably go. Like, now." She holstered her pistol, then crouched to search him.

Jax pulled open the basement door and shouted down the all clear while the remaining soldiers gathered the supplies.

"Grab the radio," Georgie called to Piper as she stepped outside. "We need to go find the Humvee."

"It can't be far," Piper answered as she stood, shouldering the dead man's rifle, the snow coming down around her in fluffy white flakes. "We just—" A gunshot cut the sentence short, and Piper's gaze dropped to the red spreading across her chest.

"No!" Georgie shouted, drawing her pistol. A shape raced across the yard, and she emptied her clip, trying to hit it. When the figure rounded the corner of the house, she almost followed, but Piper staggered and collapsed. Georgie lurched forward and landed beside her, rolling her onto her back and pressing her hands to the gunshot wound.

"Jax!" The name spilled out on a sob, and a second later, he was kneeling in the grass beside her.

There was so much blood, and no matter how hard she pushed, it just kept coming.

Georgie watched helplessly as Piper bled out, eyes wide with fear and pain. It was useless. She could be the best medic in the world, and it wouldn't have mattered—not with a bullet to the chest. But she still kept trying.

"It's okay," Georgie lied, trying to keep her voice steady. "Hey, you're okay."

Finally, Piper stopped struggling, and the silence pressed in around them. Her lifeless eyes were fixed on the dark sky, her face bathed in the orange glow from the flare.

Alvear's face flashed in Georgie's mind, those same blue eyes and light hair, the warm colors of sun through stained-glass windows painted onto the floor around him.

A quick burst of gunfire echoed across the yard, snapping her back to herself.

"All clear." Banks's voice called.

Georgie sat back, tears streaming down her face. This time, she didn't try to stop them or wipe them away.

She had witnessed so much death.

It followed her everywhere.

She lost her best friend. Stood helplessly as Desmond executed her mother. She watched her own people kill each other during the uprising and saw the life drain from her patients' eyes as she and Grayson fought to keep them alive. She saw Alvear and Grayson mercy-killed, witnessed Ortega's murder and hundreds of her people gunned down.

But it never got any easier.

As she gently brushed the light hair from Piper's face, her blood-covered hands left a trail of deep red behind.

Another good person was dead because of Desmond, and it wasn't going to stop. Not until he was gone.

Anger surged through her like wildfire, consuming everything else.

"Find the Humvee," she told Jax, wiping the blood on the frozen grass before pushing to her feet. She plucked the radio from the dead man's hand and passed it to him. "You can contact Indiana if you want, but we're leaving. Now."

They needed to get the survivors to Indiana, needed to make sure they were safe.

After that, she'd make Desmond pay for everything he'd done—and she would savor every fucking moment of it.

9

They hadn't even been driving half an hour when the pickup sputtered to a stop, the needle on the gas gauge well past *E*. It was nearly three in the morning, so they left the truck and parked the Humvee out of sight, planning to search the town first thing in the morning for gas. With only two blankets in tow, they sought refuge from the bitter cold in a small pet supply shop, grateful that it at least provided a barrier against the biting wind and snow.

Georgie pulled her bag close, unzipping it to check on the plant as Jax and Banks pulled the shades on the front windows. None of the others knew about the plant. It seemed wrong to give them hope before they could be sure it would lead anywhere, so they'd kept it hidden. She'd been able to keep it alive using water from the farmhouse's stash and sunlight through the window of an empty bedroom, but the cold was taking a toll. The leaves were wilting and breaking off at an alarming rate. If they didn't get it somewhere warm, it was going to die. Then again, the same could be said for all of them.

A flashlight was propped up to face the ceiling, the light diffused by a sheer piece of clothing, the space illuminated just enough to see while they settled in. Everyone found a spot to sit in silence, dazed and hollow and afraid. Everyone except Thompson, who paced the length of the shop. The motion reminded Georgie of Ortega after the attack in the alley. Except, while his restlessness was fueled by worry and guilt, Thompson's felt volatile, and it made Georgie nervous.

They were all on edge. How could they not be? They'd lost twelve people, including their doctor, in the span of a day. They couldn't even stick around to bury the ones at the house. Didn't get a second to grieve. To process the loss.

Fifteen left. Three soldiers, an almost-medic, and eleven people who had little-to-no experience with weapons.

"This is one of ours," Banks said as he inspected the handheld radio they'd taken from the dead man's body.

Jax absently rubbed his arm. "We should contact Indiana. See if they can meet us somewhere."

Banks switched the frequency, then handed it over. "This channel's secure, and any coordinates will be encrypted, but there's a chance Emery has access to the rest of the conversation, so careful what you say."

"I'm just gonna tell them what happened. I'm sure they'll help."

"You really think they will?" Banks asked.

Jax hesitated. "We've got no other options. Plus, we're all part of the Havens."

Thompson snorted, still pacing. "You're not."

"We should do this in private," Jax said, not acknowledging her jab, and Banks gave a quick nod.

When Thompson moved to follow, Jax said, "We'll handle it."

"We need you to stand guard while we make the call," Banks added before Thompson could argue. "I'll fill you in when we're done."

"Fine," the soldier muttered through clenched teeth.

Jax and Banks headed through the store, their flashlight beams leading the way, and Georgie followed. She stepped into the alleyway and let the heavy door swing shut behind her. Towering piles of garbage and overflowing dumpsters lined the narrow alley, and the snow was coming down faster now, dusting the asphalt.

Jax held the radio out to Banks. "You sure you don't want to do the talking?"

"*Your* idea," Banks answered. "Plus, you're better with people."

Jax heaved a sigh, switched the frequency, then held the radio to his mouth and pressed the button. "INH, this is ILH-H5. Does anyone copy?"

The quiet settled like the snow around them as they waited, until finally, a flicker of static and then a voice.

"ILH-H5, this is INH-C1. Reading you loud and clear. Be advised, this frequency is reserved for senior command or emergency traffic. Your call sign is unrecognized, so I'll assume an emergency situation. What is the nature of your transmission?"

Jax scowled. "There's no senior command *left*. The Illinois Haven's gone. Over."

A beat of silence before the voice replied. "Roger that. Acknowledged. That is an unfortunate development."

Georgie bristled at the indifference in the man's voice. The lack of surprise, like he expected it to happen. Her home was gone, the people wiped out, and the best word he could come up with was *unfortunate?*

She bit down on the inside of her lip to suppress her rising temper.

The soldier on the other end continued. "Confirm if you still have custody of the charge. Over."

Did Indiana already know they had the plant? No, how could they?

Jax's gaze flicked to Georgie, his expression impossible to read, before landing back on the radio. "Negative. Over."

"Do you have a fix on its current coordinates? Over."

"He's not interested in helping. Over."

Georgie's face twisted into a frown. *He?*

"I don't give a shit," the man responded. "Lieutenant Vega reported affirmative on the solution. Preparations are underway, and the resettlement operation is already active. Civilians are relying on this mission's success. Locate the charge, then establish comms for extraction. Over."

"We don't have the charge," Jax said, "but we have a way to make a vaccine. A plant created by Elaina Wicks's team. We have proof it works, but the people that attacked our Haven, they're looking for it. They've already tracked us down once and they'll do it again. There are fifteen of us left. We need protection and a place to stay. Over."

There was a prolonged silence before the man finally spoke again. "I can deploy a convoy for rendezvous, but we'll need time to prep and stage. There's a secure location northwest of Chicago. We can meet you there. I'll relay the exact time and coordinates in twenty-four hours. Keep that plant secure until we arrive. Over."

"Our vehicle isn't running. Any chance of you sending that convoy to us? Over."

"Negative. Secure alternate transport. Out."

Jax switched off the radio, avoiding Georgie's glare.

He was keeping secrets again.

"We'll talk about it later," he said before she could ask. He clipped the radio to his belt and pulled open the door.

"No," she said as she followed him inside through the storage room and into the main section of the store where the others were gathered.

"We're going to talk about this *now*. What charge? Who was he talking about?"

Thompson stopped pacing and gave her a sharp smile. "Oh, I'd love to fill you in," she said, loud enough to catch the attention of the entire group.

"Now's not the time," Jax spat.

"So many secrets." Thompson clicked her tongue. "If you don't want to talk about this one, we can talk about the other."

"Fine." Jax spun on Georgie and pulled in a breath to temper his frustration before continuing. "When we thought Emery was working on a vaccine, the council made sure we knew it may only be a temporary solution."

Georgie folded her arms, considering this. There was always the risk that vaccines could lose potency. Especially vaccines against fungal infections. Until a decade ago, they weren't really a thing, so it was a guessing game at this point how long it would last before the fungus outsmarted it. A few years? A decade? Hopefully long enough for the fungus to die out.

"So," he continued, "when Vega got a radio call saying we had someone with natural immunity inside our walls...well, according to him, it was like winning the lottery. He sent out a call to every walkie, letting us know what was going on."

"Natural immunity?" Georgie's tired mind reeled, trying to piece it together.

"The council had already contacted Indiana about needing their immunologist. They figured they could study what was causing the immunity to find a lasting solution, but he wanted nothing to do with the Havens." Jax paused. "We had orders to stop him from leaving, but I didn't think it was right, holding someone against their will, so I showed him a way out."

Thompson's eyes were venomous. "You *what*?"

The realization hit Georgie then. "Adam." She shook her head. "But he isn't immune. He's vaccinated."

There are no immune, Cassira had assured her.

"Turns out, he's not."

Georgie rubbed beneath her eyes, exhausted, her head throbbing.

"We should all get some rest," Jax said. He gave the others a reassuring smile. "In the morning, we'll find fuel for the trucks, then we're heading out to meet a convoy from Indiana."

Thompson perked up. "They're coming to get us?"

"We have to meet them northwest of the city," Jax explained. "They'll contact us in twenty-four hours for an exact location. We need to keep the radio off until then because we don't have a way to charge it."

"*If* they show up," Georgie muttered. She hadn't meant to say it out loud, but the knowledge of what her own Haven had tried to do left her with a heap of doubt.

"They'll be there," he said.

Since when was Jax the optimistic one?

"We have something they need," he added. "They wouldn't risk us dying out here somewhere, because if we did, they'd never get their solution. We all want the same thing."

Desmond's words crept into her head like smoke. *Project Noah was always about reestablishing control.*

"Do we?" she asked.

Jax lowered his voice, the next words clearly meant just for her. "It's either this or give up, and I'm sure as hell not ready to do that. Are you?" His eyes bore into hers, filled with desperation, like he was depending on her next words to keep him afloat. The same look he'd given her that night. *I can't make it through whatever happens next without you.*

Maybe, like her, he was barely hanging on, and this plan was his life raft. He needed to believe it.

Georgie sighed. "You're right. We'll find gas for the truck in the morning, then head toward the city."

Jax turned to the others. "Everyone get some sleep. I'll take first watch."

Thompson straightened. "Uh-uh. My turn. You had your shift."

Jax looked like he wanted to argue, but exhaustion clouded his expression, and after a moment, he nodded. "Yeah, okay. Wake us up at sunrise. We need to get moving."

"Roger that." The response was tinged with bitterness.

They all settled onto the hard linoleum floor, huddled beneath the blankets, their bodies crammed together too close for comfort. Georgie kept the backpack close, her arm looped through the strap. She really hoped he was right. Hoped this wasn't a dead end. She didn't know if they could count on Indiana, but the truth was, right now, they had no other options. The people around her were what mattered, and she owed it to them to see this through, even if nothing came of it.

The shared body heat stopped her shivering, and within minutes, Georgie drifted into a deep, dreamless sleep.

10

Oliver searched through six houses before he found the part he needed, the endeavor taking most of the morning. The subdivision across from Spring Valley had already been cleared out, probably a long time ago.

As he slipped through the door and back into the cold, he pulled off his hat, pushed his hair back off his forehead, and tugged it back overtop as he scanned the neighborhood. The snow had started sometime last night, light at first, but now, the ground was buried beneath a thick layer of white.

Townhouses lined both sides of the street, cars parked in every driveway, a row of them abandoned at the entrance of the subdivision where large concrete barriers blocked them in. It was one of the many ways the National Guard had tried to cut off the infection after so many refused to take the quarantine seriously. They took the choice out of the equation.

Oliver wrapped his gloved fingers around the transformer in his pocket as he headed down the street, eager to be back in his room. This place reminded him of his old home, and it was drawing forward memories that he'd been doing his best to avoid.

His own subdivision had been cut off from the rest of the town, which was probably why it held out so long after the collapse. That, and his parents' prognostication. Not that they were preppers or anything like that. They didn't dig a fallout shelter in their backyard and cram it full of provisions. More like, they'd lived through a pandemic once and learned from the experience. Hoarding had been a huge issue then, apparently, and they didn't want to have to fight over toilet paper again, so their basement was stocked with Costco-sized...well, everything.

After the grocery stores emptied, their neighbors started running low on food, and his parents did their best to help because that was the kind of people they were.

For I was hungry and you gave me something to eat, I was thirsty and you gave me something to drink, I was a stranger and you invited me in. That was his father's favorite verse.

His father, being a reverend, had raised Oliver and Patrick with the same set of morals. He taught them that people were good at heart, if given the opportunity.

Though, over the past couple years, people had been keen to prove his father wrong, and Oliver had to work hard to keep his faith, to keep trusting, to keep believing that humans weren't just awful. After all, it was Oliver's trust in people that got his family killed.

No, it was what got his *parents* killed.

His brother, that was purely *him*.

Oliver rubbed his thumb over the transformer, his steps crunching beneath him despite his efforts to stay silent. It was hard to be invisible in a half foot of snow.

What would his parents say if they could see the world as it was now? If they knew about the Hub and the things those people put Adam through? The hundreds of people Cassira killed in God's name? Would they still believe people were good?

And what about Oliver? Would they still believe *he* was good after everything he'd done? He wasn't sure, but he knew they would find the words to make him feel better, regardless. They always handled things with understanding and patience. Always knew just what to say.

When Oliver was fifteen, he'd confided in them about a crush. A boy in his class that didn't know he existed.

"You like boys, then?" his dad had asked gently, and Oliver remembered frowning at the question. He'd never really considered what the crush meant. He didn't think about what it would mean to tell his parents.

"I like *him*," he answered plainly. But Oliver had felt things for other people before then, and gender had never impacted those feelings.

For a moment, he'd panicked as he grasped the gravity of the conversation he had unintentionally stumbled upon. But his parents wrapped him in a tight hug and spent the afternoon talking it out, providing their guidance, free of any judgements.

God, he wished they were here.

Oliver rounded the corner of a house, the tree line of Spring Valley coming into view, but froze when he saw a girl in the middle of the street, wearing flannel pajama pants and a tank top. No coat. No shoes. Like she'd just wandered out of bed.

He ducked back around the corner. Should he say something? Should he go talk to her? Offer to help?

For a long time, the girl stayed rooted to the spot, swaying a little as the wind and snow whipped past her, until she finally turned and shuffled in his direction. Her dark hair covered most of her face, but she couldn't have been older than thirteen. What was she doing out here by herself?

Help her.

Oliver swallowed back the awful feeling in his gut and stepped out into the street, hands deep in his pockets. She hadn't noticed him yet, so he waited, studying the unsteady way she moved, the tight grimace on her face. She was in pain, but she didn't look wounded.

Was she sick?

The girl inched closer, and when Oliver finally caught a glimpse of her face, he recoiled, his heart pounding. Thin, pale stalks protruded from one nostril, a line of blood trickling down over her lips. Her eyes were white, with more stalks growing from behind them, crawling up her forehead, and her cheeks were streaked with tears.

He clamped a hand over his mouth, stifling the whimper that almost made it out. If she'd noticed him, she didn't show it.

Could she even see?

She stumbled forward, tripped, and landed on her knees, hands buried in the snow.

Oliver took a slow step backward, and then another, and on the third, the girl's gaze shot up.

When she spoke, the word was a raspy whisper. "Hello?"

He straightened, holding his breath, and when her eyes found him, her expression shifted.

Okay, she could definitely see him.

The girl climbed back to her feet, struggling to regain her balance. "Can you help me, please?"

He wagged his head, taking another step back. "Stop."

But she didn't. "Please," she repeated, face twisted in a frown. She took another step forward. "I'm scared."

Oliver spun on his heel and ran, and when he reached the edge of the forest, concealed from view, he curled forward, hands on his knees, struggling to pull in air as he tried to make sense of what he'd just seen.

The girl was clearly infected, and not newly infected. She was, like, *infected* infected. He knew little about biology—he much preferred machinery and circuitry to muscles and organs—but he had a decent understanding of how the infection affected the human body. She should've been paralyzed by this stage, locked in place until, eventually, she died.

So why was she still moving? Why was she wandering the streets?

It was all wrong. Was the infection changing?

At least, creepy as the girl was, Oliver was vaccinated. She wasn't a threat to him. He was safe.

Leaning against a tree, he stared into the forest with wide eyes. The subdivision was so close to Spring Valley. The infection was going to make it there. That was clear. It was mobile. How many people were out there like that girl? How long before it started wiping out communities?

This was bad. This was really bad.

Where was he supposed to go if this place fell?

Haven, he thought. He'd go to Haven. This new information would be a major cause for concern, even for them. If it spread all the way out there, it would only be a matter of time before it made it inside.

They'd need a solution. Like his purifier.

This could actually help Oliver's case. How could they turn him away now?

He just needed to get it working before someone at Spring Valley got sick, because he wasn't eager to test the effectiveness of the vaccine.

When his pulse finally settled, the roar of engines kicked it up again.

There were still people out here, communities speckled across the city and suburbs, so it wasn't unheard of to run across others. However, most of them this close to the city didn't bother with cars.

The upkeep was a constant struggle. Not to mention all the barriers and quarantine zones and permanent traffic jams.

As Oliver glanced around the tree, a black car with tinted windows raced by, followed by a silver SUV. They decelerated and veered towards the entrance of Spring Valley.

Oliver scurried through the trees toward the farmhouse. By the time he made it, the vehicles were parked in the gravel driveway and Vivian was already outside. Hal stood at her side, wearing the same sour look that he'd had during their argument yesterday.

Avoiding the brittle branches and snow drifts, Oliver moved slowly to the back of the shed, edging along the side until he was close enough to hear.

"Relax. We're all friends here, are we not?" The voice was smooth and calm.

And *familiar*.

He rounded the corner, surprised to find Desmond Emery standing in front of Vivian. He was supposed to be at Haven with Georgie and Adam. What was he doing out here?

A large, muscular man with a massive gun stood a few feet away, a girl half his size beside him, her hood pulled up, blocking her face.

Were they *all* from the Haven?

"It's not pickup day," Viv said.

"No, it isn't, but I'm told you declined this week, so I thought I'd offer you a chance to resolve the matter."

Oliver frowned. Desmond was with the people protecting Spring Valley? Since when?

"It's just a misunderstanding," Viv replied. "I'm handling it."

"We made a deal, Vivian. You don't get to go back on it."

"I know. And I'm not. We have our contribution ready."

"Double," Desmond said, then added an indifferent shrug. "For the inconvenience."

"How—" Hal started to say, but Vivian held up her hand.

"We can't spare that much, Emery," she said. "We barely have enough for our own people."

"Then I suggest you figure something out."

"We lost four people," Hal snapped. "To a group *you* were supposed to be keeping in check."

Desmond smiled brightly. "Hey, look at that. Four fewer mouths to feed. You have supplies to spare now."

That set Hal off, his face turning a bright shade of red as he stepped in close to Desmond. "We're handing over a portion of our supplies, and you can't even hold up your end of the fucking deal. Find somewhere else to get your shit."

Desmond's gaze slid slowly to Vivian. "Is that how *you* feel?"

"No," she answered without hesitation. "Hal, go. Get the supplies."

"Double," Desmond added in a sing-song tone.

"Double," she echoed.

"But I—" Hal started, but she gave him a warning look.

"Now."

"No." Hal grabbed the lapel of Desmond's jacket, and at the same moment, his head kicked violently to the side, leaving a vivid splatter of red across the snowy ground.

Oliver gasped and stumbled back, nearly losing his balance.

He hadn't even seen any of them draw their guns. Which one fired?

Desmond's attention jumped abruptly to Oliver, and recognition flickered across his face before shifting into something else. He raised an eyebrow as the corner of his mouth turned up, and though Oliver couldn't quite decipher the meaning behind the expression, he knew he didn't like it.

Run.

Oliver turned and ran toward the house without looking back.

11

People will always give up their freedom for the promise of security. Desmond had told Adam that during his first few days at Jardine. At the time, he'd thought it was ridiculous, but now, watching these people make a pile of pre-packed crates, he wasn't so sure.

They were so willing to hand over their supplies for the illusion of safety.

That was all it was, though. An illusion.

He kept the reticle over the gray-haired woman as she nodded along with whatever Desmond was saying, obviously working hard not to look down at the body at her feet.

Leon, a brick wall of a man who reminded Adam a little of a Saint Bernard in both looks and personality, picked up the crates and headed down the gravel driveway toward the cars. When Des and Eris turned to leave, the handful of people outside the farmhouse watched them go, nobody moving an inch until they were back in their car.

Adam's reaction time was sluggish, and his attention had drifted more than once during the interaction, the noise in his head distracting. He'd let the man get too close. If he'd had a knife, the shot could've been too late.

You're slipping.

He's going to realize it and replace you.

Lowering the rifle, Adam let out a heavy sigh. He needed sleep.

When Des had invited him to come, he'd agreed wholeheartedly, hoping to get a chance to use his gun. He thought it'd make him feel better, the way it had with the dealers. A quick burst of satisfaction, followed by a brief moment of peace when sleep didn't feel so unreachable. But he'd felt nothing when he pulled the trigger. Still nothing when the bullet found its target.

It just didn't have the same effect.

At least Des was taking him on runs again.

If Adam proved his usefulness, it might push Desmond to act on the Hub. If Des realized he needed Adam, he wouldn't be so indifferent about him staying or leaving.

He couldn't afford to mess up again, couldn't disappoint him like before.

His first week at Jardine, Adam had been perched on a balcony, watching as Desmond, Leon, and Eris met with one of the newer groups in the city.

A pack of lowlifes who've teamed up seemingly for the sole purpose of irritating me, Desmond had explained.

One of them had spotted Adam. They'd snuck up on him, and dragged him down, using him as leverage to force the others to leave.

Desmond had planned to kill a few to send a message, but they left the place in ruins—a complete massacre. He could've let them shoot Adam and stuck to the plan. It would've been his own fault. But Des didn't. He sacrificed two of his own people to save him, and Adam would always owe him for that. For treating him like he mattered. Now that Desmond trusted him enough to bring him along again, Adam had to prove he deserved it.

And he'd almost messed it up again.

The cars rolled to a stop at the end of the gravel drive, and Adam placed his rifle in the trunk, then slid into the backseat.

"So, did you smooth it over?" he asked.

Des flashed a smile in the rear-view mirror. "Of course."

The car sped forward, leaving Spring Valley behind, the suburban houses blending into a monotonous stream outside the window. Adam propped his elbow on the curve of the car door, his head cradled in his hand as his mind wandered and his thoughts blurred.

When someone said his name, he jolted upright, disoriented and panicked as he took in the room around him. *His* room. But how? He couldn't even remember arriving at Jardine.

Desmond was leaning against the door frame, arms folded casually across his chest as he gave Adam an evaluative look.

Pull it together.

"You need something?" Adam asked. "Or did you just miss my face?"

Desmond's mouth tilted up at the corner, but there was a hint of something heavy behind it. "Come with me. I want to show you something." He turned and headed back into the hallway before Adam could answer.

Do as you're told.

Shut up. Adam pushed up from his bed, his legs unsteady, every inch of him weak with exhaustion as he followed.

Good soldier.

Shut up shut up shut up. He winced, gritting his teeth as he trailed a few steps behind. When Des came to an abrupt halt, Adam was so focused on the voice that they almost collided. He quickly shaped his face into a calm mask as Desmond punched in a code. When the keypad beeped, he pulled open the door and gestured for Adam to go first.

The small office had been converted into a makeshift lab with stark white walls. It reminded Adam of something he'd seen in a movie once, complete with a bulky microscope and fridges and fancy science equipment.

"Our quarantine room," Desmond explained.

"We have a quarantine room?"

"We do."

Adam frowned. "If someone's infected, why not just shoot them?"

"Science," Des replied plainly as he approached the window across from the entrance. "Fungi are fickle things. Any changes in the environment or the preferred host can affect the virulence. Ophiocordyceps Luminalis displays notable dissimilarity from the majority of present-day fungi, as expected, considering it essentially time traveled three million years in ice, but I figured it wouldn't deviate too far from the usual pattern." He glanced back at Adam. "Given the abrupt and significant decline in the number of hosts, I knew it was inevitable that it would reconsider its approach. And I was right."

Adam blinked. "You lost me."

"The infection is changing. Its effects are a lot faster than when it first surfaced." Des motioned to the window. "He was exposed three days ago."

Adam crossed to the window and stared at a man hunched forward on a medical cot inside the next room, eyes shut tightly, face locked in a contorted grimace. He'd seen him before. One of Desmond's people. Long, thin mushroom shoots sprouted from the man's mouth and nose, and off-white fuzz covered his chin and half his face.

"Three days?" Adam had watched this thing tear through everyone at O'Hare, and it had taken around ten days after the first symptoms before they made it to this stage.

"The last one only made it to day seven before his heart stopped. And that's not even the strangest part." He gave a sharp whistle and the man in the other room shot up, a cloudy film over his eyes, pupils barely visible.

Adam flinched back. "Holy hell."

"They stay mobile," Des said, gesturing like he was revealing a magic trick. "Right up to the end. All the contagion, zero constraints."

Adam's gaze snapped to Desmond. No wonder it was spreading again.

The man shouted from the other side of the window, begging for help, for mercy, pleading for them to make the pain stop, but Des ignored him and whirled around.

"Walk with me." As Desmond headed out the door, he waved over his shoulder. "Hang in there, Eric."

They headed down the hall, the man's voice fading behind them, and Des slowed his pace to match Adam's, walking in step beside him.

"There are air and water purifiers integrated in the building," he explained, tone bright and conversational. "That's why I chose this place. But the communities, the people providing our supplies, it's only a matter of time before this thing clears them out. I'm not keen to rethink our strategy, as this one has been working so well, so it's of the utmost importance, for everyone here, that we track down the strays and take back my plant."

Adam knew Reese had taken the plant the night Haven fell because he'd come to him for help, terrified that Des would come looking. Wanting nothing to do with Reese *or* the plant, Adam had sent him after some of Haven's soldiers. Meaning Georgie and the others had it. But Adam had already told Des he didn't know where they were.

"Why are you telling me this?"

"Because I need your help."

The simple statement sent a thrill through Adam that was swiftly replaced by a heavy weight in his stomach, and he forced himself to ask the question. "Do I have a choice?"

Desmond stopped walking and turned to face him, his brow furrowed slightly. It was the closest Adam had seen him get to a frown. "Of course you have a choice. I'm asking for a favor, Adam, not giving orders. I would be incredibly grateful for your help, but I'm not forcing you into anything."

There was something about having Desmond's full attention. A sense of importance and belonging, and the thought of it going away made Adam nauseous. This was the perfect chance to prove he was worth keeping around.

So he agreed. "What do you need me to do?"

"Get it back for me."

"Right," Adam said dryly. "And how am I gonna do that?"

Desmond motioned to a door a few feet ahead, and Adam pushed through into Comms. Mismatched computer monitors lined one wall—security footage on each, mostly from the perimeter of Jardine. He already knew about those cameras, and had studied them as he walked the length of the pier.

But there were a few that were clearly somewhere else. Footage of empty streets from traffic cams that were somehow still working. His eyes caught on one. A familiar room with floor to ceiling windows. The lab he'd gone to with Georgie. Had he seen them there? Was that how he'd found Georgie?

"Colette," Des said to the blue-haired Hispanic girl hunched over the desk beneath the monitors.

Colette Muñoz was one of the only two people at Jardine younger than Adam. Eris being the other.

The girl perked up, her brown eyes bouncing between them. "Hey Des. Didn't even hear you come in." She set her folded elbow on the desk, using it to slide a handheld gaming console to the side. "What's up?"

"Would you mind showing Adam what you found?"

"Yeah, of course, let me just pull it up." She rolled the chair to a laptop at the opposite end.

Colette and Eris had been together since before the collapse, running minor heists since middle school, never taking enough to warrant any attention. With Colette's mastery of security systems and Eris's ability to blend in, they were a force to be reckoned with.

Her finger tapped against the keyboard, and a second later, a window opened on the screen with a long row of blue lines of varying heights.

"What am I looking at?" Adam asked.

Excitement lit up Des's face. "Wait for it."

Colette clicked something, and a voice came through the speakers.

"Confirm if you still have custody of the charge. Over."

Adam didn't recognize the first voice, but the second was familiar. "Negative," the voice replied. "Over."

"Do you have a fix on its current coordinates?" the first asked.

"He's not interested in helping."

He recognized the voice, then.

Hale.

A shock surged through Adam, and suddenly he felt like he was falling. Like he'd miscalculated a jump, and now the ground was racing up to meet him.

Were they talking about *him?*

It took every bit of restraint he had to keep his expression steady as adrenaline fizzed through him.

They were still looking for him.

Did Des know?

Was that why he brought him in here? To show him *this*?

Adam swallowed back the sick feeling creeping up his throat.

Deep breath.

He was being paranoid. They could've been talking about someone else. A little self-centered to assume it was him.

He turned his focus back to the conversation, praying to a god he didn't even believe in that Hale wouldn't use his name.

"I can deploy a convoy for rendezvous," the other voice said, "but we'll need time to prep and stage. There's a secure location northwest of Chicago. We can meet you there. I'll relay the exact time and coordinates in twenty-four hours. Keep that plant secure until we arrive. Over."

Oh. This wasn't about him or his immunity. "They're giving someone the plant."

Des nodded once, lips pressing flat, and something dark flickered in his eyes. "A Haven, of course."

"Why not just take the place out like you did with the other two?"

"The Indiana Haven is different from the others." He leaned against the table, facing Adam now. "It's not as simple. We need to find them before they make it there."

"How am I supposed to help with that?" Adam asked.

"I'd really like to have a chat with Georgie. The strays have a radio now, thanks to the incompetence of a select few individuals on my team. You could ring her, and we could all have a lovely little reunion."

"She hates me." The words cut as he said them. "She'd never agree to meet me."

"She likes to play at being a hero, just like her mother. Ask for her help. She'll come."

If he agreed to this, it would almost definitely get Georgie killed.

She was going to shoot you. She thinks you're a monster.

Adam shook his head. "I can't." It was too much. He didn't need more things to keep him up at night.

You're weak.

He waited for the backlash, expecting threats or possibly violence, but Desmond simply said, "I understand."

Adam's gaze flicked to Colette and back again. "Really?"

"I told you, I'm asking. Not ordering. You're your own person." His eyes narrowed a fraction. "I don't *own* you."

The words sent a jolt through Adam, then hung uncomfortably in the air. Desmond knew about his past. At least that it involved the Hub. These words felt carefully hand-picked, just for him, and he wasn't sure if it was meant to be comforting or threatening. But it felt like a perfect blend of both.

He was letting Des down again. Why was Adam so worried about Georgie? She didn't care about him. But Desmond did. And he needed Adam's help. He had a chance to really be part of this place, and he was turning it down for someone who abandoned him.

Desmond's face turned serious. "You don't look well, Adam," he said gently. "Are you sleeping at all?"

Adam tugged at the elastic on his glove. "Yeah, I sleep." Not exactly a lie, though he was pretty sure Desmond didn't mean one hour intervals.

"Sleep deprivation is—"

"I *sleep*," he cut in.

Des gave him a look that said he didn't believe a word, but he let it go. "Why don't you go grab something to eat."

"I will," he lied, turning to leave. His stomach felt hollow—how long had it been? But the thought of eating made him queasy.

"Oh, and Adam?"

"Hm?" He dragged his heavy gaze back, but didn't hear the reply because Desmond's near-black eyes were coated over in a sickly greenish-white film. Fungus stalks pushed out from his gaping mouth, and patches of his tawny skin disappeared beneath a glowing fuzz.

Adam pulled in a sharp gasp as he stumbled backward. He blinked, and as quickly as the fungus came on, it vanished, and he found Desmond watching him, brow creased.

Hey, there it was. An *actual* frown.

"What—"

"I'm fine," Adam interrupted. "I—" He stopped, then turned and left without bothering to finish the sentence, nearly losing his balance as he slammed through the door.

12

What was happening?

Adam's head was swirling, his hands shaking.

You're losing your mind.

He was so tired, and it was going to keep getting worse. His head was too loud.

He wanted it to stop. Wanted all of it to stop.

He hurried away from the lab, toward the front of the compound, curious gazes shifting to him as he passed.

Look, they're all watching you. You're crazy, and they know it. They're laughing at you.

"Shut up."

You can make it stop. Not like anyone would miss you.

Adam winced. *Mean.*

It wasn't the first time he'd considered ending things. He could quiet the chaos in his head. Quiet everything.

But honestly, the idea had lost its appeal after the failed attempt at O'Hare.

You can make the pain stop.

Yeah, but he had a better way. One that required a lot less...well...death.

The cafeteria was small, more of an employee lounge, and he easily found Leon's hulking shape at a table with a handful of other people he vaguely knew.

"Hey-a," Adam chirped as he slid into a seat. "How's everyone's Thursday going?"

"It's Monday," Leon replied.

"That's good," Adam said, not listening.

"What do you need, Adam?"

"I'm all out of oxys."

"That so?" Leon's voice was flat with indifference, his eyes still on the TV.

"Yep," Adam replied, popping the *p.* The heel of his boot bounced impatiently.

He's ignoring you.

Couldn't he see that this was urgent? Adam needed a fix.

Now.

Yes, he had other pills tucked away in a plastic bag in his room, but they weren't the *right* pills. The only ones that would give him any actual relief, make the pain go away, were gone.

He needed that moment when the drugs hit just right and everything ground to a stop, the world with it. Needed to quiet the voice. Because if this kept up, he might do something stupid.

Make him listen.

Adam slammed his hands down onto the table with a loud bang. "I'm not just making conversation. I need more."

Finally, Leon's attention turned to him, brows drawn together. "You really went through all that in a week?"

Adam shrugged. "We have plenty."

There was a small community that sent a box full of medications a few weeks back. Apparently, right at the beginning, after the collapse, they'd hit every hospital and pharmaceutical company for miles and had been hoarding it ever since. Adam respected the strategy.

Now, they were using that hoard to buy protection, because drugs wouldn't keep the violence away, but Desmond *would*.

"We won't for long at the rate you're going," Leon countered.

The last thing Adam needed right now was a lecture. Especially from a glorified drug dealer. Just because Leon was a pharmacist before the collapse, that didn't give him the right to judge anybody.

"I had a rough week."

The man's face softened. "You're going to kill yourself. This shit's no joke."

"I'll be fine."

Leon sighed. "No more for at least three weeks. Make it last." He dug through the inside pocket of his jacket, pulled out a bottle, and set it on the table.

"Three weeks? It's half empty!"

"Think of it as half full."

Adam glared at him, teeth clenched.

Shoot him and take the rest.

"You think you're the only one depending on me for this shit?" Leon asked, gaze sliding back to the TV. "I've got to spread it out."

Adam exaggerated a pout, tipping the bottle from side to side. "I thought we had something special."

The corner of Leon's mouth lifted. "Fuck off. I'm trying to hear this."

Adam glanced at the TV, watching a couple dance across the screen as the man sang and the woman swooned. He rolled his eyes, twisted open the bottle and downed two pills, then pushed up from the chair.

That was enough of that.

He slipped through the exit into the hall, eager to get back to his room.

The short walk seemed to take hours, and when he finally made it, he ducked inside and slumped against the door, legs threatening to give in.

Adam let his eyes close as he pulled in a breath, but when he opened them again, he was back in the hallway at the opposite end of the compound, standing in the stairwell that led down to the parking garage.

He tensed, and spun around, disoriented.

What the hell?

You're losing it.

Footsteps sounded on the stairs, fading as they headed away from him, and without intending to, he followed, descending into the concrete underground. The cold met him as he made it to the last step, his eyes scanning for the source of the sound.

The footsteps had stopped, and just as he wondered if he'd imagined them, a voice came from behind him.

Adam.

His breath hitched as he spun around, searching for the face the soft voice belonged to, but Oliver wasn't there.

But he knew he heard footsteps. Those were real.

Right?

What is wrong with you? You're such a mess.

Adam pushed deeper into the garage, the overhead florescent lights barely reaching the ground before being devoured by the shadows.

There. More footsteps echoed off the cement walls. He drew his knife, then followed the sound, and when he edged around a thick pillar, he flinched back.

Bruised circles beneath blue eyes on the quick blur of a face.

"Stop," Adam snapped as he clamped his eyes shut. "Stop it!" His voice echoed off the concrete, and when he pried his eyelids open again, he had to squint against the gray daylight flooding through large windows.

He was back in the cafeteria, which was now mostly empty. No Leon, and the TV was off.

What was happening? How long had he been wandering?

Sleep. He needed sleep.

But he *couldn't* sleep. Why couldn't he sleep?

He started back to his room—again—focusing on details in his surroundings to ground himself: a poster on one wall displaying the layout of Jardine, a defibrillator in a box on the opposite wall, and pull-down fire alarms and fire extinguishers every fifty feet.

When he finally reached his door, he found Eris standing there, just about to knock.

She turned toward him, folding her arms across her chest. "There you are. Des wants to talk to you in his office."

"Again?" Adam asked. Was he going to push the Georgie thing? "What does he want?"

"I don't know," she said with a frown. "Ask *him*."

Adam sighed and walked with her toward Desmond's office, his feet dragging but his head clearer. As they approached, the door swung open, and a man stepped out.

Adam froze, his nerves sparking.

The man's face, lined with deep wrinkles, was partially hidden behind a thick, dark beard, and beneath the corner of his right eye, the small heart tattoo.

He knew the man, had seen him every day in another life.

A steward, that was the title they were given, the ones with heart tattoos.

Another hallucination? No, his thoughts felt steady, unclouded.

He was really there.

But how?

He met Adam's intense glare and recoiled, though there was no hint of recognition. Just unease. A reaction to whatever expression Adam had been too preoccupied to keep from his face.

Of course the man didn't recognize him. His role was to know the visitors, not the products. To keep everything running smoothly. Adam was one of the dozens of faces he would've never bothered to learn.

Run away, little mouse.

Adam's muscles tensed, his body aching with the ghosts of long-healed injuries.

He clenched his fists.

Or stop being such a helpless coward and make him pay.

Des's words echoed in his head. *Don't ever let anyone make you feel powerless. Because you're not.*

He wasn't a scared kid anymore.

And he was definitely not powerless.

Adam grabbed a fire extinguisher from the wall and lurched forward. He swung, but the man ducked away from the blow and the extinguisher hit the wall with a loud *clang* that echoed down the hall.

"The fuck?" the man spat.

Someone yanked the fire extinguisher free of Adam's grasp, and two bystanders drew weapons.

The noise pulled a handful of people from the room across the hall.

"What's all this?" Desmond asked from the doorway of his office.

"He's out of his damn mind," the man said, and Adam's mouth lifted into a smile. *Not wrong.*

"Put the guns away," Desmond said, and the two bystanders immediately holstered their weapons.

"What is *wrong* with you?" the steward snarled.

You don't need fixing, Desmond's voice reminded him, the memory fortifying his resolve. *There's nothing wrong with you.*

With his eyes locked on the steward, Adam tugged off his gloves and tossed them aside, pulling his sleeves halfway up his forearms to reveal the Roman numerals on his wrists.

Finally, the man seemed to understand. His frown fell away.

"I see," Des said. With a simple hand gesture, he directed the steward to move closer, and the man complied.

"He—" the man started, but Des held up a hand.

"I didn't ask you to speak," he said, voice low. "Turn around and get on your knees."

"Wh-what? No, I didn't..." The sentence dissolved as fear unfurled on the man's face.

Des raised his eyebrows. "I get bitchy when I have to repeat myself."

The man turned around, movements jittery. "What are you going to do?" he asked, his voice breaking over the question as he lowered to the ground.

"Well, if I told you," Des chimed, "it'd ruin the surprise." He extended a hand to someone behind him, and when he turned back to the steward, it was gripping a wooden baseball bat.

"I didn't do anything to you, Emery."

"No, but I'm pretty sure you know exactly what you did to *him*." Desmond twirled the bat in one hand and exchanged a meaningful glance with Adam. "And I will not tolerate anyone mistreating my people."

The words settled over Adam like a heavy blanket, warm and reassuring. *My people.*

"I don't work for them anymore," the man said as he folded forward. "I work for *you* now. I'm sorry, okay? Please, forgive me."

Adam thrilled at the desperation in the man's voice as he begged.

He thought of all the times he pleaded for them to let him go. All the times they responded with violence.

They made you into this.

"Forgiveness is a ridiculous concept," Desmond replied with a casual smile, passing Adam the bat. "If someone dropped a knife while trying to slit your throat and then muttered an apology, would you pick it up and give it back?"

The man whimpered.

Good.

Show him it's his fault.

"Sit up," Des ordered.

The steward straightened his shoulders. "Please. Don't."

Show him what he created.

Adam stepped forward, fingers wrapped tightly around the bat, feeling the comforting weight of it in his hands, the smooth wood beneath his fingers. He thought of Stanton. Of his small room at the Hub. Of the helplessness he'd felt every single day.

But this time, the memory didn't threaten to fracture him down the middle.

This time, it lit a flame.

Make him pay.

Adam pulled back the bat, then swung. The wood connected with the man's skull with a satisfying *thud*, and he collapsed to his side, shoulder slamming against the linoleum. All at once, everything Adam had shoved behind his mask came rushing out, spilling over the brim. He swung the bat again and again, arcing it down into the man's head until it reverberated from the impact of the floor beneath.

He'd killed a few collectors and dealers, but this felt different. More personal. This man had left bruises on Adam's face, had threatened him, had unlocked the door to his room and let monsters inside. This wasn't blindly killing, this was targeted revenge. And it was the best high of his life.

Adam's chest heaved, and he pitched forward, dropping to his knees, some strange mix of a sob and a laugh tumbling from his throat as the bat rolled out of his grip.

"As you were," Des said airily to the crowd that had formed, the sound muffled by the pounding in Adam's ears. The rest of the people in the hall dispersed.

"How'd that feel?" Desmond asked.

Adam's face split into a bright grin. One that he didn't have to fake. "Incredible."

It was more than that, though. He'd always felt trapped, suffocating under the burden of his past. But in that moment, he felt free.

What were the odds that a Hub steward would end up here? Especially *that* one. Adam didn't believe in fate or karma or divine intervention of any kind, but he still sent a silent word of gratitude out into the universe. Maybe tonight, he'd actually get some sleep. Maybe the nightmares would leave him alone for a while. And when the peace from this kill faded, he would find more.

He'd track down Stanton, break him slowly, piece by piece until he was pleading, like the man had.

To do that, he needed Desmond's help. And he knew one way to ensure he'd get it.

But if he helped with this, he'd be responsible for Georgie's death. Was that something he could live with?

He cared about her—as much as he didn't want to. But he was also so mad at how she'd treated him. How she'd automatically assumed the worst.

She was going to shoot him. Why should he protect her when she obviously wouldn't do the same?

Adam had a chance to take out the Hub. To stop them from hurting more people. That was worth crossing some lines.

He needed this place too much. Why should he ruin it for a selfish Havenite?

"I'll make the call," Adam blurted. "To Georgie."

Desmond looked genuinely surprised. "You will?"

He nodded.

The surprise was gone in an instant, replaced by an approving smile. "I'm glad to hear it."

13

The smell of something savory dragged Georgie from a deep sleep. She shivered against the cold, her fingertips stinging, even beneath the thick blanket. For a moment, her gaze lingered on the squares in the ceiling, trying to place them.

When she remembered where they were, remembered what had happened the night before, she sat up straight, first checking on Jax, then the plant in her bag. It looked worse than yesterday, but it was there.

Gray daylight pushed through the gaps of the window shades, illuminating the small shop. Reese stood in his full winter gear, heating something in a pan over a chafing dish warmer, and when he noticed her, he gave a sad, tilted smile.

"Good morning." He was the only one awake, and it looked like he'd been up for a while. His eyes were bloodshot, but she couldn't tell if it was from sleeplessness or tears. Possibly both.

"Morning," Georgie mumbled. She considered asking if he was okay, but it was a stupid question. None of them were okay.

She glanced down at her watch. It was already after ten. They'd lost most of the morning. Thompson was supposed to wake them at sunrise. Despite her body's objections, Georgie threw back the blankets, then peeled herself off the floor to look out the window.

The snow had picked up, covering the ground, the street hidden beneath perfect, glittering drifts.

"Jax," she said without turning around.

He replied with a groan.

"We need to go before we get snowed in."

Blankets rustled, and a few seconds later, he and Banks were both beside her, the familiar lines appearing between Jax's eyebrows. When she turned back to the room, to the others who were starting to come awake, her heart plummeted.

They were missing people.

She counted quickly in her head. Seven. Eight were missing.

"Where are the others?" she asked Reese.

"They left."

"What? When?"

"A while ago."

Jax cursed, searching the store as Banks stormed outside without a word.

"Where'd they go?" Georgie asked.

Reese shrugged, still stirring whatever was in the pan. "I don't know. None of you tell me anything."

"And you didn't think to wake us?"

"Thompson was with them, so I figured it was part of the plan. I'm just doing my best to stay out of everyone's way."

The door chimed as Banks pushed back inside. "The trucks are gone."

"Along with everything else," Jax added, nodding to the place where their bags were piled the night before.

"How'd they get the truck running?" Georgie asked.

"Thompson didn't stay up to keep watch." Jax rubbed his temple. "She wanted to go look for gas. I should've stayed up with her."

Georgie surveyed what remained of the group.

Thompson blamed her and Jax for using the vaccine.

Banks had ordered her not to talk, and Levi was his family.

Wren would have never agreed to abandon anyone.

Reese was an outsider.

Thompson had singled out the ones she knew would go with her, the ones she trusted, woke them up, and took everything. Left everyone else to starve or freeze to death.

"They're meeting the convoy without us," Georgie said.

The others didn't have the plant. What would happen when they showed up empty-handed? Indiana would think Jax was lying.

Georgie grabbed her scarf and hat. "We have to get to the city before the convoy leaves."

"On foot?" Wren's eyes cut to the window. "We'll freeze."

"We can't get snowed in here," Jax said. "We have nothing."

"We have breakfast." Reese looked down at the pan, then gave them a tired smile. "I hope you like beans."

The snow drifts swallowed Georgie's feet as she trudged forward, the weight of hopelessness growing heavier with each step. Her pants and socks were soaked through, her toes numb. She re-wrapped the scarf to cover her nose and mouth and pulled her hat down as far as it would go, narrowing her field of vision to the small space between.

The only things they had left were the ones they kept close while they slept. Pistols and knives, gas masks, the clothes on their backs. And the plant. That was it.

Georgie's stomach was already growling, the small portion of breakfast barely making a dent in her hunger, but there was no food and stopping to search houses would cost time they couldn't afford to lose.

They quickly checked cars as they passed, hoping someone had left a set of keys tucked in a visor. But so far, nothing. Even if they lucked out and found one, there was no guarantee that it would start.

How far was it to the city? They still had time before Indiana was set to make contact again, but could they find the others before then? They had nothing more than a vague direction, a rough idea of where to go, and without the radio, they'd miss the call with coordinates.

Ciri clung to Banks's back, one blanket draped over her, the other across Levi and Wren, while the others burrowed in their winter coats. They were moving slowly, and the snow was still coming down.

As usual, Georgie's mind oscillated between two sides—a constant cycle of anxiety and anger. She knew she had to get these people and the plant to Indiana. But she wasn't sure how to handle what had to come after.

One part of her, the part that burned hot, wanted to track down Desmond. She could feel her parents in that side, and it felt good. But the other part, the one that she definitely didn't get from genetics, wanted to go with the others, hide behind another Haven's walls and hope he never found them.

Desmond won't come after Indiana was followed by *of course he's going to come after them.*

I should let go and start fresh, followed quickly by *nothing matters more than ending him.*

The cycle was nearly as exhausting as the walk.

Footsteps crunched in the snow beside her.

"How you holding up?" Jax asked.

"I'm fine," Georgie mumbled into the wool of her scarf. Before she could stop herself, she blurted, "I'm not staying in Indiana." The words felt final, like she'd made it concrete by saying it out loud.

His steps faltered, and as he caught back up, he shook his head. "What do you mean you're not staying? You're not actually still thinking about going after him."

"Of course I am."

"We have a safe place to go," Jax said. "A way to stop the infection. A chance at a normal life. Why would you throw that away?"

"He has the notebooks. What if Indiana can't figure out the vaccine without them?"

"They'll figure it out. We're bringing them the biggest piece of the puzzle."

"I have to do this."

"No, you don't."

She scowled and tugged down her scarf, the cold air stinging her lips. "What if he goes after Indiana, Jax?"

"Then Indiana will handle it."

"What if they can't? We thought our Haven was untouchable, but it wasn't. Our people deserve somewhere safe, and as long as Desmond is still alive, we can't promise them *anywhere* is."

Jax was quiet a moment. "What can we do? We don't stand a chance against them."

She sighed. "I don't know. But I can't just let it happen."

"After everything," he said quietly, rubbing his arm. "All the things that happened. How does this idea not terrify you?"

Georgie stopped short. She didn't mean to, but the question had caught her completely off guard. "Are you kidding?"

Jax's frown deepened.

"Of course the idea terrifies me—*everything* does. I'm scared all the time. But they shouldn't suffer because of it. It's *my* fault Haven's gone." When he tried to argue, Georgie cut him off. "It *is*, at least partially. I owe them this." She blew out a long breath that plumed like smoke. Her eyes drifted over the trees that had popped up seemingly out of nowhere, and her attention caught on something half hidden beneath the snow. "What is that?"

Jax followed her gaze, then motioned for the others to wait. Banks handed Ciri off to Wren and grabbed his pistol while Jax and Georgie drew their own.

The memory of the alleyway forced its way forward, the voice calling for help, luring them in, and her entire body tensed.

Was it a trap?

Jax inched forward, and Georgie followed close behind. It was a blue storage bin with large handwritten letters on the side that read, *Take what you need.*

That definitely felt like a trap. Georgie looked around, searching the trees, watching for any movement, any shadows in the forest.

"It could've been out here for months," Jax said.

Another few steps, then Georgie crouched in front of the box, wincing against the pain in her stomach. She pushed, sliding the corner of the box back.

"There's snow underneath."

"There's snow everywhere," he shot back.

"There wouldn't be snow under the box," Georgie explained curtly, "unless it was placed here *after* the snow started."

Jax glanced back at the others. "Then we need to keep moving."

Curiosity dug its hooks in, and Georgie swiftly popped open the lid. When she glanced inside, she let out a relieved laugh.

"It's a blanket," she mused. She holstered her gun and dug out the blanket, standing and shaking it out before handing it to Jax. Tucked further into the box was a pair of heavy winter boots, two pairs of thick socks, two water bottles—the liquid not yet frozen—and a pastel yellow and blue knitted beanie.

Jax put his gun away, then draped the blanket over Georgie's shoulders, a small gesture that felt so significant.

"Why would someone leave this here?" he asked. The others were beside them now, drawn in by Georgie's reaction.

"To help people stuck in the blizzard," Reese answered cheerfully.

"Why?"

His nose wrinkled. "Empathy. Kindness. There *are* still good people out here, you know."

Jax hesitated. "I don't trust it."

Georgie grabbed the beanie. "Me either. But you don't have to trust it to make use of it." She tugged the pastel-colored hat over Jax's snow-covered hair and bit back a smile. "It's very *you*."

Jax responded with a sullen look, but left the hat on.

The peaceful stillness was broken by a sharp huff of breath, one that Georgie placed immediately.

What the hell?

Her mind sputtered, leaving her completely disoriented as she tried to make sense of the sound and what she had connected it to in her head.

What the fuck would a horse be doing out here?

Georgie watched with a frown as a gorgeous gray mare strutted out from the forest, and it took another breath for her brain to snap back into gear.

There was no rider, but its mane was well-groomed, and a saddle was strapped to its back. It clearly belonged to someone, but they were in the suburbs. There hadn't been a farm in hours. Had someone ridden all the way out here to put out some boxes?

Why?

The horse may have belonged to someone, but right now, it was alone. And they needed it. One of them could ride ahead, try to meet up with the others to get the radio back before Indiana made contact.

Georgie knew how to handle horses thanks to the lessons Mabel's aunt used to give them through the summers.

She handed Wren the blanket. "Stay down."

"What are you doing?" Jax asked.

"Keep your eyes on the trees. Whistle if you see anyone." Before he could argue, she added, "Trust me."

His frown stayed put, but he nodded, and they all ducked into the shallow ditch along the road.

Georgie moved cautiously, circling around to approach the creature from an angle, exactly how she'd been taught.

"Hey there," she cooed. "It's okay, I won't hurt you." The horse backed up a step, but its ears were perked, its demeanor calm. "Where's your rider?" Her eyes jumped to the trees. There were no other sounds. No footsteps. Only the rattling of the frozen branches. "We could really use your help."

Slowly, gently, Georgie reached out and touched the horse's shoulder.

Jax's sudden whistle made her jump, causing the horse to startle. She rushed back and ducked down beside him as the shape of a person stumbled out into the open, face concealed behind a scarf and hat. Jax and Banks already had their guns drawn.

The figure was injured, struggling to stay upright as they trudged through the snow. And they were alone.

"We need that horse," Georgie whispered.

"They're not just gonna hand it over," Jax replied.

"We're armed and they're outnumbered."

Jax fixed her with an incredulous glare. "We're not shooting some stranger to steal their horse."

"I'm not saying we *shoot* them. Just strongly *suggest* they let us have it."

"And leave them stranded out here?"

"*We're* stranded out here, Jax."

"Shut up," Banks hissed. "Both of you."

The figure tripped and let out a pained cry as they sank into the snow. When the horse turned to look, they tugged off their hat.

It was a boy in his early teens with ash blond hair and round glasses.

Jax and Banks lowered their guns simultaneously.

"Yasha," the boy called. "Wait." The horse watched for a moment, then turned and strolled away as the boy struggled to his feet. "Please!"

Georgie sighed. They couldn't steal a horse from a kid.

She stood and headed toward him. As soon as the boy noticed her, he unshouldered a bow she hadn't noticed, nocked an arrow, and drew it back, the sharp point trained on her chest.

She stopped, heart leaping into her throat. "Woah, easy."

"Back up," the boy ordered.

"I'm trying to help." She swallowed, then settled her voice into something with a bit more conviction. "Put the bow down and *let* me before your horse gets too far."

The boy didn't budge. "Are you alone?"

"I'm not." She glanced over her shoulder, and when Jax and Banks rose to their feet, he looked them over like he was assessing his chances.

Finally, he lowered the bow. "Guess I don't really have a choice, do I?"

She snatched the hat from the snow and tossed it back to him. "Yasha, right?" She gestured to the horse, and the boy nodded.

Georgie approached the horse again, and after getting Yasha comfortable, carefully led her back.

"What about you? What's your name?"

"Owen."

"Hi, Owen. I'm Georgie."

"Don't talk to me like I'm a kid."

She smiled. "Understood. Sorry. How bad are you hurt?"

"I'm fine." Owen touched the back of his head and when he pulled his hands away, his fingers were slick with blood. He paled. "Shit."

"Shit," Georgie echoed. She handed the reins to Banks. "Let me see." Calmly, she tugged off her gloves and shoved them in her pockets, then rounded the boy, sweeping the sticky strands of hair aside to find the wound. "What happened?"

"I must have fallen. I don't know."

"Did you lose consciousness?"

He spun to face her. "I don't know," he repeated, louder, panic coating the words. His wide eyes flicked back to the blood on his hands.

"Head wounds bleed a lot," Georgie told him. "It makes it seem pretty scary, but it's a small cut. You may need a stitch or two, that's all." No response. "Hey, did you hear me?"

Owen gave a quick nod.

"Do you know how to get home from here?"

He looked around, finding a street sign. "Yeah."

"How far?"

The boy's face darkened, suspicion overpowering the fear. "Far enough."

She smirked. Smart kid. "I want to be sure you can make it."

He grabbed the reins from Banks. "I'll be fine." As he tried to hop up in the saddle, he stumbled again, then leaned forward, grabbing his stomach. "I think I'm gonna be sick."

There was no time for a detour. If they missed that radio call, they'd have to walk to Indiana. In this weather, they might not all make it. As bad as she felt for the kid, she couldn't risk messing things up for her own people.

Her gaze jumped to the horse.

Although, if he came from a farm, it was possible they had some sort of transportation. A pickup truck or even a tractor. Anything would be faster than walking.

If they helped Owen, whoever he was with might feel inclined to help them in return.

"Let us help you get back," Georgie said, gently taking the reins.

Jax shot her a look that she ignored.

Owen hesitated, clearly weighing his options. "Okay, yeah, but *only* you."

No way in hell. She'd learned her lesson about strangers.

"Tell you what. I'll take you, but if you pass out, I won't be able to get you back without someone helping. So this guy here,"—she motioned to Jax—"he's going to follow us."

The boy reluctantly agreed.

"How far is it?" she asked again.

"It's through the forest. Fifteen minutes that way."

"How many people?"

"Enough to take you on," Owen spat. "So don't do anything stupid."

Georgie turned to Banks. "We'll meet you at the house we just passed. If we're not back in an hour, come *find* us." She hoped the infliction would also serve as a warning to Owen.

Banks tapped his fingers on his holstered handgun. "Oh, I will."

14

The dense forest opened into a wide yard, revealing, to Georgie's surprise, a full-fledged farm nestled right in the middle of the suburbs.

Snow pelted her face as they crossed the yard, and she rubbed her gloved hands together, trying to warm them as she scanned the barns and outbuildings. The forest encircled the farm, and at its border, an old, rusty pickup truck.

There it was. She knew they'd have something. The question was, did it run?

Owen stopped in front of the picturesque farmhouse, and within seconds, a woman with a long, gray braid came bursting through the front door.

"Hello there," the woman said, her suspicious eyes sliding from their faces to the dried blood on Georgie's coat. "Who are you, and why are you on our property?" She had a gun in her hand, a revolver that looked like something from a cowboy movie.

"Just returning Owen to you," Jax replied.

"He hit his head," Georgie added. "Might need a few stitches, but he's okay."

The woman turned her attention to the boy. "What were you doing out in a blizzard?"

"I made care packages."

Her crow's feet deepened as she frowned, but Owen straightened, his expression confident and unapologetic.

The woman blew out a frustrated breath. "Put Yasha away, then find Eduardo to fix you up." After Owen disappeared, she gave a gentle head shake. "He's got a good heart, that one."

"Not a lot of people left that do," Jax said, his demeanor softening, mouth lifted into a sweet lopsided grin that was so out of character, Georgie had to catch the laugh before it tumbled out. "And in the spirit of that," he added, "is there any chance you have a radio here we can use?"

Georgie's eyebrows lifted in surprise. She hadn't considered asking for a radio. They wouldn't have to race to catch up with the others if they could contact Indiana themselves.

"No." A stern look etched across the woman's face, hardening her features. "Thank you for bringing Owen home, but you need to leave."

"We still got a long way to go," Jax said. "And more people out there waiting for us. If there's anything you can offer to help, anything at all, we'd be incredibly grateful."

"I don't know you," she said. "Judging by that hat, you already found a care package. Keep whatever was inside and get out."

"We have kids with us," Jax pushed. "Please."

The woman's expression shifted at that. "How many people?"

"Seven."

"Where you coming from?"

"We're just passing through, ma'am."

"You picked a funny time to travel."

"Didn't have much of a choice," Jax explained. "We were attacked. Barely made it out alive."

She seemed to consider this, eyes going back to the dried blood. "You understand, I can't let you inside my home. You could be infected. Dangerous."

"We understand that, but—"

"*But*," she interrupted, "we've got a cabin on the property we're not currently using." She holstered the gun. "You and your group can stay there tonight to wait out the storm."

"No," Georgie said, checking her watch. It was already after three. "We need to keep moving." Haven would be making contact in less than twelve hours, and they needed to track down the others before then. "Thank you, but there's somewhere we need to be."

"It'll be dark in a few hours," Jax argued. "Temperature's dropping, and the snow's still coming down. Those people need to rest. We all do."

Georgie yanked Jax aside, voice a sharp whisper. "We can't miss that call."

"There's no way we're gonna find them in time anyway," Jax said. "We have a general direction, and nothing else."

"So, you're giving up?"

"No, I'm taking a night to figure out our next move. We need to be realistic about this. Wandering around the suburbs in a blizzard isn't the solution."

"What if they meet up without us?"

"Then they'll have nothing to offer," Jax said. "*We* have the bartering chip. Not them."

"They'll think we lied."

"No," Jax corrected her. "They'll think Thompson lied."

How would Indiana's soldiers react when the others showed up without the plant? Would they still take them in, or leave them to fend for themselves in the city?

"When we show up at the Haven," Jax added, "we'll have the plant."

Georgie shifted her weight, glancing back at the truck. The thought of staying here, surrounded by god knows how many strangers put her on edge, but that didn't change the fact that he was right. And if they stayed the night, that would give her the chance to check the truck. If it worked, they could leave first thing in the morning and be in Indiana by lunchtime.

"Okay," she said with a nod. "Just for the night."

Jax turned to face the woman again. "We'll take you up on that offer. Thank you, ma'am."

"*One* night," the woman clarified.

Jax nodded. "Understood."

She gave them a gentle smile. "Vivian Campbell."

"Private Jaxon Hale."

"What was this place?" Georgie asked, ignoring the expectant look on Vivian's face.

"A replica of simpler times," she answered proudly. "And you are?"

"Georgie."

"Well, Georgie. Private Hale. Once you bring your people here, I'm gonna need you all to surrender your weapons."

They both straightened.

"No way," Georgie snapped.

"We can't do that," Jax added. "I have a responsibility to keep my people safe."

Vivian's eyes narrowed. "Yeah, so do I."

"So, you understand, then," Jax said. "We lost a lot of people when we were attacked, and that was *with* our guns. What if something happens? We'd be defenseless."

"Our settlement is protected," Vivian said. "Any groups big enough to be a threat know better than to step foot here."

Georgie frowned. "What the hell does that mean?"

"Do you want to stay the night or not?"

"Fine," Jax relented. "Okay. Thank you for your hospitality."

"Go get your people," Vivian said. "I'll have someone get the fire going so the cabin's nice and warm when you get back."

"I'll go," Jax offered, meeting Georgie's gaze. "If you're okay with it, I mean. You can wait here, go warm up."

It wasn't an order or a demand. It was a genuine offer. The wound in her stomach felt like it was on fire, and her face hurt from the cold, so she agreed, and Jax was gone a second later.

Vivian held out her hand, and despite every instinct telling her not to, Georgie reluctantly handed over her gun.

The front door of the farmhouse swung open and a thin boy in a brown coat scurried down the porch steps, his dark hair swallowing his pale face.

"Perfect timing, Mr. Brennan," the woman called to him. "I need you to do something for me."

Startled, he looked up and his light eyes widened as they met Georgie's.

Her breath hitched, the shock of recognition hitting her like a physical blow, almost sending her stumbling back.

No way.

"Oliver?" she said, the name slipping out as almost a laugh.

What was *he* doing here?

15

A hundred thoughts collided at once in Oliver's head.

First Desmond, now Georgie.

His gaze slid past her, searching, but it was only her. No Adam.

"What the hell?" Georgie asked. "Why aren't you at the Campus?"

Adam didn't tell her?

"I left," Oliver answered. He shoved his hands in his pockets and rocked back on his heels, fighting the urge to ask how Adam was doing, because he wasn't sure he could take the answer, whatever it may be.

"I see that," she said. "Where's Adam?"

The question sent a jolt through Oliver, like a hundred volts of electricity traveling through his nerves all at once.

"What?" He forced himself to look her in the eyes, hoping to catch a hint that she was kidding. He had a hard time grasping when people were telling jokes. That had to be what was happening. He was just missing the joke.

"Is he still at the Campus?" she pressed. "Did something happen?"

Oliver gave a small, frantic head shake. "I-I don't..." What was she talking about?

Vivian set her hand on his shoulder, and he flinched away. "Oliver, you look like you're gonna be sick. Why don't you sit down a minute?"

He ignored her. "Adam's not here. You *know* that. He stayed with *you*."

If this was a joke, it was a terrible one, and he wanted her to stop.

Georgie's face drew into a tight frown. "He left, Oliver. I haven't seen him since that night."

"You're lying." Why was she lying to him? Why was she doing this? It wasn't funny. It was *mean*.

"I thought he would've gone back to the Campus."

"No," Oliver argued. "He's safe. He's at Haven, and he's safe."

Vivian let out a strained sound, something close to a laugh. "You're from a *Haven*?"

Georgie hesitated. "We *were*."

"Were?" Oliver asked.

"You don't know?"

"Know *what*?"

"Where do I even start?" She dropped both hands to her sides. "Desmond."

Vivian straightened at the name.

"He tricked us. Adam's deal, Union Station, it was him. All of it was him." She shook her head. "He *used* me to get into Haven. The night of the party, he let his people in. We lost nearly everyone. Adam vanished during the chaos, and Reese said he was going to find *you*."

Oliver's stomach twisted. The weight of their stares felt like a searing heat on his skin, like they were burning right through him.

Adam wasn't safe.

He wasn't at Haven.

He was gone.

Adam was gone.

He was going to find you. The words caught in his mind, and his skin crawled, trying to escape.

Oliver had ended things with Adam. Left so he would stay at Haven and *not* come looking for him, but he did anyway. He did, and Oliver wasn't there.

This was wrong. This was all wrong.

He dragged himself back to the porch, dropping onto the step as his head spun and the snow soaked through his jeans.

Too much.

He hugged himself tightly and rocked, trying to make the feeling stop, and when Georgie sat beside him and asked if he was okay, he erupted.

"Just go away!" Oliver shot up from the step, fists clenched. "You ruined everything."

Before she had a chance to respond, he bolted inside and up the stairs. When he was in the safety of his room with the hatch shut tight, he crumbled.

Everything came crashing down on him like a truckload of bricks, burying him for what felt like forever.

Finally, as the light in the room began to dim, the tears stopped, and that terrible pressure, the vise-grip on his head, eased. The jumbled static of his thoughts steadied to something somewhat comprehensible.

Oliver had genuinely believed that he was doing the right thing.

He thought he was helping by pushing Adam away, but he wasn't. He was gullible and naïve, and his good intentions had destroyed everything.

Just like they had with his parents.

His brother.

This wasn't how his plan was supposed to go.

Oliver was so close to finishing his purifier. Haven was supposed to let him stay. They'd both be safe. Protected. Together.

But there *was* no Haven.

Where would Adam have gone?

Georgie's words rang in his head. *It was him. All of it was him.*

The answer was obvious. Desmond. Adam had nowhere else to go, and he hated being alone. But they weren't good people. They were extorting settlements and killing anyone who argued.

Adam wasn't like them.

He shut his eyes, remembering the way Adam had looked when they'd first met. Oliver had been so scared, standing face to face with the boy who had massacred fourteen of his family members with terrifying efficiency. The boy who would have already added him to the count if not for Oliver's exceptional talent for vanishing.

He looked violent, angry, dangerous, but in a blink, the mask split and fell away, and he dropped to his knees, body trembling. At that moment, Oliver saw the boy for what he really was. Beaten down, exhausted, alone. Lost.

Oliver had a chance to run, to get back to the train station, back to his home. Because that's what it was at the time. His home. Cassira and Malacai and Isaiah, they were his family.

But he stayed and threw it all away to help a stranger who turned out to be the most extraordinary person he'd ever met. And from then on, there was nothing he wouldn't do for him.

Which was the whole reason he'd told Haven about Adam's immunity. Because he was better off there.

But there was no Haven. No more plan. Oliver was on his own. There was no safe place to hide. No protection.

He had to find Adam and explain why he did it. They could find somewhere safe to go together.

Would Adam be mad at him? Would he forgive him?

He had to understand, right?

Was Adam safe? Desmond's people were dangerous. What if something happened to him?

No, he was okay. They needed him. That was the whole point of his deal.

Oliver would find him, and they'd be together.

He opened his eyes, mind already searching for a way to fix it.

Okay, think it through.

There was a problem set in front of him—something broken that needed to be fixed. Oliver was terrible at a whole lot of things, but fixing was what he did. What he knew. He could solve this problem. He had all the information, now he needed to shape it into something he could use.

His plan for the purifier was important, especially with the infection changing. But it wasn't the solution he needed right now. It wouldn't get Adam back.

He'd figure this out. There was *always* a solution.

He just had to find it.

16

After a shower to scrub away the mess of blood from his face and hair, Adam tried the radio, hoping Georgie would answer, but the only thing that responded was static. He was determined to keep his word.

Georgie was going to the Indiana Haven soon. If he couldn't get her to meet him before then, they'd lose their chance to get the plant back, and he'd let Desmond down. So, he stayed in Comms with Colette, pacing endlessly and trying the radio again and again until she finally had enough.

"They're probably keeping the radio off to save power," she told him, clearly frustrated, but too nice to tell him to get lost. "They said twenty-four hours. Three in the morning. It's only six. We have time.

If they use it before then, I'll know." She dragged her gaze up to Adam as he tapped his fingers impatiently on the table. "And then I'll let *you* know. You don't need to stay here."

With nothing better to do, he tucked himself away in his room and managed two full hours of sleep, uninterrupted.

Adam sat on his bed now, his back against the wall, boots propped up and crossed at the ankles. He felt better than he had in a long time. The thrill of the steward's death had lifted his mood, and the nap had settled the ache in his nerves.

But after a good high came a hard crash, and he expected this one to be hell. Boredom and restlessness were already setting in.

He wanted to stretch this out, keep the quiet peace in his head.

There was still no word from Colette about the radio, and sitting still, cooped up in his room for this long was driving him crazy.

He grabbed his flask, spun the cap open, and took a large swig, the liquid warming his chest on its way down. Adam didn't know much about alcohol, particularly when it came to quality, but this one was a soft caramel color, smooth and warm, where the moonshine from the Campus was harsh and burned like kerosene.

After another pull of whatever it was, he let his head fall back against the wall, eyes sweeping lazily over the room. It was mostly bare and still had that stuffy office feel to it, but it was his. And that was enough.

Adam had no need for the heavy wooden dresser, so it sat empty on one side of the room, the drawers bare, except for the bag of extra pills he didn't bother with anymore. The small kitchen cabinet was empty, the hotplate and kettle never used, and there were no sentimental items to keep safely tucked away. Almost everything he owned fit inside the pockets of his tactical vest.

His sniper rifle rested against the wall beside his bed. He set the flask aside and pulled the gun into his lap, relishing the familiar weight.

A vague shape appeared at the edge of his vision, and Adam squeezed his eyes shut.

"Please, leave me alone."

You know I'm not really here, right? Oliver asked, his voice so clear, so real.

"I know that. I'm not crazy." When he opened his eyes, the shape was gone.

Adam drained the rest of the flask in one go and screwed the lid closed before climbing off the bed. He needed to move, to get away from...whatever that was.

He made his way down the hall toward the cafeteria, eying the spot where the steward's blood had pooled earlier.

Of course, it was pristine now.

At one of the round tables in the cafeteria, a small group of people had gathered, with cards and various items spread out in front of them. A man spewed a line of curses, then threw his cards down and stomped away.

Adam checked his watch. It was a little after nine and still no word from Colette. He would check in with her again later, try one more time, but other than that, there was nothing he could do. Nothing to keep him busy.

After refilling his flask with the same liquor—brandy, according to the label—he dropped into the now empty chair and slid up the sleeves of his hoodie, tugging the gloves up over the tattoos on his wrists.

"Deal me in."

The man beside him, a plain-looking guy with graying brown hair, gave Adam a thorough once-over. "You don't even know what we're playing."

"Don't care. Deal me in."

"You got anything to wager?"

Adam thought for a moment, eyes sliding from his new watch to the silver flask. He wasn't risking either of those.

The last time he'd played cards, he bet a bag of stale cheddar flavored chips he'd found at the bottom of a broken vending machine. He'd won every game that night, and though he still shared the chips, he held onto the—*Oh!* Adam perked up and dug through his vest pockets until he found a small cylinder lighter. It was shiny silver with a design engraved all around it.

His thumb traced the intricate engraving, transporting his thoughts from the cafeteria to a cozy apartment kitchen, the wooden table bare, save for a neatly stacked deck of cards and a pair of flickering candles.

"How do you keep losing?" Adam had asked, flicking the lighter and watching the flame dance in his breath.

"I have horrible luck," Oliver had responded. "If I play honestly, I never win."

Adam's mouth quirked. "*If* you play honestly?" When Oliver responded with a shrug, Adam tucked the lighter in his vest pocket and leaned forward, intrigued. "Wait, hold on. You can't cheat at Gin. Luck is the whole point of the game."

"When luck's always against you, you learn to make your own."

"Show me."

"No," Oliver answered, a heaviness falling over his face.

"Oh, come on. You can't throw that at me and then not prove it."

"I don't do that anymore."

"Why not?"

"It's wrong. I promised I wouldn't."

"It's not wrong if the game's just for fun. We won't bet this round. Plus, I'm okay with it. I *want* you to cheat."

Oliver hesitated, lips pursed to the side as he considered. "I guess. Okay."

He shuffled and then dealt the cards, and minutes into the game, his were all laid out in front of him in matches.

"How?" Adam asked, staring at his own cards in disbelief.

"A mixture of stacking the deck and double-drawing."

"But I watched you the whole time."

"I used to be really into magic," Oliver admitted with a cringe. "Card tricks and stuff. Lots of practice. It's stupid."

"Mechanical engineer, lock picker, *and* magician." Adam gave him a sly smile. "So, you're all around good with your hands, then."

Oliver's cheeks turned cherry red.

"Are you in or not?" the man asked, dragging Adam back to the present.

Adam sighed and set the lighter on the table. "I'm in."

Over the next few hours, while powering through three flasks of brandy, he lost the lighter, a gold coin, a rainbow circle pin, and a charm that was shaped like a building from some city he didn't recognize. He'd only played poker a handful of times before, and unlike Oliver, he didn't know how to turn the odds in his favor. Was it even possible to cheat in poker? Honestly, he wasn't sure. When he was out of items, his vest pockets empty of everything but his pills, he called it.

The room swayed as Adam pushed up from the table and slid groggily down the hall. He needed sleep.

When he stumbled into his room, he popped an oxy and had barely reached the bed when a knock came from the other side of the door.

Adam pulled it open and smiled when he found Eris and Colette on the other side. "Did they use the radio?"

"Not yet," Colette answered, "but the twenty-four-hour mark's almost here. They're bound to turn it back on soon." She lifted her hands out at her sides, a handheld receiver in one, and a bottle of some kind of blue alcohol in the other. "Figured we could wait it out together."

Adam focused on trying to steady the room.

"You really gonna make us wait out here?" Eris asked, her voice light, even when it was tinged with irritation.

"Sorry, right, yeah." He leaned back against the door to hold it open.

Eris dropped onto the bed and Colette plopped down flat beside her, head on her leg.

"Well, come on, *mano*," Colette lifted the bottle. "You having a drink with us or not?"

"So," Colette said, gesturing with the neck of the bottle clenched in her fist. "You lived in Chicago your whole fucking life, and you never tried a Chicago Style hotdog? *Qué vaina.*" She stared at him, dumbfounded.

Adam shrugged.

The three of them sat against the wall, shoes scattered on the floor, legs sprawled across the bed, one of Colette's overlapping Eris's.

They'd tried the radio twice with no response, and it sat on his pillow now, within his reach.

Adam reached past Eris to take the bottle back from Colette. His movements felt too slow, his limbs too heavy, and now that the conversation had veered toward food, his stomach turned. Maybe he should slow down. The bottle was nearly empty, and neither of the other two had taken more than a few sips.

He took a drink, then gave Eris a tilted glance. She'd been quieter than usual. Not even a single quip at his expense.

"I was eleven when we moved here from Colombia," Colette went on. "And I remember it was the first place we went. Some shady-looking stand on the side of the road. The best ones, though, were from this place in West Town. Eris and I used to go all the time." Colette pivoted so she was facing them and ran a hand through her blue hair. "Remember that place? What was the name of it?" When Eris didn't answer, Colette nudged her.

Eris's gaze darted up like she'd caught her off-guard. Which was weird, because nothing ever caught Eris off guard. "Sorry, what?"

"The hot dog place in West Town."

"Oh, um, Fatso's. And it was Ukrainian Village."

Colette threw up her hands. "That's right! Fatso's. Ugh, I miss that place."

Adam took a swig before remembering that he was supposed to slow down. "My uncle had a deli down the street from that place." He set the bottle on the bedside table. "The best *deruny* I've ever had."

"I thought you grew up with fosters," Colette said. "You had family in the city?"

"Yeah, well, just because I was family didn't mean he wanted to deal with me."

Her frown deepened. "*Hijueputa.* If he wasn't already dead, I'd send Eris after him."

The sudden shift in mood left an awkward heaviness, and without meaning to, Adam burst out laughing, which cause Colette to do the same. Eris shook her head, but when he hiccupped mid-laugh, even she couldn't stop herself.

"I need to lie down," Adam muttered when he finally caught his breath. Eris and Colette pulled up their feet to make space as he melted onto the outer edge of the bed.

An easy silence settled over them, and Adam had to fight to keep his eyes open.

"Adam," Eris said suddenly, "there's something you should know."

He frowned at the intensity of the words and pushed up to his elbows. "What?"

"It's almost time," Colette interjected, giving Eris a look he couldn't read. She grabbed the radio and handed it to Adam. "We should try again."

He laid flat on his back, then pushed the button and held the receiver to his mouth. "ILH," he started, using the abbreviation he'd heard them use. "Are you there? Do you copy?"

A long pause, and then finally someone answered. A feminine voice, but not the one he was hoping for. "This is ILH-T4. I copy. Who is this?"

"That's not Georgie," Adam told Colette. "What do I do?" His brain was too fuzzy to think.

"Parar Bola." Colette pointed a thin finger at him, and then at herself. "Okay? Listen to me. This is our only shot. Respond to her. Tell her you're a friend of Georgie's and that you need her to meet you. It doesn't matter where they pick. Agree to it."

Adam nodded quickly, then pushed the button. "Hi, uh, I'm a friend of Georgie's. I need to talk to her. It's important."

"She's not here. Who the fuck are you?"

Adam looked expectantly at Colette. "What now?" Georgie wasn't there, and they had an hour before the other Haven said they'd make contact. These people had no reason to trust him. There was no way they'd agree to meet him somewhere.

They were going to miss their chance.

"Tell them your name," Colette said. "They'll meet you."

The girls exchanged another unreadable look, and he watched them, confused, feeling like he was missing something.

But he pushed the button again. "My name is Adam Kulyk. I need to talk to you. Can we set a time and place to meet?"

To his surprise, the woman agreed immediately.

17

Icy morning air stung Adam's nose as he stepped outside. The navy sky was starting to lighten, and it must have snowed all day yesterday because the ground was hidden beneath a heavy layer. Adam zipped his coat, then threw up his hood.

As he crossed the yard, he found Desmond and Eris waiting outside a black sedan in the wide circle of light from the security gates. He tucked his sniper rifle gently in the trunk, then climbed into the backseat beside Jay, who muttered something under his breath, still obviously upset about Adam's problem-solving during their meeting.

Desmond slid behind the wheel while Eris rode shotgun, and as the car purred to life, a gray SUV pulled up beside it.

Eris had contacted Des after the call to tell him where they were meeting, then after waiting around for a radio transmission from the Indiana Haven that didn't come, Colette had gone back to comms and Eris had gone to prep. Despite Eris's insistence that he get some rest and sober up, Adam stayed up and finished the bottle. A choice he was really regretting now.

"You remember what to do once we arrive?" Desmond asked Eris, who responded with a glare.

"It's not my first time, Des."

"I'm only being thorough."

"You're *being* a pain in the ass."

Desmond gave her a tilted smile, then turned back to the road. "Well, that's just rude."

Eris ignored him and turned to look at Adam. "You're in the building across the street. Stay hidden."

Of course. Far back, away from everything, out of danger. The thought of sitting still put him on edge.

Adam leaned forward, elbows on his knees. "I want to go in with you."

"No," Eris replied without missing a beat. ***They don't trust you. And why should they?*** "We need to make this quick, so the element of surprise is key."

"Are you saying I'm not subtle?"

"I'm saying you don't listen, and you have the attention span of a toddler."

"Mean," Adam muttered. It was a relief to have Eris back to her normal self.

"Stick to what you're good at," she added as she turned back around. "We've got the rest covered."

He sank back into the seat, arms folded.

"And stop sulking."

He scowled at the back of her head, and when Jay let out a smug chuckle, Adam redirected the bitter look his way, wondering how pissed Des would be if he got blood on the nice leather seats.

They drove through downtown as Adam fidgeted with his vest pockets, watching the buildings go by in a blur as his antsy muscles ached to move.

The handheld radio crackled to life. "Des, Eris, we got a problem." Colette's voice.

Eris grabbed the radio. "Listening."

"Computer picked up a transmission twenty minutes before we contacted the strays, but thanks to an encryption I've never seen before, it glossed right over it. Didn't notify me."

"Can you tell who it is?"

"No, but I can guess. There's a way to re-key encryptions over the air using a program called KMC. I use it sometimes to switch up our own encryptions. If Indiana was going to make contact to give a specific location, they may have thought to use a fresh encryption for that session, one nobody knows. It'd be right on brand for them."

"Can you decrypt it?"

"No, well, yes. I can run it through the algorithms, but it'll take time. We're talking days. I think you should abandon the current plan and come back here until we figure this out."

"What's your take, Des?" Eris asked.

"We're not turning around."

"What if the convoy shows up?"

Desmond tapped a finger on the steering wheel. "Oh, it will. If it's not already there."

Eris studied him a moment before lifting the radio. "We're continuing as planned. I'll keep you updated."

"Got it," Colette replied. "See you when you get back."

"Why do you think it'll be there?" Adam asked. They didn't know when or where the Haven told the others to meet.

"The strays agreed to meet you," Des explained. "No questions asked. No demands. They're overconfident. Which tells me they have backup. The transmission happened *before* your call, so they already knew where the convoy would be and when they'd be arriving. They fed you the same information so you'd show up to a welcome party of armed soldiers."

"Can we handle this?" Adam asked. Indiana was dangerous. Even Des had said as much. Should they really be picking a fight with armed soldiers?

"We can."

"Won't Indiana retaliate?"

Desmond's gaze met his in the rear-view mirror. "Perhaps. But *we* had nothing to do with the attack."

Adam's face tightened into a frown, and amusement glinted in Desmond's eyes at his confusion.

"If the Havenites find their soldiers *and* the strays all dead, yes, there's a chance, albeit small, that this could come back to us."

"Exactly."

"However," Desmond continued, guiding the car gracefully around a turn with one hand on the wheel, "if the strays aren't there..." The end of the sentence lifted as he looked back in the mirror expectantly, like he was waiting for Adam to finish the statement.

Adam shifted uncomfortably, feeling like he was back in high school, staring at a test he didn't understand. He had trouble focusing, but he wasn't stupid, and he hated when people made him feel like he was. And now, with the world spinning and his body numb, he didn't have the patience or mindset for riddles.

"I don't know," he groaned.

"They'll blame the strays."

"You're letting them walk away?" To his surprise, Adam felt a wave of relief wash over him.

"Of course not," Des answered. "But their bodies won't be there."

Their bodies.

Georgie's would be one of those.

Good. She wants you dead.

Adam knew this would be the outcome. He knew Des would kill her if he found her. And he thought he was okay with it.

Why, then, was he suddenly so bothered by the thought?

He'd agreed to this.

It was the right thing to do. A means to an end.

Taking down the Hub. That was what mattered. And this was a necessary step if he wanted Desmond's help.

When the car crawled to a stop, Des twisted to face Adam. "The shipping warehouse is on the opposite side of this building, so you should have a decent vantage point from the top floor, as long as they stay outside, which I expect they will. Don't move from this spot, and refrain from firing unless I indicate otherwise."

Adam shoved the car door open, but paused, debating whether to ask again about joining them.

"If something goes wrong," Des said, "I'm counting on you."

And with those words, Adam's stubbornness dissolved. He climbed out and grabbed his rifle from the trunk, then shrugged the strap over his shoulder, and by the time he scaled the two sets of stairs and pulled open a window, the car was gone. He flipped his rifle around, extending the bipod and resting it on the windowsill, then settled in to wait.

They were early. Would he really have to sit here for a half hour? His knee bounced at the thought, his muscles itchy.

The sun was still below the horizon, but the soft glow brightened the world enough to see the massive white box of a building across the street. The location the strays had given seemed random at the time, but now, looking at the fencing topped with barbed wire spirals, he realized it probably wasn't random at all. The warehouse parking lot was expansive, with a handful of semis parked throughout, their backs open and empty. There was a loading dock on the side closest to him, the roll-up doors sealed.

Adam pulled back the bolt handle, sliding a bullet into place, the sound comforting, and he couldn't help hoping something would go just a little wrong, so he'd have a chance to shoot.

You shouldn't be here. The sudden sound of Oliver's voice in the quiet room was startling, and as Adam looked up, his gaze collided with a pair of disapproving blue eyes and a familiar face so real he felt like he could reach out and touch it.

Even through the tipsiness, the pain left him breathless. He blinked hard and Oliver vanished.

"Don't do that," Adam muttered to the empty room, his voice shaky. He was losing it. The darkness was creeping back in around him.

Make it stop.

He popped an oxy, then finished his flask in one go before peering through the scope.

Two vehicles, a Humvee and a pickup truck, were now parked outside the fence, tire tracks in the snow behind them. He should've been paying attention. How long had they been there?

The exhaustion and alcohol blurred the edges of the shapes, but he was close enough that it shouldn't matter.

Still no sign of the convoy. Maybe Des was wrong. Maybe the encrypted call wasn't them.

Adam caught sight of three of Des's people, silhouettes appearing for only a fraction of a second before they vanished around the side of a building.

A few minutes later, the silence was shattered by the rumble of two bulky, cream-colored military trucks barreling down the street. As they neared the gate, it slid open with a loud creak.

Adam cursed quietly. Des was right. Of course he was right.

But if the strays knew they were on their way out, why would they agree to meet with him? What did they have to gain from it? Why not just tell him no? It didn't make sense.

It was the first time since the call that he'd taken a second to think about it.

Tell them your name. They'll meet you.

Why would his name make a difference? Because of Georgie?

No, wait. The Haven knew he was immune. "Thanks to you," he added out loud, looking back at the room. The soldiers had orders to keep him from leaving that night, so they probably knew his name.

That was why they'd agreed to meet. This was all a plan to drag him along to Indiana. To do whatever sciency bullshit they'd planned on doing.

The military trucks parked in front of the building, right outside the loading doors, and Adam counted as they stepped down into the snow.

Six soldiers, all in gray uniforms with bulletproof vests, heavy assault rifles in their hands.

He really hoped Desmond knew what he was doing.

Tell them your name.

Adam frowned. The Haven soldiers knew he was immune, but Colette...Nobody at Jardine knew. Why had she said that?

One soldier moved forward and signaled for the strays to pull into the lot, and once they were past the gate, it slid shut behind them. Dressed in heavy coats and winter hats, the strays poured out of the vehicles and cautiously approached the soldiers.

He scanned the figures, trying to pick out which one was Georgie.

Georgie, who had been his friend. Who had listened to him when he spoke, listened like what he said mattered. Like she cared.

You don't deserve any of the shit that's happened to you. That was what she'd told him. *You're a good person. It's not fair.*

She was lying. You deserve all of it and she knows it.

The booze churned in his stomach as his mood soured, the pleasant buzz turning heavy.

No. Desmond and the others. They were the ones who cared. Not her. They were the ones he *needed*.

Oliver's voice crept in again. *They're murderers, Adam.*

"So am I." Adam replied without looking up, echoing the answer he'd given when the real Oliver had made the same argument, the memory still sharp around the edges.

No, you're not. Not like that.

But that was even less true now than it had been then.

You're better than this. You don't actually want her dead.

Adam's leg bounced faster.

She didn't *need* to die for Desmond to get his plant. That was what he was really after, right? That was the whole point of all this.

If Adam could get down there, maybe he could...

Could what? It's too late. You already killed her.

No, she wasn't dead yet.

Adam grabbed his rifle and flipped it around his back, then stood and, when the room stopped spinning, he bolted down the stairs and out the door.

He tried to come up with a plan as he went, but his thoughts were sluggish and slippery.

It was fine. He'd improvise.

Keeping out of sight, he went the long way around, skirting the side of the adjacent building and following the footprints in the snow along the back of the warehouse until he found a hole cut in the fence.

Adam ducked inside and was almost to the corner of the building when a hand grabbed his hood and yanked him back.

18

“What the fuck are you doing?” a voice hissed, slamming him back against the wall and grabbing the front of his coat to hold him in place. “You can’t be down here.”

Ugh. Of course it was Jay.

“I need to get in there,” Adam said.

Jay jabbed a finger toward the fence. “Get the fuck out. Now.”

Adam was running out of time. His eyes flicked to Jay’s tactical vest, loaded with gear.

That could work.

In one quick motion, Adam snatched a frag grenade, pretended to pull the pin, then quickly dropped it between them.

Jay reflexively let go and lurched back before it even hit the ground, realizing too late that Adam was very obviously bluffing. "Jesus fucking Christ. What is wrong with you?"

Adam flashed him a smile, then turned and ran.

A single gunshot echoed through the lot, kicking up his pulse. He had to hurry.

After rounding the corner of the warehouse, he ducked behind a semi and scanned the group at the trucks.

Georgie wasn't there.

Adam laughed with relief, clutching the truck to steady himself.

She wasn't there.

One of the strays was sprawled on the ground while the others stood perfectly still, their guns at their feet. None of the Indiana soldiers looked concerned about the dead man, or even about who was firing at them, which seemed a little strange.

A wave of nausea hit Adam all at once. He pitched forward, sure he was going to hurl, but instead, the world tilted, and he lost his footing, stumbling out from behind the semi.

And into view of the Haven soldiers.

He caught his balance, then froze as their guns all trained on him.

Not good.

Adam flinched as a burst of automatic gunfire erupted behind him, dropping two soldiers and throwing the others into chaos. The strays scattered as the soldiers ducked out of sight, firing around the sides of the vehicles.

Get out, Oliver pleaded.

Yeah, that was probably a good idea.

A bullet flew past, too close, as Adam hopped into the back of a semi. He flipped around his rifle and peeked back outside, the crosshairs sweeping over the vehicles before a gunshot rang out from behind him, deafening in the metal container. Adam spun around to face a woman with short black hair and light skin at the back of the container. Her gun was pointed at his chest.

"Ow!" His nose wrinkled as the sound rattled around inside his skull. "A quick *hey you* would've worked. Holy hell. That was so loud."

She motioned with her pistol, closing the distance. "Gun on the ground."

"Sorry," he shouted dramatically, giving her a withering look. "Can't hear you over the ringing in my ears."

The woman adjusted her posture and squared her shoulders, like she thought it'd make her more intimidating. "Seriously, I *will* shoot you."

She was a soldier, dressed in worn camo pants instead of the sleek uniforms the ones from Indiana wore. One of the strays, then.

"You *can't* shoot me," Adam reminded her. "You need me alive."

She lowered her aim to his knees. "A lot of places I can shoot without killing you. Weapon down. Now."

Think, Adam.

The gunfire tapered off, and the world fell silent.

He let out an exaggerated sigh and set his rifle on the floor of the truck.

The woman kicked it away, then inched toward the opening of the trailer, her aim locked on him as she peered outside. "You're gonna save my ass. As soon as the soldiers take care of this, I need you to tell them who you are."

"Mm-hm, yeah, I'll definitely do that," he replied sarcastically.

"Any other weapons you got, put them on the ground and slide them over."

Adam ignored her. "Where's Georgie? Why isn't she here?"

Irritation tightened the soldier's face. "Alive. We left the others back in Elgin. They were headed this way on foot." She motioned with her gun. "Empty your holsters."

"Okay. I just..." He trailed off as his eyes shifted up over her shoulder, widening slightly in feigned fear before he threw up his hands in surrender. She took the bait, head turning to follow his gaze, and Adam drew his pistol and fired a round that buried itself in her chest.

It wasn't where he was aiming, but it worked.

The sound echoed off the walls of the hollow truck, amplifying the pain in his head.

Gasping for air, the soldier staggered back, her hands desperately clutching her chest. But she was still on her feet.

Adam steadied himself against the side of the truck to regain his balance before he stepped in closer and fired. This time between her eyes.

The soldier crumpled.

He winced, teeth clenched against the pain, as the rattling in his skull escalated to an agonizing level.

When the ringing faded enough for Adam to gather his thoughts, he holstered his handgun, then grabbed his rifle and threw it over his shoulder. He tugged the radio from her belt and clipped it to his vest before jumping down from the trailer.

Des and Eris stood at the rear of a military truck, two bodies lying in the snow nearby. As Adam approached, Desmond's dark eyes fixed on him with a piercing intensity that locked Adam in place.

"Don't move," Des growled. He adjusted his grip on his Desert Eagle before he turned, stepping up onto the loading dock and over the body of a soldier in the now open doorway.

Adam's muscles tensed. He messed up.

You are to do as you're told.

What was he thinking?

I'm counting on you.

Desmond had trusted him, and he blew it.

When the others met back at the convoy, Jay lunged forward and shoved Adam hard, sending him stumbling, his back slamming against the truck.

"Stupid fucking kid."

Make him stop.

Adam drew his hunting knife from his boot. "Put your hands on me again and I'll cut them off."

The man straightened as his hand twitched, clearly considering going for his own weapon.

"Well," Des said as he reappeared, pulling a middle-aged man by the front of his trench coat, the tension gone from his voice. "That was certainly messier than I'd hoped."

He kicked the man's knees out from under him, sending him off the side of the dock to the snow-covered ground below before stepping down beside him.

"Where are the others?" Des asked, lifting his gun.

"I-I don't—"

Desmond fired a shot, and the sentence broke off in a scream as the man clutched his now bleeding hand. "Care to try again?"

The man wagged his head, face contorted in fear and agony. "Please. Don't."

Desmond holstered his gun and drew his switchblade from his jacket, and as he flicked it open and stepped in closer, Eris and Jay yanked the man to his feet. "Where is my plant?"

"I don't know anything about a plant."

The tip of the narrow blade hovered, almost touching the wrinkled skin beneath the man's eye. Des tilted his head, considering him. "I'm not sure I believe you. I recommend thinking really hard."

"I—"

The blade lurched up, piercing the man's eye, and he let out a blood-curdling scream, fighting against the hands holding him.

Des pulled the knife free. "Do you remember now, or should I move on to the other?"

"I don't know anything! You have to believe me."

Des's mouth lifted into a warm smile. "See, now I *do* believe you." He grazed the tip of the blade along the man's cheek. "But what you're telling me is you're useless."

The man's sobs shook his entire body as tears streamed down his face.

"And that's unfortunate for both of us." Des jammed the blade hilt-deep into the man's neck.

Adam's attention drifted to the bodies and the stained snow, then to their own people—one of which had been shot in the side and was being patched up by another. And it was because of him and his stupid decision.

After wiping the knife clean on the dead man's coat, Desmond clicked it shut and returned it to his pocket, then smoothed his tweed jacket.

His gaze slid to Adam. "Was it unclear what was expected of you?"

Adam shrank back and shook his head.

Was Desmond going to yell? He'd never seen him yell. The thought was unsettling. Would he shoot Adam right there and be done with it? Leave him here to rot?

But Desmond only gave a decisive clap. "All right, bring the cars around and search the warehouse. They chose this location for a reason. It's either a cache or a refueling station. Figure out which. When you're finished, handle the strays. Quickly. It's freezing, and personally, I'm sick of all this snow."

Jay scoffed. "Your pet almost got himself killed, Emery. Almost got us all killed. He shouldn't have been here."

Desmond raised a brow. "I don't remember asking for your opinion." The man opened his mouth to respond, but Des interrupted, voice lower. "Do I need to repeat my instructions?"

Jay's expression flickered from anger to uncertainty before he turned and stomped away.

"Brilliant." As everyone broke off in different directions, Des turned back to Adam. "What was all that about?"

Adam didn't know how to answer. He couldn't tell Des that he was trying to protect Georgie. That wouldn't go over well. "I wanted to help."

"If you want to help, then do the job you were brought on to do."

Adam nodded.

"Did I make a mistake assuming you could handle this?"

"No."

"Good, because this was to be a mutually beneficial arrangement, and while I'm glad to have you with us," his expression darkened, eyes suddenly venomous, "to assume I can't manage without you would be a grave mistake."

A knot twisted in Adam's already nauseous stomach.

"When we get back, you're going to spend every waking hour in Comms until you figure out where Wicks and my plant are. Understood?"

Adam nodded again.

That, he thought, *sounded an awful lot like an order.*

Desmond's expression settled into its usual calm, and he gave Adam a gentle smile, then swiftly turned and walked away.

"Really, though," Des chimed to Eris, his tone light and animated as she matched his stride. "Seven years here and I still haven't adjusted to this weather. In London, the most snow we ever saw..." His voice faded as they crossed the parking lot toward the gate.

Adam burrowed deeper in his coat.

The rest of the group was busy searching through the military vehicles, stripping the weapons from the corpses, but Adam stayed planted in that spot.

You really messed that up.

He had to fix this.

Des was assigning him back to radio duty, still fixated on finding that plant, which meant the Hub would stay on the back burner. And after a screw-up like that, Adam couldn't be sure Des even planned to keep his promise. Why would he? What had Adam done to prove himself?

But he could fix it.

The soldier had told him where Georgie was last, so he had a vague idea of where to find her. Or at least a direction to head.

He could tell Des now. But then he was back to the same problem. If Des found Georgie, he'd kill her.

Unless Adam tracked her down himself. He could steal the plant and bring it back. It would prove he was worth the trouble and free up the resources to finally take out the Hub.

All he had to do was head toward Elgin.

He could do it. He could make this right.

Adam surveyed the lot one more time, then vanished around the warehouse and slipped back through the hole in the fence.

19

Vivian seemed to soften a little after the interaction with Oliver, and Georgie wasn't sure if it was the fact that Oliver knew her or that they were from a Haven, but she seemed less on edge. She grabbed fresh water and crackers and sent Georgie with a middle-aged woman to a cabin through the woods while she waited for Jax at the farmhouse.

When the others arrived at the cabin, looking frozen and worn down, the fire was just beginning to take.

Jax and Banks brought out the blankets from the bedrooms, and Vivian lingered by the door, watching everyone settle in near the fireplace to thaw.

Georgie leaned against the arm of the couch, still processing the reunion with Oliver.

"You've really been through hell, then," Vivian said.

"Yeah," Georgie answered. "You could say that."

"Do you have somewhere to go?"

"We do, but our ride fell through." More like terrible people ruined it for them.

Would she run into Thompson at the Indiana Haven?

She really hoped so.

"That's why we asked about the radio," Jax said. "We need to contact them so they can meet us."

Georgie glanced at the others. She knew they'd get everyone to Indiana, even without a convoy to take them, but it still weighed heavily on her to be sitting around.

"Come to the farmhouse in the morning," Vivian said, folding her arms. "We'll see if we can figure something out."

Georgie studied the woman. "Why are you letting us stay? Why help us at all?"

Jax shot her a glare, but she shrugged sharply in response. Georgie knew he was thinking the same thing. There had to be an angle.

"I guess I'm getting soft," Vivian said with a chuckle. "Maybe Owen's rubbing off on me."

"Well, we appreciate it," Jax said.

After Vivian left, Georgie filled Jax in on what Oliver had said, how he'd thought Adam was at Haven all this time, and then she spent the rest of the evening obsessing over the question she was too afraid to ask out loud.

Desmond had told her at Haven that he was the one who'd made the deal with Adam. If Adam wasn't at the Campus, and he wasn't with Oliver, could he have gone with Desmond? The question carved away at her thoughts so much that it bled into her dreams.

When she woke the next morning, there were only dying embers in the hearth, though the room still held some of its warmth.

Jax was planted at the front door, keeping watch, and Georgie's tired body fought against her as she peeled herself off the floor.

"Morning," she whispered, stepping carefully over sleeping mounds scattered on the floor. They needed to go, but she didn't have the heart to wake them. Not yet.

Jax's face was etched with exhaustion. "Morning."

"Did you sleep at all?"

He shrugged, and she took that as a no.

Georgie sat at the small table and scanned the room, her gaze catching on the eerie deer head mounted over the fireplace. "Think Indiana made contact?"

Jax shrugged again. "We'll get there," he assured her. "Once we get a radio, we'll explain what happened and have them pick us up."

Someone knocked on the front door and Jax spun around, reaching for a gun that wasn't there.

"Anybody hungry?" a voice called from outside.

Jax carefully opened the door, and Georgie shot up.

"Kye!"

"Small world, huh?" Kye said with a grin as she stepped inside, a platter of food in her hands and a canvas bag hanging around her shoulder. She set the platter down, and Georgie's eyes widened. Cured meat, slices of cheese, bread, and fresh butter. They'd been living on canned goods for two months, and the sight of fresh food made her want to cry.

She dragged her attention back to Kye. "Oliver told me he left. I didn't realize you did, too. What happened?"

Kye blew out a sharp breath before answering. "We lost some people in an attack from one of the gangs that popped up after the cult disappeared." She set the canvas bag down on the floor. "Some clothes for you guys," she explained before continuing. "We dealt with it, and

I figured that was the end of it, but then a new group came along with a deal. When I refused to trade our supplies for their protection, it was like opening the floodgates." Kye grabbed a slice of bread from the platter, tearing off a small piece and popping it in her mouth. "Doubt the sudden target on our backs was a coincidence."

Our settlement is protected. Was that what Vivian had meant?

"Are they the same ones protecting this place?"

She nodded. "Vivian thinks this deal is for the best, but I don't trust them." Kye popped another piece of bread into her mouth and dropped into a chair. "Desmond especially."

The name hit like a punch to the chest. "Desmond?"

"Yeah," she said with a frown. "I'm so sorry, guys. Viv told me what happened to Haven. That he was involved. I should've seen right through his bullshit the first time he showed up at our doors."

Georgie's heart hammered against her ribs.

They needed to get away from this place.

Now.

"The truck in the yard," Georgie said. "Does it run?"

Kye shook her head. "That thing has been there since I was a kid."

"What about a radio?" Jax asked. "Vivian said she might be able to help us find one."

"Oliver has some up in the attic," Kye said. "Not sure if they work, but you can go ask. I'll take you."

Georgie wasn't sure he'd want to talk to her. He was really upset yesterday. But they needed a radio. Plus, the question was still eating away at her, and if anyone knew where Adam might have gone, it would be him.

Reese threw off the blankets and hopped to his feet, a smile lifting on his face. "Kye?" As he crossed the small room, she pushed up from the chair and met him with a tight hug.

"You can't just disappear on me like that," Kye chided. "I thought you two were dead." When she pulled back to look at him, his expression dropped.

"It's only me."

Jax had been the one to break the news to Reese after their first trip to Haven.

Georgie was well-acquainted with loss, so she felt for him, but his sister deserved the bullet that someone put in her head.

Kye's face tightened, and she tugged him back in. "I'm sorry, Reese." When she finally let him go, she asked, "Are you okay?"

"Are any of us?"

With a sigh, she turned to Georgie. "Come on, I'll show you where Oliver's room is, then Reese is going to fill me in on what I missed."

After grabbing a piece of bread and a chunk of cured meat from the platter, Georgie followed Kye outside, down the path through the woods.

"Does Desmond come here?" she asked between bites, eyeing the forest around them.

Kye ducked beneath a low-hanging branch weighed down from snow. "He came with last time, but I guess that's not the norm. There was an issue, and he came to hand out threats. Viv says they do pickups once a week, but they usually stay at the edge of the property." She gave Georgie a reassuring smile. "Don't worry, you guys are safe here."

Georgie didn't believe that, but the fear receded a little, knowing she wouldn't randomly run into him here.

Once they made it to the second floor of the farmhouse, Kye pulled a string, causing a strange device with two metal wheels to spin. When she released it, an arm-like rod tapped a plastic ball against the hatch above before gradually coming to a stop.

Georgie studied the device as footsteps sounded above them.

The hatch swung open, the ladder unfolding on its own, and Oliver called down without looking. "What do you want?"

"I'll catch up with you later," Kye said before turning and heading back downstairs.

Georgie hesitated.

Would Oliver even be willing to help? Would she trust him if he said he wanted to? He'd already sold them out once before. Would he be willing to do it again?

She didn't know what to expect, but he had a radio, and unless she wanted to keep dragging her people through the snow, she needed to borrow it. So she climbed cautiously up into the attic and took in the room.

The morning sunlight seeped through cracks in the walls and flooded through the single window. A small desk sat against one wall, the paint on the front worn and chipping in places, and Oliver was perched on the chair in front of it.

"Hey," she said.

He mumbled a response without looking up from whatever he was working on.

The room was small, every bit of space utilized by metal cabinets and toolboxes and shelves packed with books. Two radios sat on one shelf—big, bulky things like the one her dad had in his tent, and beside them, a handheld receiver.

There we go.

"Can we talk?" she asked.

"We *are* talking," Oliver replied.

She crossed to the desk, eyeing the radios. "How are you holding up?"

"Fine."

"This place seems nice."

Oliver finally tore his eyes from his work to give her a baffled frown. "Is that really what you came all the way up here to talk about?"

"I'm just making conversation."

"Why?"

She shrugged. "I don't know."

"I'd rather you didn't. I don't like small talk and I'm kind of busy." He turned back to the box on the desk.

"What is that?"

"Are you still making conversation, or do you actually want to know?"

"I'm curious."

"That's not an answer."

A smile tugged at her lips. "Are you always this difficult?"

"I guess."

"I genuinely want to know, Oliver."

He scooted the chair to give her a better view of the metal box, the side open to wires and microchips and fans. "It's a high-efficiency particulate air purifier, but I've added a UV light here to increase the efficiency. I had an issue with the transformer, and it set the whole thing back, but I figured it out."

With a quick glance in her direction, he paused, like he expected her to tell him to stop talking.

"So, how does it work?" she asked, leaning on the desk.

The corners of his mouth ticked up as the words poured out in a steady stream, and even though Georgie didn't understand most of it, she listened.

"It can only filter the air in one room at a time," he added. "But if I can figure out a way to enhance it, to make it bigger, it could potentially keep an entire house spore free. Imagine if we could install these in every home. Every greenhouse."

That she understood. If he could pull that off, it'd be world changing.

Georgie shook her head in amazement, mind reeling with possibilities. "Has anyone ever told you you're a genius?"

His expression flattened. "Yes."

Her gaze drifted around the room, landing again on the radios.

"I'm not," Oliver said, his voice tinged with frustration, brows drawn together. "Just because I know a lot about one thing, it doesn't mean..." He let the sentence trail off, then shrugged.

"I didn't mean anything by it, Oliver."

"Everybody automatically assumes because I can build things, I'm really smart or something, but I'm not, and it always seems to disappoint them." Oliver closed the side of the purifier and flipped the latch. He grabbed a pair of old safety goggles, twisting the worn strap around his fingers. "I'm not—I like fixing things, that's all."

Georgie chewed the inside of her lip, unsure how to respond.

"What did you really come up here for?"

She glanced at the radios, but when she opened her mouth, the question tumbled out. "Is Adam with Desmond?"

Would he have really gone with them? Even after what they did to her? To her home?

Oliver hesitated, then tilted his head to look at her, his light eyes only making it to around her chin before stopping. "I think so."

Georgie exhaled sharply, heat flooding her veins as she pushed away from the desk, rattling everything on top.

How could he do that? How could he betray her like that?

She was quickly running out of people to trust.

"Don't blame him," Oliver said. "He didn't have anywhere else to go."

"He had *you*. Why didn't he go home?"

Oliver was quiet a moment before answering. "I told him not to."

That she didn't see coming. "Why the hell would you do that?"

He shoved to his feet and paced the length of the small space. "Adam was miserable and there were dangerous people who wanted to take him away, and I was so afraid that something really bad was going to happen. So, I made a choice."

The radio call to Haven.

"You told Vega that he's immune."

Oliver stopped abruptly and wrapped his arms around himself. "I thought he'd spend some time being mad at me, and then after a while, he'd realize how good he had it there. He'd have a life with everything he'd always wanted. If they hadn't come along and ruined it all, he would've been happy."

Her anger dissipated.

Adam came to her, probably looking for help, and what did she tell him?

Go. Before my common sense kicks in and I shoot you where you stand.

He had nowhere else to go.

"I'm going after Desmond," Georgie said.

Oliver frowned. "What?"

"I'm going to Jardine and ending this."

"You really do make terrible decisions."

"Yeah, so I've heard."

"Wait, Jardine? The water treatment plant?"

Georgie nodded. She thought back to the roof of her mom's lab and the handful of dim lights spread throughout the empty city. She'd seen it then, the long strip of land beside Navy Pier, the building lit up against the darkening sky.

Reese had told them everything about his time there, which wasn't much. He'd only seen a small portion of the place.

A controller on the bed drew Georgie's attention. "Oh!" She tucked her hand in her coat pocket and pulled out the small metal cube. "I found this at Haven. It's broken, but maybe you can fix it."

"BUG!" Oliver snatched the cube from her hand. "I don't..." He trailed off as he looked up at her. "Thank you."

She smiled and watched as he turned BUG over to inspect each side.

"I'll help you," Oliver said suddenly. "If you're going after Desmond. I'll do whatever I can. I have a dart still—the kind the cult used. And the device to shoot it. You can have both, or anything else you need, but you have to promise to bring Adam home."

She looked back at the radios. "Can I borrow one of those?"

"Why?"

"If we're going to dig that idiot out of the shit he's gotten himself into, I need to get my people somewhere safe first."

Oliver stepped in close to the shelf, his fingers moving slowly across the devices.

"Here," he said, pulling a bulky radio free of the stack and passing it to Georgie. "This is the only one that works at the moment. You'll need a generator to power it." He grabbed a box from his desk and unplugged a cord from an outlet in the front. "It should have enough charge left." He set it on top of the radio.

Georgie gave him a grateful smile. "Thanks, Oliver."

He dropped back into the chair, attention already back on his project. "Don't break it."

"I'll do my best."

"How about now?" Banks asked from behind the radio.

"Still nothing." Georgie sat slouched in a wooden chair, elbow on the table, chin resting in her hand. They'd been trying to figure out the radio for an hour with no luck, and she was starting to lose patience.

The others had scattered, all finding something to keep them busy while they waited. Wren and Ciri had gone to the farmhouse to offer help with lunch, Reese and Kye to talk to Dr. Ramirez, and Levi had headed to the barn to see the animals.

"Are you sure it works?" Jax mumbled sleepily.

"Oliver said it does," Georgie answered.

"He could be wrong."

"I doubt it."

"Then, maybe he's lying."

"Why would he lie about a radio?"

"I don't know. Because he's a liar and we probably shouldn't trust a damn thing that comes out of his mouth."

"He's trying to help, Jax."

"He was actively trying to get us killed, like three months ago. Sorry if I have my doubts."

Georgie didn't fully trust him either, but Oliver was the reason Jax was still alive. Plus, he wanted to get Adam back. He wouldn't do anything to mess that up. Not that she could use that argument. She had decided it was probably best not to mention to the others that Adam was with Desmond. Not yet.

"How about now?" Banks asked again after a few minutes. The light flickered, and this time, it stayed on.

"You got it," Georgie said with a smile. She grabbed the square microphone and held it out to Jax, only to find his eyes closed, his head cradled in his hand, the lines between his eyebrows finally gone. Her gaze shifted to Banks, who sighed and plopped into the chair across from her before taking the microphone.

"INH, this is ILH-B5. Do you copy? Over."

A moment later, a gravelly voice answered. "ILH-B5, this is INH-C1. Reading you loud and clear. What's the sitrep on extraction? Are you with our troop? Over."

A frown creased Banks's forehead. "Negative. Need rendezvous coordinates. Over."

"Our convoy scheduled rendezvous this morning. They should've linked up with you already. Why aren't you with them? Over."

Georgie deflated. She'd hoped they'd catch them in time. Now, how long would they have to wait? Where were they supposed to stay until they sent another?

"Part of our group split off," Banks replied. "*We* have the plant, not them. Redirect troops to pick us up. Over."

"Lost comms with the convoy at extraction time. We can't send additional assets until the situation is clear. You need to deliver the plant to our location. Over."

"You're fucking kidding," Georgie grumbled. They were offering to hand over a solution that could possibly save everyone, and these bastards couldn't be bothered to send someone to get them? She narrowed her gaze at the radio as heat rose in her cheeks. No. She was so done with this.

"My turn." Georgie held out her hand, and Banks handed her the mic.

"Alright, listen," she snarled. "We have been through hell. Literal. Fucking. Hell. We're offering you something you need, so get off your asses and make an effort. My people are safe where they are and I'm not dragging them back on the road without the promise of a ride. If you want this thing, come and fucking get it."

She slammed the mic onto the table, jolting Jax awake.

With an amused smirk, Banks grabbed the mic and added, "Over."

After a moment, the voice replied. "Roger. Requesting additional time. Will contact when en route with coordinates. Out."

Georgie beamed. That was more like it.

20

With the assurance that their ride was coming soon, Vivian agreed to let the seven of them stay at the cabin for a couple more days, as long as they pulled their weight.

They were almost in the clear, and knowing the others would be behind Haven's walls before Desmond's people sent for the next pickup made Georgie feel a little better. However, what she had to do after continued to send her thoughts into a tailspin.

The snow tapered off, and they spent the day finding a sort of flow in the tasks of the homestead.

Georgie spent two hours helping Banks and Levi clear the snow from the chicken run while Jax was on radio duty, but her heart still jumped into her throat every time she picked out the shape of a person in the yard.

As the evening shifted into night, the Spring Valley residents disappeared inside the farmhouse, and Vivian stopped Georgie before they headed back to the cabin to invite them for dinner.

"I need to pop into the greenhouse to pick some herbs," Vivian said. "I'll meet you at the house."

Georgie straightened. "I can do it." The plant was sitting in the cold cabin, hidden away in one of the bedrooms. She needed to keep it safe until Indiana sent new coordinates.

Vivian handed her the key, then rattled off the list, and a second later, she was gone.

"Want help?" Jax asked.

She gave him a gentle smile. "I don't think we need two people to pick herbs. I won't be long."

He nodded, but stayed put, clearly wanting to say something else.

"Talk to me, Jax."

He glanced at the farmhouse, then back at her. "You said Indiana lost contact with the convoy. Doesn't that seem a little strange?"

She hadn't thought much about it, honestly. "Yeah, I guess."

"Do you think it was Emery?"

The question left a heavy feeling in her stomach. "They lost contact, that's all. It doesn't mean they were attacked."

"You don't just lose contact with a military convoy unless they're dead."

Was he right? Could it have been Desmond?

"You see how insane it is to think we can go after them ourselves?" he asked. "If we go into Jardine, we're dead."

"We don't *have* to go into Jardine," she said. "I have a plan. Or at least the beginnings of a plan. This place is under his protection, right? If we can find a way to disrupt things, maybe Desmond will come deal with it personally. We'll have the upper hand."

"We're not even allowed to carry weapons. What are we gonna do when he shows up?"

"If we tell Vivian, explain what—"

"If she hears anything about this, she'll kick us out on our asses."

"I'm not giving up on this, Jax." She rested her hands firmly on her hips, lips pressed into a line.

He looked her over, his gaze lingering on her pursed lips for a moment before his expression softened.

"What?" she asked with a frown.

"I missed you."

The words left Georgie instantly disarmed. Her cheeks warmed and her hands fell to her sides. "I missed you too."

The quiet pushed in around them, until he finally said, "We have dinner plans."

She nodded. "We do. And I have herbs to pick."

"You sure you don't want help?"

"I've got it covered. I'll meet you at the farmhouse."

He lingered a moment, eyes on her, and when he turned and started across the yard, she watched him go, the three words lingering.

I missed you.

Maybe she hadn't lost him yet. He was still here, still trying.

Jax may have pushed her away over the past few months, but she couldn't ignore the fact that she had pushed him away first. She kept him at a distance because she was afraid.

But keeping him at arm's length didn't prevent the pain when she thought she had lost him. It still hurt like hell.

And losing Mabel didn't lessen the value of their years together. She was lucky to have so many memories to cling to.

Georgie swung by the cabin to grab the plant, then headed to the greenhouse with it tucked safely in her bag.

It was a simple structure—metal poles and an opaque tarp. Nothing like the building they had at Haven, but it was enough to protect the crops from the cold weather and contamination.

Would the verti-farms at the Indiana Haven resemble the one at her own?

She carefully pulled the plant from her bag. It looked rough. Broken, tattered, wilting.

Same, thought Georgie.

"Hang in there," she told it. "You're the key to everything."

This plant would change the world. Her mom's hard work was going to save everyone.

After watering it and tucking it out of sight, she followed the row of wooden planters to one with labels for various herbs, crouching to pluck a few sprigs of rosemary, thyme, and parsley.

Her mom used to grow rosemary in their apartment. She didn't cook much, but she loved the smell of it.

Georgie ran her fingers over the planter, loosening and turning the top layer of the damp soil, stirring up the subtle, earthy aroma. The one that used to remind her of her mother.

But it conjured a different memory now.

A charming smile, kind dark eyes, a smooth lilting voice.

Dance with me.

The mask that hid the monster underneath.

An icy chill crawled up her spine and lifted goosebumps on her arms, the terrible feeling of something ominous lurking just beyond her line of sight, waiting for the moment she let her guard down.

What if Desmond *did* show up here? What if Indiana didn't come? What if they were on their own?

Even if she had the element of surprise, it wouldn't matter.

What was she thinking? How did she plan to take on someone strong enough to scare entire settlements into siding with him?

How stupid was she to think she stood a chance?

She shifted back and sat on her heels, queasy and trembling. Panic swept over her like a sudden gust of wind, leaving her breathless and disoriented, and though it didn't last, she stayed there on the floor of the greenhouse for a long time before she felt steady enough to stand. When her pulse finally settled, she shuffled out into the frigid air.

The moon hung bloated in the sky, partially hidden behind heavy clouds, and shadows crept in from the forest like claws. She hurried across the yard as the wind rustled through the trees like a chorus of anxious whispers, glancing over her shoulder every few steps.

Georgie paused on the porch, drawing a deep breath to try and shake off the feeling of being watched before opening the farmhouse door.

The warmth of the fireplace and the inviting scent of food in the oven met her as she stepped inside. A Christmas tree stood tall in the sitting room, its branches adorned with dozens of small red ribbons, and she stopped and studied it with a frown.

Was it Christmas? She had lost all sense of time.

In the kitchen, a handful of people were already busy cooking. Conversations hummed alongside the clattering of pots, and despite its enormous size, the room felt cozy, the warmth of the cast-iron stove radiating throughout. Dried meat hung from twine along the far wall, and the cookware that filled the shelves looked like something straight out of her history books.

Jax stood at the counter wearing a beige oversized knitted sweater. He pulled a potato from a bowl of water and handed it to Owen, who chopped it while talking. The boy seemed to be feeling much better.

When Jax lifted his head, his eyes connected with hers across the room, and a soft smile touched his lips. "Hi," he mouthed.

She smiled back, the tension melting away. "Hi."

Vivian was beside her a moment later. "Find the right ones?"

Georgie pulled the handful of herbs from her coat pocket. "Where should I put them?"

"Chop them and take them to Merritt." She motioned to a man in his late thirties, his ash blond hair tied up in a messy bun. Tattoos covered his arms and neck, his face half hidden by a thick beard. Beside him, Reese watched attentively as the man wrapped a roast with a long piece of string.

While the meal cooked, Vivian opened a bottle of wine, and Kye passed out glasses.

The conversation flowed seamlessly from brief introductions to their lives prior to the collapse.

Merritt and Owen had lived in a tiny apartment on the north side, and when the world fell apart, they hopped in Merritt's food truck and headed away from the city.

Vivian had worked at Spring Valley for twenty years before the collapse and had been close friends with Kye's mother. She lost her husband to the infection, way back at the beginning.

Kye had just started college at the University of Chicago, and her professor, Lloyd, had blocked off the campus and offered it as a safe place for anyone with nowhere else to go.

Jax told them about the tiny town he grew up in, how he'd lost his mom when he was little, and his dad last year. He didn't talk about Haven or the things that happened after.

Wren talked about Ciri's dad, a nurse who refused to come home during the pandemic, sleeping at the hospital every night because he didn't want to put his girlfriend and daughter at risk.

Georgie stuck with vague details—that she grew up downtown, that she was studying to become a doctor when the pandemic hit. She wasn't about to tell her life story to a group of strangers who didn't trust her enough to let her carry a weapon.

When it was Reese's turn, his expression sobered. "I can't."

Kye pulled him against her and softly patted the side of his head—the movement protective and tender.

When the meal was ready, the rest of the Spring Valley residents crammed into the kitchen. Georgie spotted a few familiar faces from the Campus. Among them was Dr. Ramirez, the man who'd saved her life when she showed up with an infection after escaping the cult. He greeted her with a warm hug.

Vivian raised her long-stemmed glass. "Happy Christmas Eve," she began, addressing the couple dozen faces. "We've faced our share of losses this year, including some beloved members of our community. But we've gained a lot too, and tonight, we focus on that. After dinner, you're all welcome to join us in the living room. We've got wine, music, and a warm fire, and seeing as how we're still here, still breathing, we have a good reason to celebrate." She smiled. "Now, enjoy the food because it'll be another year before we eat like this again."

The meal surpassed anything Georgie had ever tasted—succulent pork, garlic mashed potatoes, and warm, crusty bread slathered with fresh butter.

Oliver popped in long enough to eat a quick serving while perched at the counter, then disappeared without a word.

Georgie spent the entire meal with her toes wiggling happily inside her shoes. It felt incredible to put everything that had happened and everything that was going to happen away for a night, and savor the present.

The room slowly emptied as everyone finished eating, and after she and Jax cleaned up their plates, they followed. Pillows were strewn across the living room floor, the couches pushed back to make more space. Georgie settled on the floor against the far wall, and Jax sat beside her as Ciri fluttered around the room like a butterfly with two others around her age.

Banks grabbed a violin from the top of a large wooden piano and Georgie's face split into a grin. She hadn't heard him play in years.

He studied the instrument a moment, then his gaze flicked to Levi. "Come on."

The boy hesitated before he dropped onto the piano bench, finger gently tracing over the keys.

Banks started first, the bow gliding smoothly across the strings, and Levi joined in a moment later. The melody of *Have Yourself a Merry Little Christmas* filled the room—it was Mabel's favorite. Georgie could almost see her there, standing beside her brothers, could almost hear her beautiful voice singing along.

Christmas had always been Georgie's favorite holiday. Her mom would have a couple days off, and her dad would do his best to be there if he was in the country. They'd get together with Mabel's family and have a big dinner, play Christmas songs like this, followed by hours of the adults drinking spirits while the kids watched Christmas movies and binged on cookies and eggnog and hot cocoa. For a while, she'd feel like a normal kid with a normal life.

Now, the only ones left were Chris, Levi, and her.

Her heart ached for everyone they had lost—before the collapse, during the first year at Haven, and the hundreds more in the last few months.

But they still had a lot to fight for.

Going after Desmond wasn't only for her. It was for her people. These people who had gone through hell with her. Who had lost everything.

Ciri stopped in front of Banks, eyes following the bow as it slid back and forth over the string, and he crouched down to her level, took her hand, and set it on the side of the instrument. When he began again, Ciri looked back at Wren, beaming, her smile taking up most of her face. She stayed like that for the length of the song, eyes closed as she focused on the vibrations of the strings against the wood.

Jax handed Georgie a glass, then picked up his own from the floor. "To us?" he said, the last word lifting at the end.

"That wasn't a toast. That was a question."

He shrugged. "Yeah, I guess it was."

She lifted her glass and softly clinked them together. "To us." They both took a long sip, and when Georgie lowered her glass, she fixed her gaze on the dancing flames in the fireplace, her eyelids heavy. "I don't understand how they keep this place running and still have energy for all this. I'm exhausted."

"Yeah. Me, too." After finishing his wine, Jax climbed to his feet and offered his hand. "Can I walk you home?"

She slipped her hand into his, using him as leverage to pull herself off the floor. Her healing stomach wound sent a clap of pain through her as she did, and she stumbled forward into him.

"Are you okay?"

She laughed and steadied herself. "Yeah, I'm fine."

Before they left, Georgie waved goodbye to Vivian, mouthing a thank you. She let Jax lead her outside, and as the door closed behind them, it drowned out the noise. When they made it down the steps, he turned to face her, the lines suddenly back between his brows.

"I need to..." The sentence fell away, and he breathed a sharp sigh, then tried again. "I'm sorry for being an ass. Can we call a truce, go back to how it was? I really need you here with me."

"I never went anywhere," she responded.

He looked like he wanted to say something else, the lines turning into a full frown as he looked back at the farmhouse.

"What's wrong?" she asked.

The frown softened. "It's nothing." His eyes met hers and he smiled. "It's Christmas Eve, and we all deserve a night to breathe. We can worry about everything else later."

Every inch of space between them seemed to hum with electricity as Georgie became acutely aware of just how close they were standing. Jax's gaze dropped briefly to her lips, and she wondered what would happen if he actually kissed her right then, because the way she felt, muscles tingling from the proximity, she was certain she'd short-circuit like a toaster in a bathtub.

Before she could find out, someone plopped onto the bottom porch step with a heavy sigh.

She scowled as she turned, but her frustration vanished in an instant.

Adam swiped the wavy caramel hair off his forehead and as he glanced up at her, the dim light pushed back the shadows on his face, revealing a strikingly vivid shade of purple across his cheekbone.

The corner of his mouth lifted. "Sorry to interrupt."

21

This was a mistake.

What was he doing?

Adam shifted on the steps as Georgie stared, the sound of muffled piano music seeping beneath the door.

His exhaustion was overwhelming, and the pounding headache from the hangover still clung tight, despite the oxys he'd taken on his way here.

After leaving the warehouse, Adam had headed west, confident that he could track her down, but as he sobered up, it quickly became clear how stupid his plan was. He'd decided to get a little sleep, and then head back to Jardine, barely making it inside a townhouse before collapsing.

He had completely forgotten about the radio clipped to his vest until a voice shook him awake. The soldiers spoke back and forth, and when Georgie's voice came on, barking orders, he sat up, listening carefully.

"My people are safe where they are," she'd said, and Adam's mind had gone immediately to this place. The location added up with what the soldier had told him, and it would take a lot for Georgie to feel like they were safe. It made sense.

It was a gut feeling, but he had nothing else to go on.

When Adam finally made it to Spring Valley, he sat against the barn, waiting. Watching. And it had all paid off. He'd tracked her down all on his own.

Now, Georgie spat a frantic sort of laugh and yanked him to his feet, throwing her arms around him.

"You're okay!" She clung tight for a long moment, and then, abruptly, she shoved him away. "What the fuck, Adam?"

She hates you, the voice growled.

He needed to find the plant. Needed to get it back to Desmond. If Adam found them this easily, no doubt Des would figure it out soon enough.

She'd never forgive him for stealing it, but it was the only way she wouldn't end up dead.

And it was the only way Desmond would ever act on the Hub.

He needed this.

"Adam," Georgie said, snapping her fingers in front of his face. "You with us?"

"Uh-huh. Just tired." He gave a forced smile and then looked at Hale, checking for any weapons. From what Adam could see, he was unarmed.

"Are you alone?" Georgie's question pulled his attention back.

"Yep, just me."

"Does he know we're here?"

Adam tensed.

Did she know about Desmond? About where he'd been? No, how could she?

He tilted his head, feigning ignorance. "Who?"

"Don't bullshit me, Adam. Does he know?"

Hale's expression darkened as he understood. "Are you fucking *kidding*?"

"Jax," Georgie warned.

Adam let the heaviness fall back over his face. Why bother? She knew he betrayed her, and he was too tired to keep the mask in place, anyway.

"He doesn't know you're here," Adam answered. "Or me, for that matter."

The muscles in Hale's jaw tensed, and Adam was pretty sure if he had a gun, he would've drawn it right then. "I saved your ass when *his* guy beat the shit out of you."

They hate you. They know what you are.

Adam's mouth tilted into a wry smile, which set Hale off even more.

When the soldier stepped in too close, Adam fought the urge to recoil.

"I should've known better," Hale said. "Should've left you to die on that damn street."

"Yeah, you probably should have. But then again, thinking's not really what soldiers are for, is it?"

Hale shoved him so hard that he stumbled backwards, his boots hitting the bottom step. He grabbed the wooden railing to steady himself.

Make him stop. You have a weapon, and he doesn't.

Adam drew his pistol and focused his aim, his finger resting on the trigger. "Don't touch me."

"*Enough,*" Georgie snapped. "Give me the gun, Adam. Now."

Shoot them both.

No. He didn't want to hurt her. He just needed the plant.

His hand fell to his side.

"The gun," Georgie said again.

"I'm not giving you my gun," he said flatly.

"I wasn't asking."

He cast a glare in her direction, but she met it with an equally fierce one.

"Or you can leave," she added. "This place has rules. No guns while on the property."

Adam snorted. "Seriously?" No wonder they needed to buy protection.

"Yeah, well, I guess people tend to get stupid with their weapons." She gave him an accusatory look. "They'll be locked away, safe in a room with ours."

He needed that plant. Needed to fix things.

Dragging in a breath, he slapped the pistol into her open hand.

"The rifle, too."

It was only while he searched for the plant. He'd get the guns back before he left, even if they didn't give them willingly.

Adam shrugged off the rifle and handed it to her.

"Jax, can you take these inside and have Kye put them away?"

Kye was here?

Why?

With a scowl, Hale shook his head. "I'm not going anywhere."

There was a weighted silence and a shared look before she added, "I need a minute. Please."

"Fine," he grumbled, gaze cutting back to Adam. "If something happens, *I* don't need my gun to put you down."

He clipped Adam's shoulder hard as he passed.

Georgie dropped onto the steps and Adam sat beside her. How could he get her to tell him where it was?

"You can't point your gun at people like that," she scolded.

"Then your soldier should keep his hands to himself."

"He shouldn't have done that, but can you really blame him for being mad?"

Adam shrugged, and silence crept in, hovering for a moment before she spoke again.

"Did you go willingly?"

After a beat of hesitation, he nodded.

"Do you regret it?"

"No." The answer tumbled out before he thought to lie, and her face twisted in disgust. "What other options did I have?"

"You could've come with us."

"You treated me like the enemy."

"Yeah, well," she gestured toward him, "I guess I was right."

He winced at the words.

"I thought we were friends, Adam."

"Yeah, me too."

"Then how could you do that?"

"How could *I?*" challenged Adam, the question echoing through the yard.

She was the one who told him to leave.

She was the one who drew her weapon.

She didn't get to put this on *him*.

Adam took a deep breath, settling the mask back into place. This was going to end badly, and before it did, he needed to know where the plant was.

They were alone.

The weight of the knife in his boot tugged at him. Could he *make* her tell him where the plant was? She had a lot here he could threaten. A lot of leverage to press on. But he was by himself. She was stronger than him, and Hale was close by. There were too many ways it could go wrong.

What was he thinking? This wasn't going to work.

Adam pushed to his feet. "This was obviously a bad idea. I should go."

"No," she snapped, standing to face him. "Fuck you, Adam. You don't get to show up here and drop this bullshit in my lap and then run back to him."

"Don't worry, I won't tell him anything."

"I don't trust you."

The words sliced through him.

"Are you going to force me to stay?" he challenged.

"No, of course not. I just...what am I supposed to do? You put me in a terrible position." She sighed and weaved her fingers through her hair. "Have you talked to Oliver yet?"

Adam's expression dropped. "What?"

"That's why you're here, right?"

The question knocked the air from his lungs, and the world screeched to a standstill.

Oliver was *here*?

When Adam realized she was watching, he nodded. "Yeah, that's why I'm here."

"And then what?" she asked. "Are you staying?"

She kept talking, but Adam had stopped listening.

Oliver was here.

It doesn't matter.

Had he been right here the whole time? Adam looked over his shoulder at the door.

He doesn't want you.

None of them want you.

Please stop, he begged silently, but the voice was relentless.

You have nobody.

You're alone.

Stop.

You destroy everything.

"Stop," Adam snarled, this time out loud, causing Georgie to recoil. He met her gaze and forced a smile. "Sorry. Not you."

Her scowl faltered. "You're kind of scaring me, Adam. What's going on?"

"Nothing," he answered. "Just tired. Long walk. Can we talk more tomorrow? I really need to sleep."

"So, you're staying?"

"Yes, I'm staying," he lied. "Can you show me where to go?"

Georgie studied him intently, her eyes assessing before she sighed. "Top floor. Come on."

22

I don't want you to follow me. Those were Oliver's words.

It was over.

So why, then, was Adam standing below a hatch in a ceiling trying to build up the nerve to knock?

He should go. He should focus on what he came here to do.

Georgie lingered a moment, then wordlessly slipped back down the hallway toward the stairs.

Hale had refused to let him stay without someone monitoring him, so Banks was leaned against the window frame at the end of the hall. Adam could feel his gaze boring into the side of his skull, the sensation intensifying the throbbing behind his eyes.

He felt too light without his guns. It was a stupid rule, making everyone give up their weapons. If it weren't for the knife tucked in his boots, he would've never agreed to it. That and the knowledge that he could pick the lock and get them back whenever he needed.

Adam popped an oxy, his eyes never straying from the hatch.

I don't want you to follow me.

I don't want you.

His jaw clenched, his fingers curling into fists at his sides.

Okay, yeah, fine, it was over. Oliver had left like Adam always knew he would. Painful, but inevitable.

Whatever.

But he'd also sold him out to a Haven. A fucking Haven! And he was too much of a coward to tell Adam to his face. Didn't even give him the opportunity to respond.

Adam at least deserved the chance to speak his mind.

He straightened and tugged the string, and as the hatch flew open and the ladder unfolded automatically—an Oliver creation, no doubt—he stepped back, out of view.

"What now?" Oliver's voice called from above.

Turn and go, his mind pleaded.

Adam stared at the ladder as the footsteps above receded, his feet locked in place, then glanced back at the soldier whose expression was stone.

No, he had to do this, had to get this closure. If he didn't, it would hang over him forever.

Finally, he gathered the nerve to step onto the first rung, gripping the ladder so hard, his fingers ached.

He didn't scare easily, but this...this was terrifying.

A deep breath through his nose, then he willed himself forward, heart pounding in his chest.

When Adam stepped into the small room, his gaze immediately fixed on Oliver's hunched figure, his elbows on the desk, one hand tangled in his dark hair.

This was a bad idea. Why was he here? He shouldn't have come here.

Leave.

A spark surged through Adam's nerves like a lit fuse as Oliver looked up.

Run.

Oliver blinked in surprise, then shot up from his chair. His mouth opened like he was about to say something, then closed again.

He looked tired, and the bags beneath his eyes were more prominent than ever. But he was still the most infuriatingly beautiful person Adam had ever seen, and it suddenly seemed impossible that he'd managed to survive the past two months without seeing that stupid, maddening, gorgeous face. Oliver's hair was slightly longer now, curling around his ear and sweeping over his forehead, partially covering one of his eyes, and Adam fought the urge to go to him and brush it away, because how dare it hide something so incredible.

"Hi," Oliver said on an exhale.

As he stepped closer, Adam backed away, maintaining a safe distance and keeping his arms firmly at his sides.

"Don't." The cold snap of his voice made Oliver recoil.

"I-I didn't—" Oliver stammered, his eyebrows pulling up in the center.

"This was a mistake." Adam shook his head. "I'm gonna go."

"No, wait." Oliver took another step closer, lips lifting in a lopsided smile. "I missed you."

Adam spat a bitter, hollow laugh. He hadn't realized how much resentment he'd been holding onto, but it all came rushing to the surface now, burning red hot, the fuse finally finding gunpowder. "You don't get to say that." The words were sharp. Acidic.

Oliver's smile fell away, and a puzzled frown took its place. "You're mad."

"Of course I'm mad! I'm mad and I'm hurt and I'm fucking broken, Oliver. You broke *everything*!"

"I-I *had* to," Oliver stammered, eyes panicked. "But it's different now. You can stay here." He reached out, pulling up short before touching Adam's hand. "With me."

"No." Adam knocked his hand away. "You ended it, Oliver. You don't get to take it back."

"But, you—" Oliver raked a hand through his hair, both of those stupid gorgeous eyes visible now. "Everything was so messed up…I was trying to fix it."

"I didn't need you to fix it," Adam snapped. "I needed you to *stay.*"

"I'm sorry."

"Good."

"Let me fix it. What can I do?"

"Nothing. It's over, remember. There's nothing to fix."

"But, I love you. You *know* that."

Adam staggered under the weight of the words, the pain echoing through his body. "See, that's the problem," he said, hand splayed across Oliver's chest as he pushed him back. "You're *convincing*. I believed you for so long. Believed everything you told me. But you were never mine. Not really. I realize that now."

Adam swiped a traitorous tear from his cheek with the back of his gloved hand, and before Oliver could say another word, he spun and tore down the ladder, then the stairs, ignoring the soldier in the hallway telling him to wait—not slowing until he was outside.

The dam threatened to break, and he sniffled, trying to stop the tears from overflowing.

Why did he come here? This was so stupid.

He's lying. He doesn't love you. He never loved you.

"I know that!" Adam shouted. Something in the snow snagged the toe of his boot and he fell to the ground, arms buried up to his elbow. "Ugh!" He sat back on his boots, his breathing ragged.

The door to the farmhouse opened, and Adam squeezed his eyes shut because if he saw Oliver's face again, he might lose the strength to leave.

"Go away."

"Adam?" It wasn't Oliver.

He dragged himself back to his feet, pulled off the wet gloves, and tossed them aside, then turned toward the voice. Kye and Reese were standing on the front porch.

Perfect. Amazing. Wonderful. Why *wouldn't* it be more ghosts from his past? He wrinkled his nose, then turned and walked away, shoving his hands deep in his coat pockets.

Footsteps followed behind him. "Where've you been?" Reese asked. "Are you okay?"

"Leave me alone."

"Come inside and warm up," Kye tried, matching his pace.

Adam slammed to a stop, teeth gritted. "Leave. Me. Alone."

"We're trying to help you."

"I don't need help." He pulled out a flashlight and clicked it on, the cold stinging his fingers. "I'm leaving."

"You can't go," Reese said.

Adam spun around and narrowed his eyes, glaring at Reese from below his lashes. "Are you gonna stop me?"

The question was a dare neither of them seemed willing to take. Reese took a careful step back, and there it was. That look. The same one Georgie had given him at Haven.

They see what you really are.

They're afraid of you.

Good, thought Adam. *They should be.*

He turned and left, desperate to get away before he cracked and shattered into a million pieces, picking up speed with every step until he was running, but he only made it to the end of the gravel driveway before his legs threatened to give out.

Adam slowed, then stopped, folding forward, hands on his knees.

He was so damn tired.

More footsteps.

Seriously? Why wouldn't they listen?

You could make them stop. Make them listen.

In one fluid motion, Adam drew his knife, whirled around, and leveled it at Reese, who slammed to a stop.

"Wait." Reese squinted against the flashlight. "It's just me."

"I *know* it's you. Why are you following me?"

"I'm making sure you're okay," Reese said. "Have you *seen* yourself?"

"*Pfft,* always the flatterer."

"We're worried about you, Adam. Come back. There's food and a warm fire." Reese perked up and motioned back the way they came. "Oliver's there. Did you know that?"

He let out a bitter laugh. "Yeah. I know."

"It's Christmas Eve."

Adam rolled his eyes. He'd spent last Christmas training at O'Hare so Elias would keep supplying the pills. The Christmas before, he was the brand new item at the Hub. Every Christmas before that varied from non-existent to disappointing to outright traumatic. So Christmas didn't mean much to him.

A sound behind him caught his attention, and his grip tightened on his knife. Kye followed, too?

"I'm really not in the mood," Adam shouted toward the sound, flashlight sliding across the snow until it landed on a bulky figure beside a black sedan.

"Look what you found," Leon said cheerfully.

"Did you *follow* me?"

"You took off without a word. It piqued Emery's interest, so Colette tracked you down through the feeds and sent me to meet you. What happened?"

Adam shrugged. "I had a hunch, so I followed it, but I was wrong. There's nothing here."

Leon shot Reese a look. "Well, that's not completely true."

"He doesn't have the plant," Adam muttered.

"And the rest? Where are they?"

"How should I know?" A pit formed in Adam's stomach. "Let's just go."

Leon chuckled, then drew a handgun and pointed it at Reese. "You heard him. Let's go."

Reese's eyes bulged. "No."

"He doesn't have it," Adam said again. "And he doesn't know where it is. There's no reason to bring him back."

Leon's face lost its humor as he closed the gap and locked eyes with Adam. "You wanna make amends for your fuck-up? Then take the win and get in the damn car."

Adam was messing everything up. And for what? Reese made his choice when he stole the plant. He knew how it would end. This was *his* fault, and Adam wasn't going to ruin everything because of Reese's stupid decision.

A low, eerie whine carried on the soft breeze. Adam spun around, the flashlight beam landing on a slender girl in pajamas.

"Stay where you are," Leon ordered, but the girl didn't react, just trudged clumsily forward through the snow. Leon grabbed Reese's arm to hold him in place, then turned the gun on her. "Stop moving."

"Help me," she pleaded.

A chill skittered up Adam's spine. Why was she out here in the dark, and how did she seem completely unbothered by the cold?

"I said stop." Leon fired a warning shot into the ground by her feet, but she just kept coming.

A sob tore from the girl, heavy with pain and desperation.

As she lifted her head, the flashlight caught her face, and Adam's heart lurched. Stalks jutted from her nostrils and curled out from behind her eyelids. He flinched back reflexively, dropping the flashlight, which sank into the snow at his feet. As the world around them plunged into darkness, the girl's face took on the unsettling pale green glow of the fungus. Unlike the Shinies, who were always speckled with spores, this covered entire patches of her skin.

"The hell?" Leon muttered.

She was like the man at Jardine, Adam realized. The mutated infection.

"I need—" she started, but a violent, chest-deep cough cut off her words.

Adam dug the flashlight out of the snow, and when he shined it back at the girl, she was uncomfortably close. He could see the skin of her eyelids bulging around the stalks, the dried blood beneath her nose. Her lips were chapped to the point of cracking, and her eyes, which were hidden by a cloudy film, were looking directly at him.

"Please," she begged. A ragged breath. Another cough. "Why won't anyone help me? I think I'm sick."

Leon fired, and as the bullet tore through the girl's chest, a burst of spores erupted, creating a disorienting curtain around the three of them. The cloud lingered in the air, swirling and shifting before it was finally whisked away by a gust of wind.

Had those all been *inside* her?

She stayed upright for a moment, wide eyes still on him. Adam swallowed hard and looked away as she crumpled.

Gross.

23

"Wait!" Reese shouted, his feet digging deep in the snow, fighting against Leon's unyielding hold. It was pointless. The man barely seemed to notice the resistance as he opened the car door and effortlessly shoved Reese inside.

Adam's jaw tensed, and he stood there, frozen, unsure what to do.

"Come on, let's get home," Leon called to him before sliding into the driver's seat.

Home. The word bounced around in Adam's head. That wasn't quite right. Jardine didn't feel like home. Nowhere did. But the people there—Eris, Desmond, Leon, Colette—they felt safe, and he figured that was something like home. A strange sort of family.

You don't deserve them.

He wanted to make things right with Desmond. Wanted to make him proud, because he craved the way it felt when that warmth was directed at him. But it was more than that. He *needed* Desmond to get to Stanton.

Finally, Adam relented. He edged along the car, climbing slowly into the passenger seat.

"Adam, please," Reese begged, his voice trembling. "You're better than this."

Monster, the voice taunted—grating and low.

He closed his eyes, trying to block out Reese's shouting from the back seat and the growling of the voice in his head.

You deserve to be alone.

"Stop," he pleaded under his breath. He couldn't win. Couldn't make the voice go away, no matter what he did. "Just stop."

Somehow, when Adam opened his eyes, they were already pulling into Jardine, the security check-in spotlights bathing the car in white light. Sleet hit the windshield, and the wipers screeched as they cleared it, the sound jarring.

He glanced back at Reese, who had gone eerily quiet, and when his eyes met Adam's, there was no anger. No hatred. No blame. Only a sad sort of acceptance.

Adam knew he should feel...something.

He knew this was his fault. Knew it was wrong.

But instead of guilt or shame, he felt numb. Empty. The nagging discomfort of the void where those emotions should have been was more unsettling than the look on Reese's face.

The car came to a stop, and Adam climbed out. Sleet pelted his face as he watched Leon pulled Reese from the backseat and lead him to the gate, the lights plastering their shadows on the ground behind them.

Shouldn't he try to stop this? There were only two guards.

His hand went automatically to his holster, but his pistol was gone. He'd forgotten to get his guns back from Spring Valley.

He could grab Leon's gun. Drop him, then the guards. But if Leon was gone, where would he get his pills?

Also, Des wouldn't be happy. Not only would he refuse to help with the Hub, but he'd probably kill Adam, too.

"Call Emery," Leon told the guards. "Have him meet us out here." He pushed Reese effortlessly to his knees.

Look at what being your friend gets people.

After a while, Adam gave up trying to stand and sank, exhausted, into the wet snow.

Finally, the gate slid open with a grating sound of metal against metal, and Des greeted them with his usual easy smile. His eyes swept over the three of them, and his grin widened when he spotted Reese.

"Reese Sanders. It's been a while. How've you been? How's the sister?"

Reese glowered.

"Oh, I'm sorry." Des's expression fell. "That was too far. Forgive me?"

"Eat shit."

The smile returned. "To what do I owe the pleasure of this visit? Did you come to return what you stole from me?"

"Your plant's gone," Reese said. "It wilted and died."

"Sure it did." His attention shifted to Adam. "We *have* vehicles, you know. I could've given you a ride."

"Something happened," Leon said. "Think you need to know about it." He told Des about the girl, the glowing, the stalks growing from her face. "Never seen anything like it."

So, Des hadn't told him about the mutation. Had he told anyone else?

"Did she touch you?" Des asked.

"No," Leon answered. "But she basically exploded when I shot her. Spores everywhere."

Desmond's eyes ignited with enthusiastic curiosity. "Oh, brilliant." He considered the new information, then, in an instant, his face turned serious and he took three large steps backward. "How close were you? Did you breathe it in?"

Leon shrugged. "Don't matter. We're vaccinated."

Adam knew Des had given the few vials of Cassira's—well, *his* vaccine to his closest people as soon as they'd taken it from the train station. The ones he needed the most. Leon. Eris. Colette. He didn't know how many others. And they all assumed Adam was vaccinated like Oliver during the cult's judgment.

"But I figured you'd want to deal with this one out here," Leon nodded to Reese. "Since he's not."

Des gave each of them a thorough, evaluative look before his smile resurfaced. "Right. So, first order of business." He drew his Desert Eagle, holding the barrel a few inches from Reese's head. Reese winced, but didn't make a sound. "Are you going to tell me where the strays are?"

You did this.

"I'm not telling you anything," Reese answered.

Adam considered speaking up, stopping this, but he couldn't get himself to say anything at all.

Coward.

It wouldn't matter, anyway. Reese stole from Desmond. He wasn't going to let that go.

Besides, Reese was infected. He was going to die either way. Why should Adam ruin his good thing when it wouldn't even make a difference?

Honestly, a gunshot was a better ending than the other option. At least this was quick. It was kinder to just let it happen like this.

"And if you kill me," Reese continued, his voice steadying, "you'll never find your plant."

Amusement glinted in Desmond's dark eyes. "People really have a tendency to underestimate me."

To Adam's surprise, he lowered the gun.

Was he letting him go?

"I'm not going to kill you," Des told him. "It will be far more satisfying to have you experience the repercussions of your actions firsthand." He turned to a guard. "Escort him to Quarantine Room Two."

No.

The guard grabbed Reese, and as he pulled him to his feet, Adam closed his eyes and gritted his teeth.

They were going to let Reese suffer. Let him die a slow and excruciating death.

"Now," Des said, "because I'm not one to take chances, you're both spending the next twenty-four hours in quarantine. Spend a few extra seconds in the UV light at the door and grab a mask on your way inside. You've already contaminated one of my favorite cars."

Leon scoffed. "I'm not sitting in some room. I've got shit to do."

"Or you can stay out here in the cold." Des shrugged, gaze sliding back to Adam. "But that seems imprudent."

Adam pushed to his feet, and Des responded with an approving nod.

"Smart choice."

24

The walk back to the cabin was heavy with tension, and Georgie was grateful when the small structure finally appeared in her flashlight beam.

After helping Jax get the fire going, she collapsed onto the couch, pulling a blanket up to her chin. The cold pierced through her body, making her shiver, and the dampness of the sleet weighed down her hair.

Jax remained crouched by the fireplace, the soft crackling of the flames emphasizing the silence hanging between them.

Georgie understood why he was angry with Adam. She was, too. But she wasn't going to turn him away, and she knew there was nothing she could say that would get him to leave while Oliver was here, anyway.

"You really trust him?" Jax asked finally.

"No." The answer was easy. She *didn't* trust him. She had a hard time trusting anyone anymore. "But, I *want* to. I want him to be telling the truth, because my faith in people as a whole is pretty low right now, and I'd really like to be proven wrong."

She planned to talk to Adam more tomorrow, to ask the rest of the questions she was dying to ask, and hopefully he'd have something a little more convincing to say.

Jax shook his head, shoving another log into the fireplace.

"Plus," she added, "Adam might be the key to getting my mom's notes back. And maybe he can help us figure out a way to kill Desmond."

Jax stood and crossed the room, joining her on the couch. "What if killing him doesn't make a difference? What if they still come after the plant? After Haven?"

"Without him, the people at Jardine won't have the inside knowledge of the Havens. They won't be as much of a threat."

Jax leaned back, sinking into the couch, gaze fixed straight ahead. "*If* we can even pull this off."

"We're going to stop him," she said. "We're going to make sure they're safe."

His face tightened, the muscles around his jaw clenching, and the fear in his eyes was unmistakable.

"You don't have to stay," she said, and without meaning to, Georgie's gaze dropped to the arm strapped in the sling. "I mean, I'd understand if you want to go with them to Indiana."

Jax turned, frowning. "My dad was all I had left. He had nothing to do with the vaccine or Project Noah or any of it, and Emery killed him to make a fucking *point*."

Everyone at that safehouse died because Desmond wanted the key code for the lab. All those people had been collateral damage. She hadn't even considered that Jax had just as much reason to want Desmond dead as she did.

Georgie swallowed. "I'm sorry, I—"

"Don't," he interrupted, expression softening. "Instead, let's make sure Emery *is*."

"Okay. Together, then."

He rubbed his arm.

"How's it feeling?" she asked.

"It's fine." Jax stood and walked back to the fireplace.

"And *you*?" Before he could give the same answer, she added, "Don't bullshit me. You're a terrible liar."

"I just..." he started, the quiet words hanging in the air for a long moment before he continued. "I feel like I'm ruined, like I can't measure up anymore."

She hopped up, letting the blanket tumble to the floor. "Jax—"

"Georgie." He turned to meet her gaze, eyes gentle and pleading. "This is the first time I've had the nerve to talk about it. Please, let me."

She nodded, then joined him at the fire.

"Being a soldier, it gave me a purpose. It felt like, for the first time in my life, I was part of something important. Like what I was doing actually mattered. And I was *good* at it. But now, it's like there's a piece of me missing, and there's this constant nagging voice in my head saying I'm broken. That I'll never be whole again. That I'm worthless."

Quiet settled in around them, and she took that as her cue to talk. "You're right. You'll never be the same. And yes, you're broken."

He scowled.

"But so am I. You know how many panic attacks I've had in the last two months? Me either. I've lost count. I'm so hell bent on going after Desmond, but even the thought of facing him sends me spiraling. I'm permanently marked with Cassira's stupid fucking cross, and even after all this time, her face still creeps into my dreams, whispering beautiful words that part of me still clings to. And the others, Wren and Levi and Banks and Reese, I don't think they've gotten a full night's sleep since that day."

"That's not—"

"No," she said, pressing a finger to his chest. "It's my turn."

The corner of his mouth quirked.

"My point is, we're all broken, Jax. But somehow, despite the odds, after all the shit we've been through, we're still alive. Still fighting. And a huge part of that is because of *you*. You're the one keeping us going. The one skipping sleep to make sure the rest of us are safe. I am *so* sorry about your arm, and I know I can't even begin to understand what you're going through. But your worth isn't based on how good you are with a gun or how well you can fight. We're depending on you. And I can't make it through whatever happens next without you."

The smirk tilted into a full smile at the familiar words.

"So, from now on, if something's bothering you, tell me. We're in this together. Okay?"

His eyes stayed fixed on hers as he gave a sharp nod. "Yes, ma'am."

Georgie mirrored his smile, but when Jax brushed a strand of hair away from her face, his finger grazed her cheek, and she reflexively took a step back.

His gaze fell. "Sorry."

She paused for a moment, fighting to gather the thoughts he'd just sent into a whirling spiral. "I didn't..." The sentence tapered off into silence. She was so bad at this.

Dammit. Why was this so difficult?

She knew she wanted this, knew she needed to stop pushing him away. But the impulse to run was still there.

"It's okay," Jax said. "You don't have to say anything. I shouldn't ha—"

Georgie threaded her fingers through his hair, pulled him in close, and kissed him.

For a moment, all she could focus on were the sparks, the way he tasted, the soft feel of his lips. This was what she'd wanted for so long.

What had she been so afraid of?

She sank into him, and he felt so right that she couldn't imagine ever not having him beside her.

Then the ground dropped out beneath her.

What was she thinking? She had already wrecked one friendship this way.

Her muscles stiffened, and she pulled away, the cold flooding back in around her.

"This is a terrible idea."

His eyes searched hers. "Why?"

"Because I love you, you idiot. Do you really not know that by now?"

"And *that* makes this a terrible idea?"

"Yes. Because I can't handle losing you."

"Why would you lose me?"

She looked down at her feet. "Because I make stupid mistakes and mess things up. I destroy everything I touch, Jax. Why would this be any different?"

He gently touched beneath her chin, tilting her head up to look at him. "You make mistakes because you're so afraid of failing—of letting people down—that you don't give yourself time to think. That fear makes you reckless, causes you to make bad decisions."

"Great. Thanks." She frowned and pushed him away. "Do I owe you for this therapy session, Dr. Hale?"

"You asked why this would be different," he continued as she folded her arms across her chest. "And that's how. This time, you're not rushing in blindly. You've thought it through, right? When you take the time to think first, your decisions are usually pretty sound. So, now you need to figure out what that decision is."

She gnawed at her lip, watching the flames dance in the fireplace.

"I'll respect whatever you decide," he added. "You're my best friend, so you're stuck with me. But you need to figure out what it is you want, because I can't keep doing this."

What *did* she want?

To stop losing people. To stop being so afraid.

To stop pushing him away.

"Is there anything you're not good at?" she grumbled. "It's infuriating."

"I'm told I'm a terrible liar," Jax answered with a shrug.

"Oh, come on. That doesn't count."

He gave her a half-hearted smile. "Let's get some sleep. It's been a busy day."

Stop pushing him away.

"But I know what I want."

His eyebrows furrowed. "You do?"

She let her hands fall to her sides. "I want you to kiss me."

Jax's face softened. He swiftly closed the distance, sliding his hand over the small of her back and pulling her close.

And this time, when their lips met, it was surprisingly effortless to let go. To stop being so afraid. He was her best friend, and he was safe, and when they were together, nothing was too much to handle.

The kiss was gentle, the electricity a low hum, and the warmth of his lips dissolved the tension that had been so tightly wound inside her.

But gentle wasn't what she wanted—not now, after all this time. She'd fought this too damn long.

Georgie dug her nails into his back through his sweater, drawing him flush against her, the arm fastened against his chest the only barrier between them. With a low, quiet groan, Jax deepened the kiss, and her breath hitched as his hand slid beneath her layers of thick clothes, fingertips tracing the curve of her spine.

They fumbled back through the hallway to the bedroom, and Jax closed the door behind him, plunging the room into sudden darkness. He walked her back until her calves hit the edge of the bed, and she sank into sitting.

"Shit, that's cold!"

"Sorry," Jax muttered. "I can get a—"

Georgie grabbed the front of his shirt and yanked him down to her, their lips colliding as he caught himself. She shifted back to the center of the bed, pulling him with her, not breaking the kiss.

His body pressed down on top of hers.

"I love you, too, by the way," he whispered against her lips.

Her cheeks flushed with warmth as the words wrapped around her like a blanket.

"Well, yeah," she teased. "I knew *that*."

As Jax kissed her again, heat swept through her body, burning away the last of her lingering doubts.

25

Oliver had been sitting on the wooden floor of his room for what felt like hours, replaying the conversation with Adam over and over and over, searching for the error. The place where he'd messed up.

He'd had an idea of what would happen when Adam came back. In his head, it was romantic and happy, and nothing like what had actually happened.

It wasn't *fair.*

Oliver had never seen Adam so angry. Why didn't he understand? All of it was for him.

His skin felt squirmy, like it was trying to peel itself away from his muscles. The sounds from downstairs had faded to a dull hum, but it was still too loud.

If Adam would just let him explain.

He wiped his cheeks with his sleeve and pressed his hands to his temples, but it didn't help. Frustrated, he shook them out, trying to rid himself of the horrible sensation. It wasn't until his back began to ache that he realized he'd been rocking.

Oliver knew he messed up. He thought he was helping, but he was destroying everything.

As his eyes closed, his hand instinctively found the corner of his shirt, running his thumb over the smooth flannel fabric, the comforting feel of it gradually calming his frayed nerves, until finally, his skin stopped trying to escape.

He jumped as a sudden knock echoed through the room.

Scrambling up, Oliver raced to the hatch and pulled it open, but it wasn't Adam looking up at him as the ladder lowered.

He deflated and dropped back onto the floor, and a second later, Kye was beside him.

"Are you okay?"

"Peachy," he croaked.

"Mind if I join you?"

He shrugged, and she lowered herself onto the floor beside him.

"Did he leave?" Oliver whispered.

Kye nodded. "Reese went after him, but I doubt he'll be able to catch up."

"I ruined everything." Oliver felt himself start to rock again and forced himself still. "I thought I was saving him, but I was pushing him right to them."

"I'm obviously missing a lot of the story, but I'm here if you'd like to talk about it."

No use in hiding it now. The truth was there, staring him in the face. He was selfish and awful, and he'd lost Adam forever.

With a heavy sigh, Oliver wiped his cheeks, then let everything come rushing out. What he'd done at the Campus for Cassira, Adam's deal with Desmond's people, his immunity, the call to Haven.

And it sounded just as terrible out loud.

He was such a coward.

Kye was quiet for a moment as she processed. "Adam's mad," she said finally, "and he has every right to be. You broke his trust."

Oliver dropped his head into his hands. She was right. What was he thinking? It didn't matter if he was trying to save Adam. He broke a promise. How could he do that?

"But give him time," Kye added. "Reese told me about Emery's people, about the things they do. Adam's too good for them. And your intentions were good. He knows that, even if he can't see it clearly yet. He'll be back."

"No, he won't," Oliver mumbled. "He hates me." The way Adam had looked at him...Oliver would never recover from that look.

Kye shook her head. "I don't believe that for a second. The only time I ever saw peace in his eyes was when he looked at you. He could never hate you."

Oliver didn't know how to reply, so he stayed quiet.

Eventually, Kye stood and pulled her jacket shut. "I'm right downstairs if you need anything. Give yourself some grace. You're doing your best."

When Oliver was alone again, he grabbed BUG from the desk and plopped flat on his bed, staring up at the beams in the ceiling. He'd been working on fixing him when Adam showed up, re-soldering a few of the wires that had come loose, and now, when he pressed the power button, BUG greeted him with illuminated green eyes. But he couldn't muster the excitement that his favorite creation deserved.

It didn't matter. None of it mattered.

Oliver sighed and spread his arms out to his sides, letting BUG fall from his hand onto the floor.

Maybe losing Adam was his punishment. His atonement. For betraying Hale and Georgie and Kye. For the awful things he did for Cassira.

For his parents and his brother.

He grabbed the pillow and pulled it over his head.

His family had made it through the worst of the pandemic in their house in the suburbs. They lasted a year after the world collapsed and the news stations fell silent. An entire year. Then someone knocked at their door, claiming to be National Guard. They said they wanted to help, that they had a safe place where they were bringing survivors. Oliver believed them and let them inside.

They stole everything they could fit in their bags and when his parents came downstairs demanding they leave, the strangers shot them.

Oliver freaked out and ran to his parents' room. He hid in the closet, where he found the shotgun his dad used for hunting, along with the shells to load it. He had been hunting a few times—back when his dad was searching for a common interest to share with him—so he knew how to use the gun.

He loaded two shells, pointed the barrel at the door, and waited. When he heard the footsteps enter the room, he steadied himself and closed his eyes.

The door flung open, and he fired.

The image of how his brother looked, his chest shredded, blue eyes wide, had haunted Oliver every single day since.

Everything he had was torn away all at once. And it was his fault.

When Cassira found him wandering the streets, he was so scared and desperate, he ate up everything she said. She spoke about God and a plan to make the world better, and Oliver wanted so badly to believe her.

At the time, it was only Cassira, Malacai, Isaiah, and a handful of others at the train station. Isaiah had fled a violent settlement with enough supplies to keep them fed and had given them access to vials of the infection to test for immunity.

Of course, Oliver knew better now. Knew that Isaiah had somehow gotten his hands on a vaccine. It had all been a lie.

But for a while, that train station felt like home. It was safe.

"You're one of a kind, Oliver," Cassira had told him so many times.

She made him feel loved. Wanted. Less alone. Gave him something to look forward to.

A few months later, when Cassira asked him to build her something, he didn't even think twice. He didn't consider the people they would hurt with those dart guns. The deaths that would be his fault. He didn't question any of it, even as he watched it happen. He was complacent because he was a coward.

Oliver pulled the blanket over himself and curled up on his side. What if he was no better than the people he was trying to save Adam from?

At least *they* could keep him safe.

Which was more than Oliver could say he was doing for this place. He'd told himself the air filter was to protect Spring Valley, but clearly that was a lie.

He was selfish. As soon as he'd realized it couldn't help him get Adam back, he'd cast it aside.

The infection was mobile now. How long before the fungus showed up in the corners of the farmhouse, spreading through these people? Or in the greenhouse, turning the plants toxic? The only thing keeping this place from destruction was pure luck.

I was a stranger and you invited me in.

Vivian had let him stay here. And what was he doing to help them? He was wallowing in self-pity. He had always been dependent on everyone else to keep him safe, but now it was his turn.

Oliver was going to fix it. Not for himself, not because it would benefit him, but because these were good people, and they deserved better.

But the little filter wasn't going to cut it. He needed to think bigger.

And he needed help.

26

The next morning, Georgie woke to the sun in her eyes. For a second, she panicked, unsure of her surroundings before she found Jax beside her, his face peaceful in sleep.

She rolled onto her side, head propped on one hand, delicately tracing the contour of his jaw with her fingers. His eyes fluttered open, going through the same split-second of alarm before finding her.

"Hi," she whispered.

Jax's green eyes lit up, his mouth curving into a tilted smile.

"Hi." He reached up and brushed a strand of hair out of her face, like the night before, but this time, she felt no resistance. Nothing telling her to run.

The way he looked at her hadn't changed, but it pushed past the barrier she had built, and Georgie let herself revel in its warmth instead of trying to squirm away.

His fingers lingered at her temple before following her cheek down to her chin, drawing her in for a soft kiss. "Merry Christmas."

Everything felt ripe with newness. She thought it would be difficult, the change in their dynamic, but it was unbelievably easy, like they'd always been this way.

"Merry Christmas," she echoed. "What's the plan for the day?"

"Definitely more of this." His hand trailed her shoulder, down over the thick lines of the scar on her forearm, before coming to rest on her hand, their fingers intertwining.

A knock came at the front door, barely audible from the bedroom. Jax sat up automatically, listening.

"Let the others get it." She pulled him back down and as she kissed him again, he smiled against her lips.

A second later, the knocking was at the bedroom door, followed by Banks's voice.

"Get Up. You've got company."

Jax climbed out of bed, and she watched sleepily as he pulled on his worn jeans, then tugged his gray t-shirt over his head, the everyday motions taking some effort. She wanted to offer help, but didn't know if it would bother him.

He grabbed her clothes from the floor and crossed back to the bed, leaning over to give her a deep kiss before he handed them to her.

"Can you help with the sling?" Jax asked as he grabbed it from the floor.

Georgie smiled. "I'd love to."

When they reached the living room, Georgie found Banks and Levi on the floor, a chessboard between them. As Levi touched the top of a pawn, he hesitated.

"Think first," Banks said softly. "Actions have consequences. If you move your pawn, what are the repercussions?"

Levi pulled his hand back, eyes moving over the board, studying the pieces.

Oliver hovered in the entryway, brow tight, eyes on his fidgeting hands.

She really thought he'd look happier now that Adam was back.

When he noticed her, he straightened. "I need your help."

"With?"

"I need to make a run. It's not far, but the last time I went out alone, it didn't go well, so I need you to come with me."

Georgie frowned. "Why me?"

His eyes darted to Jax, then dropped. "Because as far as I know, *you* don't want me dead. And Kye has a lot on her plate."

"Why can't you ask Adam?"

Oliver pursed his lips to the side, then tucked his hands in his pockets. Finally, he mumbled, "Because he left."

"He *left*?" She glared at Banks. "I thought you were keeping an eye on him."

"I was there to make sure he didn't hurt anyone," Banks answered as he moved a chess piece. "And he didn't."

"Why didn't you tell me?"

Banks gave her a wry look. "You were busy."

Her cheeks burned, and she quickly turned back to Oliver. "What happened?"

He responded with a shrug.

"Where did he go, Oliver?" More silence, which told her everything. Her hands clenched into fists. "Goddammit. I'm going to kill him."

So much for having Adam's help. She swallowed back the urge to yell. Taking it out on Oliver wouldn't do a damn thing.

What if Adam was lying about everything? What if it was a trick?

What if Desmond was on his way here right now?

"We need to contact Indiana," Georgie said, snatching her bag from the floor before remembering the plant wasn't in there. "If he tells Desmond where we are, we're fucked. I'm done waiting. We need to get the others out of here. Now."

Oliver's face contorted at the comment. "Adam wouldn't do that. You know he wouldn't."

"Apparently, I don't know anything about him."

How long would it take for Desmond to get here?

"Banks," Jax said. "We need to have someone running perimeter checks at all times."

Banks moved another chess piece, then climbed to his feet. "On it."

"No," Georgie said. "We need to leave. Call Indiana."

"Indiana already made contact," Jax said.

Georgie's gaze snapped to him. "When?"

"Yesterday afternoon."

She took a relieved breath. "Great. Where are we meeting?"

Jax sank onto a kitchen chair and rubbed the bridge of his nose. "We're not."

"What do you mean?"

"They changed their minds. They're not coming."

Her stomach dropped with a sickening lurch.

"Did they say why?" Banks asked.

Jax shook his head.

"Why didn't you tell me?" Georgie asked.

"I wanted to give everyone *one* night where they didn't have to worry."

She sat on the chair beside him. "Okay," she muttered, her brow furrowed in concentration as she weighed their options. "We'll head to Indiana on our own." There was bound to be a working car somewhere around here.

"We can't go to Indiana," Jax said, rubbing his arm.

"What? We have to."

"They won't let us in."

The words were like a physical blow, leaving her reeling and disoriented.

"What about the plant? What changed?"

Jax didn't answer.

Indiana was going to send someone to pick them up. Now, they weren't even allowed inside.

What about the rest of their people? Where would they go?

"What are we going to do?" she asked, voice taut.

Banks and Levi joined them at the table, and Georgie desperately tried to keep her composure as the room pushed in around her, the dark water lapping at her feet.

There was nowhere to go. They were on their own. How was she supposed to keep her people safe now?

"So, will you come with me?" Oliver asked, breaking the silence.

A muscle twitched in Georgie's cheek as her narrowed eyes locked onto him. "Read the room, Oliver."

"I swear, I wouldn't be asking if it wasn't important."

"No!" she snapped. "I'm not leaving my people to go on some run with you. We need to figure out what the hell we're going to do. Where we're going to go."

"If you help me," Oliver pressed, "I can convince Vivian to let you stay here."

Banks perked up at that. "This is a good place."

"And when Desmond shows up?" she asked.

"Adam won't tell him," Oliver said.

"What if he does?"

"Then we come up with a plan," Banks said.

"You wanted Emery to come to us," Jax added.

"Not like this!" She pressed her palms to her temples. "Not until they were safe in Indiana."

"Please," Oliver begged. "I need to do this, and I need your help. It won't take long."

Her fists slammed down on the table. "What the hell is so important?"

Oliver hesitated a moment, his fingers tapping against his legs. "I need to find parts for another air filtration system, one big enough to protect this place."

A sharp laugh burst from her lips. "We're worried about being hunted down and you want me to leave to help you with your science project?"

His brows drew together. "The infection is different. If I don't finish this, things here are going to get really bad."

"Different, how?"

"Last time I was out there, I saw a girl. She was infected. Like, late stage infected, but she was still mobile and talking. I couldn't even tell she was sick until I saw the mushrooms growing from her face."

"That's not possible," Georgie argued. She'd studied the infection enough to know how it worked. "The fungus paralyzes the host before that stage. There's no way."

Oliver threw up his hands. "I don't know. I guess it changed its mind. I wouldn't lie."

"You have before," Jax said.

"I'm not lying. I'm trying to do the right thing. The infection is mobile. Who knows how much time we have before it makes it here. That's why I need to do this now." When nobody answered, he added, "The people here can't help you if they're all dead."

Georgie frowned. "Are you sure she was infected?"

"Of course, I'm sure. I don't think mushroom eyes are a common occurrence."

She bit at her thumbnail as Jax and Banks shared a look.

"Levi and I will walk the perimeter," Banks said.

Jax nodded. "I'll let Wren and Reese know to come to the cabin. It's pretty well hidden out here. And I'll keep watch just in case."

"Are Desmond's people watching this place?" Georgie asked Oliver. "Is it safe for us to go out there?"

"Vivian sends people out occasionally," he answered. "It wouldn't really stand out." His gaze lifted to her hair. "Just, maybe wear a hat."

This was a terrible idea. She should be working on a plan, not out wandering the streets with Oliver.

"Go," Jax told her as he stood. "We've got it handled here."

The steadiness of his voice pushed back the dark water.

It was a short trip. They wouldn't be gone long.

"You're sure?"

"This is important."

She let out a sharp breath and pushed out of the chair.

"I need to talk to Vivian first," Georgie said. "I need my gun." How much should they tell her? What would she do if she knew Desmond was looking for them? "Can we trust her not to sell us out?"

Oliver considered the question. "You guys trust Kye, right?"

"Of course," Georgie replied. She owed Kye and Dr. Ramirez her life. Banks and Jax nodded in agreement.

"Well, she trusts Vivian enough to bring the few people she has left here."

Georgie sighed. "All right. Let's go fill her in."

Banks and Levi zipped their coats and headed out the door.

Jax wrapped his arm around her waist, drawing her close. "I'll figure out the thing with Indiana. I'll fix this. I promise."

Georgie planted a soft kiss on his lips, and when she pulled back, her eyes slid over Jax's tousled hair, his quick smile, and she had to summon every ounce of willpower to get herself to walk away.

27

"So, what exactly are we looking for?"

Oliver flinched as Georgie's voice resounded down the quiet street, her footsteps too loud behind him. The sleet had turned the top layer of snow into a melting mess that soaked right through his shoes. His socks were sopping wet, and the feeling made him want to tear them off and throw them.

He stopped, searching their surroundings as he answered in a whisper. "There's a high-tech hospital not far from here." His fingers traced the metal cube hanging from his belt loop. It was good to have BUG back.

"Wouldn't people have already taken everything?"

He glanced back at her, wishing she'd talk quieter. They'd made it through the subdivision without coming across the girl, but he doubted she was the only one out here.

When Georgie caught up, he said, "I don't think they would've taken what I'm looking for."

"Which is?"

"The HVAC systems. They're top of the line, with air purifiers that use a combination of UVGI and HEPA filters powerful enough to protect the whole building." He'd heard about it a few years before the pandemic. It was big news. A test of a very expensive, innovative new system. "If I can get a look at it, scavenge some parts, I can implement them at Spring Valley." The greenhouse would be his first goal. If the fungus got inside and infected the crops, everyone at Spring Valley would be sick within days. How long before that happened? How fast was it spreading now?

It felt good to be helping. Good to be part of the solution, not just a burden in need of protection. And the distraction was keeping him grounded, keeping the pain of everything with Adam pushed to the back of his mind.

"Have you been there before?" she asked.

"No." Oliver took off again, keeping his steps silent. Not that it mattered with his present company.

The hospital was in the next town over, and by the time they saw the first sign with a red *H,* Georgie's steps had slowed, her hand clutching her abdomen like she was in pain. The air was so cold it burned Oliver's skin and lungs, and his mushy socks were going to make him lose his mind.

"Hold on," he said, slamming to a stop. He untied his shoes, and one at a time, pulled them off to remove the sock before shoving them back on. It wasn't much better, but at least the insides of his sneakers were less...squishy. He abandoned the wet socks on the ground and retied his laces. "Okay. Ready."

Georgie drew her pistol and removed the magazine, studying it a second before reinserting it. "How's your ammo?"

"I don't have a gun."

Georgie frowned. "Why *not*?"

He wasn't about to get into that, so he shrugged. "I don't like them."

"I'm not a fan either, but I like the idea of dying a lot less." The corners of her mouth turned downward, and something flashed across her face, though he couldn't pick out the exact emotion. She shook her head. "Wait, so, it's all on me to keep us both alive? You realize how stupid that is? How do you not have a gun?"

A heaviness settled over him. "I had Adam. I didn't need one."

"Well, you *don't* anymore," she snapped, her voice sharp, and Oliver winced. "If you ask me to come along on a run, you need to pull your weight. I can't have the pressure all on me. It's too much."

Oliver dropped his gaze to the toes of his shoes. "We're almost there," he mumbled.

He took off across the street, but as he turned the corner, he froze in place.

No.

Georgie's footsteps stopped beside him.

He stared at the large structure at the end of the block. The building's frame was still mostly intact, but it was bent and twisted in places, and the few remaining walls were scorched and blackened. Tattered yellow quarantine zone barriers flapped angrily in the wind.

Two military trucks sat outside in a state of disrepair, and the street was littered with the remnants of bodies. Hundreds, Oliver guessed, all reduced to bones and cloth. He inched forward to get a better look at the interior of the hospital, but there was nothing left.

There had been a field hospital in his own town that burned down not long after everything went dark. A riot, his parents had told him.

The remnants were messy and chaotic, some of the tents left intact while others were burned to nothing.

But this looked nothing like that. This was thorough.

When he looked back at Georgie, her eyes were wide, and her face had gone pale.

28

When the shock faded, Georgie walked the length of the massacre, taking in the destruction.

Skeletons, debris, and bullet casings covered the street in front of the hospital. Large cement barriers blocked the building off from the street, and two military vehicles rested in front. Cars were scattered across the wide road, with no method to the layout, like they'd parked in a hurry, most of them riddled with large bullet holes. The kind left by heavy military artillery.

Back when the pandemic was in full swing, hospitals had been severely overwhelmed. She knew they had to turn people away, and that some had reacted violently, but what she'd seen on the news before the stations shut down was nothing like this.

She rounded back to Oliver. "A fire?" she guessed.

His eyes squinted against the daylight as he craned his head, studying the structure. "No, the frame's damaged."

He was right, of course. Georgie had a sinking feeling in her gut that she wished she could ignore.

She clenched her teeth, gaze sliding over the skeletons, the realization twisting her stomach. They were all running away, trying to escape. Some were wearing scrubs, others remnants of hospital gowns. Doctors, nurses, patients. Children.

The military was supposed to keep people safe. Why would they open fire on civilians?

Georgie could see the horrible logic behind it, claims of the greater good and clearing out the infected. Pressing the reset button on the city by culling the sick.

This was an attack. A bombing.

The soldiers had been outside, waiting to gun down anyone who tried to escape as they leveled the hospital.

Her head swam as she fought against the rising nausea.

All she wanted to do was get away from here, back to Spring Valley. To Jax.

"I'm going back," she said, her voice trembling.

Oliver didn't look at her, but he nodded once.

Georgie didn't bother trying to stay quiet on the walk back. She was too busy grappling against the panic, trying to keep her thoughts from spiraling out of control. Oliver followed close behind, and neither of them said a word.

As they reached the entrance of the subdivision across from Spring Valley, a gunshot shattered the silence. Oliver dropped instinctively, hands covering his head.

"Run!" she ordered, grabbing Oliver's arm and yanking him to his feet. They sprinted down the street, and ducked inside a house with an open red door.

She slammed the door behind them, locking the deadbolt as Oliver slid to the floor, clutching BUG tightly.

"What the hell?" she gasped, drawing her pistol. Who was shooting at them? Had Adam sold them out? Did Desmond send people after them?

Georgie moved to the window, pulling the curtain aside to peer out at the street. She had three bullets and terrible aim, and Oliver wouldn't be any help. Keeping them both safe fell on her.

Too much pressure.

If it came to a fight, she could guess how it would end.

Georgie swallowed hard. What was she supposed to do now?

Why had she agreed to this?

Her nerves were frayed and raw, her muscles slow to respond, legs barely keeping her up.

What if they were headed to Spring Valley?

What if Desmond was already there?

Jax had assured her they'd be okay, that he could handle it, but what if he was wrong?

Run.

They could already be dead and she was sitting here, terrified, and god, why had she believed Adam? How could she be so stupid?

A noise at the back of the house snapped her out of her thoughts, and her eyes darted to the sliding door in the kitchen, where a shape moved behind the curtain.

Shit.

The door slid open, the curtain shifting aside, and Georgie, acting on pure instinct, lifted the gun and squeezed the trigger, startled when the bullet actually found its mark.

Barely.

The man staggered back, howling in pain as his gun clattered onto the cement patio. He clutched his jaw, which now hung at an unnatural angle.

So much blood.

The man's frantic gaze jumped from Georgie to the gun at his feet.

"Don't," Georgie warned, keeping the gun leveled, her body shaking with the effort.

His hand shot up in surrender, the other still gripping his shattered jaw, blood running down his arm and dripping from his elbow.

"Are you with Emery?" she asked.

The man gave her a confused frown, then wagged his head, which must have hurt because he folded forward, another cry erupting. He tried to speak, but the words were lost in the gore.

Georgie swallowed hard. She was going to be sick. "I can't understand you."

He tried again, and though his speech was sloppy and slurred, this time she could distinguish two words. "My family."

Bile forced its way up. She turned and vomited into one of the ceramic planters flanking the entryway.

He was protecting his family, and she shot him.

She wiped her mouth with her coat sleeve and took a shaky breath.

Help him. "I'm a medic," she told the man, trying to regain her composure as she stepped forward. "Let me—"

Oliver grabbed her arm, stopping her mid-step. "Where's your family?" he asked quietly, a strange sort of knowing in his eyes.

The man shook his head again, carefully this time. "Sick."

Georgie cursed and took an instinctive step back. "Are *you* sick?"

He hesitated, then shook his head again, clearly lying.

The back of her neck prickled.

The infection is different.

If Oliver was telling the truth, that meant the fungus was mutating. Would the vaccine still be as effective?

She had no desire to test it.

The man was still standing outside the back door, but to be safe, she pulled off her winter hat and held it over her mouth and nose with one hand while the other kept her gun on him.

"Oliver, cover your face and get that door open. We need to get the hell out of here."

"Please." The man took a step closer.

"Stop," Georgie commanded, and he did. "Back up."

The man's eyes were pleading. Scared. "Help?"

She blinked, and in an instant, the image of the bodies at the hospital tore through her mind, scattering her thoughts, pulling her away from the room, the house, the man, as if her connection to the present had been abruptly severed.

Had her dad been aware of what the military was up to out here while they were tucked away at Haven?

He knew. Of course he knew.

Project Noah was the emergency protocol. The Havens were the biggest part, but there were also the efforts outside, the commands to be followed as the military worked to combat the threat.

Project Noah had orchestrated the hospital bombing.

There was no way he didn't know.

Her mom knew, too.

The panic didn't creep up on Georgie this time. It hit her all at once, like a speeding train.

She pulled in a strained breath, and her arms fell limply at her sides.

They knew.

"Georgie," Oliver said from somewhere a million miles away. "Come on!"

But she'd lost control of her thoughts, and they were spinning at a hundred miles an hour.

They knew.

They both knew.

Hypocrites.

They played the heroes, condemning the governor when their own people had wiped out fucking hospitals.

For so long, Georgie had tried desperately to emulate her parents—idolizing them, shaping her entire goddamn personality around who she believed they were. But in truth, she didn't know them at all.

Everything she thought she knew had been a lie.

Was Desmond right?

I may not be the good guy, but at least I don't lie to myself about it.

The world tilted, her throat closed, and she sank to her haunches, unable to escape the onslaught of images flooding her mind.

Bistro lights and loud music.

Desmond's smile. *Dance with me.*

Screaming and gunfire.

They stood back and let the world burn.

No, they didn't let it burn. They fucking torched it themselves.

Her parents knew. They knew and they let it happen.

How many deaths were on their hands? On Project Noah's hands?

At least I don't lie to myself about it.

Maybe it was for the best that Indiana turned them away. She wanted nothing to do with any of them.

"Georgie."

A hand grabbed her wrist, pulling.

"Get up."

She didn't budge. She couldn't.

The gun vanished from her grasp, and her gaze lifted to the man.

Was he closer? He was definitely closer. He was inside the house now.

Get up get up get up.

"I don't want to shoot you." Oliver's voice, still distant and hollow.

Georgie's pulse pounded in her ears as the man took another step. She gasped for breath, trying to tell him to stop, but the word couldn't make it through.

Bang.

A gunshot?

The sound brought Georgie back to herself, and the world snapped into focus, leaving her disoriented, her mind sputtering to catch up.

"Sorry. Don't. Please." The man was backing toward the sliding door, his free hand back in the air.

"Georgie," Oliver pleaded, his voice right beside her now. "Come on! Please! We need to go."

She found him, face tight with fear, her gun in his outstretched hand, pointed at the man. The front door was open behind him.

Run.

Slowly, Georgie struggled to her feet, her legs wobbly, eyes locked on the man across the small house.

Go. Now.

The man abruptly spun around, causing him to lose his footing as he made a desperate grab for the pistol on the ground. Oliver fired off a shot before he could reach it.

He missed terribly, but it was enough to send the man running.

That was her last bullet.

Georgie drew a slow breath, the air finally making it through, and exchanged a meaningful look with Oliver.

"Okay," she whispered. "Go."

29

"Turn that fucking thing down."

Adam ignored the order, his attention on the shapes closing in from all sides. His eyes darted between the lumbering figures, mind racing to devise a strategy, but it was too late, and there were too many.

He wiped out a handful of them before the screen turned red and the zombies tackled him to the ground.

"Ugh!" He tossed the controller onto the cot. "I can't get past this stupid part."

"My head is killing me," Leon growled, running a hand over his tattooed scalp. He stood and pounded on the window, yelling at the empty room on the other side. "Emery!"

"Yep, yelling will fix that headache," Adam chirped.

"It's been a fucking day. I've got shit to do."

Adam grabbed the controller and held it out to the man. "Give it a try. It makes the time go by faster."

Leon knocked it out of his hand and it clattered to the ground.

"Or don't," Adam mumbled, rolling his eyes as he reclined on his cot, arm bent behind his head. That only lasted a couple seconds before his skin started to crawl. He shot up and paced the tiny room, reminding himself that this wasn't a prison. It was a precaution. He'd be out soon.

He wasn't a prisoner.

But whenever he gave his mind a second to wander, it would end up back in his room at the Hub.

You're trapped.

Not trapped. Quarantined.

You can't leave.

Temporary.

Prisoner.

He'd be out soon.

Adam thought of Reese, alone and dying in the next room.

Nope. Too much.

He pulled the bottle of pills from his vest pocket, then used the top of the TV to crush an oxy, because he needed the extra kick today. After taking the line, he sank back onto the cot, zipping and unzipping his hoodie until, a few seconds later, the high hit. Numbness rose over him like water, and he released a deep exhale.

Better.

He let his eyes drift closed, savoring the nothingness as everything fell away.

After a while, the high settled to a dull constant.

"This is your fault." Leon growled, his meaty hands going to his temples. "Emery!" he shouted again, but this time, the name was cut off by a violent, wet cough from deep in his chest. When Leon caught his breath, his eyes went round.

Adam sat up and wrinkled his nose. "That doesn't sound good."

He'd been coughing for most of the day, but this one was damning.

Leon grabbed him by the collar and yanked him up from the cot. "Why aren't you coughing?" The anger took Adam by surprise. Leon was usually easy-going. The kind of guy who laughed too hard at his own jokes and actually listened to the answer when he asked how someone was.

"That is an excellent question." The door on the other side of the glass clicked shut and Des's gaze jumped between them. "Everything okay in here?"

Leon shoved Adam aside and lurched at the window. "I need out of here, Emery."

"That's not going to happen."

"I can't be sick. I'm vaccinated."

"Intriguing, isn't it?" The calm in Desmond's voice seemed to stoke Leon's frustration.

"Do the test. You'll see."

"Unnecessary. The vaccine is clearly obsolete."

"No, then he'd be sick, too." Leon shoved a thick finger in Adam's direction.

Des's attention cut to Adam, then back again. "You'd think so."

Leon erupted, but he doubled over before he could even get a word out, wracked by another violent coughing fit.

"It *is* unfortunate," Des said. "I was really hoping to have more time."

"That's it?" Leon spat. "What the actual fuck, Emery."

A fair point. Even for Des, that was too calm of a response. He'd been so determined to track his plant down. Why wasn't he upset that the vaccine didn't work?

"I have a backup plan," Desmond explained. "Sorry to say it won't be much help to you." He threw a remorseful glance at Leon. "You deserve better."

Leon sank onto the cot, muttering something under his breath.

"Adam, there's a change of clothes in the next room." Desmond crossed to the second door and pressed a button on the wall. "Change, then throw your clothes back in there with Leon. The UV light will do the rest."

Adam happily agreed and made his way into the decontamination room as the purple lights flickered to life. The fresh clothes were comfortable and clean, the hoodie soft on the inside with sleeves that hung past his fingers. When Des opened the door to let him through, Adam lifted his bare hands in front of him, the baggy sleeves sliding down his thin forearms. "I need new gloves." He'd left his at Spring Valley.

Desmond's mouth quirked. "We'll get you some gloves."

Adam studied him for a second, waiting for him to question the lack of symptoms, already trying to conjure up a lie through the haze in his head.

"You and I need to have a chat."

There it was.

Adam gestured broadly. "Chat away."

"I want to commend you for tracking down Reese."

Adam grimaced.

"You're sure the strays weren't at Spring Valley?"

"I'm sure." The lie came so effortlessly. "Like I said, Reese told me they split up weeks ago."

Desmond's inquisitive eyes sent a flutter of insecurity over Adam.

He knows you're lying.

Des could pick out a lie from a mile away.

But if he knew, he didn't let on. "All right. I'll have Colette continue to monitor the cameras."

Adam ran a hand over the back of his neck. "Why are you still looking for them if the plant doesn't work?"

"Whether or not it works is irrelevant. It belongs to *me*, and they took it."

"*Reese* took it," Adam corrected. And he was definitely being punished for it.

"They're all accountable."

He was still going after her.

Des gave a dismissive wave. "But that's a problem for tomorrow. Go get some rest."

"Aren't you curious why I'm not sick?"

"Should I be?" He crossed to the door with the keypad.

Adam frowned, a little offended. "I *thought* so."

"It's possible you got lucky."

There was no way Desmond actually believed that.

"What is going on?" Adam asked. "I thought you'd want to know."

"Know what?" When Des turned to face him, there was a subtle glint of amusement in his eyes. "Is there something you'd like to share?"

"No."

He arched a brow.

"Okay, yes."

"I'm listening," Desmond said, folding his arms and leaning against the wall.

Adam hesitated, then finally forced the words out. "I'm not vaccinated. I'm immune."

A beat of excruciating silence, and then Des responded with a nonchalant, "Huh."

Adam searched his expression, the terrible realization hitting all at once. "You *knew*."

He was the backup plan.

Desmond's lips curved into a smile. "I didn't until we got back here after the party. Colette shared Oliver's little radio conversation."

Adam was never actually free to leave. He was an asset. Desmond kept him close, not because he cared, but to be sure he didn't go anywhere. Everything he'd said, every promise, every kind word, it was all a lie.

"That's why you had Eris trail me," Adam said. "And Leon. You were making sure I came back."

"I was trying to keep you alive while letting you have enough freedom to feel content here," Desmond said. "A task that turned out to be more challenging than I had anticipated."

"You were *using* me."

"No," Des responded, his expression suddenly serious. "I was making sure the Havens *didn't*."

Adam scoffed.

Tell them your name. Colette used his immunity to get the strays to meet them. She knew they'd show up. Knew they'd try to take him.

Everybody uses you, the voice jabbed.

"That's the only reason you wanted me here."

Desmond tilted his head. "Don't be daft. I wanted you here long before I knew about your immunity. You're a valuable part of the team. Which is why I have been nothing but accommodating, despite your inability to follow even the simplest of instructions." He stood up straight and slid a hand through his hair. "Why don't you go get something to eat, and we'll talk more later."

"I'm leaving."

He won't let you. You're still a prisoner.

"Is my assistance with the Hub no longer required?"

Adam's shoulders stiffened. "No, I'll do it myself."

You can't do anything by yourself. You're a mess.

"Go get some rest, Adam."

"Did you not hear me? I'm leaving."

"You have nowhere else to go."

The words tore through him. Desmond was right. He had nobody left. He couldn't go back to Spring Valley. They'd know he was responsible for Reese's disappearance. How could he explain that? Georgie had given him a second chance, only for him to ruin it.

He'd had a moment, an opportunity to choose differently. To choose something better. Instead, he chose this place and these people.

He'd chosen a prison.

You'll only ever be as good as what you can do for others.

None of this was real.

He thought of the steward and the convenient way he'd appeared outside of Desmond's office at just the right time. What if it wasn't random at all? What if it was Desmond's way of manipulating him into agreeing to contact Georgie?

Of course you have a choice. I'm not forcing you into anything.

Adam never actually had a choice. Desmond was lying. Using him.

Ugh, he was so stupid.

Des wasn't family. He was a toxin that had eroded away every bit of sense Adam had gained throughout his life. But his thoughts were suddenly clear, and he could see Desmond for what he was. A manipulative liar. Selfish like everyone else.

Adam leaned against the wall, the way Des had a moment ago, and folded his arms. "You know, it's funny," he started, trying to keep his voice steady. "You hate the people at the Havens so much, but you're really no better than them."

Desmond lowered his voice, his words slow and measured. "Go back to your room."

"Just another asshole on a power trip. At least the Havens are honest about holding me captive."

Desmond's mouth tilted up into a dangerous smile. "You're about to cross a dangerous line, Adam, and I guarantee you will not like the consequences."

"Maybe when I find Georgie, I'll go with her to Indiana." It was a bluff, of course, but it didn't matter.

The smile vanished, and Desmond lunged forward, slamming a hand against the wall inches from Adam's head.

"Enough." The word was venomous, and the sudden change was unnerving.

Despite the pounding in his chest, Adam kept his composure. "Don't forget," he taunted. "You *need* me."

"If you choose to behave like a child," Des said, leaning in close, eyes fixed on Adam's, "then I'll treat you as such." He snatched the pill bottle from Adam's vest pocket and held it up between them. "I'll hold on to these, and you can stay right here until you feel a little more agreeable."

You did this.

Adam's gaze jumped to Leon on the other side of the glass, and his façade crumbled.

"You can't leave me here. He's infected."

"And you're immune." Desmond shrugged, then turned and keyed in the code. "I'm sure he'll be happy to have company." The keypad beeped and Des pulled open the door, stepping out into the hallway.

Adam scrambled forward, but he was too slow. The door latched, and the keypad beeped as the lock let out a damning click.

The blood drained from his face, and the room spun around him.

Prisoner.

"Wait!" Adam shouted.

No no no.

The air was heavy and suffocating, leaving him struggling for breath as the walls closed in.

You are to do as you're told.

"Please," he begged, sinking to the floor.

There had to be another way out. Adam scanned the room.

Nothing. Just the two doors.

He pulled his knees up to his chest, and when he closed his eyes, he was back at the Hub.

"Welcome to your new home." Stanton's voice, cold and empty.

It had been two years since he walked willingly into that brick mansion, but everything about it was still perfectly clear in his head. They promised a safe place. But that had also been a lie.

You deserve it, the voice growled.

Then Reese's silvery tone added, *you deserve all of it.*

"I know," Adam whispered, pressing his forehead to his knees. "I'm so sorry."

30

It took another day of coughing fits before a cloudy film formed over Leon's eyes, the first stalks growing out of his nose. He never seemed to stop making noise, between the pained cries and the low groans, and Adam hadn't been able to sleep at all since the conversation with Desmond the day before.

Eris had stopped by a few times through the night. Two knocks, and then a check-in through the closed door. The same four questions. Was Leon still alive? Was he still mobile? Had Adam shown any symptoms? Was he okay?

His answers were always the same. Yes. Yes. No. Always.

Three simple truths, one massive lie.

And then, just like that, she'd leave him alone again with the growling in his head.

The second hand on his watch seemed to vibrate his entire arm with every click, emphasizing the excruciatingly slow passage of time. Or maybe it was in his head. It was hard to tell anymore.

His eyes jumped to the window as Leon sat up on his cot. Adam had thought about going back into the room. At least the cots were more comfortable than the cold tile floor, but he lost the nerve every time. Memories of O'Hare and all the people he'd watched die seeped into his thoughts. All the others he'd put out of their misery. At least back then, by this stage, their muscles were paralyzed, their bodies basically corpses even before their hearts stopped beating.

Leon was still moving, still talking, and Adam couldn't get himself to go in there. Especially knowing once he went in, he wouldn't be able to get back out.

For a while after Desmond left, Adam had been so angry. At Desmond, at himself. At Eris and Colette, and everyone else in this place. He paced the room like an animal caught in a trap.

You did this.

You ruined everything.

Now, the prickle of withdrawal had grown into a clawing that made everything hurt. Adam swore the room was suddenly smaller, pressing in against him.

And then there was Leon, banging his fists on the window, begging for help.

Bang, bang, bang.

The sound bounced around the tiny room, too loud, pounding in time with the throbbing in Adam's head.

Stop it. He pressed his palms to his eyelids.

Make him be quiet.

Bang. Bang. Bang.

"Stop it!" he shouted, and when Leon didn't listen, Adam climbed off the ground and slammed his hand against the button. He pushed open the door, and then the next, and when he stepped into the quarantine room, he drew his knife and slashed it across Leon's throat.

Blood spattered against his cheek, and Adam scowled, wiping at it with the back of his hand.

"I. Said. Stop."

Leon's cloudy eyes went wide, and the small puff of spores hung in the air. Wrecked sounds poured from his mouth as his thick hands clasped desperately over the gash. Blood cascaded down his chest and he staggered backwards, shoulders connecting with the wall. Once there, his knees gave out, and he slid to the ground.

When he finally stopped moving, stopped making noise, Adam shoved the knife back into its sheath, not bothering to wipe it first.

He crouched beside Leon and searched the pockets of his jacket, hands sticky with blood, but came up empty.

Come on.

Of all the days to have nothing on him.

Desmond was your only chance at getting to Stanton. You ruined it.

After one more thorough check, just to be sure, Adam crawled onto the cot and curled up on his side, his muscles and bones and skin all aching.

He could've locked you in here months ago, but he didn't. You're the one who tried to leave. This is your fault.

Why had he gotten so mad at Desmond? He was lucky to have this place. Lucky Desmond cared enough to want him here, to give him what he needed to hold the darkness in his head back. Why did it matter what his reasoning was?

He's going to cut off your supply.

Adam was being ungrateful. Selfish.

Worthless.

Sorry.

You need Desmond.

I'm sorry.

When Adam closed his eyes, Alice was there, humming gently, her hand smoothing back his hair like she used to.

I'll make it right. I'll fix it.

Within seconds, sleep pulled him violently under.

The sound of the door in the next room shook Adam from a nightmare. He shot up from the cot, the room tilting as he stumbled to the window.

Desmond looked past him, eyebrows slightly raised as he surveyed the room.

"That's one way to solve the problem."

"Can I go to my room now?" Adam croaked. His mouth was dry, his throat sore.

So tired.

"And what have we learned?" Des crooned as he settled onto the stool opposite the glass. He placed the bottle of pills on the counter in front of the window, sending the voice into a frenzy.

Adam stared for a moment, and when he looked up to meet Desmond's gaze, his chest tightened.

You'll listen.

"I'll listen." He swallowed hard, trying to settle his stomach. "I'm sorry."

Des's dark eyes swept over Adam, assessing the mess down his front before pocketing the pills. "Clean off in the decontamination room. I'll get you some new clothes." He offered a warm smile. "Gloves, too this time."

After the blood and grime were gone from his skin, Adam pulled on the fresh clothes and followed Des out of the quarantine room, into the wide hall.

"Come with me."

Adam wanted to go back to his room and sleep, but Desmond still had his pills. Plus, he was already walking a thin line, and the last thing he wanted was to be put back in that prison, so he followed without a word.

You are to do as you're told.

The silence was painful as they walked from one end of Jardine to the other, and Adam's gaze kept pulling to Desmond, waiting for him to spare a single glance in his direction.

Though he didn't show it on his face, Des emitted an unmistakable aura of irritation that radiated off him like heat waves from the pavement in summer.

Eris joined them, but she avoided looking at Adam. Was she mad, too?

The tension grew with every minute that passed, until Des finally stopped and pulled open a door, motioning for Adam to go first.

Cautiously, Adam stepped inside, scanning the large room. Sunlight streamed through the windows, painting thin strips of light and shadow across the laminate floor. The room was empty, save for a thin man with long silver hair that sat hunched in a chair, head bowed.

Desmond leaned against the wall, arms folded, while Eris let the door close behind her with a soft click.

Adam didn't understand what was going on, why Des would've brought him here—until the man's head lifted and his eyes fluttered open.

Stanton's gaze lifted, connecting with his, and Adam inhaled sharply.

Holy hell.

Des had kept his end of the deal. This was really happening. Adrenaline surged through Adam's veins, and a grin broke across his face.

Was Desmond making up for locking him in that room? Maybe he did care.

"Apologies for the belatedness," Des said, voice edged with something that wasn't usually there. A small, almost frown flickered on his face. "Kind of sad you weren't with us for it. I know how much it meant to you."

Adam's mind spun briefly, struggling to catch up, and when he finally understood, his smile vanished.

The Hub.

Desmond went without him.

All that time waiting, looking forward to the day he could see it end.

He swallowed the disappointment and gave a small nod. It was fine. That was what he wanted, right? It didn't matter how. Only that they were gone. He should be grateful.

"It's still burning," Desmond added. "You can probably see the smoke from here."

Adam's stomach lurched, and his tired legs almost faltered.

"No," he said on a breath. "You weren't supposed to do that." He thought of the tiny rooms with sealed windows, the doors locked from the outside. All those people. Prisoners like him.

"You wanted it gone."

"I wanted the people running it gone. Not everyone inside."

"Oh," Des said, then pursed his lips in a pantomime of sympathy. "You really should have been more specific." He shrugged.

Adam's gaze slid back to Stanton, temper flaring. All those deaths, they were on Stanton. It was *his* fault, and Adam would make him pay for it. For everything he'd done—to Adam and everyone else in that place.

He'd get his closure. Replace the images that haunted his nightmares with ones of the man dying at his feet.

And he'd finally be able to sleep.

Adam drew the knife from the holster in his boot, his grip tightening around the handle, pulse quickening with an exhilarating rush.

You are nothing.

The man's pointed features hardened as recognition sank in. Adam was going to draw this out, make Stanton suffer like he had.

You are a number.

He slid his tongue along his top teeth as he stepped closer.

An object.

Where should he start?

A toy to be discarded once you're too broken to use.

His pinky finger, Adam decided, remembering the all-encompassing bolt of pain he'd felt when Stanton had snapped his. He'd take his pinky finger and keep it as a fucking trophy.

And he would take his time. He wanted to savor this.

He'd earned this moment.

The man's thin lips lifted into a smile, and Adam wanted so badly for him to speak. To beg. But he didn't say a word.

That's okay, Adam thought, smile twisting into a grimace.

There was time.

He'd get him to beg.

Adam flinched as a gunshot echoed through the empty room, the sound jarring and deafening. The impact kicked Stanton's head back, his lifeless eyes fixed on the high ceiling overhead.

"No!" Adam shouted, gaze snapping to Desmond, whose hand gripped the Desert Eagle with white-knuckled intensity. His muscles coiled, and his body surged forward, but Eris grabbed his arm, stopping him in his tracks.

"Adam," she pleaded. "Don't."

He yanked his arm free, his eyes locked on Desmond, vision blurring.

Adam's voice, barely a whisper, struggled to break through the suffocating weight of the air as it bore down on him, threatening to crush him. "How could you do that?"

"I warned you that you wouldn't like the consequences," Des said, brow tight. "I don't like being ignored."

You did this.

It's your fault.

Adam swiped away a tear, his jaw clenched so tight it hurt.

In a breath, Desmond's frown vanished, his calm settling back into place like a curtain. "You had a good thing here. I went out of my way to make sure you were happy, and yet you treated me like the enemy."

The disappointment in Desmond's voice coursed through Adam like a poison, draining his strength and dousing the fire.

You ruined it.

"I assume you would choose your own room over the quarantine facilities."

Adam nodded.

"Then, I expect there won't be any further issues."

When Adam shook his head, Des nodded once and held out his bottle of pills.

"Good. We're done here. Go grab something to eat."

31

Adam sat at an empty table, a plate of food in front of him. He didn't dare let himself look at it, afraid he'd lose the battle against his nauseous stomach. His nerves were wound tight, his muscles buzzing. Sitting still hurt, but he was too achy to move.

Why were the pills taking so long to kick in?

After popping another, he abandoned the untouched meal and dragged himself to the bar, grabbing the nearest bottle and dropping onto a stool.

When someone sat beside him, he breathed a frustrated laugh.

"He's still afraid I'll leave?"

Eris leaned forward, her hood up over her dark hair. "He really *does* care about you, you know. About all of us."

Adam took a long drink, ignoring her.

"You still look like hell," she said, and when he responded with an irritated glare, a faint smirk tugged at the corners of her lips. "Go get some rest."

"Can everyone stop treating me like a kid?" he snapped.

Her face soured. "Yeah, sure. When you stop acting like one. You pretend you have it so bad, but you get special treatment that the rest of us never do." When Adam didn't respond, she softened her tone and tried again. "You've had a rough couple of days. Please, try to get some sleep."

He studied her for a moment. "Why do you care what I do?"

"You die of exhaustion, we're all screwed."

He scoffed. "So you know, too."

She flattened her lips, then nodded once. "I was with Colette when she picked up the call."

You're only as good as what you can do for others.

Adam folded his arms on the bar and rested his chin on top. "My head's too loud to sleep."

"How about some fresh air?" Eris hopped gracefully to her feet.

"Am I allowed?" he asked, his tone laced with bitterness.

"I'm responsible for you at the moment, and *I* want to go for a walk. I can't leave you alone, so get your ass up."

Adam pushed slowly up from the stool. He felt heavy as he followed Eris through the hall, his boots dragging under the weight.

As they stepped outside through the back exit, the cold air pricked at his lungs and bit his skin. He zipped his hoodie as far as it would go and closed his eyes, listening to the soothing sound of birds chattering and water lapping at the pier.

When he opened them again, a camera pointed at the doors caught his attention, and a thought forced its way to the front of his blurry mind.

He turned back to Eris. "Why did you ask me those questions?"

Her eyes narrowed. "What?"

"There are cameras in the quarantine room," he clarified. "Why walk all the way over there?"

"I don't understand. What questions?"

"Last night. You asked about Leon. About symptoms. But why would you go out of your way when you could've had Colette check the feed and saved yourself the trips?"

She was quiet a moment, searching his face, her own unreadable. "When was the last time you slept?"

The subject change threw him. "I—"

Eris's walkie went off, and she gave him one more evaluative glance before she grabbed it and responded.

Adam rolled his eyes, then plodded through the snow to the side of the pier. He let the tips of his boots hang off the edge, his gaze dragging up to the Ferris wheel on the pier across the water.

He'd never been on a Ferris wheel, but he was sure he would've liked it. Shame it wasn't running.

A second later, Eris was beside him. "Des needs me."

"I'll be fine out here."

"He's sending Birk to take my place." The silence lingered for a brief moment between them before she asked, "Honestly, though, are you okay?"

Without missing a beat, he gave his usual answer. "Always."

She gave him that look again, like she was searching for something or waiting for the answer to a question she hadn't asked.

"What?" he snapped, throwing his hands out at his sides.

All the hard edges on Eris's face fell away. "I didn't go anywhere near the quarantine room last night, Adam."

Slipping.

Falling.

Losing your hold.

"Oh." He pulled up his hood, desperately trying to hold the mask in place. "Must have been someone else."

She offered a tight smile and a quick nod and left it at that.

They stayed like that, eyes forward, neither saying a word, until a lean man with long hair and a narrow face joined them. Eris disappeared, and after a minute, Birk flicked his cigarette into the water.

"It's fucking freezing. Time to go back in."

Adam didn't budge.

Crazy.

Falling.

"Hey. You hear me?"

"I did," Adam said. "Just choosing not to listen. Haven't you heard? I'm not great at following instructions."

When Birk reached out to grab his arm, Adam flinched away, his nerves sparking. "Don't touch me."

The man's face hardened. "Then move."

It won't stop.

It'll never stop.

"I'm staying here," Adam said flatly. "You can go back in."

"Emery said not to let you out of my sight. He *really* seems to like you." The corners of Birk's lips lifted slightly as his eyes narrowed. "Makes me curious what you do for him."

Adam's muscles tensed, and the voice snarled in his head. "I could show you." He pulled his smile into place, closing the distance between them.

The man shot a weary look back at the building. "No, I didn't—I was just—"

Before Birk could finish his response, Adam's knife was burrowed up beneath his ribs. He held the man's gaze for a long moment, then pulled the knife free and shoved him into the water, wondering what the last part of that sentence would've been.

He's going to put you back in that room.

Adam pulled his bottle of pills from his hoodie pocket and took two.

No. He wouldn't go back. He couldn't handle another minute in there.

Desmond's voice filled his head. *You're about to cross a dangerous line.*

He held the bottle close as he watched the man struggling to stay afloat, blood spreading in the water. Des was going to take his pills again.

His grip tightened on the bottle.

You are to do as you're told.

Finally, Birk stopped fighting, his body slowly sinking, his hair the last thing to be swallowed by the dark water.

Adam tilted his head, eyelids drooping.

It looked so peaceful.

Adam, Oliver's voice pleaded. *Walk away.*

He dropped the pills on the ground at his feet. "I...don't want to."

It'll never stop.

Aren't you worried you'll fall? Georgie's voice asked.

He frowned, then looked down at his boots, the water below sloshing against the concrete. The truth was, he was never worried he'd fall, but he always kind of hoped he would.

What would it feel like to drown?

You're sinking anyway.

What do you have left?

He was never going to be able to sleep. Desmond ripped away his only chance at peace. Stole it from him. Now what did he have?

Please, Adam, Oliver begged.

Adam had always liked the quiet that surrounded him underneath the water.

Maybe it would be like going to sleep.

Sleep. The word tugged at him. Enticing. Welcoming.

Walk away.

"I just want to sleep." He shoved the hood back.

You can make it stop.

One last look at Navy Pier. The Ferris wheel. The sun hanging low over the jagged teeth of the city. Then Adam lifted his arms out to his sides, closed his eyes, and stepped off the ledge, the frigid water coming up to meet him.

Pain blew through him all at once, stealing his breath, a thousand knives cutting into his skin.

He hadn't expected it to hurt so much.

Adam swallowed the shock, grappling with his survival instincts as his body fought to push back through the surface.

It would fade. He had to make it through the initial pain, and then it would all disappear.

He emptied his lungs, letting himself sink.

I just want to sleep.

It was quiet here. He tried to focus on that, but everything hurt.

His chest was screaming. Why did this have to hurt so much? It wasn't calm. It wasn't like going to sleep. His body ached for breath, sending panicked signals through his nerves, alarms that were impossible to ignore.

Slowly, the pain faded, the frenzy finally settling into a sleepy calm.

So tired.

Adam's eyes lifted to the rippling sky above as a shape, barely visible, leaned over the ledge.

You're too late.

He was dying.

Alone.

But he wasn't ready to die.

The thought slammed into him with enough force to shake off the sleepy haze.

What was he doing?

After everything, he was really going to quietly disappear? Sink to the bottom of Lake Michigan?

He wasn't ready to die.

Yeah, living hurt. It was more painful than the icy water against his skin. But he wasn't done.

He. Wasn't. Done.

Don't disappear on me.

The shape above solidified. Familiar dark hair against the sky.

Adam's mouth opened, and he pulled in an involuntary breath, but there was no air. Only water. He panicked, clawing his way back to the surface.

He grabbed the ledge as he fought to pull in a wet gasp, his body roaring in pain. The rasping turned to coughing and eventually subsided into strained breathing.

There was nobody around him. No Oliver. No anybody.

Of course there wasn't.

Alone.

As Adam dragged himself up onto the ledge and collapsed onto the concrete, his teeth chattered so hard, he thought they might shatter in his mouth.

He sat up and stared at the Ferris wheel, his entire body trembling.

Coward.

What happens now?

"I'm so tired," Adam whispered, dropping his head onto his knees.

You have nothing.

The Hub was gone. Stanton was gone. And after what he'd just done, Desmond was going to lock him back in that room.

What was he supposed to do? It was never going to stop. He was trapped.

And tired. So tired.

He needed to feel less.

Adam scrambled to the bottle of pills and twisted open the lid.

You're stronger than you think, Oliver's voice said softly.

"I'm not."

Desmond was using him, and Adam was allowing it because he was weak and desperate to belong.

It was so easy for everyone to use him. To manipulate him. To break him.

He made it so easy.

Adam's body shook violently as he stared at the open bottle clenched in his fist.

No, *these* made it easy.

Elias used them to make him compliant.

Flora used them to buy his silence.

Desmond used them to punish him.

It was so easy.

But it didn't have to be.

A sharp jolt surged through his nerves, like static crackling under his skin, and he shoved up from the ground, hurling the open bottle with every bit of strength he had left. The pills disappeared into the dark water, and the bottle landed, floating on top.

What did you do?

Adam watched in horror as the water devoured the orange bottle.

No no no.

His breathing stuttered, and an invisible hand tightened around his throat.

Desmond was going to lock him in with Leon's corpse, and now he had nothing to numb the sharp edges.

Run, Adam, Oliver's voice pleaded.

Adam's eyes flicked to the garage entrance. There were plenty of cars, but even if he knew how to drive, he'd never make it through the gate.

Goddammit, Adam, Georgie shouted in his head. *Just fucking go!*

He balled his fists as his gaze slid toward the city.

I don't like being ignored. Desmond's voice was like smoke seeping in, holding him in place.

"I don't know what to do," Adam whispered.

Please, Oliver begged. *Come home.*

Home.

Oliver.

All at once, the hold loosened. Adam swiped the dripping hair from his face and ran.

32

Georgie and Oliver made it back to Spring Valley shaken, but unscathed. He immediately disappeared up the stairs, and after turning in her gun, Georgie headed to the greenhouse to sit and calm down before facing the others.

When she finally dragged herself to the cabin, she told Jax what they'd found—the attack on the hospital and the man in the subdivision.

"I'll try Indiana again," Jax said. "We need somewhere to go before the infection makes it here."

"They already told us no."

"I said I'd fix it, and I will. Just trust me."

Even if Georgie believed he could convince them, she wasn't sure she wanted to go. Not after what she'd seen. Desmond's words had put a flicker of doubt in her head, and the scene at the hospital had solidified it.

"I think we should talk to Vivian about staying here," she said. "Project Noah, they're not what we thought they were."

Did she want to hand the plant over to people who would do something like that? Would they really use it to make things better, or would they hoard it for themselves?

She was furious at Indiana for blowing them off, her parents for their hypocrisy, Project Noah and the military for their callousness, and herself for believing all the bullshit she'd been fed.

Jax studied her expression. "They're not perfect, but we *need* them."

As much as she wanted to argue, she dropped it because it didn't matter what either of them thought. Indiana didn't want them.

The rest of the day was spent splitting perimeter checks and helping with chores. Her and Jax dedicated their downtime to brainstorming ways to handle Desmond—none of which led to a viable solution.

Georgie stopped by the greenhouse every few hours, obsessively checking on the plant. Thank god the thing was bred for resilience. It was already beginning to perk back up.

Banks found the infected girl Oliver had told them about shot dead on the outskirts of Spring Valley. That was one less concern, and the man wouldn't be around much longer.

But there were bound to be more. And without the hospital to scavenge, Oliver didn't have the parts he needed for his purifier.

Vivian allowed them to have their weapons while running patrols, thankful to have an added layer of security against this new threat. Desmond's deal didn't protect them against the infection.

Kye relayed the news that Reese had gone after Adam and still wasn't back, told them to keep an eye out while making their rounds.

"Maybe he went back to Jardine with Adam," Kye said, trying to pretend like the thought didn't terrify her.

But that made no sense. Reese was terrified of Desmond, sure that if he ever saw him again, he'd be dead.

It was possible he already was.

Judging by the look on Kye's face, she was thinking the same thing.

The day after was pickup day.

Knowing Desmond's people would be there, they waited it out in the subdivision across the street, with Kye ready to raise the alarm if anything seemed off. But they came and went without incident. For now, it seemed Oliver was right—Adam hadn't told Desmond they were there.

Today, Georgie felt calmer, the pressure easing, just a little. She spent most of the day helping Dr. Ramirez. They discussed the plant, the infection's shift, and the future of the vaccine now that Indiana was no longer in the picture. Neither of them had a clue how to get from one to the other, but at least she felt a little less alone in the endeavor.

After dinner at the farmhouse, Ciri asked her to play a board game, and she agreed. They settled on the floor around the coffee table, Wren and Vivian watching from the couch and talking about some show they both used to watch.

Oliver passed through the sitting room and disappeared into the kitchen. Georgie hadn't seen him since the hospital trip and was starting to worry how he was coping with the disappointment.

When he returned a moment later, he paused behind her, and she glanced over her shoulder to see him signing something to Ciri.

Georgie angled her cards away from him. "What'd you tell her?" she asked as Ciri gave Oliver a mischievous grin.

He shrugged. "I didn't say anything."

"No, but you *signed*. You cheaters."

"I don't know what you're talking about." He met her gaze for a second, mouth tipped up, while Wren and Vivian both laughed.

Georgie cast Ciri a playful scowl. "I see how it is."

Oliver signed again, and Ciri nodded.

"Okay, go ahead," Georgie said. "Let's get it over with. I know when I've lost."

Ciri played a card, setting it on the game board, and sure enough, it was one Georgie had no way to block.

"How'd you even know what to tell her?" Georgie asked. "I'd never seen this game before today."

"My brother and I used to play." He signed something to Ciri, then headed up the stairs.

"He seems better today," Vivian said when he was gone, leaning forward to help gather the cards.

Georgie's eyes lingered on the staircase. "Yeah."

Was he still working on his air purifier?

The longer they stayed here, the more Spring Valley grew on her. It was the kind of place that proved something good could still exist. And though there were a couple crucial steps to handle before they could even think about staying long term, the idea of going anywhere else grew less appealing by the minute.

These people could've turned them away, but instead, they had offered them not only a place to stay, but food and kindness.

Vivian handed over the cards and gave her a brief smile.

"Thank you," Georgie told her.

"No problem, hon."

"No, really." Georgie's brow cinched. "Thank you. For everything. You saved us."

"I took a risk, and it paid off. Not like it's charity. You all pull your weight."

Georgie added the cards on top of her own pile. "If there's anything else we can do to help, please let me know."

Vivian nodded. "I'll do that."

Jax appeared in the sitting room, bundled in his coat, exhaustion painted across his face.

"I'll be back in a few hours," he said.

He seemed to be taking more shifts than anyone else, and it was clearly taking a toll.

"It's my turn," she told him. "You take my place here. Maybe you'll have better luck." Georgie gave Ciri a smile, then signed a quick *thank you.*

Jax hesitated, but as his eyes drifted to the plush couch, he nodded. "Okay. Thanks."

Georgie stood and pulled her heavy winter coat over the green jacket.

"Be careful," he said as he took her hand and drew her in for a kiss.

After collecting her pistol, Georgie headed outside.

The sky was the same dull gray it had been for days, but today was colder, and the layer of slush had hardened into a thick sheet of ice.

As she walked the perimeter of Spring Valley, a constant swarm of anxious thoughts buzzed in her mind.

Why did Indiana change their minds? How would she get the notebooks back without Adam's help? Could she make a vaccine without them? Between her and Dr. Ramirez, could they figure it out?

If they could, would it still work against the mutation?

She shivered at the thought, then forced her brain to change direction to the more urgent problem.

Desmond.

If they lured him here, how could they kill him without anyone getting hurt? Would Kye be willing to help, knowing that they'd be messing with Vivian's deal? They didn't have many weapons. Adam left his sniper rifle locked away with the others, but could any of them even use it?

Her thoughts veered again at the mention of Adam.

Why did he leave, and why did Reese follow?

Were they okay?

She tucked her hands in her pockets, that last thought sticking with her.

The sky had darkened to a moody charcoal by the time Georgie finished the check. She made her way back through the forest toward the cabin, bracing against the gusts howling through the frozen trees.

She slowed her pace as she neared the lake, watching the wind ripple across the dark surface before she noticed a shape on the wooden dock. A person curled up on their side, facing the water.

The man from the subdivision?

Georgie pulled off her gloves and drew her gun.

"Hey," she barked, her muscles tightening as she fought the urge to run.

The shape didn't move.

Maybe he was already dead. They'd have to burn the body to prevent contaminating anything.

Or maybe it was Reese. Maybe he never actually left. But then why hadn't any of the others found him?

She inched closer, gun pointed as she rounded the figure and cautiously pulled back the hood, exposing a chaotic mess of caramel brown hair that whipped wildly in the biting wind.

"Shit," she said on a breath as she crouched down, angling his head to get a better look. "Adam, open your eyes."

He looked like a corpse, face chalky, lips tinged slightly blue. Georgie pressed the back of her hand against his forehead, recoiling at the icy chill of his skin. Her movements were frantic as she checked for a pulse, and when she finally found it, she heaved a sigh of relief.

He was alive.

It was freezing, though. He should have been shivering, but he wasn't. Possibly Hypothermia.

What the hell was he doing out here?

"Adam," she said again. Still no response.

Georgie pushed to her feet and grabbed his hands, trying unsuccessfully to sit him up, the movement sending lightning bolts of pain through her abdomen.

"Come on." She pushed his shoulder, rolling him onto his back. "Work with me, dammit."

He groaned.

Good. It was something. "Get up. You stay out here, you're going to freeze to death. Open your eyes."

"Let me sleep." The words were quiet and grating.

"Nope. Fuck that. Not happening. Get up." She gripped his hands again and pulled, and this time, he managed to sit up.

Georgie grabbed his face with one hand, squeezing probably a little harder than she should've. "You have some fucking explaining to do. Now get your ass up."

Adam's eyes fluttered open, and the sadness in them was jarring.

"Stop yelling at me," he muttered, his squished cheeks mashing the words into something barely comprehensible.

"I'm not yelling!" She sighed. "Okay, yes I am." Her hand fell away, and he folded forward, head on his knees. "What are you doing out here? Where'd you go? Where's Reese?"

"I went back," he said without lifting his head.

She figured, but heat still rose in her chest at the words. Georgie swallowed back the urge to shout, reserving it for when he wasn't half conscious.

"Did you tell him where we are?"

He shook his head.

"Are you alone?"

A subtle nod.

She had to get him inside.

Georgie shut her eyes, feeling the pressure building behind them. Adam had betrayed her twice. There was a possibility he was lying to her now—though in this state of mind, it was unlikely.

Still, the smart thing would be to leave him out here. Let him figure it out. It was *his* choice to leave. Let him deal with the consequences.

But if she did, he'd die.

"Can I trust you, Adam?"

Another shake of his head. "I don't even trust me."

"Not very reassuring." She sighed. "Let's get you warmed up, and then you can explain to me what the actual fuck you were thinking."

Suddenly, he looked up, grabbed her wrists, and pulled her down to his level.

"I'm sorry," he muttered. "I didn't know what to do. I still don't. I just—" A ragged sob cut the sentence short. "I want it all to stop, but I'm a coward and the lake was too cold and it hurt. Everything hurts."

Her shoulders softened, the fire dissipating in a breath, and as Adam released his grip, Georgie wrapped her arms around him and pulled him close. He sank against her, his entire body uncoiling.

"It's okay," she whispered. "You're going to be okay."

33

The sound of hushed arguing dragged Adam awake, and his muscles ached as he tensed. He resisted the urge to open his eyes and instead concentrated on the voices, trying to figure out who was in his room.

"I couldn't leave him to die."

A girl's voice. Eris? No. Eris had an airy way of speaking. This voice had an edge to it.

He frowned as he placed it, because there was no way Georgie was at Jardine. It was his mind messing with him again.

"You put everyone at risk by bringing him back here." Hale's voice? *Ugh*, was everyone in his head now?

Adam wanted to move, but even the thought of it exhausted him. His skin hurt. His head hurt. God, everything hurt. He felt like a human pincushion.

"He was unarmed and half dead," Georgie argued. "He's not a threat."

The gentle crackling of a fire pulled his attention.

He wasn't at Jardine.

Why wasn't he at Jardine?

Adam shivered as the memory rushed back—the pier, Lake Michigan, the walk through the city. The last thing he remembered was bunkering down in an apartment to rest, sure he'd freeze to death there, all alone.

And now he was here. But where was *here*?

Georgie was at Spring Valley, so if she was actually here with him, if she wasn't in his head...had he walked all the way to Spring Valley from the city?

These memory lapses were really screwing with his head.

"What if it's a trick?" Hale asked. "What if he told Emery everything?"

"If he told him where we are, we'd know it by now."

That was for sure.

But even if Desmond didn't know yet, he would soon. He'd figure it out.

Adam brushed the thought away. He couldn't handle worrying about *that* particular problem right now.

"What about Indiana?" Jax asked, lowering his voice to a near whisper. "They're looking for him. We need a way to convince them to let us in. Maybe we could use this in our favor."

Adam's jaw clenched.

"He'd never be okay with that."

No freaking kidding.

"If they find out he's here, he may not have a choice."

Run.

Leave.

He couldn't go to Indiana. He couldn't be trapped at another Haven.

"How would they find out?" she asked. "I'm sure as hell not telling them. And neither are you."

Adam caught himself before the grateful smile lifted on his face.

They both went quiet for a long moment, and he was about to open his eyes when Georgie asked about Reese.

He winced.

"Still not back," Hale answered. "Why don't we ask *him*?" The tone was pointed. Accusing.

"Reese is dead," Adam mumbled, surprised at the roughness of his voice, like sandpaper on stone. It wasn't exactly a lie, and it felt easier than the horrible truth.

When he opened his eyes, Georgie and Hale were staring with matching scowls from the table across the room.

They really were perfect for each other.

"What happened?" Georgie asked.

As Adam pushed to sitting, Hale shot up and positioned himself between the couch and the front door, like he expected him to bolt.

"He followed me," Adam said. "I told him to go back, but he wouldn't listen."

A shadow fell over her face. "Goddammit, Adam," she muttered as she shoved out of the chair. "Reese was a good person. And he cared about you." Her fingers pressed hard against her forehead.

"I know," he whispered.

"He needs to leave," Jax said.

"Kye's never going to forgive you," Georgie said. "I don't even know if she'll let you stay. Hell, I don't know if *I* want you to."

She paced the room twice, and when she stopped and studied Adam, his eyes dropped to the floor, the knot in his stomach pulling tight.

When he looked back up, her harsh expression softened slightly with understanding.

"It wasn't you."

Adam shrugged, the movement draining.

He might as well have done it himself. He'd climbed into that car, stayed silent, ignored Reese's pleading. He should've found a way to get into the other quarantine room. To put Reese out of his misery instead of letting him suffer.

Reese didn't deserve to die that way. Nobody did.

The relentless clawing in Adam's head intensified, sharpened by the fresh sting of guilt.

Make it stop.

His hand instinctively went for the spot where the bottle should have been, but he wasn't wearing his vest. He frantically searched his hoodie pockets, the ground dropping out beneath him when he remembered.

No.

They were gone. His pills were gone.

Adam's gaze jerked to the front door. He had to go back.

"I swear to god, Adam, if you go for that door..." Georgie left the threat unfinished.

He looked back at her. "I wasn't doing anything."

"You still wanna go?" Hale snapped. "Fine. Gladly. We can toss you back out into the cold. Not like you'd make it back to the city, anyway."

"Jax—" Georgie started, but Hale cut her off.

"No. We're not letting him stay here."

"I'm not kicking him out."

Hale shook his head. "I can't, for the life of me, figure out why you keep trusting him."

"Me either," Adam said through a yawn, and Georgie shot him a glare.

"Just because I don't want you dead doesn't mean I *trust* you. I'm a medic. It's my job to keep people alive."

She hates you.

You don't need her.

Georgie closed her eyes and blew out a breath, and when she opened them again, she said, "I'm going to get Oliver and then—"

"Don't," Adam interrupted. He couldn't handle that. Couldn't face him. He thought he'd be able to, but it was too much. It was all too much. The pain, the guilt, the bugs crawling around under his skin.

He needed to go back to Jardine.

Desmond was going to be so mad.

Why did he come here? It wasn't too late to fix it. He could beg for another chance. Des could resupply him. Make the pain stop.

You need him.

You need the pills.

Georgie dug through a medical kit on the table, then crossed the room, crouching so they were at the same level before holding a thermometer out to him.

He frowned. "I'm fine."

"Do you understand how close you came to dying?"

Leave.

Run.

"If I don't get my pills back, I'm gonna wish I *did*." The words spilled out before he could filter them.

For a moment, Georgie lingered, motionless in front of him, until finally, she sighed and sank onto the couch, leaving a noticeable gap between them. She exchanged a look with Hale that Adam was too tired to read.

Hale let out a frustrated huff, then stormed off into one of the bedrooms.

"I can help," she said finally.

She can't.

"You have people here who care about you."

She's lying.

"Just...promise me you'll stay."

Ugh.

Adam glanced at the front door one more time.

His clothes felt like needles against his skin and his head was throbbing. He wouldn't make it far if he left.

This was his doing. *He* threw his pills in the lake.

He was so sure about the decision at the time, but now, when he tried to remember the reason, he couldn't hear his own thoughts over the snarling in his head.

"Fine, I'll stay."

Again, not exactly a lie. He wasn't sure what he planned on doing yet. But his thoughts were clouding, and he just wanted to go back to sleep.

He lay back down, his head almost touching Georgie's legs, feet hanging over the armrest, then pulled the blanket up to his chin and closed his eyes.

"You're not alone," Georgie whispered, smoothing his hair back out of his face, the way Alice used to.

You're stronger than you think, Oliver's voice reminded him.

This was Adam's choice, and he knew it was the right one. At least, he was pretty sure it was.

Maybe he could do this. Maybe he could stay.

Sleep dragged him back under like an anchor, and when a nightmare shook him awake some time later, he was surrounded by a handful of sleeping strangers barely visible in the fading firelight.

Adam tensed, panic fizzing in his muscles, until he found Georgie's copper hair and remembered where he was.

Now, maybe it was time to find Oliver.

Hale had placed himself in a chair blocking the exit, but his head was tilted back against the door, his breathing slowed by sleep.

Adam moved silently to the other side of the cabin, but there was no back door—because of course there wasn't—so he slipped into a bedroom. With shaky hands, he pulled open the window and climbed out into the bitter cold night air.

34

Gray eyes watched expectantly as Oliver ran his thumb over the metal device in his hands.

The dart gun. *His* creation.

He wanted to slam it on the table. Break it into tiny pieces so she couldn't use it to hurt anybody else, but his hands wouldn't listen.

He knew it was a dream, knew he couldn't actually hurt anyone here, but the lack of control was still infuriating.

"I couldn't have done any of this without you," Cassira said, her red lips lifting into a gentle smile. She touched his cheek, and the warmth of her hand felt so real, he flinched back. The train station fell away.

Oliver sat up straight in the chair and wiped the drool from his cheek.

The work light was still on, the room illuminated in an awful bluish white, and one side of his soundless headphones had been pressing into his head while he slept, leaving a bruised feeling around his ear.

His gaze shifted to the window above his bed. The sky was beginning to lighten—not quite sunrise, but bright enough that when Oliver switched off the work light, he could still see clearly.

It wasn't an ideal way to begin the day, but at least he could get an early start, go grab some breakfast while he had the kitchen to himself. He tugged the headphones off and set them on the desk.

"Morning."

Startled, Oliver spun around in his chair, nearly toppling over.

Adam sat cross-legged on the floor beside the hatch, head tipped down, his wavy hair hanging over his forehead as his fingers fidgeted with the zipper on his sweatshirt.

"I tried knocking," he mumbled.

Oliver swallowed hard, every muscle urging him to jump up and close the distance, but the last time he'd tried that, Adam pushed him away. Literally and figuratively. So, instead, he slid slowly, cautiously from the chair to the rough wooden floor because it felt right to be at the same level, and sitting on the floor always made him feel steadier.

He pressed his back against the bed so there was as much space as possible between them. Oliver didn't know what to say because he'd already messed it up once, and he was so afraid that he'd make the same mistake and Adam would run again.

"I'm mad at you," Adam said, pushing his hair out of his face, but keeping his eyes on his lap, looking rumpled and lovely in the dim morning light.

"I know." Oliver pursed his lips in frustration at his own terrible response. What was he supposed to say? What would fix this? How could he make Adam understand? It made sense in his own head. The logic was sound, the reasoning solid. He sifted through the words, trying to pluck out the right ones.

Adam finally looked at him then. "Was any of it real?"

The question landed like a punch. "How can you say that?"

Adam drew up his knees and wrapped his arms around them. "You left."

"For *you*. I did it to—"

"No, don't do that," Adam interrupted, voice edged with irritation. "I don't care. I don't care what the reason was. I don't care what you *thought* you were doing or who you were doing it for. You. Left." His head shook, and his eyes narrowed. "And it was so *easy* for you, like I never gave you a reason to stay."

"It was *not* easy, Adam." His voice cracked over the words. "It was the most difficult thing I've had to do in my entire life."

"Am I supposed to feel sorry for you?"

Oliver wrenched back, surprised at the bitterness in Adam's voice. "I-I...No. I just, I'm trying to explain. I need you to understand."

Adam tugged on the elastic of his gloves. "I do understand."

"Then why can't we go back to the way things were?"

"Because you *left*, Oliver!" he shouted, throwing out his hands, voice cutting through the quiet of the sleeping house.

"I don't..." The words trailed off as Oliver tried to figure out what he was missing.

"I can't survive that fall again. I can't!"

"You won't have to."

Adam's voice lowered, barely audible now. "You told me...You *promised* you'd never leave."

"I know." Oliver curled forward, wiping the tears from his cheeks.

"And I let myself believe you."

"I'm sorry."

"For as long as I can remember, I've had to be on guard, constantly watching for threats, trying to stop anyone else from hurting me, and it's so fucking exhausting." Adam closed his eyes. "The only place I ever considered home wasn't a place at all. It was *you*. And then you left. You left and you told me you didn't want me anymore. You handed me over to them like I was your property to give away. I didn't think you were a threat, but clearly I was wrong." When his eyes opened again, they met Oliver's gaze, intense and unwavering. "So, yeah, I know why you did it. I know that your intentions were good. But how can I ever not see you as a threat when you hurt me more than anyone else ever has?"

Oliver's chest ached. "I'm sorry."

"I can't." Adam shook his head and pushed up from the floor.

"But you left, too."

Adam blinked. "What?"

"You were already gone before any of that mess with Haven."

The conversation was engraved in Oliver's mind. *What if they take you away?* he had asked, and Adam's response had cut like a knife digging straight into his heart.

I hope they do.

"You wanted out. You *told* me you wanted out."

Adam pressed his palms to his forehead. "No, that's not fair."

"I knew the wreck was coming, and I thought I could steer in a direction to minimize the damage, give you somewhere soft to land. Somewhere you could be happy, even if it wasn't with me."

Adam gave a resigned huff and dropped his hands to his sides. "So, what do we do?"

"You stay."

That was the only part that mattered. The only part Oliver was sure about. They could be together, and the rest they'd figure out as they went.

"A lot's changed," Adam said. "*I've* changed. I don't know if you're even going to want me anymore."

"That's stupid," Oliver blurted before he could remember to buffer his thoughts.

Adam crossed the room and dropped onto the bed, legs dangling beside Oliver. When he leaned forward, peeking over the edge, Oliver tipped his head up to look at him.

"All the things I've done," Adam said. "What if you hate me for them?"

"Try me," Oliver responded without hesitation. "Tell me everything you think is unforgivable and let me show you that none of it matters."

Adam's face tightened. "How can you be so sure?"

"Because you're here now. That means you don't *want* to be that person anymore."

Adam disappeared again over the edge of the mattress. "But what if I liked being that person?"

Oliver didn't know what to say, didn't know the right words to reassure him. He stood slowly, afraid that Adam might bolt back through the hatch.

To his surprise, Adam wrapped his arms around his waist, pulling him close and resting his head against his chest. "I need you to fix it."

"Fix what?" Oliver asked with a frown.

Adam pulled back, tipping his head to meet Oliver's gaze. "Me."

He smoothed back Adam's disheveled waves and gave him a ghost of a smile. "Fixing things is kind of what I do, so believe me when I say you're not something that needs to be fixed."

"We'll see if you feel the same tomorrow when I'm calling you all sorts of awful things."

Oliver frowned. "What?"

"I missed the first couple days of withdrawal last time thanks to the whole being unconscious thing, but I don't think I was very fun to be around when I woke up."

It took a moment for Oliver to work out what he was saying. "You're clean?"

Adam shrugged, expression heavy. “And this time, stupid me did it to myself.”

Before Oliver could remember that he was supposed to be careful, he hopped onto the bed, bent legs on either side of Adam, his face in his hands.

“That’s amazing!” he blurted. “I’m so proud of you!”

The startled look in Adam’s eyes caused Oliver to flinch back.

He dropped his hands and pursed his lips. “Sorry.”

But Adam only gave him a tilted smile. “Do you mind if I crash with you for a while?”

“Really?” Oliver’s heart fluttered. “You’re staying?”

Adam wrinkled his nose. “It’s, like, *really* cold outside.”

As Adam’s fingertips grazed Oliver’s cheek, he leaned into the touch.

There was still so much to figure out, so many outside factors that needed to be accounted for, so many problems still looming over them. But next time, he wouldn’t give up without a fight.

Adam cupped Oliver’s face and kissed him.

In that instant, the world around them, all those variables in Oliver’s mind, ceased to exist, and all he could focus on was kissing him back.

35

Daylight spread across the rough wooden floor of the attic, the house below already full of noise as the rest of Spring Valley prepped for the day. Despite the chores that awaited and the rumbling of his stomach, Oliver had no intention of moving from that bed. Possibly ever.

Why would he? Nothing beyond that hatch mattered more than the boy beside him.

Adam frowned in his sleep and Oliver mirrored it, studying him in the soft morning light.

What was he dreaming about?

Throughout their months together, Adam often woke in a panic from nightmares, and Oliver was always there to reassure him they weren't real, that he was safe. He hadn't been there for the past two months to chase the nightmares away, but he would be from now on.

He let his gaze slide lazily from the crease in Adam's forehead to the three freckles that dotted his cheekbone, to the tiny mole on his jawline. All the things Oliver had studied and committed to memory. And then he examined the new marks. The cut on his forehead, partially hidden by his hair, the deep bruise along his cheekbone, the lighter one around his throat.

What happened to him? Was it those people? Did they hurt him?

A protective anger rose in Oliver's chest, but he pushed it away.

Everything was going to be okay now. Adam was here with him, and he'd never let anything bad happen to him again.

Oliver smiled and pulled the blanket up further, but the second his eyes closed, Adam shot up, tearing the blanket off them both.

He blinked once, and before Oliver could ask what was wrong, Adam rushed across the room, dropped to his knees, and vomited into what he probably assumed was a garbage can.

It wasn't.

Oliver grimaced.

It was fine. He could clean those later.

"Sorry," Adam mumbled as he wiped his mouth with the back of his hand.

He wore a pair of Oliver's pajama pants and a cotton white t-shirt, his arms and hands bare—an unguarded version of him that only Oliver was ever lucky enough to see.

"It's okay." Oliver joined him on the floor as Adam dropped his face into his hands.

"I'm pretty sure I'm dying."

"You're not. You'll get through this."

"I won't. This was a mistake." He glanced up, eyes pleading. "I can start over. We can lower the dose again. Do it slowly."

"Is that what you really want?"

"Yes." Adam's brow knitted. "No." He curled forward and let out a frustrated groan. "Drowning hurt less than this."

Oliver's eyes widened. "Drowning?"

Adam breathed a laugh, but it warped into a pained sob. "Ow, I can't do this."

"Wait," Oliver said as he studied his expression, searching for some sort of hint that he was kidding. "*Drowning*?"

Adam yawned widely and scratched his arm. "I thought none of the stuff that happened there mattered."

"I-I mean..." Oliver wrapped his arms around himself, deciding it was best not to push it. At least not now. "Are you okay?"

"No, I'm *dying*, remember?"

"I'm sorry it hurts." He helped Adam to his feet, catching him as he pitched forward. "Come back to bed."

Another yawn as he dropped onto the mattress.

Oliver's eyes went to the bruises on Adam's face again. Did they let him leave willingly? Did they let him break his deal?

"Are they going to come looking for you?"

Adam hesitated. "It doesn't matter. They don't know where I am."

But Desmond knew Oliver was here. There was no doubt that he'd seen him. It was a safe assumption that they'd check here first.

"They'll be looking though?"

With a frown, Adam nodded. "He knows I'm immune. I don't think he'll ever stop looking."

Adam wasn't safe here.

Oliver couldn't protect him from this.

And the others, if Desmond showed up searching for Adam, he'd find them, too.

Adam had enough to worry about right now. Oliver couldn't tell him. Not yet. But this was too big to try to handle on his own. He needed to tell somebody.

Kye. She'd know what to do.

"I'm going to get you some water," Oliver offered.

Adam grabbed his hand. "Don't disappear on me again, okay?"

The words pierced right through Oliver.

"Never," he promised. And he meant it with every particle of his being. "But you need to stay hydrated."

"I *need* an oxy," Adam snapped back, letting his hand fall away. "Can you get me one of those while you're at it?"

Oliver pulled a blue flannel button-up over his shirt, followed by his coat, then placed BUG next to Adam. "I'll be *right* back," he said, tucking the controller in his sweatpants pocket. "Use BUG if you need me, and this"—he set an empty bin beside the bed—"if you need to be sick."

He lifted the hatch, then paused. "Please stay in bed."

Adam nodded and threw the blanket over his head.

The lingering scents of breakfast met Oliver on his way down the stairs, but the house was quiet. Everyone had already dispersed, thankfully, off to handle their daily chores.

The sun had finally made an appearance, and warm beams poured in through the windows.

Vivian would have a long list of things that needed handling, and she'd definitely be expecting Oliver.

Would she come get him if he didn't show up?

If she found out about Adam, would she make him leave? Would she tell Desmond in an effort to keep the peace? She let the others stay, but that was different. Vivian knew she could keep them hidden, and they were valuable to keep around. But Desmond already knew Adam was here. It was only a matter of time before he showed up.

Oliver couldn't tell anyone until he talked to Kye and figured out what they were going to do.

He pushed outside, eyes scanning the yard. Where was she?

He'd try the barn first.

Careful to stay out of sight, Oliver slipped away from the house. He was really bad at lying, so avoidance was the best option. If he didn't see anyone, he wouldn't have to lie.

Which might have worked if, as he slipped around the corner of the workshop, he didn't run straight into Georgie.

She let out an audible gasp as they both staggered backward. "You scared the hell out of me!"

"Sorry. I-I didn't...sorry."

She studied his face for a moment, and then her expression softened. "He's with you."

Oliver's gaze flicked involuntarily to the house as he stumbled for a reply. "He's not-I don't." He sighed, then nodded. There was no point in lying. She obviously already knew Adam was here.

"I'm just glad he didn't go back," she said. "How's he doing?"

"Miserable." Oliver knew he should tell her about Desmond. They weren't safe. But everything in him was pulling to Kye.

Georgie didn't trust him. But she trusted Kye. And so did he.

"I was going to get him some water," Oliver said.

"With your hands?"

He frowned. "What?"

She nodded to his fidgeting hands. "I think you forgot the pitcher."

He let out a nervous laugh. "Oh. Right."

"I need to go check on him," Georgie said. "He still wasn't back to a healthy temperature when I fell asleep. The withdrawal won't kill him, but if he keeps wandering off in the cold, hypothermia *will.*"

"Y-yeah. Go ahead. I'll be up in a bit."

He waited until she disappeared into the farmhouse before he turned and headed to the barn.

36

The hatch closed, and Adam waited for approximately ten seconds before he flung the blankets off and rolled out of bed. He expected his legs to catch him, but they didn't, and he crashed to the floor with a thud.

Real smooth.

He didn't want to leave. He was finally sure of that.

The fear of upsetting Desmond lingered, a constant, unsettling presence at the edge of his thoughts, but he didn't actually want to go back, not when Oliver was his other option.

Adam wanted to stay right here, hiding out and sharing body heat in this bed until spring came and thawed everything.

But he couldn't. Not like this.

He needed something to help with the horrifying pain that had settled in his skin. His bones. His head. Something to dial back the animalistic hunger that gnawed at his insides.

One last high to give him the boost of strength he needed to actually go through with this. That was all. He hadn't allowed himself time to prepare.

Just one quick fix, a hard reset, and then he'd give it a real shot.

There had to be something in this house.

Adam grabbed the bedframe and tried to pry himself off the floor, but his hands were shaking and his head was spinning and why couldn't he stop yawning?

Had the last time hurt like this? He didn't think so.

You're going to die.

Can't you feel it?

He would do anything for that moment of nothingness, just one more time. This was all too much.

Too much shaking.

Too much pain.

Too much thinking.

Make it stop.

Finally, Adam made it to his feet. He clumsily pulled on his gloves, then his hoodie, zipping it to his chin, then tugged open the hatch and watched the ladder slowly stretch down to the floor.

Why were his hand shaking so much? They definitely didn't do that last time. Did they?

Gripping the railing as tight as he could manage, Adam climbed carefully down to the second floor and scanned his surroundings.

Three doors.

He pushed open the first—a large bedroom—and went straight for the dresser, searching each drawer, pushing aside the contents.

Nothing.

The second door led to more of the same.

When he opened the third, he found a bathroom with a white tile floor and ugly floral wallpaper that didn't help with the nausea. There was one small window, and—*there we go.* A medicine cabinet above the sink. A quick check of the hallway, then he slipped inside and locked the door behind him.

He lifted a trembling hand to the mirrored door of the cabinet, fingers grazing the smooth surface before pulling it open.

No prescription bottles.

Not even cold medicine or over-the-counter painkillers.

Adam slid to the ground as his strength ebbed, every one of his muscles aching.

Pathetic.

Oliver would be back soon. He was running out of time. But when he tried to pull himself up, his body refused.

Find something to make it stop.

"I'm trying!" Adam curled forward, hugging his knees. He should've stayed at Jardine.

Why did he choose this? Why did he leave? He could be blissfully numb right now.

No, how could he think that?

His stomach churned, the nausea intensifying. Adam scrambled forward, retching into the toilet, but despite his body's efforts, there was nothing left to expel.

Yeah, he was definitely dying. Which was unfortunate. He'd finally found Oliver, and now he was going to die alone on a bathroom floor. He really thought his death would be more interesting.

A soft knock tapped at the bathroom door.

"Go away," he croaked, his voice echoing in the empty room as he curled up on the cold tile floor.

"Open the door, Adam." Georgie's voice.

"No."

"Then I'll wait out here."

Adam groaned in frustration. "Why won't you leave me alone?"

"Because I'm worried about you."

"Why?"

"What do you mean, *why*?"

"I mean, why do you even care? You should be mad. You should hate me."

"Oh, believe me, I'm plenty mad."

"Then go away. Run off to your new Haven and let me die in peace."

"I'm mad, but I don't hate you."

Adam rolled onto his back, staring up at the ceiling. "You should."

"Yeah, maybe. But I know despite everything, you're a good person, and you're worth the effort."

He thought of Reese's terrified face in the back of Leon's car. Imagined him alone in the quarantine room, mushrooms growing from his face as he writhed in pain.

"You obviously don't know me at all," he said. "I'm not a good person."

"I know that you came back for me that first day. At the school. You didn't know me at all, but you risked your ass to save me."

That didn't make him good. That made him stupid and cocky.

"And I know that you've been dealt shitty hand after shitty hand, but you're still here trying to be better."

The words lodged in his chest, a slow, spreading ache.

"Is that why I'm digging through a stranger's bathroom for pills?"

"Your addiction doesn't define you, Adam. Struggling doesn't make you a bad person."

Adam sat up, the simple movement painful and draining. "What if I think it was a mistake to come here? Does *that* make me a bad person?"

"You want to go back?"

He didn't. Not really. "I just want this to stop. It's too much. I miss the numbness."

After a long pause, she said, "My anesthetic of choice was vodka. Parties, loud music, anything to drown out the anxiety and the doubt and the depression. But I lost someone I cared about to that, and I refuse to lose another one to this. So I need you to open the door." When he didn't respond, desperation seeped into her tone. "Please. Let me in."

He groaned, then dragged himself to the door, reaching up to turn the lock, and as he scooted back, the door yawned open. He didn't look up, but he could feel her eyes on him.

She shut the door and sank to the floor beside him, handing him a thermometer.

"I'm fine."

"Shut up. I'm not asking."

He gave her a tilted smile, then put the thermometer tip under his tongue. Quiet settled over them as they waited, broken only when the thermometer beeped.

"Almost back to normal," she said when he handed it back, and he couldn't help but laugh because there was nothing normal about any of this.

"What was their name?" Adam asked. "Your friend."

Georgie hesitated before answering. "Her name was Mabel."

"Tell me about her." When she shook her head, he added, "I'm dying. Distract me."

She scooted against the bathtub and stretched her legs out straight, and he did the same.

"She was brave," Georgie said, her voice quiet. "Outgoing. A little wild. She had this way about her...I can't really explain it. But she always pushed me to get out of my safe little bubble."

"She sounds pretty great."

"I was in love with her." Georgie tilted her head back. "And I get so mad at the universe for taking her from me. For taking *everyone* from me."

Adam pressed his lips together. It always bothered him when people responded to someone else's tragedy with *I'm sorry*. It felt empty and meaningless, and was a useless thing to say, so he didn't. He simply nodded because he really did understand.

She sat forward and turned to look at him. "I can't lose anyone else. Okay? I *can't*. So I'm going to do whatever it takes to prevent that, even if I *am* still so fucking mad at you."

Adam's stomach twisted.

Why did he come here? He put them all in danger. Put Oliver in danger.

Selfish.

"He's going to come looking for me," Adam said.

Tension flickered across Georgie's face. "You're not allowed to leave?"

"I thought I was." Adam pulled his legs up and pressed his forehead to his knees. "But he knows about..." the sentence dissolved on his tongue. He hated saying it out loud, this thing that he had no say in, that made him valuable. "He knows I'm immune. He's going to drag me back."

Her eyes drifted as she thought. "Vivian's letting us hide out in the cabin. You can stay there. You didn't tell him where you were going, right? So he doesn't know you're here."

It didn't matter.

Desmond knew Adam found Reese at Spring Valley. It would probably be the first place he'd check.

"I think he knows."

When Georgie didn't respond, Adam lifted his head to look at her. A crease had formed in her forehead.

"I'll let him have the plant," she said finally, her voice stretched and strained, like the idea was painful. "Vivian can say Reese left it here or something. He can make his vaccine from that, and maybe it'll buy you some time."

"The vaccine doesn't work," Adam said, remembering Leon's cough, the film over his eyes. "The plant's useless."

The color drained from Georgie's face, and for a moment, Adam thought she might be sick, which sent a fresh wave of nausea through him. He swallowed it down.

"How do you know?" she asked. "Are you sure?"

"I watched someone who was vaccinated die from the infection." Adam straightened his legs and pulled at the elastic of his gloves. "Well, technically, I slit his throat, but he was definitely sick before that."

"It still doesn't affect you?"

"Apparently not."

"And Desmond knows this?"

Adam nodded. "Which is why I know he'll come find me. You guys have to go before he shows up here."

"We're not leaving."

"You *have* to." He had to make her understand how bad it would be if Desmond found them. "Reese was infected," Adam said, fixing his gaze on the door. "Desmond's so bitter about him taking the plant, he put him in a room to let him die slowly instead of just killing him. If he finds you..." Adam shook his head. "I don't want that to happen to you."

"Reese is still alive?" she asked.

"No. Well, yes, but he's days into the infection."

After a long silence, Georgie said, "We can stop him. I know we can. He's untouchable when he's at Jardine, but here, we have the advantage."

Adam gave a dismissive snort. "Believe me, you don't have the advantage."

"I was trying to figure out a way to draw him out," she went on, her words spilling out, edging toward manic. "This isn't ideal, but it'll do the trick. He still doesn't know we're here. He'll only be expecting *you*. We can do this. We can kill him."

That was probably meant to be comforting, but Adam's skull was splintering and everything hurt, and he was too mad at the world to pretend.

"You're joking, right?" he blurted. "I thought you were reckless, but maybe you're actually suicidal."

Georgie scowled. "Thanks. That's helpful."

Ugh. "I don't know what you expect me to say. That I'll help?" He pushed shakily to his feet, and she followed. "Because I won't. You have somewhere to go. Why stick around and pick a fight?"

"We don't," she snapped. "Indiana decided we weren't worth the risk. They won't let us in."

Adam tensed, frowning.

Was Desmond right? Did they blame the strays for the convoy attack? If so, Adam was partially to blame for them having nowhere to go.

"This is the only place we've got," Georgie continued. "So yeah, I'm going to fight for it. And I thought you might want to, too."

She needs you for this.

You have leverage. Use it.

He smoothed his expression and took a deep breath. "Okay, I'll help."

She gave him a wary look.

"But I need something to level me out first. I need a clear head."

"Dr. Ramirez is here," Georgie said. "He can set up the room they've been using for an infirmary. He knows better than me how to help you through this."

There was an infirmary. Which meant there was a medical supply. Where? He needed to find it, but he wasn't going anywhere near the doc. Not after the way he'd *helped* last time.

"That's not what I meant."

"I know it's not," Georgie said, her tone heavy. "But I won't help you kill yourself."

Adam's eyes narrowed into a glare. "Only because you need me as bait."

She breathed a humorless laugh. "If you don't want to help, fine. We'll manage without you. I was already working on another plan before you showed up."

He pulled open the door. "Yeah, because your plans always work out so well."

Instead of the anger he was hoping to provoke, he was met with a look of pity that made the voice growl.

"Either way," Georgie said, softening, "Desmond is going to show up. Stay hidden until we can figure this out. I'll check back in later."

She slid past him and headed down the hall, disappearing down the stairs.

He waited, listening as the front door opened and then closed. The house was silent again.

Find it.

Adam rushed through the rest of the house, searching through drawers and cabinets, but even the room he guessed was the infirmary was nearly empty. The weak desperation twisted into a violent need.

No, they had to have something. He must have missed it.

He staggered back into the upstairs bathroom and pulled open the medicine cabinet, frantically knocking aside a bottle of lotion, a tube of toothpaste, tweezers, sunscreen, letting them fall into the sink.

When the cabinet was empty, he slammed it shut, leaving his palm flat against the mirrored door.

A deep ache echoed through his muscles.

You deserve it.

You destroyed everything.

"Shut up," Adam growled, matching the voice's anger. "Shut up!" He slammed his hand hard against the glass, splintering it beneath his palm, and a fresh wave of pain, sharper than the constant agony of the withdrawal, sliced through him.

A deep cut split open his palm. Thick red drops painted the porcelain sink and everything piled in it.

That was stupid.

What was he *doing*?

Oliver would be back soon. How was he supposed to explain this mess?

Adam grabbed a hand towel and pressed it to the cut as he tried to concoct a lie, but his head was too fuzzy.

He ruined it. Ruined everything. And it had taken less than a half a day. He needed to leave. Needed to get out of here.

He needed to go back to Jardine. To make all this go away.

Adam pulled open the bathroom door, freezing in place when he saw Oliver at the ladder to his room. For a moment, he thought about running, but then Oliver turned toward him, a worried frown creasing his face.

"Hey, I was just coming to find you," Adam lied, pulling the smile into place.

Oliver's eyes dropped to the bloody towel wrapped around Adam's hand. "Are you okay?"

"Always."

"What happened?"

"It's nothing."

Leave.

Run.

But when Oliver asked if he was ready to go back up, Adam pushed the voice away and nodded.

37

Georgie hovered on the front porch, trying to collect herself. It was too much all at once, and she could feel herself slipping.

The plant was useless. The vaccine didn't work.

The sick man in that house—if Oliver hadn't kept him back, they both would've been infected. The fungus wasn't just spreading again. It was completely mobile. And her and Jax weren't protected against it.

But none of that even mattered because they wouldn't last the week. Desmond knew where they were.

He killed Reese—no worse, he locked him away to let him suffer slowly—all over a plant that was no longer viable. What would he do when he found *them*?

Georgie lowered herself onto the top step and closed her eyes.

She knew they'd have to face Desmond eventually, but she thought they'd have time. What chance did they have? He wiped out an entire Haven. Adam clearly wasn't interested in helping. She doubted anyone at Spring Valley would choose them over their safety arrangement.

"Georgie?"

Her heart leaped into her throat as her eyes popped open. Kye and Oliver stood at the bottom of the porch steps, their faces etched with concern.

"What happened?" Kye asked.

Georgie shook her head. "I can't keep..." She swallowed back the sick feeling. "I can't do this."

"Oliver," Kye said softly. "Go check on Adam."

Oliver gave a nervous nod, then slipped past Georgie. The front door closed, and Kye sat on the step beside her.

"We'll figure this out," Kye assured her, and somehow, her voice was steady and sure.

"Reese is gone," Georgie whispered. She considered telling her the full truth, but it seemed kinder to leave it at that. "I'm so sorry, Kye. I was supposed to keep them all safe."

Kye's face darkened, her eyes fixed ahead, and a long silence hung in the air before she finally spoke. "You can't blame yourself, Georgie. Not for any of it."

"How can I not? Everything I touch turns to shit."

"I couldn't save the Campus," Kye said quietly. "They trusted me to have answers, but I didn't. All of this...it's not on us. You know that, right? It's *him*."

Georgie clenched her fists. Of course, Kye was right, but she was so sick of trying so hard only to have everything crumble in her hands.

"So, what's the plan?" Kye asked.

Georgie frowned.

"You plan on staying here," Kye went on, "so I'm guessing you've been working on a way to deal with Desmond's people. Whatever it is, I want in."

"Vivian won't like us messing with her protection."

Kye stood. "Then let's show her that we don't need it."

"You think Adam's right?" Jax asked. "You think Emery knows he's here?"

Georgie nodded.

"He saw Oliver," Kye added. "He definitely knows."

Jax was halfway through his perimeter check when Georgie and Kye had caught up with him, and as they walked, his gaze swept the trees.

"Then we need to go."

Georgie threw out her hands. "Go where, Jax?"

"Anywhere but here."

"And what about Adam? What about Spring Valley?"

"Spring Valley's under Emery's protection. They're fine."

Kye shook her head. "He doesn't give a shit about anyone here. If he thinks they're hiding something, he'll tear the place apart."

"Even more reason to be gone before he shows up. We have to keep the plant away from him."

Georgie hesitated. She had to tell them, as much as she was dreading it. "The vaccine doesn't work against the mutated infection. The plant's useless."

Jax slammed to a stop, the oppressive silence of the forest pressing down as her words hung in the air.

"But at Haven," Jax said finally. "Your house. If the vaccine doesn't work, why aren't we dead?"

She thought about the glow of the rooms and the stalks in the corners. The freezer.

"Those were frozen samples from the lab released by the explosion. They wouldn't have had time to mutate."

"Emery knows about the plant?"

"He does," Georgie said. "And he knows about Adam."

Jax's eyes scanned the trees again.

"We need to figure out what we're going to do when he shows up," Georgie said. "We need a plan."

"The people here," Kye added, "they're not all as happy with this deal as Vivian. The supplies are going too fast, and he keeps increasing the payment amount. I know they'd be willing to fight with us."

"We can't *fight* them," Jax snapped.

"Maybe not all of them head-on," Georgie said. "But if we plan this right, we can take out Desmond. Deal with the few he'll bring with."

"What about the others?" Jax asked. "What if they retaliate?"

"They'll be too busy trying to figure out who's going to take over," Georgie said. "And how they're going to continue their protection agreements without him. It'll at least buy us time to fortify this place."

"I have contacts at some of the communities around here," Kye said. "I doubt they're happy being forced to give away their supplies. Maybe they'll fight with us."

Jax scoffed. "These people took out a Haven. We can't fight them."

"*Desmond* took out a Haven," Georgie corrected him. "*He's* what makes them dangerous."

"No, their *guns* are what make them dangerous."

"They depend on the communities for their resources," Georgie said. "Without them, everyone at Jardine starves. If we get the communities to side with us, then maybe we can broker a truce."

Jax's frown softened. "Reverse the hostage situation."

"Exactly. They may have the weapons, but they need these communities."

After a beat, Jax nodded. "Okay. So, how do we take down Emery?"

"Adam's not willing to help," Georgie said, "but his sniper rifle is at the farmhouse. When they show up, we'll need someone to use it."

"Banks is a decent shot," Jax said.

"Talk to him. See if he's willing." Georgie folded her arms as she thought. "Kye, figure out how many weapons are stocked away. Anyone with any experience needs to be ready to fight. I don't want to have to shoot anyone but Desmond, but if the ones he brings with him don't surrender, we need to be ready to put them down quickly."

"A few of mine have training with guns," Kye said.

"Good. We should also set up a lookout point outside the entrance, maybe in one of the nearby houses with a clear vantage point. We need to know the moment they see movement. And plan a route through the forest. When our lookout signals, Wren will take Ciri and the other kids and get them out."

"Okay," Kye said. "I'll update Oliver, too. He wants to help."

Georgie nodded, a flicker of hope igniting in her chest. "We can do this." They had to. There were no other options. "When he shows up, we'll be ready."

38

Oliver felt better after they relocated to one of the bedrooms in the cabin. Being surrounded by woods felt safer than staying at the farmhouse. Having a soldier standing guard helped, too.

Dr. Ramirez swung by to stitch up the cut in Adam's hand, and Kye brought them all some lunch, which Adam refused to eat.

The next few hours crawled by, with Adam managing only ten to fifteen minutes of sleep at a time before waking in a frenzy. But, despite the fatigue and pain evident on his face, he seemed to be coping surprisingly well. He was acting like his usual self, and Oliver was beginning to think they'd made it through the worst of it.

Around mid-afternoon, however, his entire demeanor shifted.

Oliver was about to go check in with the others to see how the planning was going when Adam woke up sobbing. His face was pale, his hair stuck to the sweat on his forehead. The frailness of him was terrifying. Oliver hurried to his side and sat on the edge of the bed, but when he tried to take his hand, Adam snapped it away.

"Don't touch me," he spat, his amber eyes burning.

"I-I'm sorry."

"Oh, are you?" Adam asked, the question dripping with disdain. "You're *sorry*?"

"Yes," Oliver whispered, fingers fidgeting nervously with his shirt hem.

Adam narrowed his eyes. "Can I ask you something?"

"Anything."

"You love me, right?"

Oliver frowned. "Of course I do."

"Then why are you letting me suffer? If you love me, why don't you want to make it better? I need your help, and you're ignoring me."

Don't do that, Oliver pleaded inwardly. Seeing Adam in pain was tearing him apart, and a part of him wanted to give in, to do anything to make him stop hurting.

When Oliver spoke, he kept his gaze locked on the floor, afraid that if he looked at Adam, he might lose his resolve. "Of course I love you, and I'm not forcing you to do anything. You were brave enough and strong enough to make this decision on your own. *You* chose this. Please try to remember why."

Adam huffed and climbed shakily out of bed. "I'm going for a walk."

"I'll come with you."

"No," he snapped, scooping his coat off the floor.

What was Oliver supposed to say? He couldn't let Adam leave, not with the possibility of Desmond showing up at any minute, but he also knew he couldn't stop him. "I'm just trying to help you. I'm worried about you."

Adam spun on him, seething. "You don't get to worry about me. You lost that right. I'm going to find *something* to make this stop, since *you* won't."

"Can we just talk for a minute?"

Adam let out a derisive snort. "You want to talk? Fine." He dropped back onto the bed, hands folded in his lap. "Let's talk about how you sold me out to a Haven."

Oliver shrank back.

When Adam was happy, he shined so brightly that he illuminated the room. So it was no surprise that he drained all the light when his mood darkened.

"No?" Adam pressed, bitterness lacing the word. "Not that? Fine. How about how you handed Hale over to the Shinies? Do you want to talk about that? He almost killed you for that. Remember? He hates you *so* much that he was actually going to shoot you." Adam shook his head, nose wrinkling in disgust. "It takes a special kind of awful to get golden boy to snap like that."

Oliver's eyes filled with tears, ready to spill over. "Why are you being so mean?"

"Because I'm a terrible person." Adam pressed his palms against his eyelids. "God, I hate this. I hate the voice that won't shut up. I hate that part of me wants to go crawling back, begging Desmond to forgive me. I hate *myself*. And right about now, I'm really regretting chickening out. I should've stayed in that lake."

"Adam..."

"No," he snarled, hands clenching into fists as they dropped back into his lap. "I might hate myself, but I hate *you*, too."

The words knocked the air from Oliver's lungs. He wrenched back, and, unsure what else to do, he sank onto the floor, back against the bed.

Oliver wanted out of that room, that house. He wanted to disappear because it was safer to be invisible, but he forced himself to stay because he told Adam he would, and he wasn't about to break that promise again.

A long time passed before he could breathe again. He wiped the tears from his cheeks and pulled in just enough air to speak. "You *hate* me?"

Adam sat on the floor beside him and crossed his legs. "I don't know why I said that," he whispered, zipping and unzipping his hoodie. "That was awful. I'm so sorry."

"It's okay."

"No, it's *not*." He let out a groan, his face drawn tight. "I don't hate you. It's just...this is so hard."

"And yet, you're doing it," Oliver said softly. "You're going to make it through this."

"How do you know?"

"Because you're the most incredible person I've ever met."

Adam rested his head on Oliver's shoulder, and they stayed like that, listening to the quiet sounds of the others moving around the living room. The cabin had been quiet all day while they were busy with chores. Georgie had volunteered to take over his today to keep Vivian from asking questions, and now that they were back, he was eager to hear if they'd made any progress with the plan.

"Come on," Oliver said, finally peeling himself off the floor. "The bed's a lot warmer."

"You know I didn't mean it, right?" Adam asked as he crawled under the blankets.

"I know, but it's alright. You can yell at me if it helps." Oliver sat on the very edge of the bed, hesitant to get too close. "You have every right to be upset. I've been a burden since we met, and it's not fair to you."

Adam's eyes met Oliver's as he reached out and took his hand. "I'm sorry if I ever made you feel like a burden. I promise I'll spend the rest of my life making sure you never feel that way again."

Oliver's cheeks warmed.

Adam slid to the opposite side of the bed. "Can you lay with me?"

"Of course," Oliver replied with a smile. He crawled in beside Adam, arm wrapped tightly around him.

After another ten minutes of writhing in pain, Adam finally fell asleep, and Oliver ducked out into the living room to catch up on what he missed.

39

The mattress was made of needles, rising over Adam's sweat-drenched skin like ice water as the voice snarled in his head.

This was worse than dying.

At least dying had an end. This seemed like it would go on forever.

40

The new day brought fresh agony, accompanied by haunting dreams of shadowy hands reaching up from dark water, clawing and dragging Adam back under, pulling him down until the surface vanished into nothingness.

Endless.

41

Adam finally slept.

Not bursts of ten minutes at a time, but a full five glorious hours.

Five hours of dreamless, uninterrupted rest.

When he woke beside Oliver, head lolled against his side, the ache in his bones and the nausea woke with him.

But he smiled despite everything, because somehow he was still alive.

The peace didn't last, and nightmares still dragged him back under, but the water's surface was finally within sight.

"I've never left Illinois, I'm allergic to shellfish, and I didn't learn English until I was in kindergarten."

Adam lay stretched out on the dock with his head nestled in Oliver's lap, watching as his lips pursed to the side, the way they always did when he was trying to figure something out.

"The third one has to be the lie," Oliver said finally, the sun bringing out a dozen different shades of brown in his dark hair as he looked down, searching for confirmation.

Adam's mouth tilted, and he shook his head. "Not the lie."

"No way," Georgie said with a smile. "What did you speak before that?"

"Ukrainian."

"Can you still speak it?" Oliver asked, eyes wide.

Adam laughed—it felt good to laugh. "*Trokhy*," he said. "A little. It's been a long time."

He hadn't thought of his parents in a while, and when he tried to picture their faces, he realized he couldn't.

They didn't deserve to be forgotten.

His parents were good people, or at least they *wanted* to be. They would have been, had life turned out differently for them. They just got lost in their addictions.

Something he understood pretty well.

"Okay," Georgie said, pressing a finger to her lips as she studied him. "The shellfish one. That's the lie."

Adam nodded, a little too fast, and the queasiness returned with a vengeance.

"So, you've really never left the state?"

"Never."

He took a slow breath, savoring the feeling of crisp air in his lungs and the warmth of the sun on his face. The air wasn't bitterly cold today, and the sky was a vivid blue that hurt his eyes. Adam hated being bundled up in layers—hated the lack of mobility—but the fresh air was worth it.

The company, too.

It was strange, the two different worlds he'd lived in over the past couple months, and for a second he wished they could overlap, just a little, because he missed Eris and Colette.

Then he remembered Eris wanted Georgie dead and had almost killed Hale. Probably best to keep those worlds separate.

Would he ever get to see them again?

He looked back up at Oliver, who met him with a bright smile that made his heart ache. He'd been trying so hard to keep Adam's mind off everything. To help bring him slowly back to life.

They both had.

If Georgie was still mad at him, she'd put it aside for the time being. She checked in twice yesterday, bringing playing cards and Tylenol, and the walk today had been her idea.

This calm, as much as he wanted to bask in it, wasn't real. It was carefully crafted for his sake. A fragile layer masking something darker beneath the surface. Georgie and Oliver tried to conceal their scheming, but Oliver's frequent, random absences and Georgie's inability to keep her emotions from her face gave them away.

But the thought of bringing it up, of shattering this, was too much, so he pretended not to notice.

"Your turn," Adam told Georgie as he readjusted his position, his bones still achy and his muscles sore. The ground was still hidden beneath a thick layer of snow, but the sun had cleared the dock, leaving the wood cold and damp beneath him.

"Okay, let's see." Her lips pressed flat as she thought, gaze drifting out over the water. "I shaved my head once, I can't swim, and I spent a weekend sharing a room with a monkey."

Adam burst out laughing. "A monkey?"

She shrugged, holding back a smile.

"That's ridiculous," Oliver said with a frown. "That has to be the lie."

"Not the lie."

"Okay," Adam said. "We're going to need more on that."

"My aunt had this awful little spider monkey named Dexter," she explained. "Horrible little thing. God, he was so loud. And mean! We visited once for her wedding, and I had to sleep in the room with the bastard all fucking weekend. Thank god he had a cage, or I think he would've killed me in my sleep."

Adam snorted. "Why did she have a monkey?"

"I don't know." Georgie threw up her hands. "For its pleasant company, I guess."

"So," Oliver said, "swimming, then. That's the lie."

"Nope, not a lie. I really can't swim. Never learned."

"I can teach you," Adam said excitedly. "This is a great spot for it."

Georgie offered him a sad smile. "Maybe someday."

A prickle of unease at her words—a warning from the back of his mind, instinct telling him that they couldn't stay.

Adam tried to shove it aside.

He wanted to keep pretending.

"I guess it's my turn, then," Oliver muttered. His eyes drifted to the side. "I, uh...oh, okay, I got it." He straightened, readying himself. "I was in a bad car accident when I was little and still have the scar from it, I started my bedroom on fire once, and I..." He frowned. "Um, I...I don't know. I'm sorry, I'm really bad at lying."

Georgie and Adam laughed, and Oliver's face went red.

"Sorry, I ruined the game."

Adam reached up and touched his cheek. "You didn't. Where's the scar?"

Oliver pushed back his hair, revealing a thin line right along his hairline that Adam had never noticed. "I had a whole bunch of stitches, though I don't actually remember any of it. I was too little." He let his hair fall back over his face.

They settled into a peaceful silence as a puffy cloud drifted in front of the sun, turning the air cold.

Adam wished they could stay like that forever. He wanted to believe it could last, but he knew better.

His feet were leaving the ground again. The fall was inevitable. And this time, Oliver and Georgie were going to plummet with him.

He couldn't just close his eyes and let that happen.

They were all painfully aware that Desmond knew he was here, and they were wasting time, playing pretend to make him feel better, and it wasn't fair to anybody.

"Banks should be back from his perimeter check soon," Georgie said as she stood. "I should probably take a turn."

"What are you planning?" Adam asked, sitting up. "Why are you guys still here? You should've run days ago. So what if Indiana won't let you in? There are other places you could go."

Georgie and Oliver shared a look before she said, "We're not leaving."

"You have to."

"If we leave," Georgie said, tucking her hands in her pockets, "do you honestly think he'd let us get far? He knows you're here, and he wouldn't take the chance of you disappearing. Yet he still hasn't come to take you back. The fact that he's taking his time tells me he's watching somehow to make sure you don't leave. We go out there, he'll notice."

Adam thought of Colette and the feeds. There couldn't be any inside Spring Valley or Desmond would've zeroed in on the strays right away. But Georgie was right. There were traffic cams. He'd have Colette watching the area. Maybe even have someone planted close by.

They were trapped. Adam was still a prisoner.

"I want to help," he said.

For a short time, Desmond had felt like family, and Adam really didn't want to be the one to pull the trigger. He wasn't sure he *could.* But he could still help somehow. He had to keep Oliver and Georgie safe, because they were what mattered. They were home.

Georgie's expression flickered through several emotions before she offered Adam a hand to help him up.

"Come on. We have a lot to fill you in on."

Before he even made it to his feet, he was already regretting the decision.

Fake or not, he missed the calm.

42

Georgie stood in the middle of the cabin's living room, biting the inside of her cheek as she watched the others.

Banks and Levi sat on the couch, and Jax stood watch by the window. Wren was settled on the floor by the fireplace beside Ciri, who was absorbed in her coloring book.

Kye had an unusual quietness about her as she lingered at the edge of the room, her face heavy and her thoughts somewhere else.

Having her on board had already proven invaluable. She'd picked out the ones who were interested in helping and added the people with weapon experience to the rotating shifts patrolling the perimeter.

She'd also been working on bringing Vivian around, getting her to understand why this was necessary.

Oliver and Adam were both seated in kitchen chairs, Oliver rocking back and forth, hands fidgeting with BUG as Adam tapped his fingers against the table.

Georgie sank into the chair next to Adam, waiting for him to say something—anything. She had briefed him on their plan, but his expression was still unreadable.

Almost three days had gone by since Adam showed up half-dead, and he was finally starting to look a bit better. Dark circles still hung beneath his eyes, and the vibrancy he once carried remained buried under the weight of everything he was going through. But at least now, he no longer seemed to be struggling just to stay upright.

"You're really depending on one of *you* making that shot?" Adam asked, finally breaking the silence.

She folded her arms on the table, trying to look surer than she actually felt. "Desmond won't be expecting a fight, so Banks will have time to line it up."

Adam's gaze cut to Banks. "Have you actually used a sniper rifle before?"

"I've been practicing," Banks responded.

Adam gaped at him. "With *my* gun?" He blinked, then waved the question away before turning back to Georgie. "Okay, say that works. You luck out, the shot lands. Then what? He'll have at least four others with him."

She shrugged. "Then we offer the others a chance to surrender."

Adam's face fell. "Surrender."

"Yeah."

"They won't."

"Then we'll shoot them, too."

"With my sniper rifle and what, two days of practice?" The condescension in his voice made Georgie bristle.

"No. We have others ready to fight. Jax and I, we'll have our pistols."

"I'm working on something," Oliver added. "A failsafe, just in case, using fuel from the shed."

Georgie winced. Why didn't she know about this? "We're not burning people alive."

"It's a better idea than facing off against them," Jax pointed out.

"It's horrible!"

"We won't use it," Oliver said quietly, "unless everything else goes wrong."

They all fell silent, the weight of the statement lingering in the air.

There was a chance everything would go wrong. Of course there was. It wouldn't be the first time, either. When had any of their plans actually worked out?

"If we want the element of surprise," Levi interjected, sitting forward, "why don't we send some of us inside Jardine? Go through the night and catch them totally off guard."

"No way," Adam said with a quick head shake. "They have cameras. Every single person inside will know you're there before you even make it to the gate."

"You made it out without being seen, right?"

"Because I know where those cameras are." Adam snapped his mouth shut, clearly regretting the words.

Jax and Banks exchanged a look.

"I'm not going back there."

"You could draw us a map," Levi pushed.

"Nobody is going inside Jardine," Georgie said. "We have a plan. We're sticking to it."

"This is ridiculous," Jax snapped, pushing away from the wall and crossing to the table. "We could have a fucking army on our side. We have leverage to get Indiana's help now. Something they'd definitely fight for. Why aren't we using it?"

"What leverage?"

Jax's gaze shifted downward, landing pointedly on Adam.

"No," Georgie said without hesitation.

From beneath heavy eyelids, Adam shot him a warning glare. "And then what?" he asked. "They drag me back to their Haven?"

"They'd give you a safe place to live," Jax pressed. "And you can help them save the world."

Adam scoffed. "I don't owe the world a damn thing. Let it burn. Serves it right."

"You're being fucking selfish," Jax growled.

"Yeah, I don't care. I'm not going to a Haven."

"Jax," Georgie warned.

He composed himself with a deep breath before facing her. "All right, what if we don't *actually* hand him over? We can lie. Tell them he's at Jardine. They'll go in and clear the place out looking for him."

Georgie shook her head. "We're not bringing him into this." As far as Indiana knew, Adam was gone, miles away, and there was no reason to change that.

"He's already in this, Georgie."

Adam tilted his head. "Stop talking about me like I'm not right here."

"We can't do this alone," Jax said, ignoring him. "We're going to end up dead. All the people here, they're in danger because of us. If we get Indiana to help, we can end this now. No more waiting, no more plotting. Think about it. Why take out one person when we could eliminate all of them?"

Georgie frowned, surprised at how nonchalantly he talked about killing so many people.

She knew he was right. Indiana would go after Jardine if they thought Adam was inside. Desmond's people would fight back, and maybe Indiana would be able to clear the place.

They could stay at Spring Valley. Have the peace that she'd been so desperate for.

But how many were inside Jardine? Had they all been part of the attack? Did they all deserve to die?

She hated how much she wanted to cave. Hated how badly she wanted to go along with Jax's plan because his way sounded much easier, and she was so damn tired.

But she would have to live with that on her conscience forever.

"Desmond is the one I want dead," Georgie said. "He's the one with a vendetta against the Havens. I don't know how many people are at Jardine, how many are actually fighters. If we send Indiana to kill everyone, we're no better than him." She would not let herself be like him.

"Emery wasn't the only one at Haven," Jax said. "Those people chose his side. They're all responsible."

"It's not that simple," Adam said, resting his head in his hand, looking suddenly drained. "There are people at Jardine who had nothing to do with that. People who manage comms or keep the power running—people who've never hurt *anyone*."

Jax tipped his head back, patience running visibly thin.

"I know it's terrifying," Georgie said, knee bouncing nervously beneath the table. "But we can do this. We have the people here behind us."

Adam sighed. "And you have someone who can actually make that shot."

"You'll do it?" Georgie asked, straightening.

"I'm not exactly at my best, so don't count on me for the others."

A quick flicker of a smile crossed her face. "It's settled then. Now we just have to wait for him to show up."

"He's making a point by taking his time," Adam said. "Playing with us. But he'll get bored of the game soon enough."

43

"How did you spend the last New Year's before shit hit the fan?"

With her head propped up in her hand, Georgie traced her finger across Jax's chest, trying to remember.

"At home, alone," she answered.

Jax studied her with the edge of a frown. "You lived downtown. Weren't there parties everywhere?"

"I don't like parties."

The frown softened into a gentle smile.

"I had an incredible view of the fireworks from our balcony, though. I sat out there with a blanket and a glass of champagne. How about you?"

He sat up, scooting back against the headboard, and put his arm out so she could curl up against him. "My friends and I, we parked our trucks on a road in the middle of nowhere, drank beer, and set off our own."

Georgie shook her head. "Beer and fireworks seem like a terrible mixture."

"Yeah, well, we were stupid with nothing to lose." He kissed the top of her head.

She begrudgingly checked her watch. Their break was over.

"It's my turn at the watch point." She grabbed her shirt and pulled it on, then went to climb over Jax, but he grabbed her waist, stopping her as she straddled him.

"You can't be a little late?" he asked with a playful smile.

"This was already a risk. We're supposed to stay ready." She leaned in and kissed him deeply, weaving her fingers through his hair. "It'll be over soon," she whispered against his lips. "Then we'll be able to spend as long as we want in this bed."

After they were dressed, they slipped out of the cabin into the bitter cold air. The sun was already sinking, and the temperature seemed to be following suit.

"Where are you headed?" she asked.

"Oliver's finishing up his failsafe," Jax answered, and Georgie cringed. "I'll see if he needs any help."

"Okay, I'll see you at dinner."

He pressed his lips to hers one more time, and as they separated, a barely audible whistle sounded from somewhere far away. A second later, a closer one echoed from the direction of the farmhouse.

Georgie's heart lurched as she met Jax's gaze, and all at once, the plan seemed stupid. Impossible.

"Ready?" he asked.

Georgie nodded—too fast—her nails digging into her palms, but she couldn't move.

He touched under her chin. "We've got this, Georgie."

Her throat felt too tight as she swallowed. "Let's go."

Adam was at the shed, searching for a part for Oliver when the whistle sounded. His eyes widened as he struggled to remember the first step.

His gun. He needed his gun.

When he made it to the house, Banks was already on the porch, sniper rifle in his hands.

How much time did they have?

The lookout point was a half a mile away. That left him a few minutes to get into position. Which wouldn't have been an issue if the pain in Adam's bones wasn't gnawing at him. Every step took too much effort. It would take him too long to make it to the barn. Even longer to make it to the loft window.

But he had another spot. The one he'd used before. It wasn't high, but it had a great view of the yard, and he'd be hidden by trees. Plus, it was much easier to get to.

He pushed forward, making it to the spot near the road just as Desmond's black sedan turned down the drive. Tires crunched against the gravel and snow. He expected another to follow—Desmond always had two vehicles—but the road was empty.

Something pricked at the back of Adam's mind, but he brushed it away, lowering the bipod and setting it on the top of a wooden fence for support. The gun was heavier than he remembered.

Everyone was counting on him to make the shot. It all depended on him. If he failed, Oliver and Georgie could die.

The pressure turned the adrenaline in his veins into a sickening, nervous energy that made him miss the numbness.

He watched through the scope as the car came to a stop.

Vivian appeared on the front porch, a smile plastered on her face as she greeted Desmond. Kye joined them a second later.

Adam frowned, scanning the yard. Des had one person with him. Just one. And it wasn't Eris.

Where was Eris?

Focus.

Inhale, find the target.

The crosshairs bobbed as Adam tried to hold them steady.

Exhale, line up the shot.

His finger hovered over the trigger, hesitating.

Something's wrong.

Adam straightened abruptly, spinning around just in time to see Eris beside him. Before he could react, she delivered a powerful kick to his stomach. He stumbled back, losing his footing and landing hard in the snow, breathless.

44

When Georgie and Jax made it to the workshop, the black sedan was already parked in the gravel drive. They ducked inside and pulled the door closed, and streaks of daylight pushed through the cracks, drawing lines across Jax's pensive face.

She shut her eyes tight, digging her nails into her palms and pressing herself against the wall, hoping Adam was ready.

Breathe.

Everyone should be in position.

With nothing to do until Adam dropped Desmond, Georgie focused on slowing her racing pulse.

This was going to work. They had a plan. And even if it somehow went off the rails, they had Oliver's failsafe to fall back on.

The engine cut off.

Breathe.

She wasn't running headfirst at this. It was going to work.

In her mind, Georgie pinpointed where the others were, reminding herself that she wasn't alone.

Oliver was in the attic, the switch in his hand. If needed, he'd flip it, and his device would create a spark that would set off small fuel-filled canisters placed around the yard.

Kye and Vivian would greet Desmond, ready to get out of range if the signal was given. Vivian still wasn't fully on board, but the rest of her people were, so she'd reluctantly agreed to play her part.

Wren and Levi hopefully had time to get the kids out of the farmhouse.

Adam was perched in the barn, lining up the shot.

Jax, Banks, herself, and six others were armed and strategically placed, ready and waiting. Once Desmond was down, they'd train their weapons on the others and offer a single chance to surrender.

Even if everything went as planned, there would still be a lot of work to do, but that was after. Right now, all that mattered was step one.

Desmond.

Voices carried from outside, and Georgie opened her eyes, leaning against the door to hear what was happening.

"...supposed to be part of a team." Desmond's voice. "I help you. You help me. It doesn't work if I can't trust you."

"We made our payment," Vivian replied.

"You did. Believe me, we'd be having an entirely different conversation if you hadn't. I'm referring to the Haven strays you've taken in."

Georgie's heart sank.

He knew they were there. How long had he known? *How* did he know?

Jax shifted his weight beside her, and she glanced up at him. Even in the dim light, she could see the lines of his frown deepen.

Come on, Adam.

"During the last pickup," Desmond continued, "Mike here asked if you'd seen any Havenites, and you explicitly said you hadn't."

"I didn't know they were from a Haven."

"Is that really what you're going with? More lies?"

A beat of silence.

"You see," Desmond said, "Kye and I, we have history, so I know for certain that *she* knew who they were when they showed up here. I find it difficult to believe you didn't know."

"If I'd known, I would've told you."

"I'm extending the double payment amount," he went on, "until I decide you've made up for the inconvenience."

"No. Absolutely not. With our numbers, we don't have enough to last through the winter as it is."

"Then I suggest you find a solution quickly. But the new arrangement stays. And if you lie to me again, I won't be as forgiving."

Silence returned, and Georgie pushed open the door a crack to see what was happening.

Desmond was in the center of the yard, and dread coiled tightly in her chest at the sight of him.

Where was Adam? He had a clear line of sight from the barn. Why wasn't he firing?

"I can tell you where they are," Vivian said finally. "They're not my people, and they've caused enough trouble for us."

No.

Georgie stiffened, her mind screaming for her to run.

"Vivian, don't," Kye warned.

"We should signal Oliver," Jax whispered.

Georgie nodded, eyes jumping to the window, but movement in the yard yanked her attention back. Adam trudged forward across the driveway, bracketed by Eris and a man in a worn-out leather jacket with Adam's gun slung over his shoulder.

No.

She tightened her grip on the door, the cold making her fingers throb.

Adam was in range of the failsafe. They couldn't set it off now.

They were fucked. Vivian was selling them out. Her people were going to die.

Her mom's face flashed in her mind, the safehouse littered with bodies.

Do something!

Anger and determination burned away the fear, and Georgie burst through the workshop door.

Desmond spun around, and his face lit up with delighted surprise. "Little Wicks," he chimed. "Funny running into you here."

"You're not taking him," she said. "And you're not hurting any more of my people."

The man beside Adam trained his gun on her, and Eris drew her knife.

"You're outnumbered," Jax said, beside her now.

Merritt and Banks pushed out onto the porch as the rest appeared, guns drawn.

Desmond's eyes stayed locked on hers. "You don't really believe that, do you?"

Georgie's stomach twisted, a cold knot tightening as his words sank in. He'd known they were here before arriving. He'd known—and yet he brought only three people. It didn't add up.

Finally, her gaze broke away, sweeping over the yard, the forest.

They never had the upper hand. Not really. Desmond was already ten steps ahead of them.

How many of his people were here? She doubted he needed many. They'd prepared to fight five, maybe six, and that was with the element of surprise.

If they fought now, everyone here would die.

In an instant, the air turned thick like honey, smothering the fragile flame. She lowered her gun, defeated, and Desmond lifted a brow.

"Now you're catching on."

Adam glanced back at the attic window, silently pleading for Oliver to flip the switch and end this. They wouldn't get another chance.

But Oliver wouldn't do it as long as Adam was in range.

Desmond was going to kill Georgie, and there was nothing he could do about it.

"Wait," Adam pleaded. "I'll go back. But you have to promise everyone here will be safe."

The corner of Desmond's mouth curled in amusement. "I have devoted a substantial amount of time and resources trying to accommodate you. I made an effort to be cordial, even kept this one alive." He waved his hand dismissively toward Georgie. "Despite my overwhelming desire to put her down like her treacherous mother, which, believe me, required immense self-restraint. All for you. And still, you betrayed me."

Adam's lips pressed flat. He should never have come here. This was all his fault. And now he couldn't fix it.

"Speaking of treacherous," Desmond said, turning to face Vivian. "You agreed to take the strays in, only to turn on them for a few crates of supplies?"

Vivian crossed her arms, her expression hardening. "I do what I have to for my people, and *they* aren't my people."

"You're spineless," Desmond said, "and you threw them under the bus to save yourself. Think your people didn't notice? The settlements I negotiate with are investments. I need capable leaders, not cowards, to ensure these investments don't fail." His gaze cut to Kye. "Shame about the Campus, by the way. There are some terrible people out there. I'm sure you understand now the importance of what we offer."

Kye scowled, but stayed silent.

Desmond grinned. "I always liked you." As he looked back at Vivian, the smile transformed. Darkened.

Adam knew this one well.

Knew it was dangerous.

Knew what was about to happen.

Apparently, so did Vivian because she threw out all restraint. "I hope the Havens *burn* you, you arrogant fuck."

"Congratulations on the promotion, Kye," Des said before drawing his gun and firing a round into Vivian's chest.

Adam recoiled, and Kye gasped.

Vivian stumbled back a step, then hung there for a moment with a dumbfounded look before dropping.

Kye's hand lingered over her pistol and Adam met her gaze, his eyes silently pleading.

Don't.

She must have decided she didn't actually have a death wish, because her hand fell back to her side.

"Now, Adam, if you're ready..." Desmond motioned toward the car. "I doubt you want to watch this next bit."

Adam glanced at Eris, but she tilted her head, purposefully avoiding his gaze, which gave him the opening he needed to grab the pistol from her holster. Turning, he leveled it on Desmond's chest.

Jay and the other man both turned their guns on him.

But they wouldn't shoot.

Desmond's smile never faltered. "You really have a flare for the dramatic."

He couldn't let this happen.

Georgie was still close to the workshop, out of range of the trap, and Oliver was safe in his room. Adam didn't want Kye to get hurt, and he definitely didn't want to die. Not now, not after he worked so damn hard to finally be okay.

But he'd led Desmond here, and now he had to fix it.

Adam lowered his aim, pointing at one of the hidden fuel canisters. "Leave, now," he said, his finger on the trigger, his muscles tense. "Or I burn us all."

Eris grabbed his arm, reclaimed the gun, and, with a swift twist, had him on the ground in an instant. But when Adam looked up, Desmond's smile was gone. His eyes shifted to the ground, scanning.

For the first time, he looked unsure.

He must not have noticed the canisters before. He hadn't planned for the trap, couldn't tell how far it reached.

All it would take was one shot from any one of the people around the yard—or one flip of a switch—and Desmond would be gone.

Yes, his people would wipe out everyone here after. He probably brought his best fighters. It would be easy.

But Desmond's priority was himself.

Oliver had saved them all.

Adam gave Desmond a proud grin as Georgie and Hale lifted their guns, each aiming at a canister.

"You should probably leave," Adam said, climbing to his feet. "It's over."

A glint of cold fury flashed in Desmond's dark eyes as they narrowed. "Do you sincerely believe you'll get this lucky twice?" With a gesture, he signaled and an SUV started down the drive. "Do you think next time I won't kill everyone here and drag you back?"

The SUV came to a stop, and the driver slid over.

"Tell you what," he added as he pulled open the driver's side door. "Get in the car, and I'll leave them be."

Adam's gaze lifted back to the attic window.

"You *will* end up back at Jardine, whether by choice or by force. I don't require your cooperation." Desmond cast Georgie a bright smile. "However, to keep breathing, *they* do. So, are you going to save them, or are you honestly selfish enough to remain here, clinging to the faint hope that perhaps you can replicate this stroke of luck next time?"

Eris hovered beside Adam until Desmond was safely in the vehicle. The others climbed in, and Eris held the back door open, waiting.

But he stayed put, listening, searching the edges of the yard.

Why was Desmond bartering if he had people waiting to take them out? Why not just end it now?

Unless it was a bluff.

He had no backup.

He hadn't planned on this being a fight.

Maybe he hadn't actually realized the strays were here until after he arrived.

Desmond was outnumbered, and the trap had made him reassess his chances.

If Adam went with now, Des would still come back for Georgie and the others. He would never let it go, especially after this. But it would at least buy them time. Time to run. Time to get away.

Adam heaved a sigh and climbed inside.

He knew what he had here was too good to last. It never stood a chance. He'd known that from the moment he arrived.

But it still hurt to leave it behind.

45

The SUV roared down the driveway and then vanished, leaving behind a silence that was so thick, it seemed to weigh down the air, and for a long moment, no one dared to break it.

And then the front door slammed open and Oliver hurried down the porch steps.

He paused, locking eyes with Georgie in a silent, meaningful exchange—a shared understanding passing between them—before turning and heading down the driveway.

He wasn't giving up.

Good. Neither was she.

But Georgie was determined not to repeat the same mistake she had made countless times before. She needed to take a second to think. Needed an actual plan.

"Oliver, wait," she called, running to catch up.

He turned to face her, his light eyes frantic. "I-I have to-I can't just—"

"Hey," Georgie interrupted. "I know. We'll get him back. Just hold on." She scanned the yard, brain whirring, her eyes landing on the black sedan in the drive.

Her brow furrowed. Why would Desmond leave his car? There was no way that was a slip-up.

Oh.

She scoffed and shook her head. The car was for *her*. He knew she would come after Adam. He wanted her to. Expected it. The car was an invitation, a show of control.

As she glanced back at Oliver, a flicker of an idea sparked in her mind.

"Do you still have that dart gun?"

Oliver frowned. "Yeah. But like I said, there's only one dart."

That was okay. There was only one person they needed out of the way if she was ever going to get to Desmond.

Adrenaline flared as the spark ignited into a plan.

Georgie didn't know how to drive, and though she could probably figure it out, now wasn't the time, so she turned and crossed the yard to Jax.

"I need your help. I have a plan, but I can't do it alone."

He shot her a disbelieving glare. "You're not really going after him."

"I have to."

Adam had saved them by going with Desmond, and she wasn't going to sit back and let him disappear again.

Jax's gaze jumped to the forest, his brow creased in thought.

"Okay, I'm with you," he said finally. "Whatever happens, we'll face it together."

She glanced back at the others. "I need to figure out a few things first. We need to talk to Oliver, see if he has a solution."

"You go ahead," Jax said. "I have to run to the cabin."

"For what?"

"There's something I need to do. I'll meet you back here."

Shadows thickened, and evening dissolved into gray twilight as the car navigated the cleared path across the bridge. Jax's hand gripped the steering wheel, his eyes locked on the road ahead.

A tense silence had consumed the last few minutes of their drive, the reality of what they were doing sinking in.

When Navy Pier came into view, Jax eased the car to a stop.

This will work.

Georgie dragged herself out of the car, then tugged her jacket closed and adjusted her hair, wincing at the uncomfortable tightness and weight of the bun on her head.

It has to work.

The words did little to calm her nerves.

Oliver checked his messenger bag, then blew out a loud breath, mumbling something she couldn't hear as his hand went to BUG on his belt loop. A second later, he vanished without a sound.

This will work.

She repeated the words over and over like a mantra on the short walk to Jardine until they felt strange and meaningless.

For her and Jax, there was no need for stealth, no point in trying to stay hidden. Desmond knew they were coming. So they took the direct path down the middle of the road, guns already in their hands.

Breathe. This wasn't some stupid split second, reckless choice, and she wasn't on her own. It was a sound plan—well, as sound as it could be with the odds so stacked against them—and they had gone over it multiple times during the drive.

She was going to end this and bring Adam home.

But her steps faltered as her mind went to the train station, to Cassira, to that feeling of walking to greet her own death. She'd failed then, almost lost Jax. Desmond's people were the only reason the cult was gone. The only reason Cassira didn't kill them all. What made her think this would be different?

She couldn't do this.

It was madness.

Her feet abruptly stopped moving.

"We can't," Georgie whispered. The darkness crept up through the cracks in the ground, wrapping around her ankles like chains holding her in place.

Jax reached for her hand, his grip steady and reassuring.

"We can turn back," he said. "Get the others from Spring Valley and run. Nobody would blame you."

Georgie swallowed hard, battling the rising panic as she focused on thoughts of Adam. She remembered him smiling at the sky from the lab rooftop, patiently teaching her to shoot outside the Campus. The pain and desperation in his eyes in the Spring Valley bathroom and the effortless way he laughed at the dock.

No. She couldn't give up on him. And she couldn't abandon Oliver.

Jax studied her a moment, then pulled in a deep breath. "Ready, then?"

"Ready."

"Hey," someone barked as they approached the large gates to Jardine. "One more step and we open fire."

There were two guards stationed behind the metal bars, armed with military-grade assault rifles, and at least one more inside the glass checkpoint booth.

She looked up at the security camera, its blinking red light confirming they were being watched.

Desmond would know they were here.

Good.

"Weapons on the ground," the guard ordered. Jax's movements were slow and careful as he set his pistol on the concrete at his feet, then kicked it away.

Why bring guns at all if you know they'll take them at the gate? Oliver had asked before they left.

Because, Georgie had answered, *every step of this depends on Desmond thinking he has the upper hand, that he's still ten steps ahead of us. It has to be believable.*

Desmond expected her to act recklessly. Expected her to come in fighting.

"Gun down," the guard called out, but she kept her eyes fixed on the camera, mouth set in a straight line as she waited.

"Fine," the guard said, taking aim, "have it your way."

"Georgie," Jax muttered in warning.

Come on. Desmond was far too vindictive to let someone take this from him.

Right on cue, the familiar lilting voice sounded from the man's walkie. "It's impolite to drop in uninvited."

Georgie scowled and flipped off the camera.

"But since you're already here," Desmond continued, "join me for a cuppa. Leave the gun, though."

Georgie rolled her eyes. "Coward." She set the pistol at her feet and kicked it away.

The guard lowered his gun and stepped toward the gate, and a moment later, it rolled open. While he grabbed their pistols from the ground, the second searched them for other weapons.

As expected.

He led them into the massive building that cut down the center of the pier.

She had to continuously urge herself to keep walking, desperately hoping her nerves would hold steady.

Normally, when staring down a blatant trap, the smart choice would be to turn around and go the other way.

But she kept pushing forward.

Not because it was what her parents would do, or because she gave a shit about what Desmond would do to Indiana if she turned back. Not for the sake of humanity or any lofty ideals of the greater good.

She was done caring about any of that.

Georgie kept walking because Adam was her family. And because nobody deserved to be used the way Desmond was using him.

She kept walking for the few of her people still left, for the residents of Spring Valley, who had offered them refuge when they had nowhere to go.

For Jax.

And for herself.

But mostly, she kept walking because the desire to wipe that stupid smile from Desmond's face outweighed any amount of fear.

Heat rose in her chest, and she lifted her chin, her steps steadier.

Anger was good. Anger, she could use.

46

Everything about this plan hinged on Desmond's arrogance, and as Georgie stepped into the large room, taking in the table surrounded by mostly empty chairs, she had to suppress a smile.

It was exactly what she'd expected.

Desmond didn't see them as a threat—at least not one that required anyone but Eris to handle—and he wanted to make sure they knew it.

He was reclined at the far end of the table, his brown Oxfords propped up, legs crossed at the ankles and a faint smile playing on his lips. Beside him, Eris stood with her hood down, black hair spilling over her shoulders, looking almost bored.

No sign of Adam.

Windows made up most of the back wall, the sky outside an inky blue, the silhouette of Navy Pier running parallel alongside Jardine.

"Have a seat," Desmond said cheerfully, lowering his feet to the floor and leaning forward. He picked up a kettle, eyes lifting to Georgie. "Tea?" When she answered with a scowl, he shrugged and set it back down. "Suit yourselves. But really, do sit. It's impolite to hover in doorways."

She glanced at Jax who was staring out the windows, eyes narrowed like he was searching for something.

Desmond sighed. "I don't like having to repeat myself. Sit. Now."

Jax tore his attention from the windows and dropped into a chair.

Georgie stayed put. "Where's Adam?"

Desmond tilted his head and gestured towards the chairs.

Cursing under her breath, Georgie chose a seat a few feet from where Eris stood, trying to ignore the persistent pull on her scalp.

Focus.

The door swung open a moment later, and a surly faced woman led Adam inside.

His eyes widened in surprise at the sight of them. Did he really think she wouldn't come after him?

The woman stepped back out, shutting the door behind her, and Desmond nudged the chair beside him with his foot, sliding it back from the table.

"Join us."

Adam crossed the room and slumped into the chair.

Georgie couldn't see the cheerful, witty version of him she'd first met, or the sharp, protective one she had caught glimpses of. She couldn't even see the determined one who had fought through the pain.

He looked broken and defeated, and it only sharpened her resolve to put Desmond down.

"So," Desmond said casually, "to what do we owe the pleasure?"

"We're taking Adam home," Georgie replied, surprised at the steadiness of her own voice.

He arched an eyebrow, his attention shifting to Adam. "Do you want to *leave,* Adam?"

Adam shot her a pleading look, clearly urging her to run, before dropping his gaze and shaking his head, disheveled hair falling over his forehead.

"Sorry, love," Desmond chirped. "Looks like you wasted your time."

"We can either walk out of here with him," Jax growled, "or we can kill everyone inside and *take* him."

That was a hell of a bluff, but she went with it. "Starting with you."

Desmond glanced down at the kettle. "Hm," he mused. "If I'm facing my own impending demise, I'm going to need something with a bit more kick."

He reached to a cabinet behind him and pulled out a half-empty bottle and two glasses.

"Single Malt Scotch Whisky," he explained as he poured a small amount in each glass. He slid one to her, then picked up his own, studying the liquid as it swirled. "It was your mother's favorite."

Georgie's muscles tightened at the mention of her.

"To Elaina," Desmond said, lifting his drink.

She grabbed her own glass and upended it, spilling the drink onto the table. "Fuck you."

Desmond took a sip, then smirked over the rim of the glass. "You really do look just like her, you know."

Georgie shoved up from the table, the heat in her chest blazing.

Eris had her knife drawn before Georgie even made it to her feet. "Down, girl."

Come on, Oliver. What was taking him so long?

Georgie sank back into the chair, but her muscles hummed with a seething anger.

"You know," she snarled, "all those settlements you're fucking over—sooner or later, they're going to see through your bullshit. They'll realize it's all just a show. And when they do, they'll tear you apart."

His smile widened. "It's that show, Little Wicks, that keeps the monsters in their dark corners. Simple, primal fear. Without me, that fear disappears. So, sure, let those settlements tear me apart. The city would surely reciprocate."

47

Invisibility was crucial for survival, now more than ever.

Oliver navigated the edge of the pier, watching for cameras while the murky water churned beside him. He made his way toward the utility building at the far end.

If he messed this up, he'd never see Adam again, and Georgie and Jax wouldn't make it out of that place alive.

No pressure.

He wasn't used to people depending on him for anything, and so far, he wasn't a fan.

But this was for Adam.

He stopped and listened, making sure it was clear before bolting across an open stretch. As he reached the exterior of the building, he caught the faint murmur of voices and froze.

They were getting closer.

Run.

Oliver scanned the building, finding an entrance a little further down. He took off, ducking inside and closing the door gently behind him. After a few steadying breaths, he assessed his surroundings.

A long hallway stretched out in front of him. Massive pipes arced overhead and high-tech gauges dotted the concrete wall. It was dark, save for the glowing blue of the meters, and he stopped at the first one to inspect it.

Amazing.

He knew the city had renovated the water treatment plant a while back, but he didn't realize the extent of it.

Oliver followed the pipes, entranced, until he made it to an enormous well-lit room with metal tubes extending up to the high ceiling. Above him, a catwalk cut down one side, leading to a—

No way.

His mouth fell open. This place had a giant, industrial-sized filtration system. One at the same level as the hospital, possibly even more advanced. If he had filters that size...his mind buzzed, already spinning ways to take the equipment apart and rebuild it again at Spring Valley.

Focus.

They were depending on him. He dragged his gaze from the filter and followed the signs to the electrical room.

Stay silent.

Stay invisible.

He was unarmed in a place with very dangerous people who wouldn't think twice about shooting him.

Oliver tensed at the thought.

Just get this done and get out.

Georgie and Hale were probably already inside. They knew they'd have no trouble with that part. But taking out Eris before she could react would prove a whole lot trickier. And leaving when they were finished even more so.

That was where *he* came in.

Taking down the power would give them a few seconds of darkness before the emergency backups kicked on. And the security cameras would probably stay down until they fixed the power.

Oliver easily found the control panel. It was extensive, taking up most of the wall, but the device he'd thrown together—though rudimentary at best—should still be sufficient, as long as he picked the right spot.

After taking a minute to study the panel, he placed the small rectangle box where he was sure it would do maximum damage and eyed the button.

"Don't fucking move."

Oliver froze, and his heart jumped all the way into his throat.

"Turn around slowly. You move your hands, I fire."

Holding his breath, Oliver turned to face a man in a leather jacket with a handgun already aimed.

He held a walkie to his mouth, keeping the gun trained on Oliver. "Des, I found someone in the control station. Doubt he's alone. Should I shoot him or bring him in?"

Oliver stiffened, hands aching to react to the awful buzzing in his nerves.

Bad bad this is bad.

After an excruciating stretch of silence, Desmond's voice finally cut through the speaker. "Bring him in."

It was better than being shot right there, but odds were it would ultimately end the same way.

The man attached the walkie to his belt and motioned with his gun. "Your lucky day. Set your weapons on the ground."

"I—" Oliver's voice caught in his throat. He swallowed and tried again. "I don't have any weapons."

"Bullshit. Face the wall."

He turned slowly, and as the man took his bag and checked beneath his coat for a holster, Oliver pressed the button on the device.

Ten seconds.

"What the hell's this?" the man asked as he unclipped BUG from his belt loop.

"It's not a weapon," Oliver said. "I swear."

The man snorted as he spun Oliver back around. "You broke in here, unarmed? To do what?"

Whispering a prayer under his breath, Oliver shoved his hands in his coat pocket and grabbed the Swiss Army knife the man had overlooked.

"What'd you say?"

Oliver ignored him, lips barely moving as he continued the prayer, carefully flipping out the small blade.

"Hey," the man snapped. "Speak up. What are you doing here? How many of you are there?"

A spark lit up the room in a sudden burst, and the man's angry curses echoed as he shoved Oliver against the control panel.

"The fuck did you *do*?"

Oliver shook his head.

Come on. Please work.

The man stepped forward, too close. "Fix it. Now."

With another spark, the device crackled, and the room went black.

Forgive me.

Oliver pulled out the knife and jammed it into what he was ninety percent sure was the man's throat, balking at the sickening warmth that poured over his hand.

I'm sorry I'm sorry I'm sorry.

He shoved the man back, surprised when he offered no resistance.

Two muffled pops.

The shots missed Oliver and struck the control panel behind him. His heart hammered in his chest as he stood there, frozen and unsure what to do. It was too dark to run. Was the cut even enough to kill the man? What if it wasn't?

The lights flickered back on at a dim emergency level, casting eerie shadows across the walls. The man stood a few feet away, his hand clasped over his throat, blood streaming down his arm as he aimed the gun.

Fudge.

Oliver tried to duck behind a row of large panels, but he wasn't fast enough. The pain hit him suddenly—sharp, hot, and overwhelming. He collapsed behind the bulky metal box, his breathing shallow and panicked.

Two more muffled shots, then silence, followed by the sound of a body hitting the floor and the metallic clatter of the gun.

Oliver pulled his coat aside, searching for the wound. The pain seemed to radiate everywhere, and red spread across the side of his flannel shirt. Gritting his teeth, he lifted the shirt, wincing as the fabric stuck to the wound.

The bullet had barely grazed him.

Thank God.

With a shaky breath, he folded his knife and slipped it into his pocket before struggling to his feet. He grabbed BUG and his messenger bag from the ground, then staggered toward the exit.

He was too panicked to bother sneaking as he pushed back out into the night. Pressing a hand against the bleeding wound in his side, he forced himself forward until he reached what looked like the entrance of a parking garage. He paused there, gasping for breath, the sticky blood on his hands turning his stomach. He wiped them on his jeans, trying to get it off his skin.

Movement at the base of the city buildings caught his eye, the shape lit only by the silver moonlight peeking through the clouds.

For a second, Oliver thought he'd imagined it. It was dark, and he was kind of freaking out.

But then it moved again.

He squinted as he tried to make sense of what he was seeing. An odd-shaped vehicle was parked in the middle of the large road with something long on top.

Oliver watched, waiting, but nothing happened.

A quick burst of distant gunfire pulled his attention back to Jardine, the sound echoing off the buildings before the quiet returned.

That wasn't good.

48

"I'd really love to know what your plan was," Desmond said, voice dripping with amusement. "You thought you'd come threaten me, take Adam, and what, walk back out the front doors?"

Adam's gaze lifted to Georgie, whose glare was locked on Desmond.

Why did they come here? They should've stayed away. They should've run.

"You missed the part where I shoot you," she replied.

"Oh, of course." Desmond grinned. "Realistically, though, you know you're not making it out of here alive."

"I came back," Adam pleaded. "You said you'd leave them alone."

"They're the ones who waltzed in here brandishing threats." He shrugged with an exaggerated air of innocence. "I can't be held responsible for their stupidity."

No, this wasn't supposed to happen. He couldn't let her die.

"Let them walk out of here," Adam said with sudden resolve. "Or the first chance I get, I'll put a bullet in your head." When Desmond's eyes met his, he fought the urge to recoil. "You know I'll find a way," he added for good measure.

Adam had hoped for anger, hoped to hit a nerve, but Des held tight to the calm.

"You want to shoot me?" He pulled the Desert Eagle from his holster and set it gently on the table. "Why wait? Do it now."

Adam's fists clenched as he looked up at Eris, who was focused on Georgie and Hale.

Would she be fast enough to stop him if he reached for the gun?

Would he have the nerve to pull the trigger if she wasn't?

If he shot Desmond, he'd have to shoot her, too. Eris, Colette, Desmond. They were like family—at least they'd felt like it once.

Desmond folded his arms, and his expression shifted, his features set in that rare, concerned frown.

"Do you honestly think they're here out of genuine concern for you? She discarded you without a second thought, and now, suddenly, you're valuable, and she decides you're worth fighting for."

Hesitation and doubt crept in and settled deep within Adam.

He's right.

She's using you.

Was that the reason Georgie was here? Because they were screwed without him?

For months, he clung to Des's words with the same intensity he clung to his pills, depending on them, craving them, killing for them. But they were lies, and Adam knew that.

He *knew* that.

Desmond didn't care about him.

He didn't care, and he was lying.

He stole Adam's only chance at revenge just to punish him.

He wasn't family.

You betrayed him.

He'd forced Adam to come back. Locked him in a room.

That was your fault, the voice growled.

In an instant, the facts that were so tangible moments before twisted into a distorted blur.

Of course Desmond had locked him away. Adam tried to kill him. He was unstable. Couldn't be trusted.

Slipping.

A voice from a walkie yanked him out of the fog.

"Des, I found someone in the control station. Doubt he's alone. Should I shoot him or bring him in?"

Adam's gaze snapped to Georgie. Who else did they bring?

Her face tightened, and when she cast him an apologetic look, the world lurched to a stop.

Oliver.

The realization was a white hot needle shoved into Adam's lungs, and the cold dread that followed was like being in that lake all over again.

He was underwater.

Drowning.

Desmond watched Georgie's reaction with a bright grin. "What do you think, Adam? How is this going to end?"

"Please." Adam winced as the word scraped its way out, his fingers gripping the edge of the table.

Des hummed thoughtfully as he reclined in the chair, his dark eyes wandering up to the ceiling. He finished his drink, then finally lifted the radio to his mouth.

"Bring him in."

49

A chill crept along Georgie's skin, her heart pounding so fiercely she felt each beat in her fingertips.

If Desmond's people had Oliver, then the plan was shot to hell. The distraction was crucial to pull this off, especially with Eris's sharp eyes tracking their every move.

They needed her out of the way.

She eyed the distance between Eris and herself. Three steps, possibly four. Georgie had angled the chair when she sat back down to make the next part easier, but Eris was already on her feet, a knife in her hand and a holstered gun on her hip. She was faster than Georgie, even without the advantage she had now.

Georgie would be dead in seconds.

This didn't work without Oliver.

Suddenly, the whirring of the vents stopped, plunging the room into silence as darkness fell over them like a curtain.

Without hesitation, Georgie's hand shot up to the bun on her head, freeing her hair and retrieving the small dart gun concealed within.

It was primed and ready.

Squinting into the darkness, she locked onto Eris's silhouette against the moonlit sky, pulled the trigger, and ducked for cover a fraction of a second before what she assumed was Eris's knife clattered sharply against the wall behind her.

Oh shit.

That was too close.

The dim emergency lights flickered on, and as Eris drew her pistol, Adam lunged for Desmond's gun on the table. Eris spun to react, but Desmond struck with lightning speed, driving his blade through Adam's gloved hand and into the solid wood of the table.

He let out an anguished cry that echoed through the room.

Taking advantage of the distraction, Jax swiftly closed the gap, landing a powerful blow to the side of Desmond's face, but he quickly retaliated, grabbing Jax's arm as he shot up from his chair, sending him to the floor with one forceful twist.

Desmond's expression soured as he massaged his jaw. "Okay, that was uncalled for."

Eris stumbled, her gun clattering to the floor as she reached out to steady herself on the table.

Georgie rushed forward and snatched the pistol, turning it on Desmond before he could reach his own on the table.

He stopped, hands open at his sides. "I should've stabbed you through the heart."

Georgie steadied the gun, savoring the sliver of anger that shone through the wry smile on Desmond's face. "Yeah, you should've."

"Don't," Jax said suddenly, climbing back to his feet. "You can't shoot him."

"The fuck I can't."

Adam yanked the knife free from his hand and slammed it on the table as Eris hit the ground.

"Please, Georgie," Jax said. "I need him alive."

Her eyes jumped to him for a moment, then refocused on Desmond. "Why?"

"The general at Indiana offered us a deal."

"A *deal*?" Georgie shook her head. "They abandoned us."

"I said I'd fix it, and that's exactly what I'm doing. They think we attacked their convoy. They think we're a threat. You know how dangerous that is for us? But I told them I could bring them the person who was actually responsible. The person who wiped out our Haven. We prove our innocence, they get to prosecute a criminal. We get a spot at their Haven. Protection, supplies, an actual life."

Desmond snorted at that, and Georgie stormed forward, shoving the gun barrel into his chest, her finger yearning to pull the trigger.

Jax set a heavy-duty zip-tie on the table, the kind they used at Haven during arrests. "What's more important? Revenge, or our people?"

That was an unfair question. This was supposed to be *for* their people. She didn't trust Indiana, and she sure as hell wouldn't be sending anyone there. But he was right. It was dangerous for Indiana to see them as a threat.

Desmond gave a theatrical sigh. "Can I at least grab myself a refill while you two sort this out?"

"Shut up," she and Jax snapped back simultaneously.

"Please, Georgie," Jax said. "I'm giving us a chance. I'm trying to make things right. Let me."

When she finally lowered the gun, Desmond smirked and brushed a hand over his tweed jacket where the barrel had rested.

Jax gently took the gun from her and trained it on Desmond while Georgie secured his hands behind his back.

That was why Jax needed to go to the cabin. He was contacting Indiana.

"Why are you just telling me this now?" she asked.

"Because I knew you'd never agree to the terms, and I needed you to get inside. To get to both of *them*."

She frowned. "Both of them?"

"This is how we survive. This is how I save you. Indiana has soldiers on their way here. We have to hand Emery over." He glanced at Adam, who was cradling his injured hand. "And Adam, too."

Georgie straightened. "*What?*"

Adam's eyes locked on Jax's, filled with an intense and fiery hatred.

"Oh, this is fantastic," Desmond mused with a wide grin. "You really should be more careful who you put your trust in, Little Wicks."

She snatched the second gun from the table and pointed it at Desmond's head. "No deal, Jax."

The walkie on Desmond's belt crackled. "We got movement on—"

A burst of gunfire, and the walkie went quiet.

"We don't have a choice," Jax said. "They're already here."

No no no.

Adam sprang to his feet. Oliver was outside somewhere. If the Havenites hurt him, he would hunt down every last one of them. Sidestepping Hale, he dashed out of the room, nearly crashing into Colette.

She stumbled back, her eyes wide with shock.

"What's going on? Where's Eris?"

Ignoring her, Adam took off again, panic making him clumsy. He had to find Oliver before something happened to him, and the fastest route outside was through the front entrance.

His boots pounded against the linoleum, and as he burst through the front doors, he skidded to a sudden halt, stunned by the amount of soldiers.

They formed a wide semi-circle, positioned far from the building, their weapons aimed at the door.

Hale stumbled to a stop beside Adam. "Wait," he shouted, setting the gun on the ground and raising his hands. "Don't shoot. I have the charge, as promised."

A soldier stepped forward, her features sharp, hair drawn back in a ponytail. "This him?"

Hale nodded once. "And Emery's secured inside. He'll be able to tell you what happened to your convoy."

"Great work, soldier." The woman lifted a radio to her mouth. "All clear."

Adam's mind spun, muscles vibrating as he tried to figure out his next move.

He couldn't go to a Haven.

He couldn't lose his freedom again.

"Step away from the building," the woman commanded, then addressed the other soldiers. "Secure the charge and transport him to the vehicle. Move quickly."

As two soldiers stepped away from the group, Adam grabbed the gun from the ground and pressed it to his own temple, eyes locked on the one giving the orders.

"Don't move," he barked.

They needed him alive.

When the soldiers froze, Adam took a slow step backward toward the door.

He needed to get back inside.

The parking garage.

He could make it out through there. He'd find Oliver, and they'd get out of here together.

A distant boom reverberated around them, deep and resonant and unlike anything Adam had ever heard. He flinched, his eyes darting instinctively toward the sound. As he spotted the massive artillery gun at the edge of the city, his stomach sank and his face went slack,

Holy hell.

Without thinking, his hand dropped.

The pain hit him like a bolt of lightning, electricity searing through his side, up his spine, and into his head, causing his jaw to clench shut.

He tried to fight against it, but it engulfed him entirely.

And then he dropped.

50

"You're denser than I thought if you actually believe they're going to let you walk into that Haven." Even with his hands bound behind his back, Desmond held the edge of a smile.

"I don't," Georgie answered. She didn't trust Indiana. Didn't understand why Jax did. There was no way she was handing over Adam. No way she was letting Desmond walk out of here.

She gripped Desmond's gun tighter. She was ending this now.

The door slammed open, and a girl with short blue hair stood in the doorway, panicked eyes taking in the room before landing on Desmond.

She drew a pistol and trained it on Georgie. "Drop it."

Gritting her teeth, Georgie reluctantly lowered the gun.

"Where's Eris?" the girl asked, and Georgie cast a pointed look at the body on the floor behind the table. Her gaze followed. "*Mierda*," she breathed, her expression tightening. "What did you do?"

"She's fine," Georgie said, and the girl darted across the room and dropped beside Eris.

A muffled *boom* echoed from outside, the sound strange and deep.

The girl shot up, terror on her face. "Des? What's happening?"

The smile dissolved from Desmond's face, his eyes turning dark and bitter. "We should probably go."

A thunderous roar slammed through the building. The windows burst. Shards of glass sprayed across the room.

Georgie shouted and dropped to a crouch, throwing her hands over her head.

When the sound of the blast settled into the faint patter of falling debris and distant shouting, she stood, trembling and disoriented.

What the fuck was *happening*?

The girl pulled on Eris's arms, desperately trying to lift her off the floor.

Go, Georgie urged herself. She had to get out. This wasn't her problem.

Run. Leave them.

Eris had tried to kill Jax. She was almost as responsible for the Haven attack as Desmond was.

But the desperation in the girl's face made her hesitate.

She was so young. Eris, too. Adam had fallen for Desmond's bullshit more than once, and she'd forgiven him, so how could she leave these two to die for the same crime?

Georgie groaned, then ran to help. She and the girl pulled Eris's arms over their shoulders, and by the time they got her up, Desmond was gone.

"Son of a bitch," Georgie growled.

They poured out into the hallway, pausing briefly to take in the destruction. To the right, a section of the building had crumbled, revealing a glimpse of the sky through the cracked ceiling.

When they turned toward the front, Desmond was there, hands free of the zip-tie.

He took Eris's arm from Georgie's shoulder and slung it over his own. "Hurry the hell up."

A handful of people ran with them. They tore through the building, and as they approached the front entrance, a few filed out.

Desmond and the girl stopped just inside the door, and Georgie inched closer, eyes going to the group of soldiers outside. An officer with angled features stood in front of the others, her uniform slightly different from the plain gray of the soldiers, her hair pulled back into a ponytail, the sides buzzed.

A sharp breath hissed between Georgie's teeth when she noticed Adam on the ground, writhing in pain, and her fist clenched tighter around the gun. Jax stood beside him, hands up in surrender.

"There are still people inside!" Jax shouted. "*Our* people. Tell them to stop firing."

The officer lifted her gun, her face expressionless, and the sound of the gunshot was lost beneath another deep resonant boom.

Jax's head snapped back, and he collapsed.

"No!" Georgie screamed, lunging for the door, but Desmond caught her arm and yanked her back. She fought against him as the sob tore from deep in her chest and everything inside her disintegrated, crumbling to dust. "Let me go! I have to—"

"Don't be stupid," he said sharply. "If anyone's going to put you out of your misery, it's going to be me. *Not* them. Go."

Gunfire erupted, and the people who had fled outside all fell, dropping like puppets with their strings cut.

Jax's shape in the snow melted into a blur as tears spilled over and streamed down Georgie's face. The pain was all-consuming, a void that devoured every ounce of strength she had left. She stopped fighting against Desmond's hold. If she went out there, they'd shoot her, too.

He released her arm and gently placed Eris on the ground. Then, wordlessly, he took the pistol from the blue-haired girl and stepped toward the door.

"Des," the girl pleaded.

He leveled the gun, and for a second, Georgie thought he planned to shoot the officer, but then his aim lowered.

To Adam.

"Don't!" Georgie shouted, a flurry of panic surging through her. She lunged forward and shoved him as he pulled the trigger, and the bullet buried itself in the snow a few feet from Adam's head.

Desmond spun around to meet her fierce glare.

"*Qué carajos?*" the girl snarled, snatching her pistol back. "Are you fucking kidding me, Des?"

Another explosion at the opposite end of the building.

He cast one last glance at the door, his mouth pressed in a grim line, before he scooped Eris up in his arms. "Come on."

They hurried into a nearby stairwell, and Georgie followed down the stairs into a large underground parking garage.

Without warning, her legs buckled beneath her, and she collapsed onto the hard floor.

Jax was gone.

He was gone.

He trusted those people, and they *killed* him.

She clapped a hand over her mouth, fighting back the ragged sobs.

They could've both made it out. They *had* it. Desmond would have been dead, and they could've been on their way back to Spring Valley. Why did he have to—

No, this all came back to Desmond.

Georgie lifted the heavy handgun and aimed it at his back. "This is your fault!" she called, her voice ringing out through the cavernous garage.

He stopped and turned to face her. "I warned you what they were."

The weight was too much, and she let her hand fall to her side, the gun resting on the ground as the tears flowed.

"Georgie?" Oliver's voice. Why was he here? Why wasn't he running? "What happened?" he asked. "What's going on?"

She folded forward, the weight of everything tethering her to the cold concrete.

"Where's Adam?"

"Gone," she whispered.

When she looked up at him, the dread on his face cut deep. She'd promised him this would work, that they would get Adam back. But now Adam was gone. Jax was gone. She'd lost everything.

"They took him," the girl said. "He's alive. But *we* won't be if we don't go. Now."

"Who did?" he asked. "The Haven?"

Desmond had the audacity to smile at the question, his face etched with bitterness. "Of course, the Haven."

"We have to get him back," Oliver said, voice trembling. "Where's Jax? He knows where to go, right?"

Georgie shook her head as another sob broke through.

"By all means," Desmond chirped, "stand around chatting about it, but I'm getting the hell out of here."

He turned and walked away, Eris still in his arms, but the blue-haired girl hesitated, gaze jumping between them.

"This place is coming down," she said. When Georgie didn't move, she bounced a moment, then muttered a curse before turning and following Desmond.

Georgie swallowed hard, fingers squeezing the handle of the gun. She couldn't let Desmond leave. Not after everything.

"Emery," she shouted, but this time he didn't stop. Grief twisted back into raw anger, and she struggled to her feet, her finger already on the trigger as she marched up to press the barrel against the back of his head.

He stopped, head cocked slightly. "Is this really the time, Little Wicks?"

Another distant *boom* echoed.

"Shit." He turned to lock eyes with Georgie, all humor gone from his face. "I suggest you put the fucking gun down, because I'm getting them out, and if you get in my way, I will end you right here." His glare hardened, and Georgie took an involuntary step back.

"Let's go," Oliver urged, jolting her back to her senses as the others hurried forward.

She nodded, and they sprinted toward the gaping exit, nearly there when an explosion tore through the underground structure.

The blast hurled Georgie forward, slamming her into the cold, unforgiving ground. White-hot pain was the last thing she felt before the world crashed down around her, plunging her into darkness.

ACKNOWLEDGMENTS

In some ways, this book felt easier to write than the first—I've lived with these characters for four years now, and they've become so familiar. In other ways, this book was more challenging. Imposter syndrome often left me questioning myself, wondering if I was doing anything right. But I made it to the finish line, and I'm so grateful for everyone who helped get me here.

I am forever grateful to my partner and my biggest supporter, Carlos. I can't express how much your support has meant. You've been there for every step, reading through early drafts, troubleshooting plot snags, and encouraging me when my own belief faltered. You know this story and these characters as intimately as I do. This book truly wouldn't be here without you.

To my children, Eleanor, Teddie, and Finley, thank you for cheering me on and lifting me up.

Thank you, Mom, for the countless ways you've helped. I'm endlessly grateful for your encouragement. Thank you for listening to my venting and for reading these stories with an understanding of just how much they mean to me.

A big thank you to my developmental editor, Cameron Montgomery Taylor, who always asks the right questions. Your margin notes always make me laugh, and your love for these characters shines through. This book—like the last—wouldn't be what it is without you.

Another thank you to my amazing cover artist, Nastya Litepla, who outdid herself with the incredible cover illustration.

Thank you to the friends in the writing and book community who have been so kind and supportive.

And finally, thank you to my readers. Your passion for this series and love for these characters makes every step of this journey worthwhile. Thank you, from the bottom of my heart.

ABOUT THE AUTHOR

Toni Duarte writes stories about queer characters navigating unraveled worlds. Originally from Illinois, she now calls the Irish countryside home. When she's not dreaming up new stories, she can be found spending time with her family or questing through video games. She loves D&D, books, and all things zombie-related.

Check out Toni's upper-YA dark fantasy, The Hollow Dark, and keep an eye out for book three of the Bioluminescence trilogy (coming soon).

Find out more at toniduartewriter.com
Follow on
Instagram, TikTok, & Threads @tduartewriter

www.ingramcontent.com/pod-product-compliance
Lightning Source LLC
LaVergne TN
LVHW031536060526
838200LV00056B/4518
* 9 7 8 1 0 6 8 7 1 6 6 9 0 *